BLAMELESS

The Parasol Protectorate: Book the Third

GAIL CARRIGER

www.orbitbooks.net

ORBIT

First published in Great Britain in 2010 by Orbit
Reprinted 2011, 2012

A CIP catalogue record for this book
is available from the British Library.

ISBN 978-1-84149-973-4

Typeset in Times by Palimpsest Book Production Limited,
Falkirk, Stirlingshire
Printed and bound by CPI Group (UK) Ltd, Croydon, CR0 4YY

Papers used by Orbit are from well-managed forests
and other responsible sources.

MIX
Paper from
responsible sources
FSC® C104740

Orbit
An imprint of
Little, Brown Book Group
100 Victoria Embankment
London EC4Y 0DY

An Hachette UK Company
www.hachette.co.uk

www.orbitbooks.net

Acknowledgments

This book really wouldn't have happened without Kristin, Devi, and Francesca. No, really, you'd be reading a big fat collection of blank pages right now. Thanks, ladies, I owe you all wine and cheese! Lots of cheese. And a million hugs to J. Daniel Sawyer, who was more helpful, more often, than he realized.

CHAPTER ONE

Wherein the Misses Loontwill Cope with Scandal in Their Midst

"How much longer, Mama, must we tolerate this gross humiliation?"

Lady Alexia Maccon paused before entering the breakfast room. Cutting through the comfortable sounds of chinking teacups and scrunching toast shrilled her sister's less-than-dulcet tones. In an unsurprising morning duet of well-practiced whining, Felicity's voice was soon followed by Evylin's.

"Yes, Mumsy darling, such a scandal under our roof. We really shouldn't be expected to put up with it any longer."

Felicity championed the cause once more. "This is ruining our chances"—*crunch, crunch*—"beyond all recuperation. It isn't to be borne. It really isn't."

Alexia made a show of checking her appearance in the hall mirror, hoping to overhear more. Much to her consternation, the Loontwills' new butler, Swilkins, came through with a tray of kippers. He gave her a disapproving glare that said much on his opinion of a young lady caught eavesdropping on her own family. Eavesdropping was, by rights, a butler's proprietary art form.

"Good morning, Lady Maccon," he said loudly enough for the family to hear even through their chatting and clattering.

"You received several messages yesterday." He handed Alexia two folded and sealed letters and then waited pointedly for her to precede him into the breakfast room.

"Yesterday! Yesterday! And why, pray tell, did you not *give* them to me yesterday?"

Swilkins did not reply.

Nasty bit of bother, this new butler. Alexia was finding that little was worse in life than existing in a state of hostility with one's domestic staff.

Entering the breakfast room, Alexia actually flounced slightly in her annoyance and turned her ire upon those seated before her. "Good morning, dearest family."

As she made her way to the only empty chair, four pairs of blue eyes watched her progress with an air of condemnation. Well, three pairs—the Right Honorable Squire Loontwill was entirely taken with the correct cracking of his soft-boiled egg. This involved the application of an ingenious little device, rather like a handheld sideways guillotine, that nipped the tip off the egg in perfect, chipless circularity. Thus happily engrossed, he did not bother to attend to the arrival of his stepdaughter.

Alexia poured herself a glass of barley water and took a piece of toast from the rack, no butter, trying to ignore the smoky smell of breakfast. It had once been her favorite meal; now it invariably curdled her stomach. So far, the infant-inconvenience— as she'd taken to thinking of it—was proving itself far more tiresome than one would have thought possible, considering it was years away from either speech or action.

Mrs. Loontwill looked with manifest approval at her daughter's meager selection. "I shall be comforted," she said to the table at large, "by the fact that our poor dear Alexia is practically wasting away for want of her husband's affection. Such fine feelings of sentimentality." She clearly perceived Alexia's breakfast-starvation tactics as symptoms of a superior bout of wallowing.

Alexia gave her mother an annoyed glance and inflicted minor wrath upon her toast with the butter knife. Since the infant-inconvenience had added a small amount of weight to Alexia's already substantial figure, she was several stone away from "wasting." Nor was she of a personality inclined toward wallowing. In addition, she resented the fact that Lord Maccon might be thought to have anything whatsoever to do with the fact—aside from the obvious, of which her family was as yet unaware—that she was off her food. She opened her mouth to correct her mother in this regard, but Felicity interrupted her.

"Oh, Mama, I hardly think Alexia is the type to die of a broken heart."

"Nor is she the type to be gastronomically challenged," shot back Mrs. Loontwill.

"I, on the other hand," interjected Evylin, helping herself to a plateful of kippers, "may jolly well do both."

"Language, Evy darling, please." Mrs. Loontwill snapped a piece of toast in half in her distress.

The youngest Miss Loontwill rounded on Alexia, pointing a forkful of egg at her accusingly. "Captain Featherstonehaugh has thrown me over! How do you like that? We received a note only this morning."

"Captain Featherstonehaugh?" Alexia muttered to herself. "I thought he was engaged to Ivy Hisselpenny and you were engaged to someone else. How confusing."

"No, no, Evy's engaged to him now. Or was. How long have you been staying with us? Nearly two weeks? Do pay attention, Alexia dear," Mrs. Loontwill admonished.

Evylin sighed dramatically. "And the dress is already bought and everything. I shall have to have it entirely made over."

"He did have very nice eyebrows," consoled Mrs. Loontwill.

"Exactly," crowed Evylin. "Where will I find another pair of eyebrows like that? Devastated, I tell you, Alexia. I am utterly devastated. And it is all *your* fault."

Evylin, it must be noted, did not look nearly so bothered as one rightly ought over the loss of a fiancé, especially one reputed to possess such heights of eyebrow preeminence. She stuffed the egg into her mouth and chewed methodically. She had taken it into her head recently that chewing every bite of food twenty times over would keep her slender. What it did was keep her at the dinner table longer than anyone else.

"He cited philosophical differences, but we all know why he really broke things off." Felicity waved a gold-edged note at Alexia—a note that clearly contained the good captain's deepest regrets, a note that, judging from the stains about itself, had received the concerted attention of everyone at the breakfast table, including the kippers.

"I agree." Alexia calmly sipped her barley water. "Philosophical differences? That cannot be true. You don't actually have a philosophy about anything, do you, Evylin dear?"

"So you admit responsibility?" Evylin was moved to swallow early so she could launch the attack once more. She tossed her blond curls, only one or two shades removed from the color of her egg.

"Certainly not. I never even met the man."

"But it is still *your* fault. Abandoning your husband like that, staying with us instead of him. It is outrageous. People. Are. Talking." Evylin emphasized her words by stabbing ruthlessly at a sausage.

"People do tend to talk. I believe it is generally considered one of the better modes of communication."

"Oh, why must you be so impossible? Mama, do something about her." Evylin gave up on the sausage and went on to a second fried egg.

"You hardly seem very cut up about it." Alexia watched as her sister chewed away.

"Oh, I assure you, poor Evy is deeply effected. Shockingly overwrought," said Mrs. Loontwill.

"Surely you mean *a*ffected?" Alexia was not above a barb or two where her family was concerned.

At the end of the table, Squire Loontwill, the only one likely to understand a literary joke, softly chortled.

"Herbert," his wife reprimanded immediately, "don't encourage her to be pert. Most unattractive quality in a married lady, pertness." She turned back to Alexia. Mrs. Loontwill's face, that of a pretty woman who had aged without realizing it, screwed itself up into a grimace Alexia supposed was meant to simulate motherly concern. Instead she looked like a Pekingese with digestive complaints. "Is that what the estrangement with *him* is over, Alexia? You weren't . . . brainy . . . with *him*, were you, dear?" Mrs. Loontwill had refrained from referring to Lord Maccon by name ever since her daughter's marriage, as if by doing so she might hold on to the fact that Alexia *had* married—a condition believed by most to be highly unlikely right up until the fateful event—without having to remember *what* she had married. A peer of the realm, it was true, and one of Her Majesty's finest, to be certain, but also a werewolf. It hadn't helped that Lord Maccon loathed Mrs. Loontwill and didn't mind who knew it, including Mrs. Loontwill. *Why,* Alexia remembered, *once, he had even—*She stopped herself from further thought of her husband, squashing the memory ruthlessly. Unfortunately, she found that the agitation of her thoughts had resulted in toast mutilated beyond all hope of consumption. With a sigh, she helped herself to another piece.

"It seems clear to me," interjected Felicity with an air of finality, "that your presence here, Alexia, has somehow overset Evy's engagement. Even you cannot argue your way out of that, sister dear."

Felicity and Evylin were Alexia's younger half-sisters by birth and were entirely unrelated if one took into account any other factors. They were short, blond, and slender, while Alexia was tall, dark, and, quite frankly, not so very slender. Alexia was known throughout London for her intellectual prowess, patronage of the scientific community, and biting wit. Felicity and Evylin were known for their puffed sleeves. The world, as a result, was generally more peaceful when the three were not living under the same roof.

"And we are all aware of how considered and unbiased your opinion is on the matter, Felicity." Alexia's tone was unruffled.

Felicity picked up the scandal section of the *Lady's Daily Chirrup*, clearly indicating she wanted nothing more to do with the conversation.

Mrs. Loontwill dove courageously on. "Surely, Alexia, darling, it is high time you returned home to Woolsey? I mean to say, you've been with us nearly a week, and, of course, we do love having you, but *he* is rumored to be back from Scotland now."

"Bully for *him*."

"Alexia! What a shocking thing to say!"

Evylin interjected. "No one has seen him in town, of course, but they say he returned to Woolsey yesterday."

"Who says?"

Felicity crinkled the gossip section of the paper explanatorily.

"Oh, *they*."

"He must be pining for you, my dear," Mrs. Loontwill resumed the attack. "Pining away, miserable for want of your . . ." She flailed.

"For want of my *what*, Mama?"

"Uh, scintillating companionship."

Alexia snorted—at the dining table. Conall may have enjoyed her bluntness on rare occasion, but if he missed anything, she doubted her wit was top of the list. Lord Maccon was a were-wolf of hearty appetites, to say the least. What he would miss most about his wife was located substantially lower than her tongue. An image of her husband's face momentarily broke her resolve. That look in his eyes the last time they saw each other— so betrayed. But what he believed of her, the fact that he doubted her in such a way, was inexcusable. How dare he leave her remembering some lost-puppy look simply to toy with her sympathies! Alexia Maccon made herself relive the things he had said to her, right then and there. She was *never* going to go back to that—her mind grappled for a description—that untrusting nitwit!

Lady Alexia Maccon was the type of woman who, if thrown into a briar patch, would start to tidy it up by stripping off all the thorns. Over the past few weeks and throughout the course of an inexcusably foul train journey back from Scotland, she thought she had come to terms with her husband's rejection of both her and their child. She was finding, however, at the oddest and most irregular moments, that she hadn't. She would feel the betrayal, like some writhing ache just under her ribs, and become both incredibly hurt and transcendently angry without warning. It was exactly like an acute attack of indigestion—only with one's finer feelings involved. In her more lucid moments, Alexia reasoned that the cause of this sensation was the unjustness of it all. She was quite accustomed to defending herself for having done something inappropriate, but defending herself when completely innocent made for a dissimilar, and far more frustrating, experience. Not even Bogglington's Best Darjeeling succeeded in soothing her temper. And if tea wasn't good enough, well, what *was* a lady to do? It was not, certainly not, that she still loved the man. That was entirely illogical. But the fact remained that Alexia's temper was tender about the edges. Her family ought to have recognized the signs.

Felicity snapped the paper closed suddenly, her face an uncharacteristic red color.

"Oh, dear." Mrs. Loontwill fanned herself with a starched doily. "What *now*?"

Squire Loontwill glanced up and then took refuge in close examination of his egg.

"Nothing." Felicity tried to shove the paper under her plate.

Evylin was having none of it. She reached over, snatched it away, and began scanning through it, looking for whatever juicy tittle-tattle had so disturbed her sister.

Felicity nibbled on a scone and looked guiltily at Alexia.

Alexia had a sudden sinking feeling in the pit of her stomach. She finished her barley water with some difficulty and sat back in her chair.

"Oh, golly!" Evylin seemed to have found the troublesome passage. She read it out for all to hear. "'London was flabbergasted last week when news reached this reporter's ears that Lady Maccon, previously Alexia Tarabotti, daughter of Mrs. Loontwill, sister to Felicity and Evylin, and stepdaughter to the Honorable Squire Loontwill, had quit her husband's house, after returning from Scotland without said husband. Speculation as to the reason has been ample, ranging from suspicions as to Lady Maccon's intimate relationship with the rove vampire Lord Akeldama, to suspected family differences hinted at by the Misses Loontwill'—oh look, Felicity, they mentioned us twice!—'and certain lower-class social acquaintances. Lady Maccon cut quite a fashionable swath through London society after her marriage'—la, la, la . . . Ah! Here it picks up again—'but it has been revealed by sources intimately connected to the noble couple that Lady Maccon is, in fact, in a most delicate condition. Given Lord Maccon's age, supernatural inclination, and legally recognized postnecrosis status, it must be assumed that Lady Maccon has been *indiscreet*. While we await physical confirmation, all signs point to The Scandal of the Century.'"

Everyone looked at Alexia and began talking at once.

Evylin snapped the paper closed, the crisp noise silencing her family. "Well, that explains *that*! Captain Featherstonehaugh must have read this. Which is why he broke off our engagement this morning. Felicity was right! This really is your fault! How could you be so thoughtless, Alexia?"

"No wonder she's been off her feed," commented Squire Loontwill unhelpfully.

Mrs. Loontwill rose to the occasion. "This is simply too much for a mother to endure. Too much! Alexia, how did you manage to bungle matters so completely? Didn't I raise you to be a good,

respectful girl? Oh, I don't know what to say!" Words failed
Mrs. Loontwill. Luckily, she did not try to strike her daughter.
She had done that once, and it hadn't worked out well for anyone.
Alexia had ended up married as a result.

Alexia stood. Angry again. *I spend a considerable time out
of temper these days*, she reflected. Only four people had known
of her unseemly condition. Three of them would never even
consider talking to the press. Which left only one option, an
option that was currently wearing the most reprehensible blue
lace dress, sporting a suspiciously red face, and sitting across
from her at the breakfast table.

"Felicity, I should have realized you wouldn't be able to keep
your trap shut!"

"It wasn't me!" Felicity instantly leaped to the defensive. "It
must have been Madame Lefoux. You know how these
Frenchwomen are! They'll say anything for a modicum of fame
and money."

"Felicity, you knew about Alexia's condition and did not
inform me?" Mrs. Loontwill recovered from her shock just in
time to be shocked again. That Alexia would keep a secret from
her own mother was to be expected, but Felicity was supposed
to be on Mrs. Loontwill's side. The chit had been bribed with
enough pairs of shoes over the years.

Lady Alexia Maccon slammed one hand down on the tabletop,
causing teacups to rattle ominously, and leaned forward toward
her sister. It was an unconscious application of intimidation
tactics learned during several months spent living with a werewolf pack. She was nowhere near as hairy as was generally
required for the maneuver, but she still managed to execute it
flawlessly. "Madame Lefoux would do *no such thing*. I happen
to know for a fact she is the soul of discretion. Only one person
would talk, and that person is not French. You promised me,
Felicity. I gave you my favorite amethyst necklace to keep
silent."

"Is that how you got it?" Evylin was envious.

"Who is the father, then?" asked Squire Loontwill, apparently feeling he ought to try and steer the conversation in a more productive direction. The ladies, fluttering agitatedly all around the table, entirely ignored him. This was a state comfortable to them all. The squire sucked his teeth in resignation and went back to his breakfast.

Felicity went from defensive to sulky. "It was only Miss Wibbley and Miss Twittergaddle. How was I to know they would go running off to the press?"

"Miss Twittergaddle's father owns the *Chirrup*. As you are very well aware!" But then Alexia's anger simmered off slightly. The fact that Felicity had held her tongue for several weeks was practically a miracle of the third age of mankind. Undoubtedly, Felicity had told the young ladies in order to garner attention, but she probably also knew such gossip would effectively dissolve Evylin's engagement and ruin Alexia's life. Sometime after Alexia's wedding, Felicity had evolved from frivolous to outright spiteful, which, combined with a gooseberry-sized brain, resulted in her being an acutely disastrous human being.

"After all this family has done for you, Alexia!" Mrs. Loontwill continued to heap recriminations on her daughter. "After Herbert permitted you back into the safety of his bosom!" Squire Loontwill looked up at that turn of phrase, then down at his portly frame with disbelief. "After the pains I went through to see you safely married. To go outside of all standards of decency like a common strumpet. It is simply intolerable."

"Exactly my point all along," stated Felicity smugly.

Driven to heights of exasperation, Alexia reached for the plate of kippers and, after due consideration of about three seconds, upended it over her sister's head.

Felicity shrieked something fierce.

"But," Alexia muttered under the resulting pandemonium, "it is *his child*."

"What was that?" Squire Loontwill brought a hand down sharply on the tabletop this time.

"It is his bloody child. I have not *been* with anyone else."
Alexia yelled it over Felicity's whimpering.

"Alexia! Don't be crass. There is no need for specifics.
Everyone is well aware that is not possible. Your husband is
basically dead, or was basically dead and is mostly dead now."
Mrs. Loontwill appeared to be confusing herself. She shook her
head like a wet poodle and sallied stoically on with her diatribe.
"Regardless, a werewolf fathering a child is like a vampire or
a ghost producing offspring—patently ridiculous."

"Well, so is this family, but you all appear to exist in accord-
ance with the natural order."

"What was that?"

"In this case, 'ridiculous' would seem to require a redefinition."
Blast this child to all four corners of hell, anyway, thought
Alexia.

"You see how she is?" interjected Felicity, picking kipper off
herself and glowering murderously. "She just keeps talking like
that. Won't admit to doing a single thing wrong. He has chucked
her over—are you aware of that? She is not returning to Woolsey
because she cannot return. Lord Maccon cast her out. That is
why we left Scotland."

"Oh, my goodness. Herbert! Herbert, did you hear that?" Mrs.
Loontwill looked about ready to have the vapors.

Alexia wasn't certain if this was manufactured distress at
Conall publicly booting Alexia or if it was genuine horror at the
prospect of having to board her eldest for the foreseeable future.

"Herbert, do something!" Mrs. Loontwill wailed.

"I have died and gone to the land of bad novels," was Squire
Loontwill's response. "I am ill-equipped to cope with such an occur-
rence. Leticia, my dear, I leave it entirely in your capable hands."

A more inappropriate phrase had never yet been applied to
his wife, whose hands were capable of nothing more complex
than the occasional, highly stressful, bout of embroidery. Mrs.
Loontwill cast said hands heavenward and sagged back into her
chair in a partial faint.

"Oh, no, you don't, Papa." An edge of steel entered Felicity's tone. "Forgive me for being autocratic, but you must understand Alexia's continued presence under our roof is entirely untenable. Such a scandal as this will substantially hinder our chances of matrimony, even without her actual attendance. You must send her away and forbid her further contact with the family. I recommend we quit London immediately. Perhaps for a European tour?"

Evylin clapped her hands, and Alexia was left wondering how much planning Felicity had put into this little betrayal. She looked hard into her sister's unexpectedly pitiless face. *Deceitful little plonker! I should have hit her with something harder than kippers.*

Squire Loontwill was taken aback by Felicity's forthright talk, but always a man to take the path of least resistance, he took stock of his collapsed wife and fierce-faced daughter and rang the bell for the butler.

"Swilkins, go upstairs immediately and pack Lady Maccon's things."

Swilkins remained motionless, impassive in his surprise.

"Now, man!" snapped Felicity.

Swilkins retreated.

Alexia made a little huffing noise of exasperation. Just wait until she told Conall about this latest familial absurdity. Why he'd . . . *Ah, yes, never mind.* Her anger once again died, buckling under the ache of a werewolf-sized hole. Attempting to fill up the void with something, she helped herself to a dollop of marmalade and, because she had nothing left to lose, ate it directly off the spoon.

At that, Mrs. Loontwill actually did faint.

Squire Loontwill gave his wife's limp form a long look and then, with due consideration, left her there for the time being and retreated to the smoking room.

Alexia remembered her mail, and since she needed a distraction and would rather do anything other than converse further with her sisters, she picked up the first letter and broke the seal. Until that moment, she had actually thought things couldn't get any worse.

The seal on the letter was unmistakable—a lion and a unicorn with a crown in between. The message on the interior was equally forthright. Lady Maccon's presence was no longer welcome at Buckingham Palace. The Queen of England would henceforth be unable to receive her. Lady Maccon's duties as a member of the Shadow Council were suspended until further notice. She no longer carried Her Majesty's confidence or authority. The position of muhjah was once more vacant. She was thanked kindly for her previous services and wished a pleasant day.

Alexia Maccon stood up very decidedly, left the breakfast room, and walked directly into the kitchen, ignoring the startled servants. With barely a pause, she marched over and stuffed the official missive into the huge iron range that dominated the room. It caught fire and immolated instantly. Craving solitude, she went from the kitchen into the back parlor, rather than back to the breakfast room. She wanted to retire to her room and crawl back under the bed covers in a tiny—well, not that tiny—ball. But she was already dressed, and principles must be maintained even in the direst of times.

She should not have been surprised. For all her progressive politics, Queen Victoria was morally conservative. She still wore mourning for her husband, dead, ghosted, and gone for over a decade. And if any woman didn't look good in black, it was Queen Victoria. There was no way that the queen would allow Lady Maccon to continue in her clandestine role of preternatural adviser and field agent, even if it remained an entirely secret and classified position. Lady Maccon could not possibly have even a hint of an association with the queen, not now that she had become a social pariah. The morning's news was probably already common knowledge.

Alexia sighed. The potentate and the dewan, fellow members of the Shadow Council, would be delighted to see her gone. She hadn't exactly made life easy for them. That, too, had been part of the job requirements. She experienced a shiver of apprehension. Without Conall and the Woolsey Pack to protect her, there were probably quite a number of individuals who would count her as better off deceased. She rang the bell for one of the maids and sent her to retrieve her parasol-cum-weapon before the butler packed it away. The maid returned shortly, and Alexia felt slightly comforted by having her favorite accessory on hand.

Her thoughts, unbidden, returned once more to her husband, who had so thoughtfully gifted her with the deadly ornament. _Damn and blast Conall_. Why didn't he believe her? So what if all known history contradicted her? History wasn't precisely revered for its accuracy at the best of times. Nor was it overflowing with female preternaturals. Scientifically, no one understood how she was what she was or did what she did even now, with all England's vaunted technology. So what if he was mostly dead? Her touch turned him mortal, didn't it? Why couldn't it also turn him human enough to be able to give her a child? Was that so impossible to believe? _Horrible man_. So like a werewolf to get overly emotional and fluff up the duster like that.

Just thinking about him and Alexia became overcome with sentiment. Annoyed at her own weakness, she dabbed the tears away and looked to her other note, expecting more bad news. However, the writing on this one, bold and entirely too flowery, made her give a watery smile. She'd sent a card round shortly after she returned to London. She wouldn't be so rude as to ask, but she had hinted at her uncomfortable domestic situation, and he, of course, would know what had happened. _He_ always knew what was happening.

"My _darling_ Chamomile Button!" he wrote. "I received your card, and given certain recent intelligence, it has occurred to me that you may be in ever-increasing need of accommodation but were far too polite to request it openly. Let me tender my most humble offer, to the _only person_ in _all_ of England currently thought _more_ outrageous than myself. You would be welcome to share my *unworthy* domicile and hospitality, such as they are. Yours, et cetera, Lord Akeldama."

Alexia grinned. She had been hoping he would read the appeal behind her formal social nicety. Even though his card had been written before her condition had become public knowledge, she suspected her vampire friend would still be amenable to an extended visit and had probably already known about the pregnancy. Lord Akeldama was a rove of such consistently shocking dress and manner that his reputation could only be amplified by taking in the now-ruined Lady Maccon. In addition, he would have her at his mercy and disposal, thus able to extract all truths from her ad nauseam. Of course, she intended to accept his offer, hoping that, as the invitation had been made yesterday—damn the irascible Swilkins—she was not too late. She was rather looking forward to the prospect. Lord Akeldama's abode and table were quite the opposite of humble, and he kept the companionship of a large collective of such shining paragons of foppishness as to make any sojourn in his company one of unending visual delight. Relieved that she was no longer homeless, Lady Maccon sent a note to that effect. She took pains to ensure that the missive was carried by the Loontwills' most attractive footman.

Maybe Lord Akeldama would know something that would explain the presence of a child parasiting about inside her. He was a very old vampire; perhaps he could help prove to Conall her upstanding virtue. The ludicrousness of that thought—Lord Akeldama and virtue in the same sentence—made her smile.

Her luggage packed and her hat and cape in place, Alexia was preparing to quit her family's house, probably for the last time, when yet more mail arrived addressed to her. It was in the form of a suspicious package accompanied by a message. This time she intercepted it before Swilkins could get his mitts on it.

The package contained a hat of such unparalleled biliousness that Alexia had no doubt as to its origin. It was a felt toque, bright yellow in color and trimmed with fake black currants, velvet ribbon, and a pair of green feathers that looked like the feelers from some unfortunate sea creature. The accompanying note boasted remarkably exclamatory grammar and, if possible, attained new heights of flowery penmanship above and beyond that of Lord Akeldama. It was, admittedly, a tad harrowing to read.

"Alexia Tarabotti Maccon, how could you behave so *wickedly*! I just read the morning paper. You had my heart in my chest, you really did! Of course, I should never have believed such a thing in all my born days! Never! In fact, I do not believe a word of it now. You understand that we—Tunny and I—would *love* to have you to stay, but circumstances being, as they say, indefensible—or it is indefatigable?—we cannot possibly tender the offer. You understand? I'm certain you do. Don't you? But I thought you might require some consoling, and I remembered how much attention you paid this adorable hat last time we were out shopping together—ah, these many months ago, in our careless youth, or do I mean carefree youth?—so I picked this out for you at Chapeau de Poupe. I had intended it to be a Christmas gift, but such an emotional crisis as you must be suffering clearly indicates that now is obviously a far more *important time for hats*. Wouldn't you say? Love, love, love, Ivy."

Alexia perfectly understood all the things Ivy hadn't written, if such a thing was to be believed possible given the length of the missive. Ivy and her new husband were committed theatricals and, quite frankly, could not afford to lose patronage through association with the now-besmirched Lady Maccon. Alexia was relieved she would not have to turn them down. The couple lived in the most horrible little set of apartments imaginable, down in the West End. They had, for example, only one parlor. Lady Maccon shuddered delicately.

Tucking the repulsive hat under her arm and grabbing her trusty parasol, Alexia made her way down to the waiting carriage. She gave Swilkins a haughty sniff as he handed her up and directed the driver on to Lord Akeldama's town house.

CHAPTER TWO

In Which Lord Maccon Is Likened to a Small Cucumber

Lord Akeldama's house was located in one of the most fashionable parts of London. A part that had probably become fashionable because it was fortunate enough to host said town house. Lord Akeldama did *everything* fashionably, sometimes to the exclusion of all else, including common sense. If Lord Akeldama were to take up wrestling in vats of jellied eels, it would probably become fashionable within a fortnight. The exterior of his house had been recently redecorated to the height of modern taste and the worshipful approval of the ton. It was painted pale lavender with gold trim swirling and flouncing around every window and aperture. An herbaceous border of lilac bushes, sunflowers, and pansies had been planted as a complement, forming a pleasing three-level effect as visitors wandered up to the front steps, even in winter. The house stood as a solo bastion of cheer, battling valiantly against the London sky, which had undertaken its customary stance halfway between an indifferent gray and a malnourished drizzle.

No one responded to Lady Maccon's knock, nor to her tug on the bell rope, but the gilded front door had been left unlocked. Waving at the driver to wait, Alexia made her way cautiously inside, parasol up and at the ready. The rooms lay in unabashed

splendor—fluffy carpets depicting romantically inclined shep-
herds, paired with arched ceilings playing host to equally
amorous cherubs painted *alla Roma*.

"Halloo. Anybody home?"

The place was completely and utterly deserted, obviously in
exceptional haste. Not only was there no Lord Akeldama, but
there was no Biffy, nor any other drone. Lord Akeldama's abode
was normally a carnival of delights: discarded top hats and piles
of playbills, the scent of expensive cigars and French cologne,
and it boasted a background hum of chatter and hilarity. The
silence and stillness were all the more noticeable by comparison.

Alexia made her way slowly through the empty rooms, as
though she were an archaeologist visiting an abandoned tomb.
All she found was evidence of departure, certain items of
importance taken down from places of honor. The gold pipe
was missing, the one that normally sat atop the mantelpiece in
the drawing room like some revered item of plumbing but that—
Alexia knew from personal experience—hid two curved blades.
The fact that Lord Akeldama saw fit to take *that* particular item
with him did not bode well for the reason behind his departure.

The only living thing on the premises, aside from Alexia,
appeared to be the resident cat. The feline in question was a fat
calico that possessed the disposition of a placid narcoleptic and
that roused only periodically to enact potent and vicious revenge
upon the nearest tasseled throw pillow. Currently, the animal lay
sprawled across a puffy hassock, the remains of three decapitated
tassels nestled near her chin. Cats, as a general rule, were the
only creatures that tolerated vampires. Most other animals had
what the scientists termed a well-developed prey response
behavior pattern. Felines, apparently, didn't consider themselves
vampire prey. This one, however, was so utterly indifferent to
any non-tassel-related creature, she could probably have tolerated
residency among a pack of werewolves.

"Where has your master disappeared to, Fatty?" Alexia inquired
of the creature.

The cat had no definitive answer but graciously allowed herself to be scratched under the chin. She was sporting a most peculiar metal collar, and Lady Maccon was just bending down to examine it closer when she heard muffled footsteps in the hallway behind her.

Lord Conall Maccon was drunk.

He was not drunk in the halfhearted manner of most supernatural creatures, wherein twelve pints of bitter had finally turned the world slightly fuzzy. No, Lord Maccon was rip-roaring, tumble down, without a doubt, pickled beyond the gherkin.

It took an enormous quantity of alcohol to get a werewolf that inebriated. And, reflected Professor Lyall as he steered his Alpha around the side of an inconvenient potshed, it was almost as miraculous a feat to attain such quantities as it was to ingest them. How had Lord Maccon finagled such an arrangement? Not only that, how had he managed to acquire said booze so consistently over the past three days without visiting London or tapping into Woolsey Castle's well-stocked cellar? *Really*, thought the Beta in annoyance, *such powers of alcoholism could almost be thought supernatural*.

Lord Maccon lurched heavily into the side of the potshed. The meat of his left shoulder and upper arm crashed against the oak siding. The entire building swayed on its foundation.

"Pardon," apologized the earl with a small hiccough, "didna see ya there."

"For Pete's sake, Conall," said his Beta in tones of the deeply put-upon, "how did you manage to get so corned?" He tugged his Alpha away from the abused shed.

"Na drunk," insisted his lordship, throwing one substantial arm across his Beta's shoulders and leaning heavily upon it. "Jush a tiny little slightly small bit'a squiffy." His lordship's accent got distinctly more Scottish in times of great stress, strong emotion, or, apparently, under the influence of vast amounts of liquid intoxicants.

They left the safety of the potshed.

The earl pitched forward suddenly, his grip on his Beta the only thing that managed to keep him upright. "Whoa! Watch that bit'o ground there, would ya? Tricky, tricky, jumps right up at a man."

"Where did you acquire the alcohol?" Professor Lyall asked again as he tried valiantly to get his Alpha back on track across the wide lawn of Woolsey's extensive grounds, toward the castle proper. It was like trying to steer a steamboat through a tub of turbulent molasses. A normal human would have buckled under the strain, but Lyall was lucky enough to have supernatural strength to call upon at times of great difficulty. Lord Maccon wasn't simply big; he was also tremendously solid, like a walking, talking Roman fortification.

"And how did you get all the way out here? I distinctly remember tucking you into bed before leaving your room last night." Professor Lyall spoke very clearly and precisely, not entirely sure how much was seeping into his Alpha's thick skull.

Lord Maccon's head bobbed slightly as he attempted to follow Professor Lyall's words.

"Went for a wee nightly run. Needed peace and quiet. Needed air in my fur. Needed fields under my paws. Needed, oh I canna—*hic*—explain . . . needed the company of hedgehogs."

"And did you find it?"

"Find what? No hedgehogs. Stupid hedgehogs." Lord Maccon tripped over a daphne bush, one of the many that lined the pathway leading up to a side entrance of the house. "Who bloody well put that there?"

"Peace, did you find peace?"

Lord Maccon stopped and drew himself upright, straightening his spine and throwing his shoulders back. It was an action driven by memory of military service. It caused him to positively tower over his second. Despite his ramrod-straight back, the Alpha managed to sway side to side, as if the aforementioned molasses-bound steamboat was now weathering a violent storm.

"Do I," he enunciated very carefully, "*look* like I have found peace?"

Professor Lyall had nothing to say in response to that.

"Exactly!" Lord Maccon made a wide and flailing gesture. "She is wedged"—he pointed two thick fingers at his head as though they formed a pistol—"here." Then rammed them at his chest. "And here. Canna shake her. Stickier than"—his powers of metaphor failed him—"stickier than . . . cold porridge getting all gloopy on the side of a bowl," he finally came up with triumphantly.

Professor Lyall wondered what Lady Alexia Maccon would say to being compared to such a pedestrian foodstuff. She would probably compare her husband to something even less agreeable, like haggis.

Lord Maccon looked at his Beta with wide, soulful eyes, the color of which changed with his mood. Currently they were a watered-down caramel and highly unfocused. "Why'd she have ta go an do a thing like that?"

"I don't think she did." Professor Lyall had been meaning to have this out with his Alpha for some time. He had simply hoped the discussion would occur during one of Lord Maccon's rare moments of sobriety.

"Well, then, why'd she lie about it?"

"No. I mean to say, I do not believe she was lying." Lyall stood his ground. A Beta's main function within the werewolf pack was to support his Alpha in all things—publicly, and to question him as much as possible—privately.

Lord Maccon cleared his throat and looked at his Beta in myopic seriousness from under fierce eyebrows. "Randolph, this may come as a shock, but I *am* a werewolf."

"Yes, my lord."

"Two hundred and one years of age."

"Yes, my lord."

"Pregnancy, under such circumstances, you must understand, is not possible."

"Certainly not for *you*, my lord."

"Thank you, Randolph, that is verra helpful."

Professor Lyall had thought it rather funny, but he'd never been much good at humor. "But, sir, we understand so very little about the preternatural state. And the vampires never did like the idea of you marrying her. Could it be they knew something?"

"Vampires always know *something*."

"About what might happen. About the possibility of a child, I mean."

"Poppycock! The howlers would have said somewhat to me at the outset."

"Howlers do not always remember everything, do they? They cannot remember what happened to Egypt, for one."

"God-Breaker Plague? You saying Alexia is pregnant with the God-Breaker Plague?"

Lyall didn't even dignify that with an answer. The God-Breaker Plague was the werewolf moniker for the fact that in Egypt supernatural abilities were rendered negligible. It could not, by any stretch of the imagination, act as a paternal agent.

They finally made it to the castle, and Lord Maccon was momentarily distracted by the Herculean task of trying to climb steps.

"You know," continued the earl in outraged hurt once he'd attained the small landing, "I groveled for that woman. Me!" He glared at Professor Lyall. "An' *you* told me to!"

Professor Lyall puffed out his cheeks in exasperation. It was like trying to have a conversation with a distracted and very soggy scone. Every time he pushed in one direction the earl either oozed or crumbled. If he could simply get Lord Maccon off the sauce he might be able to talk some sense into him. The Alpha was notoriously emotional and heavy-handed in these matters, prone to flying off the cogs, but he could usually be brought around to reason eventually. He wasn't all *that* dim.

Professor Lyall knew Lady Maccon's character; she might be

capable of betraying her husband, but if she had done so, she would admit to it openly. Thus, logic dictated she was telling the truth. Lyall was enough of a scientist to conclude from this that the currently accepted gospel truth, that supernatural creatures could not impregnate mortal women, was flawed. Even Lord Maccon, pigheaded and hurt, could be convinced of this line of reasoning eventually. After all, the earl could not possibly *want* to believe Alexia capable of infidelity. At this point, he was simply wallowing.

"Don't you think it's about time you sobered up?"

"Wait, lemme ponder that." Lord Maccon paused, as though giving the matter deep consideration. "Nope."

They made their way inside Woolsey Castle, which was no castle at all but more a manor with delusions of dignity. There were stories about the previous owner that no one entirely believed, but one thing was for certain: the man had an unhealthy passion for flying buttresses.

Lyall was grateful to be out of the sun. He was old enough and strong enough not to be bothered by direct sunlight for short lengths of time, but that didn't mean he enjoyed the sensation. It felt like a tingling buzz just underneath the skin, highly unpleasant. Lord Maccon, of course, never seemed to notice sunlight at all, even when he was sober—*Alphas!*

"So where *are* you acquiring the alcohol, my lord?"

"Didna drink—*hic*—any alcohol." Lord Maccon winked at his Beta and patted him on the shoulder affectionately, as though they were sharing some great secret.

Lyall was having none of that. "Well, my lord, I think perhaps you would have had to."

"Nope."

A tall, striking blond, with a perennially curled lip and hair in a military queue, rounded a corner of the hall and halted upon seeing them. "Is he soused again?"

"If you mean, 'Is he drunk *still*?' then, yes."

"Where, in all that is holy, is he getting the plonk?"

"Do you think I haven't tried to figure that out? Don't just stand there gawping. Make yourself useful."

Major Channing Channing of the Chesterfield Channings slouched reluctantly over to brace his pack leader from the other side. Together the Beta and the Gamma steered their Alpha down the hall to the central staircase, up several floors, over, and up the final steps to the earl's tower sleeping chamber. They managed this with only three casualties: Lord Maccon's dignity (which hadn't very far to fall at that point), Major Channing's elbow (which met a mahogany finial), and an innocent Etruscan vase (which died so that Lord Maccon could lurch with sufficient exaggeration).

During the course of the proceedings, Lord Maccon started to sing. It was some obscure Scottish ballad, or perhaps some newer, more modern piece about cats dying—it was difficult to tell with Lord Maccon. Before his metamorphosis, he had been a rather well-thought-of opera singer, or so the rumors went, but all remnants of pitch were shredded beyond hope of salvation during his change to supernatural state. His skill as a singer had fled along with the bulk of his soul, leaving behind a man who could inflict real pain with the slightest ditty. *Metamorphosis*, reflected Lyall, wincing, *was kinder to some than to others*.

"Dinna wanna," objected his lordship at the entrance to his sleeping chamber. "Reminds me."

There was no trace of Alexia left in the room. She'd cleared out all of her personal possessions as soon as she returned from Scotland. But the three men in the doorway were werewolves; they merely needed to sniff the air and her scent was there— vanilla with a trace of cinnamon.

"This is going to be a long week," said Channing in exasperation.

"Just help me get him into bed."

The two werewolves managed, through dint of cajoling and brute force, to get Lord Maccon into his large four-poster bed.

Once there, he flopped facedown, and almost immediately began snoring.

"Something simply must be done about him." Channing's accent was that of the privileged elite. It irritated Professor Lyall that the Gamma had never bothered to modify it over the decades. In the modern age, only elderly dowagers with too many teeth still spoke English that way.

Lyall refrained from comment.

"What if we have a challenger or a bid for metamorphosis? We should be getting more of both now that he has success-fully changed a *female* into a werewolf. You cannot keep Lady Kingair a secret in Scotland forever." Channing's tone was full of both pride and annoyance. "Claviger petitions have already escalated; our *Alpha* should be handling those, not spending his days falling down drunk. This behavior is weakening the pack."

"I can hold the challengers off," said Professor Lyall with no shame, no modesty, and no boasting. Randolph Lyall might not be as large, nor as overtly masculine, as most werewolves but he had earned the right to be Beta in London's strongest pack. Earned it so many times over and in so many ways that few questioned his right anymore.

"But you have no Anubis Form. You cannot cover for our Alpha in *every* way."

"Just you mind your Gamma responsibilities, Channing, and leave me to see to the rest."

Major Channing gave both Lord Maccon and Professor Lyall disgusted looks and then strode from the room, the tail of his long, blond hair swaying in annoyance.

Professor Lyall had intended to do the same, minus the long, blond hair, but he heard a whispered, "Randolph," come from the wide bed. He made his way along the side of the big feather mattress to where the earl's tawny eyes were once more open and unfocused.

"Yes, my lord?"

"If"—the earl swallowed nervously—"if I *am* wrong, and

I'm na saying I am, but if I am, well, I'll have to grovel again, won't I?"

Professor Lyall had seen Lady Maccon's face when she returned home to pack up her clothing and quit Woolsey Castle. She wasn't big on crying—practical minded, tough, and unemotional even at the worst of times, like most preternaturals—but that didn't mean she wasn't utterly gutted by her husband's rejection. Professor Lyall had seen a number of things in his lifetime he hoped never to see again; that look of hopelessness in Alexia's dark eyes was definitely one of them.

"I am not convinced groveling will be quite sufficient in this instance, my lord." He was not disposed to allow his Alpha any quarter.

"Ah. Well, bollocks," said his lordship eloquently.

"That is the least of it. If my deductions are correct, she is also in very grave danger, my lord. Very grave."

But Lord Maccon had already gone back to sleep.

Professor Lyall went off to hunt down the earl's source of inebriation. Much to his distress, he found it. Lord Maccon hadn't lied. It was, in fact, not alcohol at all.

Alexia Maccon's parasol had been designed at prodigious expense, with considerable imagination and much attention to detail. It could emit a dart equipped with a numbing agent, a wooden spike for vampires, a silver spike for werewolves, a magnetic disruption field, and two kinds of toxic mist, and, of course, it possessed a plethora of hidden pockets. It had recently been entirely overhauled and refurbished with new ammunition, which, unfortunately, did little to improve its appearance. It was not a very prepossessing accessory, for all its serviceability, being both outlandish in design and indifferent in shape. It was a drab slate-gray color with cream ruffle trim, and it had a shaft in the new ancient Egyptian style that looked rather like an elongated pineapple.

Despite its many advanced attributes, Lady Maccon's most

common application of the parasol was through brute force enacted directly upon the cranium of an opponent. It was a crude and perhaps undignified modus operandi to be certain, but it had worked so well for her in the past that she was loath to rely too heavily upon any of the newfangled aspects of her parasol's character.

Thus she left Lord Akeldama's chubby calico reclining in untroubled indolence and dashed to the side of the door, parasol at the ready. It was an odd set of coincidences, but every time she visited Lord Akeldama's drawing room something untoward happened. Perhaps this was not quite so surprising if one knew Lord Akeldama intimately.

A top hat, with attached head, peeked into the room and was soon followed by a dashing figure sporting a forest-green velvet frock coat and leather spats. For a moment, Alexia almost pulled back on her swing, thinking the intruder was Biffy. Biffy was Lord Akeldama's favorite, and prone to wearing things like velvet frock coats. But then the young man glanced toward her hiding spot—a round face sporting muttonchops and a surprised expression. Not Biffy, for Biffy abhorred muttonchops. The parasol hurtled in the unfortunate gentleman's direction.

Thwack!

The young man shielded his head with a forearm, which took the brunt of the blow, and then twisted to the side and out of the parasol's reach.

"Good gracious me," he exclaimed, backing away warily and rubbing at his arm. "I say there, *do* hold your horses! Pretty poor showing, walloping a gent with that accessory of yours without even a by-your-leave."

Alexia would have none of it. "Who are you?" she demanded, changing tactics and pressing one of the lotus petals on the shaft of her parasol, arming the tip with a numbing dart. This new stance did not look quite so threatening, as she now appeared to be about to issue a prod instead of a thwack.

The young gentleman, however, remained respectfully wary.

He cleared his throat. "Boots, Lady Maccon. Emmet Wilberforce Bootbottle-Fipps, but everyone calls me Boots. How do you do?"

Well, there was no excuse for rudeness. "How do you do, Mr. Bootbottle-Fipps?"

The self-titled Boots continued. "All apologies for not being someone more important, but there's no need to take on so vigorously." He eyed the parasol with deep suspicion.

Alexia lowered it.

"*What* are you, then?"

"Oh, no one of significance, my lady. Just one of Lord Akeldama's"—a hand waved about, indicating the general splendor of the house—"newer boys." The young gentleman paused, frowning in concentration and stroking one of his mutton-chops. "He left me behind to tell you something. A sort of secret message." He winked conspiratorially and then seemed to think better of the flirtation when the parasol was raised against him once more. "I think it is in code." He laced his hands behind his back and stood up straight as though about to recite some long Byronic poem. "Now what was it? You were expected sooner, and my memory is not so . . . Ah, yes, *check the cat*."

"That was all he had to tell me?"

Green-clad shoulders shrugged. "'Fraid so."

They spent several moments staring at each other in silence.

Finally, Boots cleared his throat delicately. "Very good, Lady Maccon. If you do not require anything further?" And without waiting for her to reply, he turned to leave the room. "Pip pip. Must, you understand, press on. Top of the morning to you."

Alexia trailed him out of the room. "But where have they all gone?"

"Can't tell you that, I'm afraid, Lady Maccon. I understand it's not safe. Not safe at all."

Alexia's confusion turned to worry.

"Not safe for whom? You, me, or Lord Akeldama?" She noticed he hadn't actually admitted to knowing his master's new location.

Boots paused at the door and looked back. "Now, don't you worry, Lady Maccon; it'll be all right in the end. Lord Akeldama will see to it. He always does."

"Where is he?"

"Why, with the others, of course. Where else would he be? Off and about, you know how it goes. A goodly numbered hunting party has gone afield, you understand, *tracking*, as it were. Gone to find . . ." He trailed off. "Oops. Never you mind, Lady Maccon. Just attend to what his lordship said about the cat. Toodles." And, with that, he gave her a funny little half bow and let himself out of the house.

Alexia, mystified, returned to the drawing room where the calico still held court. The only thing odd about the animal, apart from the creature's murderous tendencies toward tassels, was the metal collar about her neck. Alexia unclipped it and took it over to the window to examine it in the sunlight. It was thin enough to unroll into a flat ribbon and had been punched all along in an apparently random pattern of dots. It reminded Alexia of something. She ran one glove-covered fingertip along the indentations, trying to remember.

Ah, yes. It was very like the loops that fed through music machines, making those little chiming repetitive tunes that so delighted children and so annoyed adults. If this ribbon also made some kind of sound, she would need a means of listening to it. Rather than search Lord Akeldama's entire house without knowing what exact device she was looking for, and figuring the vampire in question would not be so irresponsible as to leave it on the premises, anyway, she could think of but one person who could help her at this juncture—Madame Lefoux. She headed back out to her carriage.

CHAPTER THREE

Alexia Engages in Entomology

Someone was trying to kill Lady Alexia Maccon. It was most inconvenient, as she was in a dreadful hurry.

Given her previous familiarity with near-death experiences and their comparative frequency with regards to her good self, Alexia should probably have allowed extra time for such a predictable happenstance. Except that in this particular instance, the unpleasant event was occurring in broad daylight, while she was driving down Oxford Street—not, as a general rule, the expected time or location for such an event.

She wasn't even in a rented hackney. She'd grown to anticipate regular attacks when hired transport was involved, but this time she was riding in a private conveyance. She had pinched Squire Loontwill's carriage. As her dear stepfather was giving her the royal heave-ho, she figured he wouldn't mind if she loaded his personal mode of transport with all her worldly goods and stole it for the day. As it turned out, he did mind, but she wasn't there to witness his annoyance. He had ended up borrowing his wife's pony and trap, a contraption decked in yellow tulle and pink rosettes, which was vastly ill suited to both his dignity and girth.

Her attackers didn't appear willing to follow previously established patterns in the murder arena. For one thing, they weren't supernatural. For another, they were ticking—quite loudly, in fact. Lastly, they were also *skittering*. They were undertaking the ticking because, so far as Alexia could determine, and she rather preferred not to get too close, they were clockwork, or some variety of windup mechanical. And they were undertaking the skittering because they were beetles—large, shiny red beetles with black spots and multifaceted crystal eyes, boasting nasty-looking syringes that poked upward in place of antennae.

Ladybugs were invading her carriage, a whole herd of them.

Each ladybug was about the size of Alexia's hand. They were crawling all over the conveyance, trying to break inside. Unfortunately, this did not require much diligence, as the window above the door was open wide enough for any old killer ladybug to sneak right in.

Alexia lurched up, crushing her poor hat against the ceiling of the cab, and tried to slam the sash closed, but she was far too slow. They were remarkably fast for such tubby creatures. A closer view of those antennae revealed tiny beads of moisture oozing from the tips—probably some brand of poison. She reworked her assessment of her attackers: homicidal mechanical dripping ladybugs—*ugh*.

She grabbed for her trusty parasol and bashed the first one that she could with the heavy handle. The bug crashed into the opposite wall, fell onto the back-facing seat, and scuttled once more in her general direction. Another mechanical beetle crawled up the wall toward her, and a third pushed itself off of the window sash at her shoulder.

Alexia squealed, half in fear, half in irritation, and began hitting at the creatures as hard and as fast as she could within the confines of the carriage, at the same time trying to think of some part of her parasol's armament that might help her in this particular situation. For some reason, Madame Lefoux had never specified ladybug protective measures in its anthroscopy. The toxic mist wouldn't cover enough territory to catch them all, and there was no guarantee either the lapis solaris or the lapis lunearis solutions would have any effect on the creatures. Those liquids were designed to eliminate organics, not metals, and the red and black shell looked to be some kind of shielding enamel or lacquer.

She struck out and whacked at three more of the bugs crawling across the cabin floor, holding the parasol by its tip and wielding it as though it were a croquet mallet. The carriage seemed to be positively swarming with the creatures, all attempting to stick those dripping antennae into some part of Alexia's anatomy. One of them got perilously close to her arm before she punched it away. Another climbed all the way to her stomach and struck, only to be thwarted by the leather belt of her traveling dress.

She yelled for help, hoping all the banging and clattering she was making would convince the driver to stop and come to her rescue, but he seemed oblivious. She continued to catalog her parasol options. The numbing dart was useless, and the metal and wooden stakes equally so. It was then that she remembered the parasol was equipped with a magnetic disruption field emitter. Desperately, she flipped the accessory around to its normal position and groped along the handle for the one carved lotus petal that protruded slightly more than the others. Catching it with her thumbnail, she pulled it back, activating the emitter.

It appeared that the deadly ladybugs had iron parts, for the disruption field did as designed and seized up their magnetic components. The beetles, in deference to their nature, all stopped in their tracks and turned upside-down, little mechanical legs drawn up against their undersides just as ordinary dead beetles might. Alexia sent a grateful thank-you to Madame Lefoux for her forethought in including the emitter, and began hurriedly scooping up and throwing the ladybugs out the carriage window before the disruption field wore off, careful not to touch those sticky, dripping antennae. Her skin shivered in disgust.

The driver, finally discerning that something was not quite right with his passenger, drew up the carriage, jumped down

from the box, and came around to the door, just in time to get
bonked on the head with a discarded ladybug.

"All right there, Lady Maccon?" he asked, giving her a pained
look and rubbing his forehead.

"Don't just stand there waffling!" instructed her ladyship, as
though she wasn't bumping about the interior of the carriage,
pausing only to throw enormous red bugs out of its windows.
"Drive on, you cretin! Drive on!"

Best get myself into a public place, thought Alexia, *until I'm
certain I'm out of danger. And I need a moment to calm my
nerves.*

The driver turned to do her bidding, only to be forestalled by
a "Wait! I've changed my mind. Take me to the nearest teahouse."

The man returned to his post with an expression that spoke
volumes on his feelings over how low the aristocracy had fallen.
He clicked the horses into a trot and pulled the carriage back
out into London traffic.

Showing worthy forethought, Alexia felt, under such trying
circumstances, she trapped one of the bugs in a large pink hatbox,
drawing the cords tight. In her agitation, she accidentally dumped
the box's previous occupant (a rather nice velvet riding topper
with burgundy ribbon) out the window. Her precautionary
measures were undertaken none too soon, for the disruption
field wore off and the hatbox began to shake violently. The bug
wasn't sophisticated enough to escape, but it would keep skittering
about inside its new prison.

Just to be certain, Lady Maccon stuck her head out the window
to look behind and see if the other ladybugs continued their pursuit.
They were trundling in confused circles in the middle of the street.
So was her velvet hat, burgundy ribbons trailing behind. It must
have landed on top of one of the bugs. With a sigh of relief,
Alexia sat back, placing one hand firmly on top of the hatbox.

The Lottapiggle Tea Shop on Cavendish Square was a popular
watering hole among ladies of quality, and midmorning was a

popular time to be seen there. Alexia alighted at the curb, instructed the driver to meet her at Chapeau de Poupe in two hours' time, and then dashed inside. The streets were not yet busy, so she would have to wait out the quietest part of the day until the real shopping began.

The inside of Lottapiggle was, however, quite as crowded as Alexia might want. No one would dare attack her further there. Unfortunately, while she had momentarily forgotten her ruined reputation, no one else in London had, and ladybugs weren't the only kinds of ladies with vicious tendencies.

Lady Maccon was allowed in, seated, and served, but the twitching hats and excited chattering of the women assembled abruptly ceased upon sight of her. The hats craned about eagerly, and the chattering evolved into whispered commentary and very pointed looks. One or two matrons, accompanied by impressionable young daughters, stood and left in a rustle of deeply offended dignity. Most, however, were far too curious to see Lady Maccon and were quite giddy at being in her disgraced presence. They basked in the delectable shock of the latest and greatest scandal calmly sipping tea and eating dry toast among them!

Of course, such marked attention might be attributed to the fact that said lady was carrying with her a ticking, quivering hatbox, which she proceeded to place carefully on the seat next to her and then tie to the seat back with the strap of her reticule for security. As though the hatbox might try to escape. At that, all expressions indicated that the tea-swilling ladies felt Lady Maccon had lost her sense along with her reputation.

Alexia ignored them all and took a moment to put her finer feelings back in order and soothe her ladybug-addled nerves with the necessary application of a hot beverage. Feeling more the thing, she made several forthright decisions that resulted in her requesting pen and paper from the hostess. She dashed off three quick notes and then settled in to wait out the lazy part of the morning. Several hours passed thus agreeably, with nothing but an occasional lurch from the hatbox to disturb her reverie.

Upon entering Chapeau de Poupe, Professor Lyall thought that the proprietress was looking a little tired and substantially older than when he'd seen her last. This was peculiar, as on all their previous encounters, the lady inventor had possessed that indefatigably French air of agelessness. Of the kind, of course, that did not come from actually being ageless. She was dressed in her usual odd attire—that is to say, masculine clothing. Most of them considered this shockingly inappropriate, but some were coming to expect such eccentricities from artists, authors, and now milliners. That said, Madame Lefoux may have been dressed as a man, but that did not stop her from being stylish about it, employing perfect tailoring and pleasing subtle grays and blues. Professor Lyall approved.

Madame Lefoux glanced up from an emerald-green silk bonnet she was trimming with satin roses. "Ah, she wanted to see you as well? Very good. Sensible of her."

The establishment was devoid of customers despite the excellent selection of headgear, probably because a polite little sign on the door indicated it was currently closed to visitors. The hats were beautifully arranged, displayed not on stands but dangling at the ends of gold chains attached to the arched ceiling far above. They fell to different heights so that one had to brush through them to cross the shop. The hats swayed slightly as Professor Lyall did so, simulating a pleasing undersea forest.

Professor Lyall took off his hat and bowed. "Sent a note a few hours ago. She has her moments, does our Lady Maccon."

"And you brought Woolsey's librarian with you?" Madame Lefoux's perfectly tended eyebrows arched in surprise. "That is unexpected."

Floote, having followed Professor Lyall in from the street, tipped his hat to the Frenchwoman in such a way as to indicate mild censure, which Lyall supposed stemmed from the fact that he did not approve of her choice of attire and never had.

"Lady Maccon's missive indicated his presence might be acceptable." Lyall set his hat carefully down on the edge of the sales counter, where it would not look as though it were part of the stock. It was a favorite hat. "You are aware that he was valet to Lady Maccon's father? If we are going to discuss what I believe we are going to discuss, his input might prove invaluable."

"Was he really? Of course, I knew he was butler to the Loontwills before Alexia's marriage. I don't recall her revealing anything further." Madame Lefoux looked with renewed interest at Floote, who remained stoic under her pointed scrutiny.

"Everything that has happened, up to a point, probably has something to do with Alessandro Tarabotti." Professor Lyall drew her attention back to himself.

"You believe so, do you? Including this impromptu clandestine meeting of Alexia's?"

"Isn't that always the way of things with preternaturals? Should we go somewhere more private?" The open airiness of the hat shop with its long front windows made the Beta feel uncomfortably exposed. He would feel more relaxed below the shop in Madame Lefoux's secret underground contrivance chamber.

Madame Lefoux put down her work. "Yes, Alexia will know where to find us. If you would like to—"

She was cut off by a knock sounding at the shop door. Bells jingled charmingly as it was pushed open. A cheerful-looking ginger-haired young blunt entered the room wearing a tan top hat, slightly too-tight red plaid breeches, gaiters, and a wide smile that had the unmistakable air of the theater about it.

"Ah, Tunstell, of course." Professor Lyall was not surprised at this addition to Lady Maccon's little gathering.

Floote gave Lord Maccon's former claviger a nod. Then he slipped past him to shut the shop door and check the CLOSED sign. He'd only lately been made Alexia's personal secretary and librarian; before that he'd been a *very* good butler. Sometimes it was hard to take the butlering out of a fellow, especially where doors were concerned.

"What ho, Professor? Lady Maccon's note didn't say you'd be here. What a pleasure, indeed. How's the old wolf?" Tunstell doffed his hat and gave the assembly a sweeping bow and an even wider grin.

"Floppy."

"You don't say? I should think, from what I read in the paper this morning, he'd be rampaging about the countryside, threatening to tear folk limb from limb. Why—" Tunstell was warming to his topic, striding around the room in the sentimental style, arms waving, crashing into hats. He had recently earned himself a reputation as an actor of some note, but even before his fame, his mannerisms had leaned markedly in the dramatic direction.

A humorless little smile crossed Madame Lefoux's lips, and she cut the former claviger off mid-gesticulation. "Not taking the marital separation well, your Alpha? I am very glad to hear it." It wasn't exactly rude of her to interrupt Tunstell. The redhead was a well-meaning fellow, with a perpetually jovial disposition and an undeniable stage presence, but, it must be admitted, he was prone to hyperbole.

Professor Lyall sighed heavily. "He has been *intoxicated* these last three days."

"Good gracious me! I wasn't even aware of the fact that werewolves could *become* intoxicated." The Frenchwoman's scientific interest was piqued.

"It takes some considerable effort and real allocation of resources."

"What was he drinking?"

"Formaldehyde, as it turns out. Just this morning I deduced his source. It is most wearisome. He worked his way through all of my reserves and then demolished half my specimen collection before I realized what he was up to. I keep a laboratory, you see, on Woolsey Castle grounds in a converted gamekeeper's hut."

"Are you saying that you actually *are* a legitimate professor?" Madame Lefoux tilted her head, her eyes narrowing in newfound respect.

"Not as such. Amateur ruminantologist, to be precise."

"Oh."

Professor Lyall looked modestly proud. "I am considered a bit of an expert on the procreative practices of *Ovis orientalis aries*."

"Sheep?"

"Sheep."

"Sheep!" Madame Lefoux's voice came over suddenly high, as though she were suppressing an inclination to giggle.

"Yes, as in *baaaa*." Professor Lyall frowned. Sheep were a serious business, and he failed to see the source of Madame Lefoux's amusement.

"Let me understand this correctly. You are a *werewolf* with a keen interest in *sheep breeding*?" A little bit of a French accent trickled into Madame Lefoux's speech in her glee.

Professor Lyall continued bravely on, ignoring her flippancy. "I preserve the nonviable embryo in formaldehyde for future study. Lord Maccon has been drinking my samples. When confronted, he admitted to enjoying both the refreshing beverage and the 'crunchy pickled snack' as well. I was not pleased." At which, Professor Lyall felt that nothing more was required of him on this particular topic. "Shall we proceed?"

Taking the hint, Madame Lefoux made her way to the back of the shop. In the farthest corner was a pretty marble-topped stand with an attractive display of gloves spread atop it. Lifting one of the many glove boxes, the Frenchwoman revealed a lever. She pressed it sharply down and a door swung open from the wall before her.

"Oh, I say!" Tunstell was impressed, never having visited Madame Lefoux's laboratory before. Floote, on the other hand, was untroubled by the almost magical appearance of the doorway. Very little ever seemed to ruffle the feathers of the unflappable Floote.

The hidden doorway led into neither a room nor a passageway, but instead a large cagelike contraption. They entered, Tunstell with much highly vocalized trepidation.

"I'm not certain about this, gents. Looks like one of those animal-collecting thingamabobs, used by my friend Yardley. You know Winston Yardley? Explorer of some renown. He was off down this engorged river, the Burhidihing I think it was, and came back with a ruddy great ship packed with cages just like this, full of the most messy kinds of animals. Not certain I approve of getting into one myself."

"It is an ascension room," explained Madame Lefoux to the worried redhead.

Floote pushed a lever, which closed the door to the shop, and then he pulled the small metal safety grate closed across the open side of the cage.

"Cables and guide rails allow the chamber to move up and down between levels, like so." Madame Lefoux pulled a cord on one side of the cage. She continued explaining to Tunstell as the contraption dropped downward, raising her voice above the din that accompanied movement. "Above us is a steam-powered windlass. Do not worry; it is perfectly capable of sustaining our weight and lowering us at a respectable speed."

So it proved to be the case as, with many ominous puffs of steam floating into the cage and some creaking and groaning that made Tunstell jump, they moved down. Madame Lefoux's definition of a respectable speed might be questioned, however, as the contraption plummeted quickly, bumping when it hit the ground, causing everyone to stumble violently up against one side.

"At some point, I suppose I shall have to get around to fixing that." The Frenchwoman gave an embarrassed little smile, showing small dimples. Straightening her cravat and top hat, she led the three men out. The passageway they walked into was lit by neither gas lamps nor candles, but instead by an orange-tinted gas that glowed faintly as it traveled through glass tubing set in one side of the ceiling. It was carried by an air current of some kind. The gas swirled constantly, resulting in patchy illumination and a shifting orange glow.

"Oooh," commented Tunstell, and then, rather unguardedly, "What's that?"

"Aetheromagnetic currents with a gaseous electromagnetic illuminatory crystalline particulate in suspension. I was interested, until recently, in devising a portable version, but if not precisely regulated the gas has a tendency to, well, explode."

Tunstell didn't miss a beat. "Ah, some questions are best left unasked, I take it?" He gave the tubing a wary look and moved to walk on the opposite side of the passageway.

"Probably wise," agreed Professor Lyall.

Madame Lefoux gave a half shrug. "You *did* ask, no?" She led them through a door at the end of the passage and into her contrivance chamber.

Professor Lyall sensed that there was something different about the place. He could not determine exactly what it was. He was familiar with the laboratory, having visited it in order to acquire various necessary instruments, gadgets, and devices for the pack, for the Bureau of Unnatural Registry (BUR), and sometimes for his own personal use. Madame Lefoux was generally thought to be one of the better young members of the mad-scientist set. She had a reputation for good, hard work and fair prices, her only idiosyncrasy of consequence, so far, being her mode of dress. All members of the Order of the Brass Octopus were notorious for their eccentricities, and Madame Lefoux stood comparatively low on the peculiarity scale. Of course, there was always the possibility she would go on to develop more offensive inclinations later. There were rumors, but, to date, Lyall had had no cause to complain. Her laboratory was everything that was to be expected from an inventor of her character and reputation—very large, very messy, and very, very interesting.

"Where is your son?" inquired Professor Lyall politely, looking around for Quesnel Lefoux's mercurial little face.

"Boarding school." The inventor dismissed her child with a faint headshake of disappointment. "He was becoming a liability, and then the muddle with Angelique last month made school the most logical choice. I anticipate his imminent expulsion."

Professor Lyall nodded his understanding. Angelique, Quesnel's biological mother and Alexia's former lady's maid, had been working undercover for a vampire hive when she fell to her death out of the window of an obscure castle in Scotland. Not that such information was common knowledge, nor likely to become so, but the hives were not above recrimination. Angelique had failed her masters, and Madame Lefoux had involved herself unnecessarily in the matter. It was probably safer for Quesnel to be out of town and away from society, but Professor Lyall had a soft spot for the little ragamuffin, and would miss seeing him around the place.

"Formerly Lefoux must be missing him."

Madame Lefoux dimpled at that. "Oh, I doubt that. My aunt never did like children very much, even when she was a child."

The ghost in question, Madame Lefoux's dead aunt and fellow inventor, resided in the contrivance chamber and had been, until recently, responsible for Quesnel's education—although, of course, not during the daytime.

Floote stood quietly while Professor Lyall and Madame Lefoux exchanged pleasantries. Tunstell did not. He began poking about the vast muddle, picking up containers and shaking them, examining the contents of large glass vials and winding up sets of gears. There were cords and wire coils draped over hat stands to investigate, vacuum tubes propped in umbrella stands to tip over, and large pieces of machinery to rap on experimentally.

"Do you think I should warn him off? Some of those are volatile." Madame Lefoux crossed her arms, not particularly concerned.

Professor Lyall rolled his eyes. "Impossible pup."

Floote went trailing after the curious Tunstell and began relieving him of his more dangerous distractions.

"I see there is a reason Lord Maccon never decided to bite

him into metamorphosis." Madame Lefoux watched the exchange with amusement.

"Aside from the fact that he ran away, got married, and left the pack?"

"Yes, aside from that."

Tunstell paused to scoop up and put on a pair of glassicals as he walked. Since Madame Lefoux had entered the London market, the vision assistors were becoming ubiquitous. They were worn like spectacles but looked like the malformed offspring of a pair of binoculars and a set of opera glasses. More properly called "monocular cross-magnification lenses with spectra modifier attachments," Alexia called them "glassicals," and Professor Lyall was ashamed to admit even he had taken to referring to them as such. Tunstell blinked at them, one eyeball hideously magnified by the instrument.

"Very stylish," commented Professor Lyall, who owned several pairs himself and was often to be seen wearing them in public.

Floote gave Professor Lyall a dirty look, removed the glassicals from Tunstell, and prodded him back to where Madame Lefoux leaned against a wall, arms and ankles crossed. Large diagrams drawn in black pencil on stiff yellow paper were haphazardly pinned behind her.

Professor Lyall finally realized what it was about the contrivance chamber that was so different from his last visit: it was quiet. Usually the laboratory was dominated by the hum of mechanicals in motion, steam puffing out of various orifices in little gasps and whistles, gears clanking, metal chains clicking, and valves squealing. Today everything was silent. Also, for all its messiness, the place had an air of being put away.

"Are you planning a trip, Madame Lefoux?"

The Frenchwoman looked at the Woolsey Beta. "That rather depends on what Alexia has summoned us together to discuss."

"But it is a possibility?"

She nodded. "A probability at this juncture, if I know anything about Alexia."

"Another reason to send Quesnel away to boarding school."

"Just so."

"You understand much of Lady Maccon's character, for such a comparatively short acquaintance."

"You were not with us in Scotland, Professor; it encouraged intimacy. In addition, I have made her a bit of a pet research venture."

"Oh, have you, indeed?"

"Before Alexia arrives, I take it you all read the morning papers?" Madame Lefoux switched the subject, levered herself upright from the wall, and took up a peculiarly masculine stance: legs spread, like a boxer at White's awaiting the first blow.

The men around her all nodded their affirmation.

"I am afraid they do not lie, for once. Alexia shows every sign of increasing, and we must presume that a physician has corroborated my initial diagnosis. Otherwise, Alexia would likely be back at Woolsey Castle, chewing Lord Maccon's head off."

"I never noticed any of the aforementioned signs," protested Tunstell, who had also traveled to the north with Madame Lefoux and Lady Maccon.

"Do you think said signs are generally something you're likely to observe?"

Tunstell blushed red at that. "No. You are perfectly correct, of course; most assuredly not."

"So are we agreed that the child is Lord Maccon's?" Madame Lefoux clearly wanted to find out where everyone stood on the matter.

No one said anything. The inventor looked from one man to the next. First Floote, then Tunstell, and then Lyall nodded their assent.

"I assumed as much, or none of you would have acquiesced to her request for this clandestine meeting, however desperate her circumstances. Still, it is curious that none of you challenges Alexia's veracity." The Frenchwoman gave Professor Lyall a sharp look. "I am aware of my own reasons, but you, Professor

Lyall, are Lord Maccon's Beta. Yet you believe it is possible for a werewolf to father a child?"

Professor Lyall had known this moment would come. "It is not that I know the answer as to how. It is simply that I know someone else who believes that this is possible. Several someones, in fact. And they are usually correct in these matters."

"They? They who?"

"The vampires." Never comfortable being the center of attention, he nevertheless attempted to explain himself further as all eyes turned to him. "Before she left for Scotland, two vampires tried to kidnap Lady Maccon. While she was on board the dirigible, her journal was stolen and someone tried to poison her. Most of the other incidents up north after that can be placed in Angelique's hands." Professor Lyall nodded to Madame Lefoux. "But those three episodes could not have been the maid. I believe the Westminster Hive was responsible for the attempted kidnapping and the theft of the journal, probably under Lord Ambrose's orders. It seems like Ambrose; he always was ham-handed with his espionage. The kidnappers, whom I intercepted, said they were under orders not to harm Lady Maccon, but simply intended to *test* her—probably for signs of pregnancy. I believe they stole the journal for the same reason—they wanted to see if she was recording anything about her condition. Of course, she herself had not yet realized, so they wouldn't have learned anything. The poisoning, on the other hand . . ."

Lyall looked at Tunstell, who'd been the inadvertent victim of that bungled attempt at murder. Then he continued. "Westminster would wait for confirmation before taking any action so final, especially against the wife of an Alpha werewolf. But those who are outside hive bonds are not so reticent."

"There are very few rove vampires with the kind of social irreverence and political clout needed to risk killing an Alpha werewolf's wife." Madame Lefoux spoke softly, frowning worriedly.

"One of them is Lord Akeldama," said Lyall.

"He wouldn't! Would he?" Tunstell was looking less like an actor and more like the semiresponsible claviger he'd once been.

Professor Lyall tipped his head noncommittally. "Do you remember? Formal complaints were filed with the Crown when Miss Alexia Tarabotti's engagement to Lord Maccon was first printed in the papers. We brushed them off at the time as a matter of vampire etiquette, but I am beginning to think some vampire suspected something like this might occur."

"And with the morning gossip rags printing what they did . . ." Tunstell looked even more worried.

"Precisely," said Professor Lyall. "The vampires have had all their worst fears confirmed—Lady Maccon *is* pregnant. And while the rest of the world sees this as proof of an infidelity, the bloodsuckers would appear to believe her."

Madame Lefoux's forehead creased with worry. "So the hives, originally inclined toward nonviolence, have had their fears confirmed, and Alexia has lost the protection of the Woolsey Pack."

Floote's normally dispassionate face showed concern.

Professor Lyall nodded. "All the vampires now want her dead."

CHAPTER FOUR

Tea and Insults

Lady Maccon was on her third piece of toast and her fourth pot of tea, entertaining herself by glaring at some young lady or another simply to evaluate the color of the blush that resulted. She was no closer to determining who might want her dead—there were just too many possibilities—but she had made some concrete decisions about her more immediate future. Not the least of these being that, without Lord Akeldama, her safest course of action was to leave London. The question was where? And did she have the necessary finances?

"Lady Maccon?"

Alexia blinked. Was someone actually talking to her? She looked up.

Lady Blingchester, a mannish-faced matron of the stout and square variety with curly gray hair and too-large teeth, stood frowning down at her. She was accompanied by her daughter, who shared much the same expression and teeth. Both of them were known for having decided opinions on matters of morality.

"Lady Maccon, how dare you show your face here? Taking tea in such an obvious manner with"—she paused—"an agitated hatbox for company. In a respectable establishment, frequented by honest, decent women of good character and social standing. Why, you should be ashamed! Ashamed to even walk among us."

Alexia looked down at herself. "I believe I am sitting among you."

"You should be at home, groveling at the feet of your husband, begging him to take you back."

"Why, Lady Blingchester, what would you know about my husband's feet?"

Lady Blingchester was not to be forestalled. "Or you should have hidden your shame from the world. Imagine dragging your poor family into the mire with you. Those lovely Loontwill girls. So sensible, with so much promise, so many prospects, and now your behavior has ruined them as well as yourself!"

"You couldn't possibly be talking about my sisters, could you? They have been accused of many things, but never sense. I think they might find that rather insulting."

Lady Blingchester leaned in close and lowered her voice to a hiss. "Why, you might have done them a favor by casting yourself into the Thames."

Alexia whispered back, as if it were a dire secret, "I can swim, Lady Blingchester. Rather well, actually."

This latest revelation apparently too shocking to tolerate, Lady Blingchester began to sputter in profound indignation.

Alexia nibbled her toast. "Oh, do shove off, Lady Bling. I was thinking some rather important thoughts before you interrupted me."

The hatbox, rattling mildly against its confining cords throughout this conversation, gave a sudden enthusiastic upward lunge. Lady Blingchester squawked in alarm and seemed to feel this the last straw. She flounced away, followed by her daughter, but she paused and had some sharp words with the hostess before leaving.

"Blast," said Alexia to the hatbox when the proprietress, looking determined, headed in her direction.

The hatbox ticked at her unhelpfully.

"Lady Maccon?"

Alexia sighed.

"You understand I must ask you to leave?"

"Yes. But tell me, is there a pawnshop in the vicinity?"

The woman blushed. "Yes, my lady, just down off Oxford Circus past Marlborough Bank."

"Ah, good." Lady Maccon stood, untied the hatbox, and gathered it up along with her reticule and parasol. All conversation quieted as she once again held everyone's attention.

"Ladies," said Alexia to the assembled faces. Then she made her way, with as much gravity as possible for a woman clutching an epileptic pink hatbox to her bosom, to the counter, where she paid her account. The door behind her did not close fast enough to cut off the excited squeals and babble that heralded her departure.

The road was now crowded enough for safety, but still Lady Maccon walked with unseemly haste down Regent Street and into a small pawnshop. There she sold all the jewelry she was currently wearing at a shockingly devalued rate, which nevertheless resulted in quite an obscene amount of money. Conall might be an untrusting muttonhead, a Scotsman, and a werewolf, but the man knew a thing or two about feminine fripperies. Mindful of her circumstances alone in the city, Alexia secreted the resulting pecuniary return in several of the hidden pockets of her parasol and proceeded furtively onward.

Professor Lyall looked at the French inventor with a cutting eye. "Why is Lady Maccon involving you in this matter, Madame Lefoux?"

"Alexia is my friend."

"That does not explain *your* eagerness to be of assistance."

"You haven't had many friends, have you, Professor Lyall?"

The werewolf's upper lip curled. "Are you certain friendship is all you want from her?"

Madame Lefoux bristled slightly. "That is a low blow, Professor. I hardly think it your business to question my motives."

Professor Lyall did something quite unusual for him. He colored slightly. "I did not intend to imply . . . that is, I had not meant to insinuate . . ." He trailed off and then cleared his throat. "I planned to hint at your involvement with the Order of the Brass Octopus."

Madame Lefoux rubbed the back of her neck in an unconscious gesture. Hidden under her short dark hair, just there, was a small octopus tattoo. "Ah. The Order has no direct involvement, so far as I can tell."

Professor Lyall did not miss the implication of that phrasing. Madame Lefoux might literally be unable to tell of the OBO's interests if she had been instructed to remain silent.

"But it is undoubtedly scientifically intrigued by Lady Maccon?" Professor Lyall pressed her.

"Of course! She is the only female preternatural to enter our sphere since the Order's inception."

"But the Hypocras Club—"

"The Hypocras Club was only one small branch, and their actions became sadly public. Quite the embarrassment, in the end."

"So why are you such an eager friend?"

"I cannot deny a certain fascination with Alexia as a scientific curiosity, but my research, as you well know, tends to be more theoretical than biological."

"So I was inadvertently closer to the mark initially?" Professor Lyall regarded Madame Lefoux with a wealth of understanding.

Madame Lefoux pursed her lips but did not deny the romantic insinuation. "So you will allow my motives to be, if not pure, at least in Alexia's best interest? Certainly, I care more for her well-being than that rubbish husband of hers."

Professor Lyall nodded. "For now." He paused and then said, "We must convince her to leave London."

At which Lady Alexia Maccon herself bustled into the laboratory. "Oh, no convincing needed, I assure you, my dears. The ladybugs did that. In fact, that was why I summoned you. Well, not because of the ladybugs—because of the leaving." She was clearly a little flustered. Still, all efficiency, she stripped off her gloves and dropped them, her reticule, her parasol, and a gyrating pink hatbox on a nearby worktable. "It is about time I visited the Continent, don't you feel? I thought, perhaps, one or two of you might like to accompany me." She gave them all a timid smile and then remembered her manners. "How do you do, Tunstell? Good day, Genevieve. Floote. Professor Lyall. Thank you all for coming. I do apologize for being late. There were the ladybugs, you see, and then I simply had to take tea."

"Alexia." Madame Lefoux was all concern. Lady Maccon's hair was mussed, and it looked as though there might be a rip or two at the hem of her dress. The inventor took one of Alexia's hands in both of hers. "Are you quite all right?"

At the same time, Professor Lyall said, "Ladybugs? What do you mean, ladybugs?"

"Ah, halloo, Lady Maccon." Tunstell grinned and bowed. "Do you really intend to leave? How unfortunate. My wife will be most upset."

Floote said nothing.

Professor Lyall looked at the Frenchwoman's intimate clasp on Lady Maccon's hand. "You intend to volunteer yourself as companion, Madame Lefoux?" He was thinking about the fact that all the machines in the contrivance chamber had been shut down and tidied away.

Lady Maccon approved. "Excellent. I was hoping you would agree to accompany me, Genevieve. You have the necessary contacts in Europe, do you not?"

The inventor nodded. "I have already put some thought into possible escape routes." She shifted her attention back to Lyall. "Did you think you could leave the Woolsey Pack for that long?"

"Woolsey is used to being split. We are one of the few packs that do it regularly, in order to satisfy both military and BUR obligations. But, no, you are right. I cannot leave at this juncture. The situation is most delicate."

Madame Lefoux brought a hand to her face hurriedly and

pretended to cough but could not quite hide the snicker. "Obviously, you cannot abandon Lord Maccon in his current . . . state."

"State? My repulsive husband is in a 'state'? Good! He jolly well should be."

Professor Lyall felt like he might be betraying his Alpha somewhat but couldn't help admitting, "He is practically inhaling formaldehyde in an effort to stay inebriated."

Lady Maccon's smug expression became suddenly alarmed.

"Don't concern yourself," Lyall hastened to reassure her. "It cannot harm him, not seriously, but it is certainly doing a bang-up job of keeping him utterly incapacitated in the meantime."

"Concerned." Lady Maccon turned away to fiddle with the hatbox, which had been working its way toward the edge of the table. "Who's concerned?"

Professor Lyall moved hurriedly on. "He is, simply put, not acting the Alpha. Woolsey is a tough pack to hold steady at the best of times, restless members, and too much political clout not to be a tempting prospect for opportunistic loners. I shall need to stay here and safeguard the earl's interests."

Lady Maccon nodded. "Of course you must stay. I'm certain Genevieve and I can manage."

The inventor looked hopefully at Professor Lyall. "I'd be obliged if you could find the time to look after my lab while I am away."

The Beta was pleased to be asked. "I would be honored."

"If you could stop by of an evening to check for intruders and ensure a couple of the more delicate machines remain oiled and maintained? I'll provide you with a list."

Tunstell perked up at this point in the conversation. "I'm convinced my wife would be thrilled to oversee the day-to-day operations of your hat shop, if you would like, Madame Lefoux."

The Frenchwoman looked utterly horrified at the very idea.

Professor Lyall could just imagine it: Ivy, in charge of a whole roomful of hats. Such a thing could only bring about disaster and mayhem, like putting a cat in charge of a cage full of pigeons—a turquoise brocade cat with very unusual ideas about the coloration and arrangement of pigeon feathers.

Lady Maccon rubbed her hands together. "That was one of the reasons I invited you here, Tunstell."

Madame Lefoux gave Alexia a very appraising look. "I suppose it would be better if some semblance of normal business operations continued while I was away. It would be best if the vampires did not know exactly *who* your friends are." She turned to Tunstell. "Do you think your wife equal to the task?"

"She'd be unconditionally thrilled." The redhead's broad grin was back in place.

"I was half afraid you would say that." Madame Lefoux gave a rueful little smile.

Poor Madame Lefoux, thought Professor Lyall. There was a distinct possibility she would end up with no hat shop to return to.

"Vampires? Did you say vampires?" Lady Maccon's brain suddenly caught up with the second part of the conversation.

Lyall nodded. "We believe that, now that your delicate condition is public information, the vampires are going to try and—not to put too fine a point on it—kill you."

Lady Maccon arched her eyebrows. "Through the judicious application of malicious ladybugs, perhaps?"

"Come again?"

"Ladybugs?" Tunstell perked up. "I am rather fond of ladybugs. They are so delightfully hemispherical."

"Not of these you wouldn't be." Lady Maccon detailed her recent ladybug encounter and the fact that she had only just narrowly escaped being pronged with an antenna. "This has not been a very pleasant day so far," she concluded, "all things considered."

"Did you manage to capture one for closer examination?" asked Madame Lefoux.

"What do you think is in the hatbox?"

Madame Lefoux's eyes began to sparkle. *"Fantastique!"*

She dashed off and fussed about her contrivance chamber for a moment, emerging wearing a pair of glassicals and massive leather gloves sewn with chain mail.

Professor Lyall, being the only immortal present, took it upon himself to actually open the hatbox.

The Frenchwoman reached inside and lifted out the large ticking bug, its little legs wiggling in protest. She examined it with interest through the magnification lens. "Very fine craftsmanship! Very fine, indeed. I wonder if there is a maker's mark." She flipped the mechanical over.

The creature emitted a very high-pitched whirring noise.

"*Merde!*" said Madame Lefoux, and threw the ladybug hard up into the air.

It exploded with a loud bang, showering them with bits of red lacquer and clockwork parts.

Alexia jumped slightly, but recovered quickly enough. After the type of morning she'd had, what was one little explosion added to the mix? She sneered at the resulting mess.

Professor Lyall sneezed as a cloud of greasy particulates tickled his sensitive werewolf nose. "That is vampires for you. What they cannot suck dry they explode."

Floote began cleaning up the disarray.

"Pity," said Madame Lefoux.

Professor Lyall gave the Frenchwoman a suspicious look.

The inventor raised both of her hands defensively. "Not my craftsmanship, I assure you. I do not deal in"—a sudden dimpled grin spread over her face—"coccinellids."

"I think you had better explain why you're blaming the vampires, Professor." Alexia brought the matter back to hand and gave her husband's Beta a very hard look.

Professor Lyall did explain, starting with his deductions about the poisoning, the missing journal, and the kidnapping attempt, and moving on to his belief that now that Lady Maccon's pregnancy was in print, and she was no longer officially under the

Woolsey Pack's protection, such incidents were only likely to increase in both frequency and ferocity.

Enchanting. What do I expect next? Hordes of barbaric brass bumblebees? "Why do they want me dead? I mean, aside from the customary reasons."

"We think it has something to do with the child." Madame Lefoux took Alexia's elbow softly in hand, trying to steer her in the direction of the overturned barrel.

Alexia resisted, instead turning to Professor Lyall, her throat tight with pent-up emotion. "So you believe me? You believe that this infant-inconvenience is Conall's?"

He nodded.

"'Infant-inconvenience'?" whispered Tunstell to Floote.

Floote remained impassive.

"Do you know something Conall does not?" Alexia's heart leapt with the possibility of exoneration.

Sadly, the Beta shook his head.

Hope dissipated. "Funny that you should trust me more than my own husband." Alexia sat down heavily on the barrel and scrubbed at her eyes with her knuckles.

"He has never acted reasonably where you are concerned."

Lady Maccon nodded, her mouth tight. "That does not excuse his behavior." Her face felt stiff, as though it were made of wax. An image that brought back some very uncomfortable memories.

"No, it does not," Professor Lyall agreed with her.

Alexia wished he wouldn't be so nice—it drove her pathetically close to actual wallowing. "And the only vampire likely to be on my side in this is Lord Akeldama. And he has disappeared."

"He has?" Madame Lefoux and Professor Lyall said it at the same time.

Alexia nodded. "I was at his house earlier this morning. Abandoned. And that after he asked me to stay with him."

"Coincidence?" Tunstell looked like he already knew the answer to such an idea.

"That reminds me of an old saying of Mr. Tarabotti's," offered

Floote, speaking for the first time. "'Floote,' he used to say to me, 'there's no such thing as fate—there's just werewolves, and there's no such thing as coincidence—there's just vampires. Everything else is open to interpretation.'"

Alexia looked at him hard. "Speaking of my father . . ."

Floote shook his head, glanced at Lyall, and then said, "Classified information, madam. Apologies."

"I didn't know you were an agent, Mr. Floote." Madame Lefoux was intrigued.

Floote looked away. "Not as such, madam."

Alexia knew Floote of old; he would not budge on the subject of her father. It was maddening behavior from the otherwise exemplary family retainer. "To the Continent, then." Alexia had given this some thought while in the tea shop. America was out of the question, and vampires were much more vulnerable in Europe—where few countries had followed King Henry's example and integrated the supernatural set. Perhaps they would not be quite so deadly. Or, at least, have access to fewer ladybugs.

"I do not mean to be rude," said Professor Lyall, employing the phrase most often used by those who are about to be very rude indeed, "but such travel should commence quickly. It would be no bad thing for you to leave London before the next full moon, Lady Maccon."

Madame Lefoux consulted a lunar calendar posted on the wall alongside various diagrams. "Three nights from now?"

Professor Lyall nodded. "Preferably sooner. I can use BUR agents to protect you until then, Lady Maccon, but at full moon all of my werewolves are out of commission and my secondary resources are tapped, for I cannot rely on the vampire agents. They will go against BUR orders if under the influence of a queen."

"You can store your possessions here while we are away," offered Madame Lefoux.

"Well, that is something. At least my clothing will be safe."

Alexia threw her hands up in exasperation. "I knew it was a terrible idea to get out of bed this morning."

"And Ivy, I am certain, would be happy to write to you regularly with all the latest news from London." Tunstell offered up his form of encouragement, accompanied by the expected flash of persuasive white teeth. Alexia reflected that it was a good thing her husband hadn't turned Tunstell into a werewolf. The redhead smiled too often. Most werewolves did not do smiling very adeptly; it came off as sinister.

Neither Lady Maccon nor Madame Lefoux saw fit to explain how unlikely it was that any missive would actually reach them.

"So where are we going?" Madame Lefoux looked at her friend with interest.

Alexia had also given this due consideration over her tea and toast. If she had to leave, she was going in pursuit of information. If she had to flee, she might as well flee toward the possibility of proving her innocence. Only one country knew anything substantial about preternaturals.

"I hear that Italy is lovely at this time of year."

CHAPTER FIVE

In Which Ivy Hisselpenny and Professor Lyall Are Given Too Much Responsibility

"Italy?"

"The hotbed of antisupernatural sentiment," spat Professor Lyall.

"The cesspit of religious fanaticism," added Tunstell.

"The Templars." That last was from Floote, and he whispered it.

"I think it's a perfectly topping idea," said Alexia, expressionless.

Madame Lefoux examined Alexia's face sympathetically. "You think the Templars can explain how Lord Maccon managed to get you with child?"

"Why don't you tell me? You once said you managed to read a portion of the Templars' Amended Rule."

"You did *what*?" Professor Lyall was impressed.

Floote looked at the Frenchwoman with renewed suspicion.

"They must know *something* about this thing." Alexia poked an accusatory finger at her still-flat stomach.

Madame Lefoux looked thoughtful but clearly did not want to tempt Alexia with false hope. "I think they might be so intrigued at meeting a female preternatural that they will be unguarded in their approach. Especially if they find out you are pregnant. But they are warriors, not intellectuals. I'm not convinced they can furnish you with what you *actually* desire."

"Oh, and what's that?"

"The return of your husband's regard."

Alexia glared daggers at the Frenchwoman. *The very idea!* She didn't want that disloyal fuzz-ball back in love with her. She simply wanted to prove him wrong.

"I think," said Professor Lyall before Alexia could commence a diatribe, "that you are entering a wasp hive."

"So long as it is not a ladybug hive, I shall be fine."

"I think," said Floote, "that I should come with you ladies."

Neither of the ladies in question objected.

Alexia raised a finger in the air. "Might I recommend we arrange a regular aethographic transmission date, Professor Lyall? Although that presupposes the fact that we will be able to find a public transmitter."

"They have become more popular recently." Madame Lefoux clearly approved of the idea.

The Beta nodded. "Keeping a time slot open at BUR headquarters is an excellent notion. I shall give you a list of all the names and locations of transmitters for whom we have crystalline valve frequensors, and with whom we can thus transmit. From what I recall, Florence has a good one. You understand our apparatus is not as sophisticated as Lord Akeldama's?"

Alexia nodded. Lord Akeldama had recently purchased the latest and greatest in aethographic transmitters, but BUR's was old and clunky. "I shall need a valve for your transmitter as well, for the Italian end of the business."

"Of course. I will send an agent round directly. Shall we set the appointment for just after sunset? I will have my men set ours to receive from Florence and hope something comes through from you at some point on that frequency. If only so that I know you are alive."

"Oh, that is terribly optimistic of you," said Alexia in mock umbrage.

Professor Lyall did not apologize.

"So, Italy it is?" Madame Lefoux rubbed her hands together in the manner of one about to embark on an adventure.

Lady Maccon glanced about at the four standing around her. "One should always visit one's roots once in one's lifetime, don't you feel? I expect the carriage with my things has arrived by now." She turned to leave. The others followed. "I shall have to repack. Better do it quickly, before anything else goes wrong today."

Madame Lefoux touched her arm before she could dash off. "What else happened to you this morning?"

"Aside from the announcement of my rather embarrassing condition in the public papers and an attack of virulent ladybugs? Well, Queen Victoria fired me from the Shadow Council, my family ejected me from their house, and Lord Akeldama vanished, leaving me a very terse message about a cat. Which reminds me." Lady Maccon took the mysterious metal cat collar out of her reticule and waved it at Madame Lefoux. "What do you make of this?"

"Magnetic auditory resonance tape."

"I thought it might be something like."

Professor Lyall looked on with interest. "Do you have a resonance decoding cavity?"

Madame Lefoux nodded. "Of course, over here somewhere." She disappeared behind a vast pile of parts that looked to be the dismembered components of a dirigible's steam engine combined with half a dozen enormous spoons. She returned carrying an object that gave every indication of being a very tall stovepipe-style top hat, with no brim, mounted on a teapot stand with a crank attachment and a trumpet coming out of its underside.

Lady Maccon had nothing to say upon seeing such a bizarre-looking contraption. She handed over the metal tape in mystified silence.

The inventor fed the tape in through a slit in the underside of the hat, turning the crank to run it through the device. As she did so, a pinging sound began to emerge, akin to the noise a piano might make after inhaling helium. She cranked faster and faster. The pings began meshing together, and eventually a high voice came into existence.

"Leave England," it said in a tinny, mechanical tone. "And beware Italians who embroider."

"Useful," was Madame Lefoux's only comment.

"How on earth did he know I would choose Italy?" Sometimes Lord Akeldama still managed to surprise Alexia. She pursed her lips. "Embroidery?" Lord Akeldama was never one to prioritize one vital factor, such as murder, over another, such as fashion. "I'm worried about him. Is it safe for him to be away from his house? I mean to say, I understand his being a rove detaches him from the hive, but I was under the impression roves also became part of a place. Tethered, a little like ghosts."

Professor Lyall tugged on one earlobe thoughtfully. "I wouldn't concern yourself overly, my lady. Roves have a much larger roaming ability than hive-bound vampires. It takes considerable strength of soul to break the queen dependency to begin with, and the older the rove, the more mobile. It is their very capacity for movement that keeps most roves in favor with a local hive. They are untrustworthy but useful. And since the rove needs the queen to convert his drones, they are vested in each other's survival. Have you seen Lord Akeldama's BUR file?"

Lady Maccon shrugged noncommittally. She was not above poking about her husband's office, but she did not think Lyall needed to be made aware of that little fact.

"Well, it is quite substantial. We've no record of his original hive, which suggests he has been a rove some considerable time. I should think he could easily travel outside London city limits, perhaps even as far as Oxford, with very few psychological or physiological consequences. He is probably not mobile enough to handle floating the aether or crossing the water out of England, but he is certainly capable of making himself difficult to find."

"Difficult to find? We are talking about the same Lord Akeldama?" The vampire in question had many sterling qualities—admirable taste in waistcoats and an acerbic wit to name but two—but subtlety was not among them.

Professor Lyall grinned. "I should rest easy if I were you, Lady Maccon. Lord Akeldama can take care of himself."

"Somehow I do not find a werewolf's reassurances on behalf of a vampire all that heartening."

"Shouldn't you be worrying about your own problems?"

"What enjoyment is there in that? Other people's are always far more entertaining."

With that, Lady Maccon led the way back into the hallway, up in the ascension room, through the hat shop, and out into the street. There she supervised the removal of her luggage and sent the waiting coachman off. He was clearly pleased to be heading back toward the comparative sanity of the Loontwill household, where excitable members of the aristocracy did not hurl mechanical beetles at him.

Professor Lyall hailed a hansom and directed it to BUR headquarters to continue on with what looked to be a most demanding day. Floote used the Woolsey carriage to return to the castle and collect his own meager belongings. He arranged to meet the ladies back at the Chapeau de Poupe in under four hours. They agreed that they should depart as quickly as possible, thus traveling under the comparative protection of daylight. Madame Lefoux, of course, was already packed.

Lady Maccon immediately began upending her many suitcases, with Tunstell's assistance, right there in the midst of the forest of hats. The bags had been hastily and rather upsettingly packed by the petulant Swilkins, and Alexia couldn't seem to find anything she might require for a trip to Italy. Mindful of Lord Akeldama's message, she eliminated all articles of clothing afflicted by the presence of embroidery.

Madame Lefoux contented herself with puttering about with her hats, putting them in order in anticipation of their abandonment. They were all thus agreeably occupied when an enthusiastic rat-tat-tatting at the door interrupted them. Alexia looked up to see Ivy Tunstell, black curls bouncing in her eagerness, waving madly from the other side of the glass.

Madame Lefoux went to let her in.

Ivy had taken to both married life and a considerable fall in social station with unexpected gusto. She seemed to genuinely enjoy her new role as wife to an actor of middling reputation and denizen of—gasp—*rented* apartments in Soho. She spoke with pride of entertaining poets on a regular basis. Poets, of all things! She even made murmurs about treading the boards herself. Alexia thought this might be a good plan, for Ivy had just the right kind of pleasant, animated face and inordinately melodramatic temperament to suit life as a thespian. She certainly needed little help in the wardrobe department. Always one for the outrageous hat in her unmarried state, her taste, cut free of her mother's apron strings, now extended to the rest of her attire. Today's offering was a bright apple green, pink, and white striped visiting gown, with a matching hat that boasted feathers of such epic proportions that Ivy actually had to duck slightly upon entering the shop.

"There you are, you wretched man," she said affectionately to her husband.

"Hello, magpie," was his equally warm response.

"In my favorite hat shop." Ivy tapped Tunstell coquettishly on the arm with her fan. "I wonder what could ever have brought you *here*."

Tunstell looked desperately at Lady Maccon, who flashed him an unhelpful smirk.

"Well"—he cleared his throat—"I thought you might want to pick out some new frippery or another, on the occasion of our"—he scrabbled wildly—"month anniversary?" Alexia gave him a slight nod, and he let out a sigh of relief.

Trust Ivy to see nothing but the hats and not notice Lady Maccon's copious luggage strewn about the place, or, for a few moments, Lady Maccon herself. When Ivy finally did, she was quite forward in her questioning.

"Alexia, good gracious me! What are you doing *here*?"

Alexia looked up. "Oh, hello, Ivy. How are you? Thank you kindly for the hat you sent over this morning. It was very, um, uplifting."

"Yes, well, never mind that now. Pray tell, what are you about?"

"I should think that was perfectly obvious, even to you, my dear. I am packing."

Ivy shook her head, plumage swaying back and forth. "In the middle of a hat shop? There is something amiss with such a situation."

"Needs must, Ivy. Needs must."

"Yes, I can see *that*, but what one must need to know at this juncture is, not to put too fine a point on it, *why*?"

"I should think that, too, would be perfectly obvious. I am in imminent danger of traveling."

"Not because of this upsetting business with the morning papers?"

"Precisely so." Alexia figured it was as good an excuse as any. It went against her nature to be seen fleeing London because she was thought adulterous, but it was better than having the real reason known to the general public. Just imagine what the gossipmongers would say if they knew vampires were intent on assassinating her—so embarrassing. *Look at her*, they would say. *Oh, la, multiple assassination attempts, indeed! Who does she think she is, the Queen of Sheba?*

And really, wasn't that what all disreputable ladies did in the end—escape to Europe?

Ivy knew nothing of Alexia's soulless state. She did not even know what *preternatural* meant. Lady Maccon's affliction was a not-very-well-kept secret, what with BUR and all the local werewolves, ghosts, and vampires in on it, but the majority of the daylight folk were ignorant of the fact that there was a preternatural in residence in London. It was generally felt, by Alexia and those intimate with her, that if Ivy knew of this, all attempts at anonymity would be null and void within several hours. Ivy was a dear friend, loyal and entertaining, but circumspection could not be listed among her more sterling qualities. Even Tunstell acknowledged this flaw in his wife's nature and had refrained from informing the new Mrs. Tunstell of her old friend's real eccentricity.

"Yes, well, I suppose I can understand the need to absent yourself from town. But where are you going, Alexia? To the country?"

"Madame Lefoux and I are traveling to Italy, for my low spirits, you understand."

"Oh, dear, but, Alexia, you do realize"—Ivy lowered her voice to a whisper—"that Italy is where they keep *Italians*. Are you quite certain you are adequately prepared to cope?"

Lady Maccon suppressed a smile. "I think I might just be able to muddle along."

"I am certain I heard the most horrible thing about Italy recently. I am failing to recall quite what it was, but it cannot possibly be a healthy place to visit, Alexia. I understand that Italy is the place vegetables come from—all that weather. Terribly bad for the digestion—vegetables."

Lady Maccon could think of nothing to say in response to that, so she continued packing.

Ivy returned to perusing the hats, finally settling on a flower-pot style covered in striped purple and black tweed, with large purple rosettes, gray ostrich plumes, and a small feathered pouf at the end of a long piece of wire that stuck straight out of the crown. It looked, when Ivy proudly donned said hat, as though she were being stalked by an enraptured jellyfish.

"I shall have a new carriage dress made to match," she announced proudly while poor Tunstell paid for the atrocity.

Lady Maccon remarked, under her breath, "Wouldn't it be more sensible to, for example, simply throw yourself off a dirigible?"

Ivy pretended not to hear, but Tunstell shot his wife's friend a wide smile.

Madame Lefoux cleared her throat, looking up from the transaction.

"I was wondering, Mrs. Tunstell, if you might do me a very great favor."

Ivy was never one to let down a friend in need. "Delighted, Madame Lefoux. How may I be of assistance?"

"Well, as you may have surmised"—never a good phrase when applied to Ivy—"I will be accompanying Lady Maccon to Italy."

"Oh, really? How noble of you. But I suppose you *are* French, which can't possibly be all *that* different from Italian."

Madame Lefoux paused in stunned silence before recovering her powers of speech. She cleared her throat. "Yes, well, I was wondering if you might consider overseeing the day-to-day running of the hat shop while I am away."

"*Me?* Engage in *trade*? Well, I don't know." Ivy looked about at the dangling hats, undeniably tempting in all their feathered and flowered glory. But still, she had not been raised for commerce.

"You could, of course, borrow from the stock at your leisure and discretion."

Mrs. Tunstell's eyes took on a distinctly covetous sheen. "Well, if you put it like that, Madame Lefoux, how can I possibly refuse? I would be absolutely delighted to take on the task. What do I need to know? Oh, wait just a moment, before we start, if you please. Ormond." Ivy summoned her husband with a little flap of her hand.

Dutifully, Tunstell trotted over, and Ivy issued him a complex set of whispered instructions. In a flash, he had doffed his hat to the ladies, let himself out the front door, and was off down the street about some errand at his wife's behest.

Alexia approved. At least Ivy had him well trained.

Madame Lefoux led Mrs. Tunstell behind the small counter

and spent the next half hour showing her how to cook the books.

"No need to place any new orders, and no need to open the shop for business all that frequently while I am away. I have listed the important appointments here. I understand you are a busy lady."

Ivy displayed surprising aptitude for the accounting. She always had been good with sums and figures, and she was obviously capable of being serious, at least about hats. Just as they were finishing up, Tunstell reappeared, clutching a small brown paper package.

Alexia joined them to make her good-byes. Directly before leaving, Ivy handed Alexia the package that Tunstell had just acquired.

"For you, my dearest Alexia."

Curiously, Alexia turned it about in her hands before unwrapping it carefully. It turned out to be a whole pound of tea inside a decorative little wooden box.

"I remembered that awful thing I had heard about Italy." Ivy dabbed at the corner of one eye with her handkerchief in an excess of sentiment. "What I heard . . . Oh, I can hardly speak of it . . . I heard that in Italy they drink"—she paused—"*coffee*." She shuddered delicately. "So horribly bad for the stomach." She pressed Alexia's hand fervently with both of hers and the damp handkerchief. "Good luck."

"Why, thank you, Ivy, Tunstell, very thoughtful and kind of you both."

It was good-quality tea, large-leaf Assam, a particular favorite of Alexia's. She tucked it carefully into her dispatch case to carry with her on-board the trans-channel dirigible. As she was no longer muhjah and the dispatch case could not serve its intended purpose of carrying secret and highly significant documents and gadgets belonging to queen and country, it might as well carry an item of equal value and importance.

Ivy might be a tad preposterous at times, but she was a kind and thoughtful friend. Much to both of their surprise, Alexia kissed Ivy on the cheek in gratitude. Ivy's eyes welled with tears.

Tunstell gave them yet another cheerful grin and shepherded his still-emotive spouse from the shop. Madame Lefoux had to dash after them to give Ivy the spare key and a few last instructions.

Professor Lyall had endured a long and trying day. Ordinarily, he was well equipped to cope with such tribulation, being a self-assured gentleman possessed of both mental acumen and physical prowess accompanied by the economy of thought required to choose quickly which best suited any given situation. That afternoon, however, with the full moon rapidly approaching, an Alpha out of commission, and Lady Maccon heading to Italy, it must be admitted that he *nearly*, on two occasions, lost his temper. The vampire drones were being unresponsive, only admitting to the fact that their respective masters "might not be available" for BUR duty that evening. There were three vampires on staff, and BUR was not designed to cope with a sudden loss of these supernatural agents all at once. Especially not when the four BUR-affiliated werewolves were all young enough to already be out of commission on their monthly bone-bender. To compound the staffing issue, certain supplies hadn't arrived as scheduled, two suspicious dirigible accidents needed to be investigated, and there was an exorcism to perform just after sunset. While dealing with all of this, Professor Lyall had to foil no less than eight reporters hoping to interview Lord Maccon, ostensibly about the dirigibles but undoubtedly about Lady Maccon. Needless to say, Lyall was in no mood to find, upon returning home just prior to sunset, his Alpha singing opera—or what might have been considered opera by a tribe of tone-deaf orang-utans—in the bathtub.

"You managed to break back into my specimen collection, didn't you? Really, my lord, those were the last of my samples."

"Ish good stuff, fermaldathdie."

"I thought I set Major Channing to keep watch over you. He hasn't gone to sleep, has he? He should be able to hold for one full day. He can take direct sunlight—I have seen him do it—and you are not so difficult to track, not in this condition at least." Professor Lyall looked accusingly around the bathing chamber, as though the Woolsey Gamma's blond head might just pop up from behind the clothing rack.

"He canna poshibly do tha."

"Oh, no, why not?" Professor Lyall tested the water in which Lord Maccon splashed and wallowed like some bewildered water buffalo. It was quite cold. With a sigh, the Beta retrieved his Alpha's robe. "Come on, my lord. Let's get you out of there, shall we?"

Lord Maccon grabbed his washrag and began conducting the opening sequence of *The Grand Duchess of Gerolstein*, flicking water all about the room as he did so. "Maidens, never mind us," sang the earl, "twirling round and round."

"Where has Major Channing gone off to, then?" Professor Lyall was irritated, but it didn't show in his voice. It seemed he had spent a lifetime being irritated with Channing, and given the day so far, this was nothing more than what was to be expected. "I gave him a direct order. Nothing should have superseded that. I am still Beta of this pack, and Major Channing is under my command."

"Under mine firsh," objected Lord Maccon mildly. Then he warbled out, "For you'll be left behind us, you'll be safe and sound."

Professor Lyall attempted to part pull, part lift his Alpha out of the bathtub. But he lost his grip and Lord Maccon slipped and went falling back into it with a tremendous splash. The massive tub, with its small steam-heating attachment, was extremely well constructed and had been imported from the Americas at great expense because there they *knew* steel. But it still wobbled dangerously on its four clawed feet under Lord Maccon's weight.

"If a bullet's billet, you are doomed to fall," sang out the drenched werewolf, skipping several of the words.

"You gave Channing a direct order? In this state?" Professor Lyall tried once more to extract the earl from the tub. "And he obeyed you?"

For one brief second, Lord Maccon's eyes sharpened and he looked quite sober. "I am still his Alpha; he had *better* obey me."

Professor Lyall finally managed to get his Alpha out of the water and into the robe in a desultory kind of way. The thin material stuck indecently close in places, but the earl, never one to suffer the strain of modesty under any circumstances, clearly didn't give a fig, or a fig leaf.

Professor Lyall was used to it.

Lord Maccon began swaying back and forth in time with his singing. "Take your glass and fill it, laugh and drink with all!"

"Where did you send him?" Professor Lyall, supporting the brunt of his Alpha's weight, blessed his own supernatural strength, which made the massive man merely awkward rather than hopeless to maneuver. Lord Maccon was built like a brick outhouse, with opinions twice as unmoving and often equally full of crap.

"Aha, wouldna you like ta know tha?" The Alpha did not do coy well, and Professor Lyall was not amused at the lack of a direct answer.

"Did you send him after Lord Akeldama?"

Lord Maccon came over slightly sober once more. "That pansy. Missing, is he? Good. He reminds me of limp custard filling, all cream and no crust. Never could understand what Alexia saw in that pointy-toothed ninnyhammer. My wife! Cavorting about with a crustless vampire. Least I know *he* isna the father." The Alpha's yellow eyes squinted, as if he were trying to keep from thinking about that.

Suddenly, he flopped downward with all his weight, slipped out of Professor Lyall's hold, and landed in a cross-legged heap in the middle of the floor. His eyes were starting to go completely yellow, and he was looking altogether too hairy for Professor Lyall's liking. Full moon wasn't for a couple more nights, and Lord Maccon, by Alpha rights and strength, ought to be able to resist the change easily. Apparently, he wasn't bothering to try.

The earl continued to sing even as his slurring from the drink gave way to slurring from his jawbones breaking and re-forming into those of a wolf's muzzle. "Drink and sing a ditty, good-bye to the past, all the more's the pity, if this cup's our last!"

Professor Lyall was Woolsey Pack Beta for many reasons, one of them being that he knew perfectly well when he needed to ask for assistance. A quick run to the door and one loud yell had four of Woolsey's strongest clavigers in to help him navigate his lordship, now a very drunken wolf, down into the cellar lockup. Four legs offered no improvement in the matter of the earl's wobbling, and instead of singing, he merely took to letting forth with a mournful howl or two. An aggravating day was looking to become an equally aggravating night. With Major Channing vanished, Professor Lyall really had only one recourse left to him: he called for a pack meeting.

CHAPTER SIX

Under the Name Tarabotti

It was early evening, the sun just setting, when three unlikely looking companions boarded the last dirigible for Calais, leaving from its mooring atop the white cliffs of Dover. No reporters managed to capture the departure of the notorious Lady Maccon. This may have had something to do with the swiftness of her response to the publication of her alleged indiscretion, or it may have been the fact that the lady in question was traveling incognito by means of being outrageous in entirely new ways. Instead of her fashionable but severely practical garb, Alexia sported a black floating dress with chiffon ruffles, yellow modesty straps dangling about the skirt, and a hideous yellow hat. She bore, as a result, some passing resemblance to a self-important bumblebee. It was a truly ingenious disguise, for it made the dignified Lady Maccon look and act rather more like an aging opera singer than a societal grande dame. She was accompanied by a well-dressed young gentleman and his valet. Only one conclusion might be drawn from such a party—that it was an impropriety in action.

Madame Lefoux gave herself over to the portrayal of a boy paramour with enthusiasm, affecting many acts of sycophant-like solicitousness. She donned an extraordinarily realistic-looking mustache for the charade—a large black waxed affair that curled up at each side just over her dimples. It managed to disguise much of the femininity of her face through sheer magnitude, but the protuberance had the unfortunate side effect of causing Alexia fits of intermittent giggles whenever she had to look Madame Lefoux directly on. Floote had an easier time of it, sliding comfortably back into his old role of valet, dragging behind him Madame Lefoux's boxes and his own battered portmanteau, which looked about as old as he was and much the worse for wear.

They were greeted with ill-disguised contempt by the float staff and with actively shocked avoidance by the rest of the passengers. Imagine, such a relationship openly flaunted on-board! Disgusting. The resulting isolation suited Alexia perfectly. At Floote's suggestion, she had purchased her ticket under her maiden name, Tarabotti, never having gotten around to commissioning new travel papers after her marriage.

Madame Lefoux had initially objected. "Is that wise, do you think, given your father's reputation?"

"Wiser than traveling under the name of Lady Maccon, I suppose. Who wants to be associated with Conall?" Safely ensconced in her apartments, Alexia pulled off the bumblebee hat and flicked it, as though it were a poisonous snake, across the room.

While Floote puttered about seeing to the unpacking, Madame Lefoux came over and stroked Alexia's hair, now freed from its confines, as though Alexia were a skittish animal. "Only among the supernatural set does the name Tarabotti carry much meaning. There are those who will make the connection eventually, of course. I am hoping we will move through France faster than the gossip does."

Alexia did not object to the petting—it was comforting. She assumed Madame Lefoux was simply entering into the spirit of her role. Very enthusiastic about such things, the French.

They ate a private meal in their quarters, declining to join the rest of the passengers. Judging by the rapid appearance and freshness of the foodstuffs, the staff approved of this maneuver. Most of the offerings were cooked over the steam engine—a refreshing, if bland, method of preparation.

After supper they left their quarters and made their way up to the squeak deck for some air. Alexia was amused to find that those already relaxing in the evening aether breezes hurriedly departed as soon as she and her party arrived.

"Snobs."

Madame Lefoux dimpled slightly from behind her preposterous mustache and leaned against Alexia as they both propped their elbows on the railing, looking down at the dark waters of the channel far below.

Floote watched. Alexia wondered if her father's faithful valet mistrusted Madame Lefoux because she was French, because she was a scientist, or because she was so consistently inappropriately dressed. With Floote, all three qualities were likely to engender suspicion.

Alexia herself had no such reservations. Genevieve Lefoux had proved herself a most loyal friend over the past month, perhaps a little guarded in matters of the heart, but she was kind of word and more importantly, intelligent of action.

"You miss him?" The Frenchwoman did not need to specify further.

Alexia stuck out one gloved hand and let it ride the rushing aether currents.

"I don't want to. I'm so blasted angry with him. I've come over all numb. Makes me feel slow and stupid." She glanced sideways at the inventor. Genevieve, too, had experienced loss. "Does it get better?"

Madame Lefoux closed her eyes for a long moment. Probably thinking of Angelique. "It changes."

Alexia looked up at the almost-full moon, not yet high enough in the sky to vanish behind the enormous balloon section of the ship. "It's already changing. Tonight"—she gave a tiny shrug—"hurts differently. Now I'm thinking about full moon. It was the one night we remained close, touching, the entirety of the night. Other times, I tried to refrain from extended contact with him. He never cared, but I didn't feel it worth the risk, to keep him mortal for longer than necessary."

"Were you afraid you would age him?"

"I was afraid some loner wolf with madness in his eyes would savage him before I could let go."

They were silent for a brief while.

Alexia pulled her hand back in and tucked it under her chin. It was numb. *Familiar sensation.* "Yes. I miss him."

"Even after what he did?"

Unconsciously, Alexia slid her other hand down to her stomach. "He was always a bit of a jackass. To be smart, he should never have married me in the first place."

"Well"—Madame Lefoux tried to lighten the mood by changing the subject—"at the very least, Italy should be interesting."

Alexia gave her a suspicious look. "Are you quite certain you entirely understand what that word means? I understand English is not your native tongue, but really."

The inventor's fake mustache was wiggling dangerously in the breezes. She put one elegant finger up to her face to hold it in place. "It is a chance to find out how you got pregnant. Isn't that interesting?"

Alexia widened her dark eyes. "I am perfectly well aware of *how* it happened. What it is, is a chance to force Conall to recant his accusations. Which is more useful than interesting."

"You know what I mean."

Alexia looked up into the night sky. "After marrying Conall, I assumed children were not possible. Now it's like some exotic disease has happened to me. I cannot bring myself around to being pleased. I should like to know how, scientifically, such a pregnancy occurred. But thinking about the infant too much frightens me."

"Perhaps you just do not want to become attached to it."

Alexia frowned. Trying to understand one's own emotions was a grueling business. Genevieve Lefoux had raised another woman's child as her own. She must have lived constantly with the fear that Angelique would come and simply take Quesnel away from her.

"I could be doing it unintentionally. Preternaturals are supposed to be repelled by one another, and we are supposed to breed true. By rights, I ought to be allergic to my own child, unable even to be in the same room with it."

"You believe you are going to miscarry?"

"I believe that, if I do not lose this child, I may be forced to attempt to rid myself of it, or go insane. That, even if, by some miracle, I manage to carry through my confinement, I will never be able to share the same air as my own baby, let alone touch it. And I am so angry that my great lout of a husband has left me to deal with this alone. Couldn't he have, oh, I don't know, *talked* to me about it? But, no, he gets to blunder about acting all put-upon and getting sloshed. While I—" Alexia interrupted herself. "That's a fantastic idea! I should do something equally outrageous."

At which statement Madame Lefoux leaned forward and kissed her, quite softly and gently on the mouth.

It wasn't entirely unpleasant, but it also wasn't quite the done thing in polite society, even among friends. Sometimes, Alexia felt, Madame Lefoux took that regretfully French aspect of her character a little too far.

"That wasn't exactly what I had in mind. Got any cognac?"

The inventor only smiled. "I think, perhaps, it is time for bed."

Alexia felt very worn about the edges, like an old carpet. "This is exhausting, talking about one's feelings. I am not sure I approve."

"Yes, but has it helped?"

"I still loathe Conall and want to prove him wrong. So, no, I don't think it has."

"But you've always felt that way about your husband, my dear."

"True, true. Are you certain you don't have any cognac?"

They set down in France the next morning with surprisingly little incident. Madam Lefoux brightened considerably once they landed. Her step was light and cheerful as they walked the gangplank down from the dirigible, leaving the colorful ship bobbing against its tethers behind them. The French, who, in addition to a marked preference for ridiculous mustaches, had a propensity for highly civilized mechanicals, were prepared for vast amounts of luggage. They loaded La Diva Tarabotti's trunks, Mr. Lefoux's cases, and Floote's portmanteau onto a kind of platform that floated, kept aloft by four aether-inflated balloons and pulled along by a lackadaisical porter. Madame Lefoux engaged in several protracted arguments with various staff, arguments that seemed to be more the general formula of conversation than embodying any genuine vehemence. From what Alexia could follow, which wasn't much given the rapidity of the tongue, there appeared to be some question concerning the bill, the gratuity, and the complexity of hiring transport at this time of the morning.

Madame Lefoux admitted the time of day to be unacceptably early but would brook no delay on their journey. She rousted up a youngish carriage driver, who had a particularly spectacular mustache and who met them rubbing sleepy eyes. With baggage in place and Alexia, Madame Lefoux, and Floote safely ensconced within, they drove some ten miles or so to a station where they caught the mail train on its six-hour journey to Paris, via Amiens. Madame Lefoux promised, in a low voice, there would be sustenance available on board. Sadly, the provisions on the rail turned out to be wretchedly inferior. Alexia was underwhelmed; she had heard such wondrous things about French cuisine.

They arrived in the late afternoon, and Alexia was perturbed to find, never having traveled to foreign climes, that Paris seemed just as dirty and crowded as London, only peopled by buildings more swooped and gentlemen more mustached. They did not go directly into town. Despite a most pressing need for tea, the possibility of pursuit remained uppermost in all their minds. They went to the city's main train station, where Floote pretended to purchase train tickets, and they made a prodigious fuss over catching the next high-boil steamer to Madrid. They went loudly in on one side of the train, with luggage, and then quietly off the other, much to the annoyance of one long-suffering porter who was liberally rewarded for his pains. They then exited at the back end of the station, into a large but seedy carriage. Madame Lefoux directed the driver to a tiny, rickety little clockmaker's shop nestled next to a bakery in what appeared, shockingly enough, to be the tradesmen's quarter of Paris.

Mindful that she was a fugitive and could not afford to be particular, Alexia trailed her friend into the tiny shop. She spotted the small brass octopus above the door and could not quite prevent a lurch of apprehension. Once inside, however, her fears were quickly dissipated by curiosity. The interior was littered with clocks and companion devices of all shapes and sizes. Unfortunately, Madame Lefoux pressed on through rapidly into a back room and up a set of stairs. They arrived thus, with very little pomp or circumstance, in the tiny reception chamber of a set of residential apartments above the shop.

Alexia found herself surrounded and embraced by a room of such unmitigated welcome and personality that it was akin to being yelled at by plum pudding. All the furniture looked comfortable and worn, and the paintings on the walls and side tables were bright and cheerful. Even the wallpaper was equally amiable. Unlike in England, where courtesy to the supernatural set prevailed, resulting in interiors kept dark with heavy curtains, this room was bright and well lit. The windows, overlooking the street below, were thrown open and the sun allowed to stream in. But for Alexia, the most welcoming thing about the place was the myriad of gadgets and mechanical knickknacks strewn about. Unlike Madame Lefoux's contrivance chamber, which had no other purpose but production, this was a home that also happened to be a work space. There were gears piled atop half-finished knitting and cranking mechanisms attached to coal scuttles. It was a marriage of domesticity and technology like none Alexia had witnessed before.

Madame Lefoux gave a funny little holler but did not go looking for the denizen of the abode. With the air of a regular visitor, she settled herself easily into a soft settee. Alexia, finding this familiar behavior highly irregular, resisted joining her at first, but due to the weariness of extended travel was eventually persuaded not to stand on ceremony. Floote, who seemed never to tire, laced his fingers behind his back and took up his favorite butler stance near the door.

"Why, Genevieve, my dear, what an unexpected pleasure!" The gentleman who entered the room matched the house perfectly—soft, friendly, and gadget-riddled. He wore a leather apron with many pockets, a pair of green spectacles rested upon his nose, a pair of brass glassicals perched atop his head, and a monocle hung about his neck. The clockmaker, no doubt. He spoke in French, but fortunately much less rapidly than others Alexia had met so far, allowing her to follow the conversation.

"There is something different about you?" The man adjusted his spectacles and contemplated Madame Lefoux for a moment through them. Apparently not pinpointing the enormous mustache draped atop the inventor's upper lip as the culprit, he added, "Is that a new hat?"

"Gustave, you never do change, do you? I hope you do not mind such an unexpected visit." Madame Lefoux addressed their host in the queen's English, in deference to Alexia and Floote's presence.

The gentleman in question switched smoothly into Alexia's native language as though it were a tongue as familiar to him as his own. In the same instant, he seemed to notice Alexia and Floote for the first time. "Not at all, not at all, I assure you. I adore the company. Always welcome." There was a tone to his voice and a twinkle to his blue-button eyes that suggested real truth to the social niceties. "And you have brought me guests! How marvelous. Delighted, delighted."

Madame Lefoux made introductions. "Monsieur Floote and Madame Tarabotti, this is my dear cousin, Monsieur Trouvé."

The clockmaker gave Floote a measured look and a small bow. Floote returned both in kind, after which Alexia found herself the object of bespectacled scrutiny.

"Not *that* Tarabotti?"

Alexia would not go so far as to describe Monsieur Trouvé as shocked, but he was certainly something more than complacent. It was difficult to see the exact nature of his expression as, in addition to the ubiquitous mustache, the clockmaker also wore a golden-brown beard of such epic proportions as might dwarf a mulberry bush. It was as though his mustache had become overly enthusiastic and, seized with the spirit of adventure, set out to conquer the southern reaches of his face in a take-no-prisoners kind of way.

"His daughter," confirmed Madame Lefoux.

"In truth?" The Frenchman looked to Floote, of all people, for confirmation.

Floote nodded curtly—once.

"Is it so very bad a thing, to be my father's daughter?" Alexia wondered.

Monsieur Trouvé raised both bushy eyebrows and smiled. It was a small, shy smile that barely made it through the shrubbery of his beard. "I take it you never met your father? No, of course, you wouldn't have, would you? Not possible. Not if you *are* his daughter." He looked at Madame Lefoux this time. "Is she really?"

Madame Lefoux dimpled at him. "Without question."

The clockmaker brought his monocle up, peering through both it and his spectacles at Alexia. "Remarkable. A female preternatural. I never thought I would live to see the day. It is a true honor having you to visit, Madame Tarabotti. Genevieve, you always did bring me the most charming surprises. And trouble with them, of course, but we won't talk about that now, will we?"

"Better than that, cousin—she is with child. And the father is a werewolf. How do you like *that*?"

Alexia gave Madame Lefoux a sharp stare. They had not discussed revealing the personal details of her embarrassing condition to a French clockmaker!

"I must sit down." Monsieur Trouvé groped without looking for a nearby chair and collapsed into it. He took a deep breath and then examined Alexia with even more interest. She wondered if he might try to wear the glassicals as well as the spectacles and the monocle.

"You are certain?"

Alexia bristled. She was so very tired of having her word questioned. "I assure you. I am quite certain."

"Amazing," said the clockmaker, seeming to recover some of his equanimity. "No offense meant, no offense. You are, you must realize, a marvel of the modern age." The monocle went back up. "Though, not so very much *like* your dear father."

Alexia glanced tentatively at Floote and then asked Monsieur Trouvé, "Is there anyone who *did not* know my father?"

"Oh, most people didn't. He preferred things that way. But he dabbled in my circle, or I should say, my father's circle. I met him only the once, and I was six at the time. I remember it well, however." The clockmaker smiled again. "He did have quite the habit of making an impression, your father, I must say."

Alexia was unsure as to whether this comment had an

underlying unsavory meaning or not. Then she realized it must. Given what little she knew of her father, a better question might be, to which form of unsavory meaning was the Frenchman alluding? Still, she was positively dying of curiosity. "Circle?"

"The Order."

"My father was an *inventor*?" That surprised Alexia. She had never heard *that* about Alessandro Tarabotti. All his journal entries indicated he was more a destroyer than a creator. Besides, by all accounts, preternaturals couldn't really invent anything. They lacked the necessary imagination and soul.

"Oh, no, no." Monsieur Trouvé brushed two fingers through his beard thoughtfully. "More of an irregular customer. He always had the oddest requests. I remember, once, my uncle talking about how he actually asked for a—" The clockmaker looked up at the doorway, apparently noticing something that made him stop. "Ah, yes, never mind."

Alexia glanced over to see what had caused this gregarious fellow to silence himself. But there was nothing there, only Floote, impassive as always, hands laced behind his back.

Alexia looked to Madame Lefoux in mute appeal.

The Frenchwoman was no help. Instead, she excused herself from the discussion. "Cousin, perhaps I could go find Cansuse for some tea?"

"Tea?" Monsieur Trouvé looked taken aback. "Well, if you must. Seems to me you have been in England too long, my dearest Genevieve. I should think such an occasion as this would require wine. Or perhaps brandy." He turned to Alexia. "Should I get out the brandy? You look as though you might need a bit of a pick-me-up, my dear."

"Oh, no, thank you. Tea would be perfectly suitable." In truth, Alexia thought tea a brilliant idea. It had taken well over an hour to conduct their train subterfuge, and while she knew it was worth it, her stomach objected on principle. Ever since the onset of the infant-inconvenience, food was becoming an ever more pressing concern in some form or another. She had always pondered food overmuch for the safety of her waistline, but these days a good deal more of her attention was occupied with where it was, how soon she could get it, and, on the more embarrassing occasions, whether it would remain eaten or not. Yet another thing to blame on Conall. *Who would have thought that anything could affect my eating habits?*

Madame Lefoux vanished from the room. There was an awkward pause while the clockmaker continued to stare at Alexia.

"So," Alexia began tentatively, "through which side of the family are you related to Genevieve?"

"Oh, we aren't actually family. She and I went to school together—École des Arts et Métiers. You've heard of it? Of course you have. Naturally, at the time, *she* was a *he*—always did prefer to play the man, our Genevieve." There was a pause while bushy eyebrows descended in thought. "Aha, that is what is different! She is wearing that ridiculous fake mustache again. It has been a long time. You must be traveling incognito. What fun!"

Alexia looked mildly panicked, unsure as to whether she should tell this affable man about danger of a vampiric persuasion heading in their direction.

"Not to worry, I wouldn't dare to pry. Regardless, I taught Genevieve everything she knows about clockwork mechanisms. And mustache maintenance, come to think on it. And a few other things of note." The clockmaker stroked his own impressive mustache with forefinger and thumb.

Alexia didn't quite follow his meaning. She was saved from having to continue the conversation by the return of Madame Lefoux.

"Where is your wife?" the Frenchwoman demanded of their host.

"Ah, yes, about that. Hortense slightly, well, died last year."

"Oh." Madame Lefoux did not look particularly upset by this news, only surprised. "I am sorry."

The clockmaker gave a small shrug. "Hortense never was one for making a fuss. She caught a tiny cold down the Riviera way, and the next thing I knew, she had just given up and expired."

Alexia wasn't sure what to think of such a blasé attitude.

"She was a bit of a turnip, my wife."

Alexia decided to be mildly amused by his lack of sentiment. "How do you mean, turnip?"

The clockmaker smiled again. Clearly, he had been hoping for that question. "Bland, good as a side dish, but really only palatable when there is nothing better available."

"Gustave, really!" Madame Lefoux pretended shock.

"But enough about me. Tell me more about yourself, Madame Tarabotti." Monsieur Trouvé scooted toward her.

"What more should you like to know?" Alexia wanted to ask him more questions about her father but felt that the opportunity had passed.

"Do you function the same as a male soulless? Your ability to negate the supernatural, is it similar?"

"Having never met any other living preternaturals, I always assumed so."

"So, you would say, physical touch or very near proximity with a rapid reaction time on the part of the victim?"

Alexia didn't like the word "victim," but his description of her abilities was accurate enough, so she nodded. "Do you make a study of us, then, Monsieur Trouvé?" Perhaps he could help with her pregnancy predicament.

The man shook his head, his eyes crinkling up at the edges in amusement. Alexia was finding she did not mind the copious facial hair, because so much of the clockmaker's expressions were centered in his eyes. "Oh, no, no. Far outside of my sphere of particular interest."

Madame Lefoux gave her old school chum an assessing look. "No, Gustave, you never have been one for the aetheric sciences—not enough gadgetry."

"I'm an aetheric science?" Alexia was mystified. In her experience as a bluestocking, such studies focused on the niceties of aetheronautics and supra-oxygenic travel, not preternaturals.

A diminutive maid with a shy demeanor brought in the tea, or what Alexia supposed passed for tea in France. The maid was accompanied by a low tray of foodstuffs on wheels, which seemed to be somehow trailing her about the apartments. It made a familiar tinny skittering noise as it moved. When the maid bent to lift the tray up and place it on a table, Alexia emitted an involuntary squeak of alarm. Quite unaware of her own athletic abilities until that moment, she jumped over and behind the couch.

Acting the part of footman in tonight's French farce, she thought with a bubble of panicked hilarity, *we have a homicidal mechanical ladybug.*

"Good lord, Madame Tarabotti, are you quite well?"

"Ladybug!" Alexia managed to squawk.

"Ah, yes, a prototype for a recent order."

"You mean, it is not trying to kill me?"

"Madame Tarabotti, I assure you, in my own home, I should never be so uncouth as to kill someone with a ladybug."

Alexia came cautiously back out from behind the couch and watched warily as the large mechanical beetle, all unconcerned for her palpitating heart, trundled after the maid and back out into the hall.

"Your artisanship, I take it?"

"Indeed." The Frenchman looked proudly after the retreating bug.

"I have encountered it before."

Madame Lefoux turned accusing eyes onto Monsieur Trouvé. "Cousin, I thought you preferred not to design weapons!"

"I do! And I must say I resent the implication."

"Well, the vampires have turned them into such," Alexia said. "I experienced a whole herd of homicidal ladybugs, sent to poke me in a carriage. Those very antennae that yours was using to carry the tea tray had been replaced with syringes."

"And one exploded when I went to examine it," added Madame Lefoux.

"How perfectly dreadful." The clockmaker frowned. "Ingenious, of course, but not my modifications, I assure you. I must apologize to you, dear lady. These things always seem to happen when dealing with vampires. Although it is hard to refuse such consistent customers with such prompt accounting."

"Can you reveal the name of your client, cousin?"

The clockmaker frowned. "American gentleman. A Mr. Beauregard. Ever heard of him?"

"Sounds like a pseudonym," said Alexia.

Madame Lefoux nodded. "It is rather common to use handlers in this part of the world, I'm afraid. The trail will have gone quite cold by now."

Alexia sighed regretfully. "Ah, well, deadly ladybugs will happen, Monsieur Trouvé. I understand. You can repair my finer feelings with some tea, perhaps?"

"Of course, Madame Tarabotti. Of course."

To be certain there was tea, of indifferent quality, but Alexia's attention was drawn to the food on offer. There were stacks of raw vegetables—raw!—and some sort of pressed gelatinous meat with tiny nutty-looking digestive biscuits. There was nothing sweet at all. Alexia was deeply suspicious of the whole arrangement. However, upon selection of a small mound of nibbles, she found the fare to be more than passing delicious, with the exception of the tea, which proved itself to be as indifferent in taste as it had appeared initially.

The clockmaker nibbled delicately at some of the foodstuffs but took no libations, commenting that he believed tea would make a superior beverage served cold over ice. Were ice, of course, to become a less expensive commodity. At which statement, Alexia utterly despaired of both him and his moral integrity.

He continued his conversation with Madame Lefoux, as though they had never been interrupted. "On the contrary, my dear Genevieve, I am interested enough in the aetheric phenomena to keep up with the current literature out of Italy. Contrary to the British and the American theories on volatile moral natures, blood derangements, and feverish humors, the Italian investigative societies now hold that souls are connected to the correct dermatological processing of ambient aether."

"Oh, for goodness' sake, how preposterous." Alexia was not impressed. The infant-inconvenience appeared to feel equally unimpressed by raw vegetables. Alexia stopped eating and put a hand to her stomach. Damn and blast the annoying thing. Couldn't it leave her in peace for one meal?

Floote, previously occupied with his own comestibles, immediately moved toward her in concern.

Alexia shook her head at him.

"Ah, you are a reader of scientific literature, Madame Tarabotti?"

Alexia inclined her head.

"Well it may seem absurd to you, but I believe their ideas have merit. Not the least of which being the fact that this particular theory has temporarily halted Templar-sanctioned vivisections of supernatural test subjects."

"You are a progressive?" Alexia was surprised.

"I try to stay out of politics. However, England seems to be doing rather well having openly accepted the supernatural. That is not to say I approve. Making them hide, however, has its disadvantages. I should love to have access to some of the vampires' scientific investigations for one; the things they know about clocks! I also do not believe the supernatural should be hunted down and treated like animals as in the Italian mode."

The little room in which they sat turned a pretty shade of gold as the sun began to set over the Parisian rooftops.

The clockmaker paused upon noticing the change. "Well, well, we have chatted long enough, I suspect. You must be exhausted. You will be staying the night with me, of course?"

"If you don't mind the imposition, cousin."

"It's no trouble at all. So long as you forgive the arrangements, for they will be quite cramped. I am afraid you ladies will have to bunk down together."

Alexia gave Madame Lefoux an assessing look. The Frenchwoman had made her preferences, and her interest, clear. "I suspect my virtue is safe."

Floote looked as though he would like to object.

Alexia gave him a funny look. There was no possible way her father's ex-valet could be a prude in matters of the flesh. Was there? Floote had terribly rigid ideas about sensible dress and public behavior, but he had never batted a single eye at the entirely untoward private doings of Woolsey Castle's rambunctious werewolf pack. On the other hand, he had never particularly liked Lord Akeldama, either. Alexia twitched a small frown in his direction.

Floote gave her a blank stare.

Perhaps he still mistrusted Madame Lefoux for some other reason?

Since puzzling over the matter would certainly yield no results, and talking to Floote—or, more precisely, *at* Floote—never did any good, Alexia swept by him and followed Monsieur Trouvé up the hallway to a tiny bedroom.

Alexia had changed into a claret-colored taffeta visiting dress and was just enjoying a little nap before supper when the most amazing racket awakened her. It seemed to be emanating from the downstairs clock shop.

"Oh, for the love of treacle, what now?"

Grabbing her parasol in one hand and her dispatch case in the other, she charged out into the hallway. It was very dark, as the lights in the apartment were not yet lit. A warm glow emanated up from the shop below.

Alexia bumped into Floote at the top of the stairs.

"Madame Lefoux and Monsieur Trouvé have been consulting on matters clock-related while you rested," he informed her softly.

"*That* cannot possibly account for such a hullabaloo."

Something crashed into the front door. Unlike London, the Paris shops did not stay open late in order to cater to werewolves and vampires. They shut down before sunset, locked firmly against any possible supernatural clientele.

Alexia and Floote bounded down the stairs—as much as a dignified butler-type personage and a pregnant woman of substance can be said to *bound*. There Alexia thought Paris's closed-door policy might well have its merits. For just as she entered the clock shop, four large vampires did the same by way of the now-broken front door. Their fangs were extended, and they did not look in favor of formal introductions.

CHAPTER SEVEN

The Trouble with Vampires

The trouble with vampires, thought Professor Lyall as he cleaned his glassicals with a handkerchief, was that they got hung up on the details. Vampires liked to manipulate things, but when things did not turn out as planned, they lost all capacity for refinement in the resulting chaos. The upshot was that they panicked and resorted to a course of action that never ended as elegantly as they had originally hoped.

"Where is our illustrious Alpha?" asked Hemming, sitting down at the table and helping himself to several slices of ham and a kipper. It was dinnertime for most, but for the werewolves this was breakfast. And since gentlemen were never served at breakfast, the staff merely provided mounds of meat and let the pack and clavigers see to themselves.

"He is in the clink and has been all day, sobering up. He was so drunk last night he went wolf. The dungeon seemed like the best place to stash him."

"Golly."

"Women will do that to a soul. Best avoided, if you ask me." Adelphus Bluebutton wandered in, followed shortly thereafter by Rafe and Phelan, two of the younger pack members.

Ulric, silently chomping on a chop at the other end of the

table, glanced up. "No one did ask you. No one has ever been in any doubt as to your preferences."

"Some of us are less narrow-minded than others."

"More opportunistic, you mean to say."

"I get bored easily."

Everyone was grumpy—it was that time of the month.

Professor Lyall, with great deliberation, finished cleaning his glassicals and put them on. He looked around at the pack through the magnified lens. "Gentlemen, might I suggest that a discussion of preference is better suited to your club? It is certainly not the reason I have called a meeting this evening."

"Yes, sir."

"You will note that the clavigers have not been invited?"

Around him, all the immortal gentlemen nodded. They knew that this meant Lyall wanted to discuss a serious matter with the pack alone. Normally, the clavigers were in on everyone's business. Living with several dozen mostly out-of-work actors will do that to a man's private life—that is, make it considerably less private.

All the werewolves seated about the large dining table tilted their heads so that their necks were exposed to the Beta.

Professor Lyall, aware that he now had their full attention, began the meeting. "Given that our Alpha is pursuing a new and glorious career as an imbecilic twit, we must prepare for the worst. I require two of you to take leave of your military duties to help handle the extra BUR workload."

No one questioned Professor Lyall's right to make changes to the status quo. At one point or another, each member of the Woolsey Pack had tested himself against Randolph Lyall. All had discovered the damage inherent in such an undertaking. They had, as a result, settled into the realization that a good Beta was as valuable as a good Alpha, and it was best to be happy that they had both. Except, of course, that now their Alpha had gone quite decidedly off the rails. And their reputation and position as England's premier pack was one that had to be defended constantly.

Professor Lyall continued. "Ulric and Phelan, it had best be you two. You have dealt with BUR paperwork and operational procedure before. Adelphus, you will handle the military negotiations and make all accommodations needed to compensate for Channing's absence."

"Is he drunk, too?" one of the youngsters wanted to know.

"Mmm. No. Missing. I don't suppose he told any of *you* where he was going?"

Silence met that question, broken only by the sound of chewing.

Lyall pressed his glassicals up the bridge of his nose and looked down through them at his cup of tea. "No? I suspected as much. Very well. Adelphus, you will have to liaise with the regiment and persuade them to assign Channing's majority temporarily to the nearest eligible officer. It will probably have to be a mortal." He looked at Adelphus, whose rank was lieutenant and who thought rather too well of his own abilities and rather too meanly of others'. In truth, he had fifty years more experience than most, but military protocol must be followed. "You will continue to obey his orders as you would any supernatural superior officer. Is that clear? If there is any question of improper use of pack abilities, or excess risk due to immortal prejudice, you are to come directly to me. No dueling, Adelphus, not even under the most trying circumstances. That goes for the rest of you as well."

Professor Lyall took off the glassicals and issued the table of large men a cutting glare.

They all hung their heads and focused on their food.

"Too much dueling gives a pack a reputation. Any questions?"

No one had any. Professor Lyall himself held the rank of lieutenant colonel with the Coldstream Guards, but had, in the last fifty years, rarely had cause to serve. He was beginning to regret not maintaining a more consistent presence within the regiment by letting his BUR duties supersede his military obligations. But even he, a man of considerable forethought, had not planned for a contingency wherein the regiment would be in residence *and* both Lord Maccon and Major Channing would, essentially, *not* be in residence.

He allowed the pack to continue the rest of their meal untroubled. They were nervous and a little restless. Merely through his presence alone, Lord Maccon kept them tame. Professor Lyall could fight them each individually, but he hadn't the charisma to control them en masse, and if Lord Maccon continued to remain sloshed, problems might well arise from within the pack as easily as from without it. Either that, or England would run out of formaldehyde.

Just as the gentlemen were finishing their meal, a timid knock sounded against the closed door. Professor Lyall frowned; he had left orders they were not to be disturbed.

"Yes?"

The door creaked open and a very nervous-looking Rumpet entered, carrying a brass tray with a single card resting atop it.

"Begging your pardon, Professor Lyall, sir," said the butler. "I know you said only in cases of emergency, but the clavigers don't know what to do, and the staff is in an uproar."

Professor Lyall took the card and read it.

Sandalius Ulf, Barrister. Messrs. Ulf, Ulf, Wrendofflip, & Ulf. Topsham, Devonshire. Underneath that in very small letters was one additional printed word: *Loner*.

The Beta flipped over the card. On the back had been scrawled, in the appropriate medium—blood—the fated phrase, *Name your second*.

"Oh, just wonderful." Professor Lyall rolled his eyes. And he had taken such prodigious care with his dress for the evening. "Bother."

Lyall had spent a good deal of his existence as a werewolf avoiding becoming an Alpha. Not only was his temperament ill-suited to the job, but he had no desire for that kind of physical responsibility, quite apart from the fact that he was unable to affect Anubis Form. Alphas had, he observed over the centuries, remarkably short life spans for immortals. His circumspect attitude toward brawling had served him in good stead. The devil in his current situation was that despite himself, Professor Lyall was rather fond of his current Alpha and was, as yet, unwilling to acquiesce to a regime change. Which meant that when upstart loners came to Woolsey to fight for the right to lead England's most powerful pack because the Alpha was rumored to be incapacitated, there was only one thing poor Lyall could do—fight in Lord Maccon's stead.

"Lieutenant Bluebutton, if you would attend me?"

One of the stronger and more senior pack members objected to that. "Shouldn't *I* be Gamma in Channing's place?"

"Given that the regiment is still here, it had better be a ranking officer."

Professor Lyall had to maintain military support and, with the Gamma gone, this could prove difficult. Major Channing might be a pain in the proverbial posterior as a pack mate, but he was an excellent officer with a reputation as a fire-eater, and he had the respect of both soldiers and fellow officers. Without him standing as second, Lyall needed another officer to act the part so that the pack was seen as united with the regiment, should he need to bring soldiers in to support Woolsey as a last resort. It was a truly horrible idea, using Her Majesty's army to prevent an Alpha coup. Werewolves had served their military contracts with dedication since Queen Elizabeth first integrated them, but they had always strived to keep pack protocol separate. Nevertheless, Lyall was a man of ingenuity, and he would call up the Coldstream Guards if he had to.

Hemming was no Beta, so he objected further. "Yes, but—"

"My decision is final." Professor Lyall finished his tea in one gulp, stood, summoned Adelphus to follow him, and left for the cloakroom.

There, both gentlemen stripped down to the skin and donned long wool cloaks before exiting through the front door, where an excited milling mass of clavigers and Woolsey staff waited in the cold evening air.

Professor Lyall could smell the loner even before he saw him. His scent was not that of the Woolsey Pack, nor of any distant association. The bloodline was off, making Lyall's nose twitch.

Professor Lyall went forward to greet him. "Mr. Ulf? How do you do?"

The werewolf looked at Lyall suspiciously. "Lord Maccon?"

"Professor Lyall," said Professor Lyall. And then to make matters clear to this upstart, "And this is my second, Lieutenant Bluebutton."

The loner looked offended. Lyall could tell from the man's scent that this was for show. He was neither upset nor nervous at seeing Lyall instead of Lord Maccon. He had not expected the earl to meet his challenge. He had heard the rumors.

Professor Lyall's lip curled. He loathed lawyers.

"The Alpha will not even acknowledge my challenge?" Mr. Ulf's question was a sly one. "I know of you by reputation, of course, Professor, but why is Lord Maccon himself not meeting me?"

Professor Lyall did not dignify that with an answer. "Shall we proceed?"

He led the challenger around the back of the castle, to the wide stone porch where the pack fought most of its practice bouts. Spread out and down the long sloping green of Woolsey's well-tended lawn, a vast number of military-issue white canvas tents had sprouted, clearly visible under the almost full moon. The regiment usually camped around the front of Woolsey, but Alexia had had kittens over their presence and insisted they remove themselves to the back. They were scheduled to depart for winter quarters in a week or so, having squatted at Woolsey merely for the sake of unity with the pack. Conventional niceties having been observed, pretty much everyone was now ready to move on.

The rest of the Woolsey Pack came wandering after the three men, followed by a handful of clavigers. Rafe and Phelan were looking rather haggard. Lyall suspected he would have to insist they confine themselves to the dungeon presently, before the onslaught of moon madness. Curious, a few of the officers left their evening campfires, grabbed lanterns, and meandered over to see what the pack was getting up to.

Lyall and Mr. Ulf both stripped and stood naked for all the world to see. No one commented beyond a hoot and a whistle or two. Military men were used to werewolf changes and the indecency that preceded the affair.

Professor Lyall was older than he cared to admit and had grown, if not comfortable with shape change, at least enough in control of his own finer feelings not to show how much it hurt. And it *always* hurt. The sound of shifting from man to wolf was that of breaking bones, tearing muscle, and oozing flesh, and, unfortunately, that was also what it felt like. Werewolves called their particular brand of immortality a curse. Every time he shifted, Lyall wondered if this weren't true and if the vampires might not have made a better choice. Certainly they could be killed by the sunlight, and they had to run around drinking people's blood, but they could do both in comfort and style. At its root, being a werewolf, what with the nudity and the tyranny of the moon, was essentially undignified. And Professor Lyall was rather fond of his dignity.

If asked, the surrounding men would have admitted that if anyone could be said to change from man to wolf with dignity, it was Professor Lyall. He did the regiment proud and they all knew it. They had seen their attachment of Woolsey werewolves change both on and off the battlefield, but none were as fast and quiet about it as Lyall. Spontaneously, they gave him a round of polite applause when he had finished.

The smallish, sandy, almost foxlike wolf now standing where Professor Lyall had been gave a little nod of embarrassed gratitude at the clapping.

The challenger's change was not nearly so elegant. It was accomplished with much groaning and whimpers of pain, but when complete, the black wolf that resulted was a good deal larger than Professor Lyall. The Woolsey Pack Beta was not perturbed by this discrepancy in size. *Most* werewolves were a good deal larger than he.

The challenger attacked, but Lyall was already in motion, twisting out of the way and darting in for the other's throat. There was so much to do back at BUR and he wanted to end the bout quickly.

But the loner was a crafty fighter, nimble and adept. He avoided Lyall's counterattack, and the two circled each other warily, both coming to the realization that they might have underestimated their opponent.

The men around them closed in, forming a circle of bodies around the pair. The soldiers called insults at the challenger, the officers catcalled, and the pack stood in silent wide-eyed attention.

The loner charged at Professor Lyall, snapping. Lyall dodged. The challenger skidded slightly on the smooth paving stones, his claws making an awful scraping noise as he scrabbled for purchase. Taking advantage of the skid, Lyall dove at him, hitting him broadside with enough force to knock him onto his side. The two wolves rolled over and over together, bumping into the shins of those who goaded them on. Professor Lyall could feel the claws of the other wolf tearing against his soft underbelly as he bit viciously into the creature's neck.

This was what he disliked most about fighting. It was so embarrassingly untidy. He didn't mind the pain; he would heal fast enough. But he was bleeding all over his own pristine coat, and blood from the challenger was dripping down over his muzzle, matting the fur of his white ruff. Even as a wolf, Professor Lyall did not like to be unkempt.

Still the blood flowed, bits of fur flew about the challenger's scrabbling back legs in white puffs, and the sound of growling rent the air. The wet, rich smell of flowing blood caused the noses of the other pack members to wrinkle with interest. Professor Lyall wasn't one to play dirty, but things being as they were, he thought he might have to go in for an eyeball. Then he realized something was disturbing the crowd.

The tight circle of bodies began rippling, and then two pack members were thrust violently aside and Lord Maccon entered the ring.

He was naked, had been all day, but under the moonlight, he was once more looking scruffy and feral. From his mild weaving back and forth, either a day in dry dock hadn't sufficiently eliminated the formaldehyde from his system or he'd managed to acquire more. Professor Lyall would have to have words with the claviger who'd been persuaded to let Lord Maccon out of the dungeon.

Despite the presence of his lord and master, Lyall was in the middle of a fight and did not allow himself to be distracted.

"Randolph!" roared his Alpha. "What are you about? You hate fighting. Stop it immediately."

Professor Lyall ignored him.

Until Lord Maccon changed.

The earl was a big man, and in wolf form, he was large even for a werewolf, and he changed loudly. Not with any vocal indication of pain—he was too proud for that—it was simply that his bones were so massive that when they broke, they did so with a real will to crunch. He emerged from the transformation a huge brindled wolf, dark brown with gold, black, and cream markings and pale yellow eyes. He bounced over to where Lyall still scrabbled with the challenger, wrapped his massive jaws about his Beta's neck, and hauled him off, tossing him aside with a contemptuous flick.

Professor Lyall knew what was good for him and stepped away into the crowd, flopping down onto his bloody stomach, tongue lolling out as he panted for breath. If his Alpha wanted to make a fool of himself, there came a point when even the best Beta couldn't stop him. But he did stay in wolf form, just in case. Surreptitiously, he licked at his white ruff like a cat to get the blood off.

Lord Maccon barreled into the loner, massive jaws snapping down.

The challenger dodged to one side, a glint of panic in his yellow gaze. He had banked on not having to fight the earl; this was not in his plan.

Lyall could smell the wolf's fear.

Lord Maccon swiveled about and went after the challenger again, but then tripped over his own feet, lurched to the side, and came down hard on one shoulder.

Definitely still drunk, thought Professor Lyall, resigned.

The challenger seized the opportunity and dove for Lord Maccon's neck. At the same moment, the earl shook his head violently as though to clear it. Two large wolf skulls cracked together.

The challenger fell back, dazed.

Lord Maccon, already in a state of confusion, did not register the encounter, instead lurching after his enemy with single-minded focus. Normally a quick and efficient fighter, he ambled after his bemused opponent and took one long second to look down at him, as if trying to remember what, exactly, was going on. Then he surged forward and bit down on the other wolf's muzzle.

The fallen wolf squealed in pain.

Lord Maccon let go in befuddled surprise, as if shocked that his meal should yell back. The challenger stumbled to his feet.

The earl wove his head back and forth, an action his opponent found disconcerting. The loner crouched back onto his haunches, forelegs splayed out before him. Lyall wasn't certain if he was bowing or preparing to spring. He had no chance to do either, for Lord Maccon, much to his own astonishment, stumbled again, and in an effort to regain his balance, jumped forward, coming down solidly on top of the loner with a loud thud.

Almost as an afterthought, he craned his neck around and sank all of his very long and very deadly teeth into the upper portion of the other wolf's head—conveniently spearing one eye and both ears.

Because werewolves were immortal and very hard to kill, challenge fights could go on for days. But a bite to the eyes was generally considered a no-contest win. It would take a good forty-eight hours to heal properly, and a blind wolf, immortal or no, *could* be killed during the interim merely because he was at such a grave disadvantage.

As soon as the teeth struck home, the challenger, whimpering in agony, wriggled onto his back, presenting his belly to Lord Maccon in surrender. The earl, still lying half on top of the unfortunate fellow, lurched off of him, spitting and sneezing over the flavor of eye goo and ear wax. Werewolves enjoyed fresh meat—they needed it, in fact, to survive—but other werewolves did not taste fresh. They tasted perhaps not quite so putrefied as vampires, but still old and slightly spoiled.

Professor Lyall stood and stretched—tail tip quivering. Perhaps, he thought as he trotted back to the cloakroom, this battle might be a good thing: to have it publicly known that Lord Maccon could still defeat a challenger, even when drunk. The rest of the pack could take care of cleaning up the mess. Now that the matter was settled, Professor Lyall had business to attend to. He paused in the cloakroom. He might as well run to London in wolf form, as he was already wearing his fur and his evening attire was now hopelessly wrinkled. He really *must* get his Alpha back on the straight and narrow—the man's behavior was affecting his clothing. Lyall understood a broken heart, but it could not be allowed to rumple perfectly good shirtwaists.

The trouble with vampires, thought Alexia Tarabotti, was that they were quick as well as strong. Not as strong as werewolves, but in this particular instance Alexia didn't have any werewolves fighting on her side—*blast Conall to all three atmospheres*—so the vampires had a distinct advantage.

"Because," she grumbled, "my husband is a first-rate git. I wouldn't even be in this situation if it weren't for him."

Floote gave her a look of annoyance that suggested he felt that now was not the time for connubial recriminations.

Alexia took his meaning perfectly.

Monsieur Trouvé and Madame Lefoux, having been disturbed from some detailed consultation on the nature of spring-loaded cuckoo clocks, were making their way around from behind a little workman's table. Madame Lefoux pulled out a sharp-looking wooden pin from her cravat with one hand and pointed her other wrist at the intruders. Upon that wrist she wore a large wristwatch that was probably no wristwatch at all. The clock-maker, for lack of any better weapon, grasped the mahogany and pearl case of a cuckoo clock and brandished it in a threat-ening manner.

"Quoo?" said the clock. Alexia was amazed that even a tiny mechanical device could sound inexplicably French in this country.

Alexia pressed the appropriate lotus leaf, and the tip of her parasol opened to reveal a dart emitter. Unfortunately, Madame Lefoux had designed the emitter to fire only three shots, and there were four vampires. In addition, Alexia could not recall if the inventor had told her whether or not the numbing agent even worked on the supernatural. But it was the only projectile in her armament, and she figured all great battles began with an airborne offensive.

Madame Lefoux and Monsieur Trouvé joined Alexia and Floote at the bottom of the stairs, facing off against the vampires, who had slowed their hectic charge and were moving forward in a menacing manner, as cats will stalk string.

"How did they find me so quickly?" Alexia took aim.

"So they are after *you*, are they? Well, I suppose that is hardly a surprise." The clockmaker glanced in Alexia's direction.

"Yes. Terribly inconvenient of them."

Monsieur Trouvé let out a rolling bark of deep laughter. "I did say you always brought me charming surprises, and trouble with them, didn't I, Genevieve? *What* have you gotten me into this time?"

Madame Lefoux explained. "I am sorry, Gustave. We should have told you sooner. The London vampires want Alexia dead, and they appear to have passed the desire on to the Parisian hives."

"Well, fancy that. How jolly." The clockmaker did not seem upset, behaving more like a man on the brink of some grand lark.

The vampires pressed closer.

"Now, see here, couldn't we discuss this like civilized beings?" Alexia, ever one for form and courtesy, was in favor of negotiations whenever possible.

None of the vampires responded to her request.

Madame Lefoux tried the same question in French.

Still nothing.

Alexia thought this dreadfully boorish. The least they could do was answer with a "No, killing is all we are interested in at the moment, but thank you kindly for the offer all the same." Alexia had, in part, compensated for a lack of soul through the liberal application of manners. This was rather like donning an outfit consisting entirely of accessories, but Alexia maintained that proper conduct was never a bad thing. These vampires were behaving *most* improperly.

There were plenty of tables and display cabinets in the little shop that currently stood between the vampires and Alexia's small band of defenders. Most of the surfaces of these were covered in disassembled clocks of one style or another. It was, therefore, not unexpected that one of the vampires, probably intentionally—given the general grace and elegance of the species—knocked a pile of mechanicals to the floor.

What was unexpected was Monsieur Trouvé's reaction to this event.

He growled in anger and threw the cuckoo clock he was holding at the vampire.

"Quoo?" questioned the clock as it flew.

Then the clockmaker began to yell. "*That* was a prototype atmos clock with a dual regulatory aether conductor! A ground-breaking invention and utterly irreplaceable."

The cuckoo clock hit the vampire broadside, startling him considerably. It did minimal damage, landing with a sad little "Quooooo?"

Alexia decided it was probably a good time to start shooting. So she shot.

The poisoned dart hissed slightly as it flew, struck one of the vampires dead center to the chest, and stuck there. He looked down at it, up at Alexia with an expression of deep offense, and then crumpled limply to the floor like an overcooked noodle.

"Nicely shot, but it won't hold him for long," said Madame Lefoux, who should know. "Supernaturals can process the numbing agent faster than daylight folk."

Alexia armed her parasol and shot a second dart. Another vampire collapsed, but the first was already beginning to struggle groggily to his feet.

Then the remaining two were upon them.

Madame Lefoux shot at one with a wooden dart from her wristwatch, missing his chest and hitting the meaty part of his left arm. *Hah*, thought Alexia. *I knew it wasn't an ordinary watch!* The Frenchwoman then slashed at that same vampire with her wooden cravat pin. The vampire began to bleed from two spots, arm and cheek, and backed away warily.

"We are not interested in you, little scientist. Give us the soul-sucker and we'll be away."

"*Now* you want to engage in conversation?" Alexia was annoyed.

The last of the vampires lunged for her, clearly planning to drag her off. He had one hand wrapped around her wrist when he realized his miscalculation.

Upon contact with her, his fangs disappeared, as did all of his extraordinary strength. His pale, smooth skin turned fleshy peach with freckles—freckles! He was no longer capable of dragging her off, yet no matter how hard Alexia pulled, she could not break his grip. He must have been a strong man before he changed. She began bashing at the no-longer-supernatural creature with her parasol, but he did not let go, even as she inflicted real injury upon him. He seemed to be recovering his powers of deduction and realized he would have to fall back on leverage for this task. So he shifted about, preparing to haul Alexia up and over one shoulder.

A gunshot rattled throughout the shop, and before he could do anything further, the vampire collapsed backward, letting go of Alexia in order to clutch at his own side. Alexia glanced to her left, astounded to see the unflappable Floote pocketing a still-smoking, single-shot derringer with an ivory handle. It was undoubtedly the tiniest pistol Alexia had ever seen. From the same pocket, he pulled a second slightly bigger gun. Both were horribly antiquated, thirty years or more out of date, but still effective. The vampire Floote had shot stayed down, writhing in agony on the floor. Unless Alexia missed her guess, that bullet was made of a reinforced wood of some kind, for it seemed to continue to cause him harm. There was a good chance, Alexia realized with a sick kind of dread, that a vampire could actually die from a shot like that. She could hardly countenance it, the very idea of killing an immortal. All that knowledge, gone just like that.

Monsieur Trouvé seemed momentarily captivated. "That's a sundowner's weapon you have there, isn't it, Mr. Floote?"

Floote did not respond. There was accusation inherent in the term, for "sundowner" implied official sanction from Her Majesty's government to terminate the supernatural. No British gentleman without such authorization ought to carry such a weapon.

"Since when would you know anything about munitions, Gustave?" Madame Lefoux issued her friend an imperiously quirked brow.

"I've developed a keen interest in gunpowder recently. Terribly messy stuff, but awfully useful for a directed mechanical force."

"I should say so," said Alexia, readjusting her parasol and shooting her last dart.

"Now you've wasted them all," accused Madame Lefoux, letting fly with her own, more effective wooden dart at the groggy vampire just after Alexia's projectile struck home. It hit him in the eye. Sluggish black blood oozed out from around it. Alexia felt ill.

"Really, Genevieve, must you go for the eye? It's so unsightly." Monsieur Trouvé appeared to agree with Alexia's disgust.

"Only if you promise never to use a pun like that again."

Thus two of the vampires were now incapacitated. The other two had retreated out of range to regroup, clearly not having anticipated such resistance.

Madame Lefoux glared at Alexia. "Stop stalling and use the lapis solaris."

"Are you certain that is strictly necessary, Genevieve? It seems so discourteous. I could accidentally kill one of them with such a substance. We've already had a little too much of that kind of tomfoolery." She nodded with her chin at the vampire Floote had shot, who now lay ominously still. Vampires were scarce, and generally rather old. Murdering one even in self-defense was like thoughtlessly destroying a rare aged cheese. True, a fanged and murderous rare aged cheese, but . . .

The lady inventor gave the preternatural woman an incredulous look. "Yes, final death was the idea when I designed it."

One of the vampires lurched forward again, intent on Alexia. He held a wicked-looking knife. Clearly he was adapting better to her preternatural ability than his now-inert cohorts.

Floote shot his other gun.

This time the bullet hit the man's chest. The vampire fell backward, crashed into a loaded display cabinet, and landed on the floor, making exactly the same sound a carpet makes when whacked to get the dust out.

The remaining vampire was looking both annoyed and confused. He had brought no projectile weapons. The vampire Madame Lefoux had spiked in the eye yanked out the offending optical impairment and lurched to his feet, the socket oozing blackened, sluggish blood. The two joined forces to charge once more.

Madame Lefoux slashed, and Monsieur Trouvé, finally understanding the gravity of the situation, reached around and pulled a long, wicked-looking spring-adjuster from its cradle on the wall. It was brass, so it was unlikely to do any serious damage, but it might slow even a vampire if applied properly. A sharp wooden knife had now appeared in Floote's hand—both guns being of the single-shot variety and thus out of ammunition. *Such a competent man, Floote*, thought Alexia with pride.

"Well, if I must, fine. I'll guard the retreat," said Alexia. "Buy us some time."

"What, in a clock shop?" Madame Lefoux clearly couldn't resist.

Alexia gave her a withering look. Then she opened and flipped her parasol over in a practiced motion so that she held it backward by the tip instead of the handle. There was a tiny dial just above the magnetic disruption emitter, set into a nodule. She stepped slightly forward, mindful that she could harm her friends as well as the vampires with this particular weapon. Then she clicked the dial round two times, and three ribs of the parasol began to spew forth a fine mist of lapis solaris diluted in sulfuric acid.

At first the stampeding vampires didn't quite understand what was happening, but when the mixture began to burn them severely, they backed out of range.

"Up the stairs, now!" yelled Alexia.

They all began to retreat up the tiny staircase, Alexia bringing up the rear, brandishing the misting parasol. The smell of acid burning through carpet and wood permeated the air. A few drops landed on Alexia's claret-colored skirts. *Well*, she thought, resigned, *there is one gown I won't ever be able to wear again*.

The vampires stayed just far enough out of range. By the time Alexia had reached the top of the stairs—going backward and up with both hands occupied was no mean feat in long skirts and a bustle—the others had gathered together a quantity of large, heavy objects with which to barricade the top. Alexia's parasol sputtered once, then emitted a sad little hissing noise and stopped misting, having used up its store of the lapis solaris.

The vampires renewed their attack. Alexia was alone at the top of the stairs. But Madame Lefoux was ready for them and began hurling various interesting-looking gadgets down, until, at the last possible minute, Alexia managed to sneak behind the rapidly growing pile of furniture and trunks that Floote and Monsieur Trouvé had piled at the head of the staircase.

While Alexia recovered her breath and equanimity, they built up the improvised rampart, wedging and tilting a mountain of furniture downward, relying on gravity and weight as assistants.

"Anyone have a plan?" Alexia looked around hopefully.

The Frenchwoman gave her a fierce grin. "Gustave and I were talking earlier. He says he still has the ornithopter we designed at university."

Monsieur Trouvé frowned. "Well, yes, but it isn't certified by the Ministry of Aethernautics to fly within Parisian aether-space. I did not think you actually intended to use it. I'm not sure if the stabilizers are working properly."

"Never you mind that. Is it on the roof?"

"Of course, but—"

Madame Lefoux grabbed Alexia by the arm and began dragging her down the hall toward the back of the apartment.

Alexia made a face but allowed herself to be tugged along. "Well, then, to the roof with us! Ooof, wait, my dispatch case."

Floote dove to one side to retrieve her precious luggage.

"No time, no time!" insisted Madame Lefoux as the vampires, having attained the top of the stairway, were apparently engaged in trying to bash their way through to the landing by application of pure physical force. *How vulgar!*

"It has tea in it," Alexia explained gratefully when Floote reappeared with her case.

Then they heard a horrible noise, a rumbling, growling sound and the crunch of flesh between large, unforgiving jaws. The banging on the barricade stopped as something sharp-toothed and vicious distracted the vampires. A new sound of fighting commenced as the vampires engaged whatever it was that was hunting *them*.

The little group of refugees reached the end of the hallway. Madame Lefoux leaped up, grabbing at what looked to be a gas lamp fixture but what turned out to be a pull lever that activated a small hydraulic pump. A section of the ceiling flipped down at them, and a rickety ladder, clearly spring loaded, shot down, hitting the hallway floor with an audible thump.

Madame Lefoux scampered up. With considerable difficulty, hampered by dress and parasol, Alexia climbed after her, emerging into a crowded attic richly carpeted in dust and dead spiders. The gentlemen followed and Floote helped Monsieur Trouvé winch the ladder back up, disguising their retreat. With any luck, the vampires would be stalled trying to determine where and how their quarry had attained roof access.

Alexia wondered what had attacked the vampires on the stair: a savior, a protector, or some new form of monster that wanted her for itself? She didn't have time to contemplate for long. The two inventors were fussing about a machine of some kind, running around loosening tether ropes, checking safety features, tightening screws, and lubricating cogs. This seemed to involve a phenomenal quantity of banging and cursing.

The ornithopter, for that is what it must be, looked like a most incommodious mode of transport. Passengers—there was room for three in addition to the pilot—were suspended in nappy-like leather seats the top of which strapped about the waist.

Alexia dashed over, stumbling against an inappropriately placed gargoyle.

Monsieur Trouvé ignited a small steam engine. The craft

lurched upward and then tilted to one side, sputtering and coughing.

"I told you: stabilizers!" he said to Madame Lefoux.

"I cannot believe you don't have strapping wire on hand, Gustave. What kind of inventor are you?"

"Did you miss the sign above the shop door, my dear? Clocks! Clocks are my specialty. No stabilizers needed!"

Alexia intervened. "Wire, is that all you require?"

Madame Lefoux held her fingers a short width apart. "Yes, about so thick."

Alexia, before she could be shocked by her own audacity, lifted her overskirts and undid the tapes to her bustle. The undergarment dropped to the ground, and she kicked it in Madame Lefoux's direction. "That do?"

"Perfect!" the Frenchwoman crowed, attacking the canvas and extracting the metal boning, which she passed to Monsieur Trouvé.

While the clockmaker went to work threading the wire through some kind of piping about the contraption's nose, Alexia climbed inside. Only to discover, to her abject embarrassment, that the nappy-seat design caused one's skirts to hike up into one's armpits and one's legs to dangle below the enormous wings of the aircraft with bloomers exposed for all the world to see. They were her best bloomers, thank goodness, red flannel with three layers of lace at the hem, but still not a garment a lady ought to show to anyone except her maid or her husband, a pox on him, anyway.

Floote settled comfortably in behind her, and Madame Lefoux slid into the pilot's nappy. Monsieur Trouvé returned to the engine, situated behind Floote and under the tail of the craft, and cranked it up once more. The ornithopter wiggled, but then held steady and stabilized. *Victory to the bustle*, thought Alexia.

The clockmaker stepped back, looking pleased with himself.

"Are you not coming with us?" Alexia felt a strange kind of panic.

Gustave Trouvé shook his head. "Glide as much as you can, Genevieve, and you should be able to make it to Nice." He had to yell in order to be heard over the grumbling engine. He passed Madame Lefoux a pair of magnification goggles and a long scarf, which she used to wrap about her face, neck, and top hat.

Alexia, clutching parasol and dispatch case firmly to her ample chest, prepared for the worst.

"That far?" Madame Lefoux did not raise her head, busy checking on an array of dials and bobbing valves. "You have made modifications, Gustave."

The clockmaker winked.

Madame Lefoux looked at him suspiciously and then gave a curt nod.

Monsieur Trouvé marched back around to the rear of the ornithopter and spun up a guidance propeller attached to the steam engine.

Madame Lefoux pressed some kind of button and, with a massive *whoosh*, the wings of the craft began flapping up and down with amazing strength. "You *have* made modifications!"

The ornithopter jerked into the air with a burst of power.

"Didn't I tell you?" Monsieur Trouvé was grinning like a little boy. He had a good pair of lungs in that wide chest of his, so he continued to yell after them. "I replaced our original model with one of Eugène's bourdon tubes, activated by gunpowder charges. I did say I had taken a keen interest recently."

"What? Gunpowder!"

The clockmaker waved at them cheerfully as they flapped upward and forward, now a good few yards above the rooftop. Alexia could see much of Paris laid out below her wildly waving kid-boots.

Monsieur Trouvé bracketed his mouth with his hands. "I'll send your things on to the Florence dirigible station."

A great crash sounded, and two of the vampires burst out onto the roof.

Monsieur Trouvé's grin vanished into the depths of his impressive beard, and he turned to face the supernatural threat.

One of the vampires leapt up after them, hands stretched to grab. He got close enough for Alexia to see that he had an impressive collection of jagged bite marks now about his head and neck. His hand just missed Alexia's ankle. A huge white beast appeared behind him. Limping and bleeding, the creature charged the airborne vampire, hamstringing him and bringing him back to the rooftop with a crash.

The clockmaker yelled in fear.

Madame Lefoux did something to the controls, and the ornithopter flapped two mighty strokes and surged up. Then it shifted suddenly sideways in a gust of wind, tilting precariously. Alexia lost sight of the action on the rooftop behind one massive wing. It was presently to become irrelevant, for the ornithopter reached ever-greater heights, and Paris became lost under a layer of cloud.

"Magnifique!" yelled Madame Lefoux into the wind.

Sooner than Alexia would have believed possible, they attained the first of the aether atmospheres, the breezes there cool and slightly tingly against Alexia's inexcusably indecent legs. The ornithopter caught one of the southeasterly currents and began to ride it with, blessedly, a long smooth glide and much less flapping.

Professor Lyall had plenty he ought to be doing that night: BUR investigations, pack business, and Madame Lefoux's contrivance chamber to check up on. Naturally, he ended up doing none of those things. Because what he really wanted to find out was the current location of one Lord Akeldama—vampire, fashion icon, and very stylish thorn in everyone's side.

The thing about Lord Akeldama was—and in Lyall's experience, there was always a *thing*—that where he himself was not a fixture, his drones were. Despite supernatural speed and flawless taste in neckwear, Lord Akeldama could not, in fact,

attend every social event of note every single evening. But he
did seem to have a collection of drones and associates of drones
who could and did. The *thing* that was bothering Lyall at the
moment was that they weren't. Not only was the vampire himself
missing, but so were all of his drones, assorted sycophants, and
poodle-fakers. Usually, any major social event in London could
be relied upon to temporarily house some young dandy whose
collar points were too high, mannerisms too elegant, and interest
too keen to adequately complement his otherwise frivolous
appearance. These ubiquitous young men, regardless of how
silly they might act, how much gambling they might engage in,
and how much fine champagne they might swill, reported back
to their master with such an immense amount of information as
to put any of Her Majesty's espionage operations to shame.

And they had all vanished.

Professor Lyall couldn't identify most of them by face or
name, but as he made the rounds of London's various routs, card
parties, and gentleman's clubs that evening, he became painfully
aware of their collective absence. He himself was welcome at
most establishments but was not expected, for he was thought
to be rather shy. Yet he was familiar enough with high society
to mark the difference one vampire's disappearance had wrought.
His carefully polite inquiries yielded up neither destination nor
explanation. So it was that, in the end, he left the drawing rooms
of the wealthy and headed down toward dockside and the blood
brothels.

"You new, gov'na? Like a li'le sip, would ya? Only cost ya
a penny." The young man propping up the shadows of a scummy
brick wall was pale and drawn. The dirty scarf wrapped around
his neck no doubt already covered a goodly number of bite
marks.

"Looks like you've given enough already."

"Not a chance of it." The blood-whore's dirty face split with
a sudden smile, brown with rotting teeth. He was of the type
vampires rather crudely referred to as snacky-bites.

Professor Lyall bared his own teeth at the youngster, showing the boy that he did not, in fact, have the requisite fangs for the job.

"Ah, right you are, gov. No offense meant."

"None taken. There is a penny for you, however, if you provide me with some information."

The young man's pale face became still and drawn. "I don't grass, gov."

"I do not require the names of your clientele. I am looking for a man, a vampire. Name of Akeldama."

The blood-whore straightened away from the wall. "Won't find 'im 'ere, gov; 'e's got enough of 'is own ta slurp from."

"Yes, I am well aware of that fact. But I am wondering if you might know his current whereabouts."

The man bit his lip.

Professor Lyall handed him a penny. There weren't a lot of vampires in London, and blood-whores, who made it their livelihood to service them, tended to know a good deal about the local hives and loners as a matter of survival.

The lip was nibbled on slightly more.

Professor Lyall handed him another penny.

"Word on the street is 'e's left town."

"Go on."

"An' how. Didn't suss a master could be mobile like that."

Professor Lyall frowned. "Any idea as to where?"

A shake of the head was all Lyall got in answer.

"Or why?"

Another shake.

"One more penny if you can direct me to someone who does."

"Ya ain't gunna like me answer, gov."

Professor Lyall handed him another copper.

The blood-whore shrugged. "You'd be wantin' the other queen, then."

Professor Lyall groaned inwardly. Of course it would turn out to be a matter of internal vampire politics. "Countess Nadasdy?"

The young man nodded.

Professor Lyall thanked the blood-whore for his help and flagged down a seedy-looking hansom, directing the driver toward Westminster. About halfway there, he changed his mind. It wouldn't do for the vampires to know so soon that Lord Akeldama's absence was of interest to either BUR or the Woolsey Pack. Banging on the box with his fist, he redirected the driver toward Soho, intending to call upon a certain redhead.

Professor Lyall alighted from the hansom at Piccadilly Circus, paid the driver, and walked a block north. Even at midnight, it was a pleasant little corner of the city, swimming in young people of artistic propensities, if perhaps a bit dingy and lowbrow. Professor Lyall had a good memory, and he recalled the cholera outbreak of twenty years earlier as though it had happened only yesterday. Sometimes he thought he could still smell the sickness in the air. As a result, Soho always caused him to sneeze.

The apartment, when he knocked and was duly admitted by a very young maid, proved to be neat and tidy if a tad gleefully decorated. Ivy Tunstell bustled forward to greet him in the hallway, her dark curls bobbing out from under a large lace cap. The cap had blue silk roses clustered above her left ear, which gave her an oddly rakish appearance. She was wearing a pink walking dress, and Lyall was pleased to see he had not disturbed her at rest.

"Mrs. Tunstell, how do you do? I do apologize for calling at such a late hour."

"Professor Lyall, welcome. Delighted to see you. Not at all. We keep to a sunset schedule. After he left your service, my dear Tunny never could manage to break the habit, and it does suit his chosen profession."

"Ah, yes. How is Tunstell?"

"Auditioning as we speak." Ivy led her guest into an absolutely tiny receiving room, with barely enough space to house a settee, two chairs, and a tea table. The decor seemed to have been chosen with only one theme in mind—pastel. It was a resplendent collection of pink, pale yellow, sky blue, and lilac.

Professor Lyall hung his hat and coat on a spindly hat stand crowded behind the door and took one of the chairs. It was like sitting inside a bowl of Easter candy. Ivy settled herself onto the settee. The young maid, having followed them in, gave the mistress of the house a quizzical look.

"Tea, Professor Lyall, or would you prefer something, uh, bloodier?"

"Tea would be lovely, Mrs. Tunstell."

"You are certain? I have some delightful kidney set aside for a pie tomorrow, and it *is* getting on to full moon."

Professor Lyall smiled. "Your husband has been telling you things about living with werewolves, hasn't he?"

Ivy blushed slightly. "Perhaps a little. I am afraid I have been terribly nosy. I find your culture fascinating. I do hope you do not think me impertinent."

"Not at all. But, really, just tea would be perfectly fine."

Ivy nodded to her maid, and the young girl scuttled off, clearly excited.

"We don't get many visitors of your caliber," lamented Ivy.

Professor Lyall was too much a gentleman to remark that Miss Hisselpenny's elopement, and consequent loss of what little status she'd had, made her a less than desirable acquaintance for most. Only a high-ranking original, as Lady Maccon had been, could afford to continue such an association. Now that Alexia herself had fallen from grace, Ivy must be a veritable social pariah.

"How is the hat shop coming on?"

Mrs. Tunstell's big hazel eyes lit up with pleasure. "Well, I have only had it under my charge for the one day. Of course, I kept it open this evening as well. I know Madame Lefoux caters to the supernatural set, but you would not believe the things one over-hears in a hat shop. Only this afternoon, I learned Miss Wibbley was engaged."

Prior to Ivy's marriage, Professor Lyall knew she had relied upon Alexia, who was at best disinterested and at worst obtuse, for all her society gossip. As a result, Ivy had been in a constant state of frustration.

"So you are enjoying yourself?"

"Immeasurably. I never thought *trade* could be so very entertaining. Why, this evening, Miss Mabel Dair paid us a call. The actress, you've heard of her?" Ivy looked to Professor Lyall inquiringly.

The werewolf nodded.

"Well, she came by to pick up a special order for Countess Nadasdy herself. I had no idea the countess even wore hats. I mean to say"—Ivy looked to Lyall in confusion—"she does not actually leave her house, does she?"

Professor Lyall highly doubted that a special order from Madame Lefoux for a vampire queen bore any resemblance whatsoever to a hat, aside from being transported inside a hatbox. But he perked up with interest. He had thought to ask Tunstell for information as to Lord Akeldama's disappearance, given the vampire's affection for the theater and Tunstell's previous investigative training under Lyall's tutelage, but perhaps Ivy might unwittingly have some information to impart. Mabel Dair, after all, was Countess Nadasdy's favorite drone.

"And how did Miss Dair seem?" he asked carefully.

The maid returned and Ivy fussed with the tea trolley. "Oh, not *at all* the thing. Dear Miss Dair and I have become almost friendly since my marriage. She and Tunny have appeared onstage together. She was clearly most upset about something. And I said to her, I did, I said, 'My dear Miss Dair,' I said, 'you do not look *at all* the thing! Would you like to sit, take a little tea?' And I think she might have." Ivy paused and studied Professor Lyall's carefully impassive face. "You are aware, she is a bit of a, well, I hardly like to say it to a gentleman of your persuasion, but a, um, vampire drone." Ivy whispered this as if she could not quite believe her own daring at being even a nodding acquaintance with such a person.

Professor Lyall smiled slightly. "Mrs. Tunstell, do you forget I work for the Bureau of Unnatural Registry? I am well aware of her status."

"Oh, of course you are. How silly of me." Ivy covered her embarrassment by pouring the tea. "Milk?"

"Please. And do go on. Did Miss Dair relay the nature of her distress?"

"Well, I do not think she intended me to overhear. She was discussing something with her companion. That tall, good-looking gentleman I met at Alexia's wedding—Lord Ambrittle, I believe it was."

"Lord Ambrose?"

"Yes, that! Such a nice man."

Professor Lyall forbore to mention that Lord Ambrose was, in fact, a not very nice vampire.

"Well, apparently, dear Miss Dair caught the countess and some gentleman or another arguing. A potent gentleman, she kept saying, whatever that means. And she said she thought the countess was accusing this gentleman of having taken something from Lord Akeldama. Quite astonishing. Why would a potent man want to steal from Lord Akeldama?"

"Mrs. Tunstell," Professor Lyall said very precisely and unhurriedly, "did Lord Ambrose notice that you had overheard this?"

"Why? Is it a matter of significance?" Ivy popped a sugared rose petal into her mouth and blinked at her guest.

"It is certainly intriguing." Lyall took a cautious drink of his tea. It was excellent.

"I hate to speak ill of such a nice man, but I believe he did not recognize me. He may even have thought I was a genuine *shopgirl*. Shocking, I know, but I *was* standing behind a sales counter at the time." She paused and sipped her tea. "I thought you might find the information useful."

At that, Professor Lyall gave Mrs. Tunstell a sharp look. He wondered for the first time how much of Ivy was, in fact, comprised of dark curls and big eyes and ridiculous hats and how much of that was for show.

Ivy returned his direct gaze with a particularly innocent smile. "The great advantage," she said, "of being thought silly, is that people forget and begin to think one might also be foolish. I may, Professor Lyall, be a trifle enthusiastic in my manner and dress, but I am no fool."

"No, Mrs. Tunstell, I can see that." *And Lady Maccon*, thought Lyall, *would not be so friendly with you if you were.*

"I believe Miss Dair was overset, or she would not have been so indiscreet in public."

"Ah, and what is your excuse?"

Ivy laughed. "I am well aware, Professor, that my dearest Alexia does not tell me much about certain aspects of her life. Her friendship with Lord Akeldama, for example, has always remained a mystery to me. I mean really, he is *too* outrageous. But her judgment is sound. I should have told her what I heard, were she still in town. As it stands, I judge you will make an adequate substitute. You stand very high in my husband's regard. Besides which, I simply do not believe it is right. Potent gentlemen should not go around stealing things from Lord Akeldama."

Professor Lyall knew perfectly well the identity of Ivy's "potent gentleman." It meant that this was rapidly becoming an ever more serious and ever more vampire-riddled conundrum. The potentate was the premier rove in all of England, Queen Victoria's chief strategist and her most treasured supernatural adviser. He sat on the Shadow Council with the dewan, werewolf loner and commander in chief of the Royal Lupine Guard. Until recently, Alexia had been their third. The potentate was one of the oldest vampires on the island. And he had stolen something from Lord Akeldama. Professor Lyall would wager good money on the fact that it was in pursuit of that very object that had caused Lord Akeldama, and all of his drones, to leave London.

What a fine kettle of fangs this is becoming, he thought.

Mostly unaware of the exploding steam engine she had just landed her guest in, Ivy Tunstell bobbed her curls at Professor Lyall and offered him another cup of tea. Lyall decided that his best possible course of action was to head home to Woolsey Castle and go to sleep. Often vampires were better understood after a good day's rest.

Consequently, he declined the tea.

CHAPTER EIGHT

Trial by Snuff, Kumquat, and Exorcism

Alexia's legs were stiff from the cold, but at least they were decently covered by her skirts once more, even if those skirts were now coated in mud as well as burned by acid. She sighed. She must look like a veritable gypsy with her spattered dispatch case and wild hair. Madame Lefoux also looked the worse for wear, speckled with mud, her goggles dangling about her neck. Her top hat was still secured to her head by the long scarf, but her mustache was decidedly askew. Only Floote somehow managed to look entirely unruffled as they skulked—there really was no other word for it—through the side alleys of Nice in the wee hours of the morning.

Nice proved itself smaller than Paris, characterized by a casual seaside attitude. Madame Lefoux, however, hinted darkly that the city's "Italian troubles" of ten years ago remained, hidden but unabated, and that this upsetting situation gave Nice a restless undertone not always sensed by strangers.

"Imagine! Trying to contend that Nice is really Italian. Pah." Madame Lefoux flicked one hand dismissively and glared at Alexia, as though Alexia might side with the Italians in this matter.

Alexia tried to think of something reassuring to say. "I am certain there is hardly any pasta in the whole city," was the best rejoinder she could come up with on such short notice.

Madame Lefoux only increased the pace of their skulking, leading them around a pile of discarded rags into a dingy little alleyway.

"I do hope the ornithopter will be safe where we left it." Alexia tried to change the subject as she followed her friend, lifting her skirts away from the rags. There was hardly any point in the effort at this juncture, but instinct dictated one's skirts be lifted.

"Should be. It's out of gunpowder charges, and very few, apart from Gustave and myself, know how to fly it. I shall send him a note as to its location. I do apologize for that unfortunate landing."

"You mean that unfortunate *crash*?"

"At least I chose a soft bit of ground."

"Duck ponds usually are soft. You do realize, ornithopter only *means* bird? You don't actually have to treat it as such."

"At least it didn't explode."

Alexia paused in her skulking. "Oh, do you believe it ought to have done so?"

Madame Lefoux gave one of her annoying little French shrugs.

"Well I think your ornithopter has earned its name."

"Oh, yes?" The inventor looked resigned.

"Yes. The Muddy Duck."

"*Le Canard Boueux*? Very funny."

Floote gave a tiny snort of amusement. Alexia glared at him. How had he managed to entirely avoid the mud?

Madame Lefoux led them to a small door that once might have been colored blue, and then yellow, and then green, a history it displayed proudly in crumbling strips of paint all down the front. The Frenchwoman knocked softly at first, and then more and more loudly until she was banging quite violently on the poor door.

The only reaction the racket caused was the immediate commencement of an unending bout of hysterical barking from some species of diminutive canine in possession of the other side of the door.

Floote gestured with his head at the doorknob. Alexia looked closely at it under the flickering torchlight; Nice apparently was not sophisticated enough for gas streetlamps. It was brass, and mostly unassuming, except that there was a very faint etched symbol on its surface, almost smoothed away by hundreds of hands—a chubby little octopus.

After a good deal more banging and barking, the door cautiously opened a crack to reveal a mercurial little man wearing a red and white striped nightshirt and cap, and a half-frightened, half-sleepy expression. A dirty feather duster on four legs bounced feverishly about his bare ankles. Much to Alexia's surprise, given her recent experience with Frenchmen, the man had no mustache. The feather duster did. Perhaps in Nice mustaches were more common on canines?

Her surprise was abated, however, when the little man spoke, not in French, but in German.

When his staccato sentence was met only by three blank expressions, he evaluated their manners and dress and switched to heavily accented English.

"Ya?"

The duster ejected itself through the partly opened door and attacked Madame Lefoux, gnawing at the hem of her trouser leg. What Madame Lefoux's excellent woolen trousers had done to insult the creature, Alexia could not begin to fathom.

"Monsieur Lange-Wilsdorf?" Madame Lefoux tried tactfully to shake off the animal with her foot.

"Who would be wishing to know?"

"I am Lefoux. We have been in correspondence these last few months. Mr. Algonquin Shrimpdittle recommended the introduction."

"I thought you were of the, uh, persuasion of the feminine." The gentleman squinted at Madame Lefoux suspiciously.

Madame Lefoux winked at him and doffed her top hat. "I am."

"Leave off, Poche!" barked the German at the tiny dog. "Monsieur Lange-Wilsdorf," Madame Lefoux explained to

Alexia and Floote, "is a biological analytical technician of some note. He has a particular expertise that you may find rather interesting, Alexia."

The German opened his door farther and craned his neck to see around Madame Lefoux to where Alexia stood shivering.

"Alexia?" He scanned her face in the faint light of the street torch. "Not *the* Alexia Tarabotti, the Female Specimen?"

"Would it be good or bad if I were?" The lady in question was a little distressed to be engaging in a protracted doorstep conversation in the nighttime cold with a man garbed in red and white striped flannel.

Madame Lefoux said, with a flourish, "Yes, *the* Alexia Tarabotti."

"I cannot believe it! The Female Specimen, at *my* door? Really?" The little man thrust said door wide and nipped out and around Madame Lefoux to grab Alexia warmly by the hand, pumping it up and down enthusiastically in the American style of greeting. The dog, perceiving a new threat, let go of Madame Lefoux's trouser and began yipping again, heading in Alexia's direction.

Alexia wasn't really sure she enjoyed being referred to as a specimen. And the way the German looked at her was almost hungry.

Alexia prepared her parasol with her free hand. "I would not, young sir, if I were you," she said to the dog. "My skirts have been through quite enough for one evening." The dog appeared to think better of his attack and began jumping up and down in place, all four legs oddly straight.

"Come in, come in! The greatest marvel of the age, here, on my very doorstep. This is—how do you say?—fantastic, ya, fantastic!" The little man paused in his enthusiasm upon noticing Floote for the first time, silent and still to one side of the stoop.

"And who is this?"

"Uh, this is Mr. Floote, my personal secretary." Alexia stopped staring ominously down at the dog in time to answer so Floote didn't have to.

Mr. Lange-Wilsdorf let go of Alexia and went to walk a slow turn around Floote. The German gentleman was still in his night-shirt, in the street, but he didn't seem to notice the faux pas. Alexia figured that as she had just shown her bloomers to half of France, she didn't have the right to be scandalized by this behavior.

"Is he, is he *really*? Nothing more evil than that? No? Are you certain?" Mr. Lange-Wilsdorf reached out a crooked finger and yanked down Floote's cravat and shirt, checking the neck area for marks.

Growling, the dog glommed onto Floote's boot.

"Do you *mind*, sir?" Floote looked decidedly put-upon. Alexia couldn't tell if it was the man or his dog that irritated most; Floote could abide neither a wrinkled collar nor damp shoes.

Seeing nothing incriminating, the German left off torturing Floote with his vulgar behavior. Once again he grabbed Alexia by the hand and positively dragged her into his tiny house. He gestured for the other two to follow, giving Floote yet another dubious once-over. The dog escorted them inside.

"Well, you realize, under ordinary circumstances, I wouldn't. Not a man, not so late at night. Never can tell with the English. But I suppose, just this once. Though, I did hear some of the terrible, terrible rumors about *you*, young miss." The German raised his chin and attempted to look down on Alexia, as though he were some kind of disapproving maiden aunt. It was a particularly unsuccessful look, as, aside from not being her aunt, he was a good head shorter than Alexia.

"Heard you had married a *werewolf*. Ya? What a thing for a preternatural to go and be doing. A most unfortunate choice for the Female Specimen."

"Is it?" Alexia managed to get just those two words in before Mr. Lange-Wilsdorf continued on without apparent pause or need for breath, shepherding them into a messy little parlor.

"Yes, well, we all make the mistakes."

"You have no idea," muttered Alexia, feeling a strange aching pain of loss.

Madame Lefoux began poking about the room with interest. Floote took up his customary station by the door.

The dog, exhausted by his own frenzy, went and curled in front of the cold fireplace, a posture that made him look, if possible, even more like a common household cleaning device.

There was a bell rope near the door, which the little man began to tug on, at first gently and then with such enthusiasm he was practically swinging from it. "You will be wanting tea, I am certain. English are always with the wanting of tea. Sit down, sit down."

Madame Lefoux and Alexia sat. Floote did not.

Their host bustled over to a little side table and took a small box out of a drawer. "Snuff?" He flipped the lid and offered the leaf about.

Everyone declined. But the German seemed unwilling to accept Floote's refusal. "No, no, I insist."

"I do not partake, sir," objected Floote.

"Really, I *insist*." A sudden hardness entered Mr. Lange-Wilsdorf's eyes.

Floote shrugged, took a small portion, and inhaled delicately.

The German watched him closely the entire time. When Floote showed no abnormal reaction, the little man nodded to himself and put the snuffbox away.

A disheveled manservant entered the room.

The dog awoke and, despite a clearly extensive association with the domestic staff, launched himself at the boy as though he posed a grave threat to the safety of the world.

"Mignon, we have the guests. Bring up a pot of Earl Grey and some croissants at once. *Earl Grey*, mind you, and that basket of kumquats. Thank God for the kumquats." He narrowed his eyes at Floote once more, in an "I'm not finished with you, young man" kind of way.

Floote, who was a good deal older than the German gentleman, remained utterly impassive.

"Well, this is delightful, ya, delightful. Alexia Tarabotti, here in *my* home." He took off his nightcap to enact a twitchy little bow in Alexia's direction. The action revealed a set of precariously large ears, which looked as though they rightly belonged to someone else.

"Never met your father, but I have studied much over his stock. First to breed a female soulless in seven generations, ya. It is a miracle, some have claimed, the Female Specimen." He nodded to himself. "I have the theory, of course, to do with brood female mixing outside of Italy. Brilliant choice of your father's, ya? A little of the fresh blood of English."

Alexia could hardly believe the statement. As though she were the result of some kind of horse-breeding program. "Now, I say—!"

Madame Lefoux interjected at this juncture, "Mr. Lange-Wilsdorf here has been studying the preternatural state for many years now."

"It has been difficult, most difficult, indeed, ya, to find a live specimen. My little trouble with the church, you understand."

"Come again?" Alexia checked her rage in favor of curiosity. Here was a scientist who might really know something.

The German blushed and worried his sleeping cap about with both hands. "A little—how do you say?—spot of bother. Had to move to France and leave much of my research behind. A travesty."

Alexia looked to Madame Lefoux for an explanation.

"He was excommunicated," said the inventor in a grave, hushed voice.

The little man blushed even redder. "Ah, you heard of it?"

Madame Lefoux shrugged. "You know how the Order gossips."

A sigh met this statement. "Well, regardless, you have brought me this fine visitor. A living, breathing female preternatural. You will allow me to ask you questions, young lady, ya? Perhaps, a test or two?"

A tap came at the door, and the manservant entered bearing a tea tray.

Mr. Lange-Wilsdorf accepted the tray and then waved the man away. He poured the tea, strong and redolent of the scent of bergamot. Alexia didn't much like Earl Grey; it was well out of fashion in London and was never served in any of the establishments she frequented. Vampires were not fond of citrus. Which, she realized, must be why the little man was now pressing the tea and a small pile of kumquats on the austere Floote.

"The snuff!"

Everyone looked at her.

"Ah, you decided you wanted to try some, ya, Female Specimen?"

"Oh, no. I simply realized. You made Floote take snuff as a werewolf check. They hate snuff. And now you're using the Earl Grey and the kumquats to see if he's a vampire."

Floote arched one eyebrow, took a kumquat, and popped it whole into his mouth, chewing methodically.

"You do realize, Mr. Lange-Wilsdorf, that vampires are perfectly capable of consuming citrus? They just don't like it."

"Yes, of course, I'm well aware. But it is a good—how do you say?—initial check, until sun comes up."

Floote sighed. "I assure you, sir, I am not of a supernatural inclination."

Alexia snickered. Poor Floote looked extremely put-upon.

The little German did not seem convinced by mere verbal guarantees. He kept a jaundiced eye on Floote and maintained proprietary control of the bowl of kumquats. For future use as projectile weaponry, perhaps?

"Of course, you could still be a claviger or drone-type person."

Floote huffed out a small puff of annoyed breath.

"You already checked him for bite marks," pointed out Alexia.

"Absence of the marks is not absolute proof, especially as he may be a claviger. You *did* marry a werewolf, after all."

Floote looked as though he had never been more insulted in his life. Alexia, still smarting over the "Female Specimen" moniker, sympathized.

In a lightning change of mood that seemed to characterize the little man's paranoia, the German looked with sudden new suspicion at Alexia. "The verification." He muttered to himself. "You understand, ya? Of course you do. Must verify you as well. Ah, if only I had my counter. Have this little poltergeist problem. Perhaps you could see your way to an exorcism? Should not be hard for the Female Specimen." He glanced at a small window to one side of the room, curtains thrown wide to let in the rapidly brightening dawn. "Before sunrise?"

Alexia sighed. "This could not possibly wait until tomorrow evening? I have been traveling most of the night. I suppose you could call it traveling."

The little man grimaced at her but did not take the hint, as any good host would have.

"Really, Mr. Lange-Wilsdorf, we have only just arrived," Madame Lefoux protested.

"Oh, very well." Alexia put down her tea, which wasn't very good, anyway, and half a croissant, which was buttery and delicious. If it was necessary for this odd little man to trust them in order to get some answers out of him, she was equal to the task. Alexia sighed, angry once more at her husband's rejection. She wasn't entirely certain how just yet, but she intended to blame this latest nuisance on Lord Conall Maccon as well as everything else.

The dog, Poche, led the way down several flights of stairs and into a tiny cellar, barking with unwarranted enthusiasm the entire time. Mr. Lange-Wilsdorf apparently did not notice the racket. Alexia resigned herself to the fact that it was the creature's normal mode of operation—when its eyes were open, so, too, was its mouth.

"You must think me the terrible host, ya." The German said this with an air of one attending to the requirements of society rather than one experiencing actual remorse.

Alexia could think of nothing to say in response, as, so far as it went, it was perfectly true. Any host worth his blood would have seen them decently abed by now, supernatural or not. No gentleman would insist his guest perform an exorcism without providing accommodations first, let alone a decent meal. So Alexia simply clutched her parasol and followed the German and his frenzied canine down into the bowels of his cramped and dirty house. Madame Lefoux and Floote seemed to feel their presence was not required on this jaunt and remained upstairs in the parlor, sipping at the vile tea and consuming, very probably, all of the excellent croissants. *Traitors.*

The cellar was gloomy in all the ways cellars ought to be and included, just as the man had said, a ghost in the final throes of poltergeist phase.

Above the little dog's barking came the intermittent keening wail of second-death. As if that were not bad enough, the poltergeist had gone to pieces. Alexia could not abide clutter, and, having lost almost all of its capacity for cohesion, this ghost was very messy, indeed. It was flitting about the dark musty interior as pale wisps of body parts, entirely dismembered—an elbow here, an eyebrow there. Alexia started and let out a little squeak upon encountering a single eyeball, all intelligence gone from its depths, staring at her from the top of a wine rack. The cellar also smelled badly of formaldehyde and rotten flesh.

"Really, Mr. Lange-Wilsdorf." Alexia's voice was cold with disapproval. "You ought to have seen to the unfortunate soul weeks ago and never let it get this bad."

The man rolled his eyes dismissively. "On the contrary, Female Specimen, I rented this house because of the ghost. I have long been interested in recording exact stages of *homo animus* dis-animation. And since my trouble with the Vatican, I switched the focus of my studies onto ghosts. I have managed three papers on this one alone. Now, I must admit, she has become much less. The staff refuses to come down here. I keep having to fetch wine myself."

Alexia narrowly avoided walking through a floating ear. "Which must be very vexing."

"But it has been useful. I theorize that remnant animus is carried on aether eddies as weakening of tether commences. I believe my work here has proved this hypothesis."

"You mean to say that the soul rides the aether air, and as the body decomposes, its hold on the soul disintegrates? Like a sugar lump in tea?"

"Ya. What else could explain random floating of non-corporeal body parts? I have excavated the corpse, just there."

Sure enough, a hole had been dug into one corner of the cellar floor, inside of which lay the mostly decomposed skeleton of a dead girl.

"What happened to the poor thing?"

"Nothing significant. I got much needed information out of her before she went mad. The parents could not afford grave-yard fees." He tut-tutted and shook his head at the shame of it. "When she turned out to have excess soul and went ghost, the family enjoyed still having her around. Unfortunately, they all then died of cholera and left her here for the next occupants to enjoy. Been that way until I came along."

Alexia looked about at the floating wisps. A toenail bobbed in her direction. In fact, all of the remnant body parts were floating softly toward her, as water will go down a drain. It was both eerie and unsettling. Still she hesitated. Her stomach, and its nearby problematic companion, objected to both the smell of death and the certain knowledge of what she must do next. Holding her breath, Alexia crouched down near the gravesite. The hole for the body had been dug directly into the dirt of the cellar floor with no attempt made to preserve the corpse for supernatural longevity until the German came along. The child would not have had long to be a proper ghost before the madness of decomposing flesh began taking her away. It was a cruel business.

What was left was a sad crumpled little skeleton, mostly

defleshed by maggots and mold. Alexia carefully removed one glove and reached down. She chose what looked to be the least decomposed part of the child's head and touched her there once. The flesh was incredibly squishy under her fingertip and compressed easily like wet sponge cake.

"Ugh." Alexia drew her hand back with a jerk of disgust.

The faintly luminescent wisps of body parts floating around the cellar vanished instantly, dispersing into the musty air as preternatural touch severed the last of the soul's tether to its body.

The German looked around, mouth slightly open. The little dog, for once, stopped barking. "Is that all?"

Alexia nodded, brushing her fingertip against her skirt several times. She stood.

"But I did not even have my notebook out yet! What a—how do you say?—wasted opportunity."

"It is done."

"Extraordinary. I have not observed a preternatural end a ghost before now. Quite extraordinary. Well, that confirms that you are in truth, what you say you are, Female Specimen. Congratulations."

As if I have won some sort of prize. Alexia raised her eyebrows at that, but the little man didn't seem to notice. So she made her way firmly back up the stairs.

The German trotted after. "Truly, truly extraordinary. Perfect exorcism. Only a preternatural can accomplish such a thing with one touch. I had read of it, certainly, but to see it, right there, in front of me. Do you find the effects more rapid for you, than for the males of your species?"

"I would not know, never having met one."

"Of course, of course. Ya. Cannot share the same air, preternaturals."

Alexia made her way back to the parlor, where Madame Lefoux and Floote had left her one of the croissants. *Thank goodness.*

"How was it?" asked the Frenchwoman politely, if a little coldly. The last ghost Alexia had exorcised had been a very dear friend of Madame Lefoux's.

"Squishy."

Madame Lefoux wrinkled her pert little nose. "One imagines it must be."

The German went to look out the window, clearly awaiting full sunrise. The sun was beginning to show just over the rooftops, and Alexia was pleased to see that Nice might, just possibly, be slightly less dirty than Paris. The dog vibrated its way around the room yipping at each visitor in turn, as though it had not remembered their presence, which might be the case given its apparent lack of a brain, before collapsing in an exhausted pouf under the settee.

Alexia finished her croissant using only her untainted hand and then waited patiently, hoping against hope that sometime soon they might be offered beds. It felt like a very long time since she'd slept. She was beginning to feel numb with tiredness. Madame Lefoux seemed to feel much the same, for she had nodded off. Her chin dipped down into the bow of her cravat. Her top hat, still partially wrapped with Monsieur Trouvé's scarf, tipped forward on her head. Even Floote's shoulders were sagging ever so slightly.

The first rays of the sun crept in over the windowsill and speared into the room. Mr. Lange-Wilsdorf watched avidly as the light touched Floote's trouser leg. When Floote did not immediately burst into flames or run screaming from the room, the little German relaxed for what Alexia suspected was the first time since they had knocked on his door.

With still no offer of a sleeping chamber forthcoming, Alexia took a deep breath and faced her host squarely. "Mr. Lange-Wilsdorf, why all this bother and testing? Are you a true believer? I would have thought that odd in a member of the Order of the Brass Octopus."

Madame Lefoux cracked her eyelids at her friend's direct

speech and tipped her top hat back on her head with one elegant finger. She regarded the little German with interest.

"Perhaps, perhaps. My research is delicate, dangerous, even. If I am to trust you, or help you, it is important, vital, that none of you are—how do I put this?—*undead*."

Alexia winced. Madame Lefoux straightened out of her slouch, abruptly much less drowsy. "Undead" was not a word one used openly in polite society. The werewolves, vampires, and even newly minted ghosts found it understandably distasteful to be referred to as such. Much in the same way that Alexia objected when the vampires called her a soul-sucker. It was, simply put, vulgar.

"That is a rather crude word, Mr. Lange-Wilsdorf, wouldn't you say?"

"Is it? Ah, you English and your semantics."

"But 'undead,' certainly, is not apt."

The man's eyes went hard and flinty. "I suspect that depends on what you define as living. Ya? Given my current studies, 'undead' suits very well."

The French inventor grinned. Her dimples showed. Alexia wasn't certain how they did it, but those dimples managed to look quite crafty. "Not for long it won't."

Mr. Lange-Wilsdorf tilted his head, intrigued. "You know something of relevance to my research, do you, Madame Lefoux?"

"You are aware that Lady Maccon here married a werewolf?"

A nod.

"I think you should tell him what has happened, Alexia."

Alexia grimaced. "He might be helpful?"

"He is the closest thing to an expert on the preternatural the Order of the Brass Octopus has. Templars might know more, but it's difficult to say."

Alexia nodded. She weighed her options and finally decided the risk was worth it. "I am pregnant, Mr. Lange-Wilsdorf."

The German looked at Alexia with a distinct air of covetousness. "Felicitations and condolences. You will not, of course, be

able to—how do you say?—carry to term. No preternatural
female has in recorded history. A great sadness to the Templars
and their breeding program, of course, but . . ." He trailed off at
Madame Lefoux's continued grin.

"You are implying? No, it cannot be. She is pregnant *by* the
werewolf?"

Alexia and Madame Lefoux both nodded.

The German turned away from the window and came to sit close
to Alexia. Too close. His eyes were hard and greedy on her face.

"You would not be covering up for, how you English might
say, a little indiscretion?"

Alexia was tired of all the games. She gave him a look that
suggested the next person to even hint she was unfaithful
would be receiving the worst her parasol had to offer. She
had hoped he would know something that might result in a
different reaction.

"How about," she suggested in clipped tones, "you assume I
am telling the truth in this matter and we leave you to theorize
on the subject while we attend to some much-needed rest?"

"Of course, of course! You are with child; you must sleep.
Imagine such a thing, a preternatural pregnant by a supernatural.
I must do research. Has it ever been tried before? The Templars
would not think to breed the werewolf with soulless. The very
idea. Ya, amazing. You are, after all, scientific opposites, each
other's end. With rarity of females of either species, I can see a
basis for absence of proper documentation. But if you speak
truth, why, what a miracle, what a fabulous abomination!"

Alexia cleared her throat loudly, placing one hand to her
stomach and the other on her parasol. She might think of this
baby as inconvenient, even hate it sometimes, but far be it for
some diminutive German with bad taste in pets to describe it
as an *abomination*. "I do beg your pardon!"

Madame Lefoux recognized *that tone* in Alexia's voice and
jumped to her feet. Grabbing Alexia by the hand, she attempted
to pull her friend up and out of the room.

Mr. Lange-Wilsdorf had whipped out a notepad and, oblivious to Alexia's anger, began scribbling away, all the while muttering to himself.

"We shall find guest rooms on our own, shall we?" suggested the Frenchwoman over Alexia's angry sputtering.

Mr. Lange-Wilsdorf made a dismissive movement with his stylographic pen, not looking up from his ruminations.

Alexia found her voice. "Couldn't I just whack him once? Just a little one, over the head? He would hardly notice."

Floote raised one eyebrow and took hold of Alexia's elbow, helping Madame Lefoux to remove her bodily from the room. "Bed, I think, madam."

"Oh, very well," conceded Alexia, "if you insist." She glared at Madame Lefoux. "But you had better be right about this character's character."

"Oh"—the dimples were back—"I believe he may surprise you."

"Like being served wet toad on toast?"

"He could prove you're right. That Lord Maccon fathered your child."

"That's the only possible way this could be worth it. 'Female Specimen' indeed! Sounds like he plans to dissect me with a clinkering-spud."

When Alexia finally came down to breakfast the next morning, it was, in fact, no longer morning at all, but early afternoon. Madame Lefoux and Floote were already seated at the small dining table, as was the little German scientist. He was entirely absorbed in some research while eating—*deplorable behavior*! He was positively vibrating in excitement, almost as much as his feather duster of a dog.

As it was now daytime, both the German and his dog were a tad more formally attired. Alexia was a little surprised. She'd half expected Mr. Lange-Wilsdorf to still be wearing his striped nightshirt. Instead, he looked perfectly respectable in a tweed coat and brown trousers. He wore no cravat, to Floote's obvious dismay. Alexia was, perhaps, less shocked by the missing cravat than she should have been. After all, eccentricity of dress was to be expected in foreigners for whom neckwear and cravats were regarded with suspicion, as they made it difficult to identify drones. Poche also wore tweed; a length of it was tied in a waterfall knot about the dog's neck. *Aha*, thought Alexia, *the missing cravat!* The creature greeted Alexia's arrival with the expected volley of frenzied barking.

Alexia arranged herself at the table without direction from her host and, as he did not appear to care one way or the other, she began helping herself to the repast. Today the infant-inconvenience wasn't objecting to food. Buggery thing couldn't make up its mind. Madame Lefoux greeted her with a fond smile and Floote with a little nod.

"Sir," said Alexia to their host.

"Good afternoon, Female Specimen." Mr. Lange-Wilsdorf did not look up from the open book and companion notepad upon which he was scribbling some complex formula.

Alexia scowled.

Whatever else might be said about Mr. Lange-Wilsdorf—and after his use of the term "abomination," Alexia could certainly think of a good deal that *she* might say about him—he provided a decent spread. The food laid out for luncheon was light but tasty: roasted winter vegetables, cold poultry, bread that managed to be both crispy and fluffy, and a selection of flaky pastries. Alexia had extracted from the depths of her dispatch case some of the precious tea that Ivy had given her. It had survived the journey far better than anything else. She had also, after a moment's consideration, transferred a small emergency amount into one of the pockets of her parasol, just in case. Fortunately, milk remained a cross-cultural universal, and the tea managed to taste just as delicious as it might have back in England. This resulted in a pang of homesickness so acute that Alexia actually did not speak for a good few minutes after the initial sip.

Madame Lefoux noticed her uncharacteristic silence.

"Are you feeling well, my dear?" The inventor placed a soft hand on Alexia's upper arm.

Alexia started slightly and experienced an unacceptable welling of tears. Really, at her age! It seemed to have been a very long while since anyone touched her with genuine fondness. Air kisses and three-fingered pats on the head comprised the bulk of affectionate action in the Loontwill household, and had done since she was a child. It wasn't until Conall had come into her life that Alexia became accustomed to physical intimacy. He enjoyed it immensely and had engaged in it with her at every possible opportunity. Madame Lefoux was not quite so aggressive, but she was French, and seemed to feel that verbal comfort ought to be companioned by a soothing caress. Alexia leaned into the embrace. The hand around her shoulder was not large and calloused, and Madame Lefoux smelled of vanilla and engine oil, not open fields, but beggars couldn't be choosers.

"Oh, it is nothing. I was reminded of home there for one moment." Alexia took another sip of the tea.

The German looked up at her curiously. "He did not treat you well? The werewolf husband?"

"Not as such in the end," Alexia prevaricated, never one to talk about personal matters with strange little Germans.

"Werewolves, ya. Difficult creatures. What is left of the soul is all violence and emotion. It is a wonder you English have managed to integrate them into society."

Alexia shrugged. "I am under the impression the vampires are more difficult to handle."

"Really?"

Alexia, feeling she may have been traitorously indiscreet, grappled for the right way of phrasing it. "You know how vampires get, all high-up-mucky-mucky and I'm-older-than-thou." She paused. "No, I suppose you do not know how they get, do you?"

"Mmm. I should have thought werewolves more an issue.

With the running about in armies and the marrying of normal humans."

"Well *my* particular werewolf did turn out a bit difficult. But, to be fair, he was perfectly suitable right up until the end." Alexia was painfully conscious that "perfectly suitable" was a rather understated way of putting it. Conall had been a model husband in his massive grumpy way: tender, except when it wasn't necessary, and then rough until gentleness was called for once more. She shivered slightly at the memories. He had also been loud and gruff and overprotective, but he had adored her. It had taken her a good deal of time before she believed that she was worth all that fierce affection he lavished upon her. To have it stolen away unjustly was that much more cruel.

"Isn't the end result what counts?" Madame Lefoux cocked her head. She had taken against Conall most decidedly when he kicked Alexia out.

Alexia grimaced. "Spoken like a true scientist."

"You cannot possibly forgive him for what he did?" Madame Lefoux seemed ready to reprimand Alexia.

Mr. Lange-Wilsdorf glanced up from his meal. "Cast you out, did he? Does he not think the child is his?"

"Howlers have never sung of a werewolf child." Alexia couldn't believe it, but she was actually defending her husband. "And loving me apparently wasn't enough to get him over that fact. He didn't even give me a chance."

The German shook his head. "Werewolves. Emotion and violence, ya?" Then he put down his stylographic pen decidedly and leaned forward over book and notepad. "I spent all morning with research. My records would seem to substantiate his assessment. Although, lack of corroborative cases or other information does not make for real evidence. There are older records."

"Records kept by vampires?" Alexia theorized, thinking of the Vampire Edicts.

"Records kept by Templars."

Floote gave a little wince. Alexia glanced at him. He chewed his food impassively.

"So you think the Templars might have some hint as to how *this* is possible?" Alexia gestured delicately at her midsection.

"Ya. If this has happened before, they will have records of it."

Alexia had grand romantic visions of marching into Conall's office and slamming down proof of her innocence—of making him eat his words.

"And what of your theories, Monsieur Lange-Wilsdorf?" asked Madame Lefoux.

"I believe, if I abandon the concept of undead but maintain my aetheric analysis of the composition of the soul, I might be able to explain this pregnancy."

"Will you be able to maintain the principles of epidermal contact?"

The German looked impressed. "You are indeed familiar with my work, madame. I thought you were an engineer by training?"

Madame Lefoux flashed her dimples. "My aunt is a ghost and so was my grandmother. I have a keen interest in understanding excess soul."

The horrible little dog came over to yap at Alexia's ankle, and then, to add insult to injury, began to chew on one of her bootlaces. Alexia picked the serviette up off of her lap and surreptitiously dropped it on Poche's head. The animal attempted to back out from under it, with little success.

"You believe you may have excess soul?" The German was apparently unaware of his dog's predicament.

The Frenchwoman nodded. "It seems likely."

Alexia wondered what that might feel like, knowing one was likely to end life as a poltergeist. She herself would die with no possibility of salvation or immortality. Preternaturals had no soul to save for either God or ghost.

"Then why not seek immortality, now that you live in England where such atrocities are openly encouraged?" Mr. Lange-Wilsdorf curled his lip.

Madame Lefoux shrugged. "Despite my preferred mode of dress, I am still a woman, and I know my chances of surviving a werewolf bite, not to mention vampire blooding, are extremely slim. Besides, I do not wish to lose what little skill I have as an inventor alongside the bulk of my soul. To become entirely dependent upon the goodwill of a pack or a hive? No thank you. And simply because my relatives were ghosts does not necessarily mean I, too, have excess soul. In the end, I am not that much of a risk taker."

The little dog had managed to circumnavigate the entire table without shaking off the offending serviette. Alexia coughed and rattled her dinnerware to disguise the sound of the animal bumping into various objects about the room. Floote, now within reach, bent down and removed the cloth from the dog's head, issuing Alexia a reproving look.

Alexia had never thought to ask, but come to think of it, it was indeed odd that an inventor of Madame Lefoux's particularly high creative skill level should have no supernatural patron. The Frenchwoman maintained good working relationships with the Westminster Hive and the Woolsey Pack, but she also dealt with loners, roves, and daylight folk. Alexia had thought the inventor's avoidance of metamorphosis and supernatural patronage stemmed from personal objections, not practical ones. Now she was forced to consider, had she herself been born with Madame Lefoux's options, would she choose the same path?

The German was not impressed. "I should prefer if you were a religious protester rather than an ethical objector, Madame Lefoux."

"It is better, then, Monsieur Lange-Wilsdorf, that I act to suit myself and not you. Is it not?"

"So long as the end result is one less supernatural."

"Oh, really. Must we talk politics while eating?" Alexia interjected at this juncture.

"By all means, Female Specimen, let us turn the conversation back to you." The little man's eyes were quite hard as he focused them upon her, and Alexia had a sudden sense of alarm.

"It is quite remarkable, you understand, your pregnancy. Until last night, I would have sworn that vampires and werewolves could only breed through metamorphosis. Ya? Your preternatural touch, it does not cancel out the fact that the supernatural person has, already, mostly died. It turns them mortal, ya, but not *human*, certainly not sufficient to procreate naturally."

Alexia nibbled a piece of fruit. "Obviously this is an incorrect statement you make, sir."

"Obviously, Female Specimen. So I have—how do you say?—rethought the situation. There is one line of scientific evidence to support your claim. That line is the fact that both vampires and werewolves still engage in"—the little man paused, a bright flush suffusing his pale features—"well, bedroom activities."

"Of an extensive and rather experimental nature, if the rumors are to be believed." Madame Lefoux waggled her eyebrows suggestively. Trust the only French person at the table to be at ease with this topic of conversation. Alexia, Floote, and Mr. Lange-Wilsdorf all looked painfully uncomfortable and shared a moment of awkward solidarity. Then the little German soldiered bravely on.

"There has to be a reason the procreative urges aren't eliminated post-metamorphosis. Yet, none of my books could adequately address this concern. If they really were undead, werewolves should no longer have need of that particular *biological* function."

"So how, exactly, does this pertain to my situation?" Alexia stopped eating to listen with renewed interest.

"It seems clear that your husband's capacity to continue to, er, perform, even as a werewolf, must be linked to an instinctual need to produce offspring the old-fashioned way. Modern science tells us that, thus, offspring must be a possibility, however infinitesimal. You, it would appear, are that infinitesimal possibility. The problem is, of course, the inevitable miscarriage."

Alexia blanched.

"I am sorry to say there is no way around that fact. If the Templar preternatural breeding program proved nothing else, it proved that preternaturals always breed true. And similarly that they cannot occupy the same air space. Essentially, Female Specimen, you have an intolerance for your own child."

Alexia had shared a room with a preternatural mummy once; she knew the feeling of discomfort and repulsion that would be her fate should she ever encounter another preternatural. But she had not yet felt that feeling from the embryo inside her.

"The child and I are not sharing any air," she objected.

"We are aware that preternatural abilities are a matter of physical contact. In this, the Templar records are clear, and I recall them well. All Female Specimens experimented upon over the centuries were barren or unable to carry a child. It is not a matter of *if* you will lose this embryo—it is a matter of *when*."

Alexia sucked in her breath. Unexpectedly, it hurt. Quite apart from the loss of the child, this would mean that Conall's rejection and abuse had all been for naught. It was stupid, and hopeless, and . . .

Madame Lefoux came to her rescue. "Except that this may not be an ordinary preternatural child. You said it yourself—they are usually the result of daylight and preternatural crossings. Alexia's baby has a werewolf father, and as mortal as her touch would have made him at the time of conception, he was still not human. Not entirely, for he had already lost much of his soul. This child is something *different*. It must be." She turned to look at her friend. "It is a safe bet that the vampires aren't trying to kill you simply because you are about to miscarry a soulless. Particularly not the English vampires."

Alexia sighed. "It is at times like this I wish I could talk to my mother."

"Good gracious, what good would that do, madam?" Floote was moved to speak by the outrageousness of Alexia's statement.

"Well, whatever she said, I could simply take the opposite point of view."

Mr. Lange-Wilsdorf was not to be distracted by family history. "You have felt no queasiness or revulsion for the specimen inside?"

Alexia shook her head.

The German began muttering to himself. "Something must be off in my calculations. Perhaps the aetheric exchange conduction between mother and child is limited by partial soul retention. But why, then, wouldn't a child retain part of the soul of a daylight father? Different kind of soul, perhaps?" He scratched out his careful notes with a sweeping motion of the stylographic pen, flipped to a new page, and began scribbling again.

They all watched him in silence, Alexia having mostly lost her appetite, until he stopped midnotation.

He looked up, his eyes popping wide as the second half of Madame Lefoux's statement finally worked its way into his brain. "Vampires trying to kill her? Did you say they were trying to kill her? That *thing*, sitting there at *my* table, in *my* house!"

Madame Lefoux shrugged. "Well, yes. Who else would they want to kill?"

"But that means they will be coming. They will be following her. *Here!* Vampires. I *hate* vampires!" Mr. Lange-Wilsdorf spat noisily on the floor. "Nasty, bloodsucking tools of the devil. You must get out. You must all leave, now! I am terribly sorry, but I cannot have you here under such circumstances. Not even for the sake of scientific research."

"But, Mr. Lange-Wilsdorf, what a way to treat a fellow member of the Order of the Brass Octopus. Be reasonable; it is the middle of the day!"

"Not even for the Order!" The little man stood, looking as though he were about to get just as hysterical as his dog. "You must leave! I shall give you provisions, money, contacts in Italy, but you must quit my house now. Get to the Templars. They will take care of you, if only because the vampires want you dead. I am not equipped. I am not able to handle this."

Alexia stood to find that Floote, being Floote, had at some point during the conversation sensed impending doom and vanished to their rooms. There he had obviously packed up her dispatch case, retrieved her parasol and their outerwear, and was waiting patiently in the doorway. He, at least, did not seem at all reluctant to leave.

CHAPTER NINE

How Not to Cross an Alpine Pass

Upon reflection, Alexia decided it was perhaps safer to press on toward Italy during daylight, anyway. It was becoming painfully obvious that should she expect any answers as to her current condition and situation, she would have to extract said answers from either the Templars or the vampires. And of the two, only one was likely to talk to her *before* they tried to kill her.

Another thing had also become apparent. As driven as she might be to prove Conall wrong, the fate of the infant-inconvenience was now at stake. Alexia might be frustrated with the tiny parasite, but she decided, after contemplation, that she did not, exactly, wish it dead. They'd been through a lot together so far. *Just you allow me to eat regularly*, she told it silently, *and I'll think about trying to grow a mothering instinct. Won't be easy, mind you. I wasn't ever expecting to have one. But I'll try.*

On the run from the murderous hordes, cashiered by an eccentric German, Alexia was nonplussed to find they did what anyone might have done under more mundane circumstances—they caught a cab. Hired transport, as it turned out, was much the same in France as it was in England, only more limited. Madame Lefoux had a brief but intense conversation with the driver of a fly, after which a good deal of money exchanged hands. Then the inventor sat down next to Floote, and the hansom took off at a terrific pace, heading for the coast through the streets of Nice, which were crowded with invalids and wet-weather refugees. Alexia supposed it was a sensible mode of transport when one was on the run, but the fly was a tight fit for three passengers.

The driver, up high and behind them, encouraged the horse into a fast trot with a long whip. The creature surged forward, taking turns and racketing down alleyways at quite the breakneck velocity.

In no time whatsoever, they had left Nice behind and were headed along the dirt road that wound along the cliffs and beaches of the Riviera. It was a drive Alexia might ordinarily have enjoyed. It was a crisp winter day, the Mediterranean a sparkling turquoise blue to their right. There was very little traffic, and their driver cut loose along the long slow turns and straight stretches, allowing his horse a distance-covering canter.

"He said he would take us all the way to the border," Madame Lefoux spoke into the rushing wind. "Standing me up a pretty penny for the favor, but he *is* making very good time."

"I should say so! Will we reach Italy before dark, do you think?" Alexia tucked her dispatch case more firmly beneath her legs and skirts, and placed her parasol across her lap, trying to get comfortable while wedged tightly between Madame Lefoux and Floote. The seat really was only meant for two, and while none of them was overly large, Alexia had cause to be grateful she was currently without her ubiquitous bustle. It was by no means an ideal arrangement.

The driver slowed.

Taking advantage of the more relaxed pace, Alexia stood, turning precariously backward so she could look over the roof and the driver's box to the road behind them. When she sat back down again, she was frowning.

"What is it?" Madame Lefoux demanded.

"I do not mean to concern you, but I do believe we are being followed."

Madame Lefoux stood in her turn, holding her top hat firmly to her head with one hand and grasping the edge of the hansom's roof with the other. When she sat back down, she, too, sported a crease between her perfectly arched eyebrows.

Alexia looked to her valet. "Floote, how are you fixed for projectiles?"

Floote reached into his inner jacket pocket and presented the two tiny guns. He cracked each open in turn. They were both loaded. He'd obviously taken the time to reload the single shots after their spot of vampire bother. He fished about further in his coat and produced a small quantity of gunpowder in a twist of paper and eight more bullets.

Madame Lefoux reached across Alexia and picked up one of the bullets, examining it with interest. Alexia looked on as well. They were made of some kind of hard wood, tipped in silver and filled with lead.

"Old-style sundowner bullets. Not that we will need such as these at this time of day. Any followers would have to be drones. Still, Mr. Floote, what are you doing with such things? You cannot possibly be certified to terminate supernaturals."

"Ah." Floote put the bullets back in his jacket pocket. "Let us say I inherited them, madam."

"Mr. Tarabotti?" Madame Lefoux nodded. "That explains the age of the guns. You want to get yourself one of those new-fangled Colt revolvers, Mr. Floote, much more efficient."

Floote looked with a certain degree of fondness down at the two tiny guns before tucking them back out of sight. "Perhaps."

Alexia was intrigued. "Father was an official sundowner, was he?"

"Not as such, my lady." Floote was always cagey, but he seemed to reach new heights of tight-lippedness whenever the subject of Alessandro Tarabotti came up. Half the time Alexia felt he did it out of obstinacy; the other half of the time she felt he might be trying to shield her from something. Although with vampire drones on their tail, she could hardly imagine what she might still need protection from.

Madame Lefoux pushed back the sleeve of her jacket and checked her own little wrist-emitter device. "I have only three shots left. Alexia?"

Alexia shook her head. "I used up all my darts in the clock shop, remember? And I haven't anything else left in the parasol but the lapis lunearis mist for werewolves and the magnetic disruption emitter."

Madam Lefoux sucked her teeth in frustration. "I knew I should have given it a greater carrying capacity."

"You cannot very well have done much more," consoled Alexia. "The darn thing already weighs twice as much as any ordinary parasol."

Floote stood and checked behind them.

"Will they catch us before we cross the border?" Alexia had no clear grasp on the distance from Nice to the Italian frontier.

"Most likely." Madame Lefoux, however, did.

Floote sat back down, looking quite worried.

They clattered through a small fishing town and out the other side, improved paving on the road allowing them a fresh burst of speed.

"We will have to try to lose them in Monaco." Madame Lefoux stood, leaned across the roof, and engaged in a protracted conversation with the driver. Rapid-fire French scattered on the wind.

Guessing the gist of it, Alexia unclipped the ruby and gold brooch from the neck of her traveling gown and pressed it into the inventor's small hand. "See if that will encourage him."

The brooch vanished across the roof of the hansom. The whip flashed. The horse surged forward. Bribery, apparently, worked no matter what the language.

They kept a good pace and steady distance from their pursuers right up and into the town of Monaco, a decent-sized vacation destination of some questionable repute.

The driver undertook the most impressive series of twists and turns, breaking off from the main road and dodging through some truly tiny alleys. They ran pell-mell into a line of laundry stretched across the street, taking a pair of trousers and a gentleman's shirtfront with them, in addition to a string of French curses. They ended their obstacle run, clattering out of an upper section of the town away from the ocean, heading toward the Alpine Mountains. The horse tossed off the pair of scarlet bloomers he had been wearing about his ears with a snort of disgust.

"Will we be able to cross through the mountains at this time of year?" Alexia was dubious. It was winter, and while the Italian Alps hadn't the reputation of their larger, more inland brethren, they were still respectably mountainous, with white-capped peaks.

"I think so. Regardless, it is better to stay off the main road."

The road narrowed as they began to climb upward. The horse slowed to a walk, his sides heaving. It was a good thing, too, for soon enough the track became lined with trees and a steep embankment to one side and a treacherous drop to the other. They clattered through a herd of unimpressed brown goats, complete with large bells and irate goat girl, and seemed to have shaken off pursuit.

Out the left side window of the hansom, Alexia caught sight of a peculiar-looking contraption above the embankment and trees. She tugged Madame Lefoux's arm. "What's that, Genevieve?"

The inventor cocked her head. "Ah, good. The sky-rail system. I had hoped it was operational."

"Well?"

"Oh, yes. It is a novelty freight and passenger transport. I had a small hand in designing the control mechanisms. We should be able to see it in full presently, just there."

They rounded a bend in the road and began climbing ever more steeply. Before and above them stood the contraption in all its glory. To Alexia it looked like two massive laundry lines strung parallel across the tops of pylons. It became clear, however, that the lines were more like sky-high train tracks. Straddled atop them, crawling along in a rhythmic, lurching, buglike manner on large wheels threaded with moving treads, marched a series of cabins, similar in size and shape to stagecoaches. Each cabin emitted billowing gouts of white steam from underneath. Hanging from the cabin, down below the cables, each supported a swaying metal net on long cords, loaded with lumber. Like a spider with an egg sac or a trapeze train trolley.

"Goodness!" Alexia was impressed. "Are they unidirectional?"

"Well, most are going downhill with freight, but they are designed to go up as well. Unlike trains, those cable rails require no switchbacks. One car can simply climb over the other, so long as it is not carrying a net, of course. See the way the cabling goes over each side of the cabin roof?"

Alexia was enough impressed by the invention to be distracted from her current predicament. She'd never seen or heard of anything like it—a railway in the sky!

Floote kept popping up and looking back over the cab roof like a jack-in-the-box. Alexia became quite sensitive to the pattern of his movements and so noticed when his legs became suddenly tense and he spent longer than usual standing. Madame Lefoux did as well and bounced up to lean next to him, much to the driver's annoyance. Scared of further upsetting the fly's center of balance, Alexia stayed seated, her view filled with trouser-clad legs.

She heard a faint yelling behind them and could only imagine that there were drones following. On the next switch-back, she caught sight of their enemy. Out the right side window of the cab, she could see a four-in-hand coach loaded down with intense-looking young men in hot pursuit. There was some kind of firearm equipage mounted atop the carriage roof.

Just wonderful, thought Alexia. *They have a ruddy great gun.*

She heard the pop of Floote firing off one of the tiny

derringers and the sharp hiss of Madame Lefoux doing the same with one of her darts.

Floote popped back down to change guns and reload. "Madam, I regret to inform you, they have a Nordenfelt."

"A what?"

Madame Lefoux sat down to reload while Floote stood back up and fired again.

"I have no doubt we shall witness it in action shortly."

They reached the snow line.

A whole fleet of bullets of ridiculously large size hissed by the cab and embedded themselves in an unsuspecting tree. A gun that could fire multiple bullets at once, imagine that!

Floote hurriedly sat back down.

"The Nordenfelt, madam."

The horse squealed in fear, the driver swore, and they came to an abrupt halt.

Madame Lefoux didn't even try to argue their case. She jumped down from the fly, followed by Floote and Alexia. Floote grabbed Alexia's dispatch case. Alexia grabbed her parasol. Without waiting to see if they would follow, Alexia charged up the embankment, stabilizing herself with the parasol, and began slogging through the snow toward the cable lines.

Another burst of bullets churned up the snow just behind them. Alexia let out a most undignified squeak of alarm. What would Conall do? This kind of gunfire action was not exactly her cup of tea. Her husband was the trained soldier, not she. Nevertheless, she recovered enough to yell, "Perhaps we should spread out and make for that support pole."

"Agreed," said Madame Lefoux.

The next round of fire was not nearly so close.

Soon they were too high up to be seen from the road below, even by that deadly swiveling gun. Also, the four-in-hand was even less able than the fly to handle off-road terrain. There came a good deal of shouting, probably the drones and the cab driver yelling at each other, but Alexia knew it was only a matter of time before the young men left their precious Nordenfelt behind and took to the ground in pursuit. At which point, she was at a distinct disadvantage with her heavy unbustled skirts dragging through the snow.

As they neared the cable rail, one of the laden cars came heading downward toward them. Of course the darn thing was going in the wrong direction, back into France, but it still might provide some limited refuge. The three made it, finally, to the support pole. It was furnished with flimsy-looking metal rungs, intended to be used for emergency evacuation or repair.

Floote seemed to be taking stock of their situation like some extremely dapper Roman general. "Madame Lefoux's dart emitter is the fastest weapon we have, madam."

"Good point, Floote. Genevieve, please guard the base while Floote and I climb."

The Frenchwoman nodded, looking fierce.

Alexia hated to leave her alone, but there was no other option. She hoisted her muddy skirts over one arm. Well, Paris had already seen them; she might as well show the rest of France her bloomers.

Floote and she climbed the post.

Floote paused on the small platform at the top, put down the dispatch case, and crouched to fire downward with a derringer, reloading and firing each gun in turn until he was out of ammunition, while Madame Lefoux climbed up behind them. Meanwhile, Alexia aimed her parasol at the approaching rail cabin. She could see the startled face of a driver in the window. She fully understood his confusion. She must present quite the lunatic picture— a statuesque Italian woman dressed English-style in a gown gone well beyond grubby, hair wild, and hat askew, pointing an ugly parasol at his large mechanical transport in a threatening manner.

Just as the front of the cabin drew level with the platform, Alexia pulled back on a protruding carved lotus petal in the handle of her parasol. The magnetic disruption emitter sent off its silent but deadly signal and the rail car jerked to a halt.

Inside the cable compartment, Alexia could see the engineer yelling at her in confusion. Behind her on the platform, she heard Madame Lefoux screaming obscenities in French, and the drones, now climbing up the support pole after them, were also shouting.

She turned to see if she could help her companions in any way. The infant-inconvenience kicked an objection to all her recent exertions, but Alexia disregarded it with an internal, *Pack it in, proto-nuisance. Time for that later.*

One of the drones now had Madame Lefoux by the boot. She was kicking at him while simultaneously attempting to climb the last handbreadth up onto the platform. Floote, finally out of bullets, was pulling at the Frenchwoman's shoulders in an attempt to assist.

Alexia, thinking quickly, opened and flipped her parasol. As swiftly as possible, she turned the special inset dial in the parasol's tip around to its alternate setting. Holding the parasol far out over the edge of the platform, Alexia rained a mixture of lapis lunearis and water down onto the young men climbing after them.

Dilute silver nitrate was designed for werewolves, not humans, and usually had no more disturbing a result on daylight folk than skin discoloration. But since the gentlemen in question were looking up, it had the beneficial effect of hitting the eyeballs and causing all to let go in startlement. The resulting screams may have been because they were falling, or perhaps they were the result of the chemical sting, but, as it ended with the drones writhing in the snow far below, Alexia considered the maneuver an unqualified success. Included among the writhers was the man who had had hold of Madame Lefoux's boot. He still had her boot, but Madame Lefoux was able to attain the top of the platform with a look of profound relief on her pretty face.

The three of them dashed to the rail cabin. Floote overrode the driver's objection to their presence by smashing in the front window with Alexia's dispatch case, climbing inside, and punching the poor man hard in the jaw. He fell like a stone, and his stoker, a slight, reedy boy with wide, anxious eyes, meekly acquiesced to their demands.

No one else was on board.

Alexia ripped off her bustle fall, tore the length into strips, and handed them to Floote. He showed remarkable dexterity and mastery of knot work, trussing up the boy and his unconscious supervisor with ease.

"You do that quite efficiently, don't you, Floote?" commented Alexia.

"Well, madam, being valet to Mr. Tarabotti had its advantages."

"Genevieve, can you drive this contraption?" Alexia asked.

"I only worked on the initial schematics, but if you can stoke the boiler, I will figure it out."

"Done!" Alexia thought stoking couldn't be that difficult.

Soon enough, the effects of the magnetic disruption emitter wore off, and the massive steam engine in the center of the cabin rumbled back to life. The cabin was designed with a windowed steering area at either end so that the car did not itself turn around. Instead, the engineer merely shifted position in order to drive in the opposite direction.

Madame Lefoux, after a quick review of the controls, pulled down on a massive lever at one end of the lurching cabin and then dashed to the other end, pulling a similar lever up.

An alarmingly loud horn sounded, and the contraption, cabin, and massive hanging net of lumber down below began moving backward in the direction it had come, up the mountain once again.

Alexia let out a little cheer of encouragement.

Floote finished trussing up their two prisoners. "I do apologize, sirs," he said to them in English, which they probably didn't understand.

Alexia smiled to herself and kept stoking. Poor Floote, this whole escape was rather beneath his dignity.

Stoking was hot work, and Alexia was beginning to feel the strain of having dashed across rough terrain and then climbed a pylon. She was, as Ivy had once scornfully pointed out, a bit of a sporting young lady. But one would have to be positively Olympian to survive the past three days without some physical taxation. She supposed the infant-inconvenience might also have something to do with her exhaustion. But never having run while pregnant, she did not know quite who to blame—embryo or vampires.

Madame Lefoux was leaping about the end of the cable cabin, pulling levers and twisting dials maniacally, and the rail contraption lurched forward in response to her ministrations, moving from a sedate step-by-step crawl to a kind of swaying shambling run.

"Are you certain this thing can take this kind of speed with a load?" Alexia yelled from her self-prescribed stoker's post.

"No!" Madame Lefoux hollered cheerfully back. "I am attempting to deduce how to set loose the cargo straps and net, but there seems to be a safety override preventing a drop while in motion. Give me a moment."

Floote pointed out of the front window. "I do not think we have that long, madam."

Alexia and Madame Lefoux both looked up from what they were doing.

Madame Lefoux swore.

Another loaded cart was coming down the cables toward them. It was crawling along at a sedate pace, but it seemed to be looming very fast. While one cabin could climb over another, they were not designed to do so while still lugging a net full of lumber.

"Now would be a very good time to figure out a drop," suggested Alexia.

Madame Lefoux looked frantically underneath the control board.

Alexia thought of a different tactic. She ran over to the other end of the cabin.

"How do I cut the cargo free?" she spoke in French and leaned close in to the frightened young stoker boy. "Quickly!"

The boy pointed in silent fear at a lever off to one side of the steam engine, separated from both sets of steering controls.

"I think I have it!" Alexia dove for the knob.

At the same time, Madame Lefoux began an even more frantic dance about the steering area, employing a complex series of dial-cycling and handle-pulling that Alexia could only assume would allow their cabin to climb over the other heading toward them.

They were close enough now that they could see the frightened gesticulations of the driver through the window of the other cable cabin.

Alexia pulled down on the freight-release lever with all her might.

The overrides screamed in protest.

Floote came over to help her, and together they managed to muscle it down.

Their rail car shuddered once, and seconds later they heard a loud crash and multiple thuds as the load of lumber fell down to the mountain below. Mere moments after that, there was a lurch as their cabin climbed its buglike way over the oncoming coach, swaying in a most alarming fashion from side to side, ending with one additional shudder as it settled back onto the rails on the other side.

They did not have much time to appreciate their victory, for the pinging sound of bullets on metal heralded the return of their pursuers.

Floote ran to look out a side window. "Revolvers, madam. They're pacing us by foot."

"Doesn't this thing go any faster?" Alexia asked Madame Lefoux.

"Not that I can make it." The Frenchwoman issued Alexia a demonic dimpled grin. "We shall just have to take the cable as far as it goes and then run for the border."

"You make it sound so simple."

The grin only widened. Alexia was beginning to suspect Madame Lefoux of being a rather reckless young woman.

"Italy makes for a strange refuge, madam." Floote sounded almost philosophical. He began a stately tour of the interior of the carrier, looking for any loose objects that might serve as projectile weaponry.

"You do not like Italy, do you, Floote?"

"Beautiful country, madam."

"Oh?"

"It took Mr. Tarabotti quite a bit of bother to extract himself. He had to marry an Englishwoman in the end."

"My mother? I can't think of a worse fate."

"Precisely, madam." Floote used a large wrench to break one of the side windows and stuck his head out. He received a near miss from a bullet for his pains.

"What exactly was he extracting himself from, Floote?"

"The past." Hoisting some kind of large metal tool, Floote chucked it hopefully out the window. There was a cry of alarm from below, and the young men drew slightly back, out of detritus range.

"Shame we did not eliminate any of them when we dropped the lumber."

"Indeed, madam."

"What past, Floote?" Alexia pressed.

"A not very nice one, madam."

Alexia huffed in frustration. "Did anyone ever tell you, you are entirely insufferable?" Alexia went to shove more coal into the stoke hole.

"Frequently, madam." Floote waited for the men to gain courage and catch up again, and then threw a few more items out the window. Floote and the drones proceeded in this vein for about a half hour while the sun set slowly, turning the trees to long shadows and the snow to gray. A full moon rose up above the mountaintops.

"End of the cable just ahead." Madame Lefoux gestured briefly with one hand before returning it to the controls.

Alexia left off stoking and went to the front to see what their dismount looked like.

The ending area was a wide U of platforms atop multiple poles, with cables running down to the ground, presumably used for the lumber. There was also some kind of passenger-unloading arrangement, built to accommodate the anticipated tourists. It was a basic pulley system with a couple of windlass machines.

"Think those will work to get us down?"

Madame Lefoux glanced over. "We had better hope so."

Alexia nodded and went to devise a means of strapping her dispatch case and her parasol on to her body; she'd need both hands free.

The rail cabin came to a bumpy halt, and Alexia, Floote, and Madame Lefoux climbed out the broken window as fast as possible. Madame Lefoux went first, grabbing one of the pulley straps and dropping with it over to the edge of the platform without a second thought. *Definitely reckless.*

The pulley emitted a loud ticking noise but carried her down the cable at a pace only mildly dangerous. The inventor landed at the bottom in a graceful forward roll, bouncing out of it onto her stockinged feet with a shout of well-being.

With a deep breath of resignation, Alexia followed. She clutched the heavy leather strap in both hands and eased off the edge of the platform, zipping down the line far faster than the lean Frenchwoman. She landed at the bottom with a terrific jolt, ankles screaming, and collapsed into a graceless heap, taking a wicked hit to the shoulder from the corner of her dispatch case. She rolled to her side and looked down; the parasol seemed to have survived better than she.

Madame Lefoux helped her up and out of the way just as Floote let go of a strap and landed gracefully, stopping his own forward momentum by bending one knee, managing to make his dismount look like a bow. *Show-off.*

They heard shouts behind them from the oncoming drones.

It was getting dark but they could still make out a track heading farther up the mountain toward what they could only hope was a customhouse and the Italian border.

They took off running again.

Alexia figured she might be getting enough exercise to last a lifetime in the space of one afternoon. She was actually sweating—so very improper.

Something whizzed by her shoulder. The drones were firing their guns once more. Their aim was, of course, affected detrimentally by their pace and the rough terrain, but they were gaining ground.

Up ahead, Alexia could make out a square structure among the dark trees to one side of the road—a shed, really—but there was a large sign on the other side of the road that appeared to have something threatening written on it in Italian. There was no other gate or barrier, nothing on the track to mark that they were about to go from one country to another, just a little mounded hillock of dirt.

So it was that they crossed the border into Italy.

The drones were still following them.

"Wonderful. Now what do we do?" panted Alexia. Somehow she had thought once they entered Italy, everything would change.

"Keep running," advised Madame Lefoux unhelpfully.

As if in answer to her question, the deserted pass, now heading down the other side of the mountain, suddenly was not quite so deserted after all.

Out of the shadows of the trees to either side materialized a whole host of men. Alexia only had time to register the utter absurdity of their dress before she, Madame Lefoux, and Floote found themselves surrounded. A single, rapidly lyrical utterance revealed that these were, in fact, Italians.

Each man wore what appeared to be entirely pedestrian country dress—bowler, jacket, and knickerbockers—but over this, each had also donned what looked like female sleeping attire with a massive red cross embroidered across the front. It greatly resembled an expensive silk nightgown Conall had purchased for Alexia shortly after their marriage. The comedic effect of this outfit was moderated by the fact that each man also wore a belt that housed a large sword with medieval inclinations and carried a chubby revolver. Alexia had seen that type of gun before—a Galand Tue Tue—probably the sundowner model. *It is a strange world*, she ruminated, *wherein one finds oneself surrounded by Italians in nightgowns carrying French guns modified by the English to kill supernaturals.*

The outlandishly garbed group seemed unflustered by Alexia's party, closing in around them in a manner that managed to be both protective and threatening. They then turned to face down the panting gaggle of drones who drew to a surprised stop just on the other side of the border.

One of the white-clad men spoke in French. "I would not cross into our territory if I were you. In Italy, drones are considered vampires by choice and are treated as such."

"And how would you prove we are drones?" yelled one of the young men.

"Did I say we needed proof?" Several of the swords *shinked* out of their sheaths.

Alexia peeked around the side of the Italian hulking in front of her. The drones, silhouetted against the rising moon, were stalled in confusion. Finally they turned, perhaps calculating the better part of valor, shoulders hunched in disappointment, and began walking away back down the French side of the mountain.

The lead nightgowner turned inward to face the three refugees. Dismissing Madame Lefoux and Floote with a contemptuous glance, he turned his hook-nosed gaze onto Alexia. Who could see quite unsatisfactorily far up his nostrils.

Alexia spared a small frown for Floote. He was pinch-faced and white-lipped, looking more upset by their current stationary position than he had been when they were running around under gunfire.

"What is it, Floote?" she hissed at him.

Floote shook his head slightly.

Alexia sighed and turned big bland innocent eyes on the Italians.

The leader spoke, his English impossibly perfect. "Alexia Maccon, daughter of Alessandro Tarabotti, how wonderful. We have been waiting a very long time for you to return to us." With that, he gave a little nod and Alexia felt a prick on the side of her neck.

Return?

She heard Floote shout something, but he was yelling from a very long way away, and then the moon and the shadowed trees all swirled together and she collapsed backward into the waiting arms of the Pope's holiest of holy antisupernatural elite, the Knights Templars.

Professor Randolph Lyall generally kept to a nighttime schedule, but he had spent the afternoon prior to full moon awake in order to conduct some last-minute research. Unfortunately, Ivy Tunstell's revelation had served only to complicate matters. The preponderance of mysteries was beginning to aggravate. Despite a day spent tapping all his various sources and investigating every possible related document BUR might have, Lord Akeldama and his drones were still missing, Alexia's pregnancy remained theoretically impossible, and Lord Conall Maccon was still out of commission. The Alpha was, most likely, no longer drunk, but, given the impending full moon, Professor Lyall had seen him safely back behind bars with strict instructions that this time *no one* was to let him out or there would be uncomfortable consequences.

He himself was so involved in his inquiries as to be quite behind schedule for his own lunar confinement. His personal clavigers—his valet and one of the footmen—awaited him in the Woolsey vestibule wearing expressions of mild panic. They were accustomed to Woolsey's Beta, tamest and most cultured of all the pack, arriving several hours ahead of moonrise.

"I do apologize, boys."

"Very good, sir, but you understand we must take the proper precautions."

Professor Lyall, who could already feel the strain of the moon even though it had not yet peeked above the horizon, held out his wrists obediently.

His valet clapped silver manacles about them with an air of embarrassment. Never during all his years of service had he had to bind Professor Lyall.

The Beta gave him a little half smile. "Not to worry, dear boy. It happens to the best of us." Then he followed both young men docilely down the staircase and into the pack dungeon, where the others were already behind bars. He gave absolutely no hint of the discipline it took for him to remain calm. Simply out of obstinacy and pride, he fought the change as long as possible. Long after his two clavigers had reached through the bars and unlocked his manacles, and he had stripped himself of all his carefully tailored clothing, he continued to fight it. He did it for their sake, as they went to stand with the first shift of watchers against the far wall. Poor young things, compelled to witness powerful men become slaves to bestial urges, forced to understand what their desire for immortality would require them to become. Lyall was never entirely certain whom he pitied more at this time of the month, them or him. It was the age-old question: who suffers more, the gentleman in the badly tied cravat or those who must look upon him?

Which was Professor Lyall's last thought before the pain and noise and madness of full moon took him away.

He awoke to the sound of Lord Maccon yelling. For Professor Lyall, this was so commonplace as to be almost restful. It had the pleasant singsong of regularity and custom about it.

"And who, might I ask, is Alpha of this bloody pack?" The roar carried even through the thick stone of the dungeon walls.

"You, sir," said a timid voice.

"And who is currently giving you a direct order to be released from this damned prison?"

"That would be you, sir."

"And yet, who is still locked away?"

"That would still be you, sir."

"Yet somehow you do not see my difficulty."

"Professor Lyall said—"

"Professor Lyall, my ruddy arse!"

"Very good, sir."

Lyall yawned and stretched. Full moon always left a man slightly stiff, all that running about the cell and crashing into things and howling. No permanent damage, of course, but there was a certain muscle memory of deeds done and humiliating acts performed that even a full day of sleep could not erase. It was not unlike waking after a long night of being very, very drunk.

His clavigers noticed he was awake and immediately unlocked his cell and came inside. The footman carried a nice cup of hot tea with milk and a dish of raw fish with chopped mint on top. Professor Lyall was unusual in his preference for fish, but the staff had quickly learned to accommodate this eccentricity. The mint, of course, was to help deal with recalcitrant wolf breath. He snacked while his valet dressed him: nice soft tweed trousers, sip of tea, crisp white shirt, nibble of fish, chocolate brocade waistcoat, more tea, and so on.

By the time Lyall had finished his ablutions, Lord Maccon had almost, but not quite, convinced his own clavigers to let him out. The young men were looking harassed, and had, apparently, deemed it safe to pass some clothing through to Lord Maccon, if nothing else. What the Alpha had done with said clothing only faintly resembled dressing, but at least he wasn't striding around hollering at them naked anymore.

Professor Lyall wandered over to his lordship's cell, fixing the cuffs of his shirt and looking unruffled.

"Randolph," barked the earl, "let me out this instant."

Professor Lyall ignored him. He took the key and sent the clavigers off to see to the rest of the pack, who were all now starting to awaken.

"Do you remember, my lord, what the Woolsey Pack was like when you first came to challenge for it?"

Lord Maccon paused in his yelling and his pacing to look up in surprise. "Of course I do. It was not so long ago as all that."

"Not a nice piece of work, the previous Earl of Woolsey, was he? Excellent fighter, of course, but he had gone a little funny about the head —one too many live snacks. 'Crackers' some called him." Professor Lyall shook his head. He loathed talking about his previous Alpha. "An embarrassing thing for a carnivore to be compared to a biscuit, wouldn't you say, my lord?"

"Your point, Randolph." Lord Maccon could only be surprised out of his impatience for a brief length of time.

"You are becoming, shall we say, of the biscuit inclination, my lord."

Lord Maccon took a deep breath and then sucked on his teeth. "Gone loopy, have I?"

"Perhaps just a little bit noodled."

Lord Maccon looked shamefacedly down at the floor of his cell.

"It is time for you to face up to your responsibilities, my lord. Three weeks is enough time to wallow in your own colossal mistake."

"Pardon me?"

Professor Lyall had had more than enough of his Alpha's nonsensical behavior, and he was a master of perfect timing. Unless he was wrong, and Professor Lyall was rarely wrong about an Alpha, Lord Maccon was ready to admit the truth. And even if Lyall was, by some stretch of the imagination, incorrect in his assessment, the earl could not be allowed to continue to be ridiculous out of mere stubbornness.

"You aren't fooling any of us."

Lord Maccon resisted admission of guilt even as he crumbled like the metaphorical cracker. "But I turned her out."

"Yes, you did, and wasn't that an idiotic thing to do?"

"Possibly."

"Because?" Professor Lyall crossed his arms and dangled the key to his Alpha's cell temptingly from one fingertip.

"Because there is no way she would have canoodled with another man, not *my* Alexia."

"And?"

"And the child must be mine." The earl paused. "Good gracious me, can you imagine that, becoming a father at my age?" This was followed by another much longer pause. "She is never going to forgive me for this, is she?"

Professor Lyall had no mercy. "I wouldn't. But then I have never precisely been in her situation before."

"I should hope not, or there's a prodigious deal regarding your personage about which I was previously unaware."

"Now is not the time for jocularity, my lord."

Lord Maccon sobered. "Insufferable woman. Couldn't she have at least stayed around and argued with me more on the subject? Did she have to cut and run like that?"

"You do recall what you said to her? What you called her?"

Lord Maccon's wide, pleasant face became painfully white and drawn as he went mentally back to a certain castle in Scotland. "I'd just as soon not remember, thank you."

"Are you going to behave yourself now?" Professor Lyall continued to wave the key. "Stay off the formaldehyde?"

"I suppose I must. I've drunk it all, anyway."

Professor Lyall let his Alpha out of the cell and then spent a few minutes fussing about the earl's shirt and cravat, tidying up the mauling Lord Maccon had inflicted while attempting to clothe himself.

The earl withstood the grooming manfully, knowing it for what it was: Lyall's unspoken sympathy. Then he batted his Beta away. Lord Maccon was, when all was said and done, a wolf of action.

"So, what do I have to do to win her back? How do I convince her to come home?"

"You are forgetting that, given your treatment of her, she may not *want* to come home."

"Then I shall make her forgive me!" Lord Maccon's voice, while commanding, was also anguished.

"I do not believe that is quite how forgiveness works, my lord."

"Well?"

"You remember that groveling business we once discussed during your initial courtship of the young lady?"

"Not that again."

"Oh, no, not precisely. I was thinking, given her flight from London and the generally slanderous gossip that has resulted and permeated the society papers ever since, that *public* groveling is called for under such circumstances."

"What? No, I absolutely refuse."

"Oh, I don't believe you have a choice, my lord. A letter to the *Morning Post* would be best, a retraction of sorts. In it you should explain that this was all a horrible misunderstanding. Hail the child as a modern miracle. Claim you had the help of some scientist or other in its conception. How about using that MacDougall fellow? He owes us a favor, doesn't he, from that incident with the automaton? And he is an American; he won't protest the resulting attention."

"You have given this much thought, haven't you, Randolph?"

"Someone had to. You, apparently, were not putting thought very high up on your list of priorities for the past few weeks."

"Enough. I still outrank you."

Professor Lyall reflected he may have, just possibly, pushed his Alpha a little much with that last statement, but he held his ground.

"Now, where is my greatcoat? And where is Rumpet?" Lord Maccon threw his head back. "Rumpet!" he roared, bounding up the steps.

"Sir?" The butler met him at the top of the staircase. "You yelled?"

"Send a man into town to book passage on the next possible channel crossing. It's probably first thing in the morning. And from there a French train to the Italian border." He turned to look at Lyall, who made his own more sedate way up the stairs from the dungeon. "That *is* where she has gone, isn't it?"

"Yes, but how did you—?"

"Because that is where I would have gone." He turned back to the butler. "Should take me a little over a day to cross France. I shall run the border tomorrow night in wolf skin and hang the consequences. Oh, and—"

This time it was Professor Lyall's turn to interrupt. "Belay that order, Rumpet."

Lord Maccon turned around to growl at his Beta. "Now what? I shall go by the *Post* on my way out of town, get them to print a public apology. She is very likely in danger, Randolph, not to mention pregnant. I cannot possibly win her back by dawdling around London."

Professor Lyall took a deep breath. He should have known having Lord Maccon in full possession of his faculties might result in rash action. "It is more than just the regular papers. The vampires have been mudslinging and slandering your wife's character in the popular press, accusing her of all manner of indiscretions, and unless I miss my guess, it all has to do with Alexia's pregnancy. The vampires are not happy about it, my lord, not happy at all."

"Nasty little bloodsuckers. I shall set them to rights. Why haven't Lord Akeldama and his boys been able to counteract the gossip? And why hasn't Lord Akeldama explained away my wife's pregnancy, for that matter? I bet he knows. He is quite the little know-it-all. May even be Edict Keeper, unless I miss my guess."

"That is the other problem: he has disappeared along with all of his drones. Apparently, they are off searching for something the potentate stole. I have been trying to find out what and why and where, but it has been a tad hectic recently. Both BUR and the pack keep interfering. Not to mention the fact that the vampires really aren't saying anything of interest. Why, if it weren't for Mrs. Tunstell and the hat shop, I might not even know the little I do."

"Hat shop? Mrs. Tunstell?" Lord Maccon blinked at this diatribe from his normally quietly competent Beta. "You mean Ivy Hisselpenny? *That* Mrs. Tunstell? What hat shop?"

But his Beta was on a verbal flyaway and unwilling to pause. "What with you constantly sloshed and Channing gone, I am at my wit's end. I really am. You, my lord, cannot simply dash off to Italy. You have responsibilities *here*."

Lord Maccon frowned. "Ah, yes, Channing. I forgot about him."

"Oh, yes? I didn't think that was possible. Some people have all the luck."

Lord Maccon caved. Truth be told he was rather worried to see his unflappable Randolph so, well, flapped. "Oh, very well, I shall give you three nights help sorting out this mess *you* have gotten us into, and then I'm off."

Professor Lyall emitted the sigh of the long-suffering but knew it was the closest he was likely to get to victory with Lord Maccon and counted his blessings. Then he gently but firmly put his Alpha to work.

"Rumpet," he addressed the frozen and confused butler, "call the carriage. We are going into the city for the night."

Lord Maccon turned to Professor Lyall as the two made their way through the hallway, collecting their greatcoats on the way.

"Any other news I should be made aware of, Randolph?"

Professor Lyall frowned. "Only that Miss Wibbley has become engaged."

"Should that information mean something to me?"

"I believe you were once fond of Miss Wibbley, my lord."

"I was?" A frown. "How astonishing of me. Ah, yes, skinny

little thing? You misconstrued—I was simply using her to needle
Alexia at the time. Engaged, did you say? Who's the unfortunate
fellow?"

"Captain Featherstonehaugh."

"Ah, now that name does sound familiar. Didn't we serve with
a Captain Featherstonehaugh on our last tour in India?"

"Ah, no, sir, I believe that was this one's grandfather."

"Really? How time flies. Poor man. Not much to hold on to
with that chit. That's what I like about my lass—she's got a bit
of meat on her bones."

Professor Lyall could do nothing but say, "Yes, my lord."
Although he did shake his head over the obtuseness of his
Alpha. Who, having decided all would once more be blissful
in his marriage, already referred to Alexia as his again. Unless
Lyall was wrong, and circumstances had already proved how
improbable that outcome, Lady Maccon was unlikely to see the
situation in the same light.

They swung themselves up easily into the grand crested coach
and four that served as Woolsey's main mode of transport when
the wolves weren't running.

"Now, what is this about Mrs. Tunstell and a hat shop?" Lord
Maccon wanted to know, adding before Professor Lyall could
answer, "Sorry about drinking your specimen collection, by the
way, Randolph. I wasn't quite myself."

Lyall grunted softly. "I shall hide it better next time."

"See that you do."

CHAPTER TEN

In Which Alexia Meddles with Silent Italians

L ady Alexia Maccon did not, of course, realize that they were
Templars until she awoke, and even then there was a lengthy
adjustment period. It took her several long moments to discover
that she was, in fact, not exactly a prisoner but relaxing in the
guest quarters of a lavish residence located in, if the view from
the window was to be believed, some equally lavish Italian city.
The room had a delightful southern aspect, and a cheerful spray
of sunlight danced over plush furnishing and frescocd walls.

Alexia tumbled out of bed, only to find she had been stripped
and redressed in a nightgown of such frilliness as might have
given her husband conniption fits under other circumstances.
She wasn't comfortable with either the notion of a stranger
seeing her in the buff or the copious frills, but she supposed a
silly nightgown was better than nothing at all. She soon discovered she had also been provided with a dressing gown of velvet-
lined brocade and a pair of fluffy bed slippers. Her dispatch
case and parasol, apparently unmolested, sat on a large pink
pouf to one side of her bed. Figuring that any person of refined
sensibility would have burned her unfortunate claret-colored
gown by now and finding no more respectable attire anywhere
in the room, Alexia donned the robe, grabbed her parasol, and
stuck her head cautiously out into the hallway.

The hall proved itself to be more of a large vestibule, covered in thick carpets and lined with a number of religious effigies. The humble cross appeared to be a particularly popular motif. Alexia spotted a massive gold statue of a pious-looking saint sporting jade flowers in his hair and ruby sandals. She began to wonder if she was inside some kind of church or museum. *Did churches have guest bedrooms?* She had no idea. Having no soul to save, Alexia had always considered religious matters outside her particular sphere of influence and therefore interest.

All unbidden, her stomach registered its utter emptiness and the infant-inconvenience sloshed about sympathetically. Alexia sniffed the air. A delicious smell emanated from somewhere close by. Alexia had decent eyesight and adequate hearing—although she had been remarkably capable of tuning out her husband's voice—but it was her sense of smell that set her apart from ordinary mankind. She attributed this to her oversized nose. Whatever the case, it stood her in good stead this particular day, for it led her unerringly down a side hallway, through a wide reception chamber, and out into a massive courtyard where a multitude of men were gathered about long tables to eat. *Imagine that, eating outside and not for a picnic!*

Alexia paused on the threshold, unsure. An assembly of masculinity, and her in only a dressing gown. Such a danger as this she had never before had to face. She braced herself against the horror of it all. *Here's hoping my mother never gets wind of this.*

The seated masses made for a bizarrely silent assembly. Hand gestures were the main method of communication. Seated at the head of one of the tables, a single somberly dressed monk read unintelligible Latin out of a Bible in a monotonous tone. To a man, the silent eaters were darkly tan and dressed respectably but not expensively in the kind of tweed-heavy country garb young men about the hunt might favor—knickerbockers, vests, and boots. They were also armed to the teeth. At breakfast. It was disconcerting to say the least.

Alexia swallowed nervously and stepped out into the court-yard.

Strangely enough, none of the men seemed to notice her. In fact, none of them registered her existence at all. There were one or two very subtle sideways glances, but, by and large, Alexia Maccon was entirely and utterly ignored by everyone there, and there were at least a hundred assembled. She hesitated.

"Uh, hallo?"

Silence.

True, prior familial experiences had prepared Alexia for a life of omission, but this was ridiculous.

"Over here!" A hand waved her over to one of the tables. In among the gentlemen sat Madame Lefoux and Floote, who, Alexia saw with a profound feeling of relief, also wore robes. She had never seen Floote in anything less than professional attire, and he seemed, poor man, even more embarrassed than she by the informality of the dress.

Alexia wended her way over to them.

Madame Lefoux appeared comfortable enough, although startlingly feminine in her dressing gown. It was strange to see her without the customary top hat and other masculine garb. She was softer and prettier. Alexia liked it.

Floote looked drawn and kept darting little glances at the silent men around them.

"I see they absconded with your clothing as well." Madame Lefoux spoke in a low voice so as not to interfere with the biblical recitation. Her green eyes glittered in evident approval of Alexia's informal attire.

"Well, did you see the hem on my gown—mud, acid, dog drool? I cannot say I blame them. Are these the famous Templars, then? Well, Floote, I can see why you do not like them. Highly dangerous, mute clothing thieves. Ruthless providers of a decent night's sleep." She spoke in English but had no doubt that at least some of the men around them could entirely understand her language, and could speak it, too, if they ever did speak.

Madame Lefoux went to make room for Alexia, but Floote said firmly, "Madam, you had best sit next to me."

Alexia went to do so, only to find that the continued complete disregard for her presence extended to offering her a seat on the long bench.

Floote solved this problem by pushing hard against one of his neighbors until the man shifted over.

Alexia squeezed into the space provided to find, once she had settled, that the gentleman nearest her had suddenly found himself needed elsewhere. In an organic manner, and without any obvious movement, her immediate area became entirely vacant of all personnel save Floote and Madame Lefoux. *Odd*.

No one brought her a plate of any kind, nor, indeed, any other means by which she could partake of the food currently being passed about the tables.

Floote, who had already completed his meal, shyly offered her his dirty trencher. "Apologies, madam, it is the best you'll get."

Alexia raised both eyebrows but took it. What an odd thing to have to do. Were all Italians this rude?

Madame Lefoux offered Alexia the platter of sliced melon. "Three nights of decent sleep. That's how long you've been out."

"What!"

Floote intercepted the melon when Alexia would have served herself. "Let me do that for you, madam."

"Why, thank you, Floote, but that is not necessary."

"Oh, yes, madam, it is." After which he proceeded to serve her anything she wished. It was as though he was trying to keep her from touching any of the utensils. Peculiar behavior, even for Floote.

Madame Lefoux continued with her explanation. "Don't ask me what they drugged us with. My guess is a concentrated opiate of some kind. But we were all asleep for three full nights."

"No wonder I am so hungry." This was rather worrying. Alexia glanced again at the silent, weapon-riddled men around her. Then shrugged. Food first, ominous Italians second. Alexia tucked in.

The fare was simple but delicious, although entirely lacking in any meat. In addition to the melon, chunks of crunchy, salted bread, white with flour, were on offer, as well as a hard, sharp yellow cheese, apples, and a pitcher of some dark liquid that smelled like heaven. Floote poured a portion for her into his cup.

Alexia took a tentative sip and was quite overwhelmed by an acute sense of betrayal. It was absolutely vile tasting, a mixture of quinine and burnt dandelion leaves.

"That, I am to assume, is the infamous coffee?"

Madame Lefoux nodded, pouring herself a splash and then adding a good deal of honey and milk. Alexia could not believe a whole hive of honey capable of rescuing the foul drink. Imagine preferring *that* to tea!

A bell sounded and, in a shifting rustle, most of the gentlemen departed and a new crowd entered. These men were slightly less well dressed and a little less refined in their movements, although they, too, ate in complete silence to the sound of the Bible being read aloud. And they, too, were covered in weaponry. Alexia noticed with annoyance that clean utensils were set before *them* without bother. But the staff, milling about with platters of food and additional coffee, ignored Alexia with as much thoroughness as the men seated around her. Really, it was beginning to make her feel quite invisible. She attempted a subtle sniff of her arm. Did she stink?

Just to test a theory, and because she was never one to take anything sitting down—even when she was, in fact, sitting down—Alexia scooted along the bench toward her nearest Italian neighbor, stretching out a hand in his direction, pretending to reach for the bread. In a flash, he was up off the bench and backing away, still not exactly looking at her but warily watching her movements out of the corner of his eye. So it wasn't just that they were ignoring her; they were actively avoiding her as well.

"Floote, what *is* going on? Do they think I am contagious? Should I assure them I was born with a nose this size?"

Floote frowned. "Templars." He intercepted another platter that would have bypassed Alexia and offered her some steamed greens.

Madame Lefoux frowned. "I did not know their reaction to a soulless would be quite so extreme. This is bizarre, but I suppose given their beliefs . . ." She trailed off, looking at Alexia thoughtfully.

"What? What did I do?"

"Something highly offensive, apparently."

Floote snorted in a most un-Floote-like manner. "She was born."

For the moment, Alexia decided to follow the Templars' lead and so ignored them in turn, eating her meal with gusto. The infant-inconvenience and she appeared to have reached an agreement. She was now allowed to eat in the mornings. In return, Alexia was beginning to think upon the little being if not with affection, then at least with tolerance.

At the sound of a second bell, all of the men rose and began filing out of the courtyard, going off about their business without a by-your-leave. Even the Bible reader departed, leaving Alexia, Floote, and Madame Lefoux alone in the massive courtyard. Although Alexia managed to complete her meal before the staff were done cleaning up, no servant took her now-twice-dirty trencher. At a loss, Alexia began to gather up her eating utensils herself, thinking she would take them into the kitchen, but Floote shook his head.

"Allow me." He picked up the trencher, stood, took three quick steps, and hurled it over the courtyard wall, where it shattered loudly in the city street beyond. Then he did the same with Alexia's cup.

Alexia stared at him with her mouth open. Had he gone completely mad? Why destroy perfectly good pottery?

"Floote, what *are* you doing? What has the crockery done to offend?"

Floote sighed. "You are an anathema to the Templars, madam."

Madame Lefoux nodded her understanding. "Like being one of the untouchables in India?"

"Very like, madam. Anything in contact with a preternatural's mouth must be destroyed or ritually cleansed."

"Oh, for goodness' sake. Then why bring me here?" Alexia frowned. "And one of them must have carried me down the Alpine pass and then put me into bed."

"A professional handler," answered Floote curtly, as though that were explanation enough.

Madame Lefoux gave Floote a very long look. "And how long *did* Alessandro Tarabotti work for the Templars?"

"Long enough."

Alexia gave Floote a stern look. "And how long did you?"

Floote came over all inscrutable at that. Alexia was familiar with that attitude; he got it when he was about to clam up and become his most cagey. She faintly recalled from her nightmare time locked away in the Hypocras Club, some scientist saying something to the effect of Templars using soulless as agents. Had her father really been so bad as that? To work for a people who would have regarded him as not human. *No. Could he really?*

Alexia did not have an opportunity, however, to try and crack Floote's hard, curmudgeonly shell, for someone came out into the courtyard and began walking purposefully toward them. A Templar, but this one seemed perfectly capable of looking Alexia full in the face.

The man wore practical middle-class dress twisted into absurdity through the presence of a white sleeveless smock with a red cross embroidered on the front. This absurdity was somewhat mitigated by the sinister presence of a particularly large sword. At his approach, Alexia and Madame Lefoux extracted themselves from the bench seats. Alexia's nightgown ruffles got caught on the rough wood in a most annoying manner. She tugged them away and drew the robe closed more securely.

Looking down at her attire and then back up at the man approaching, Alexia grinned. *We are all dressed for bed.*

This Templar also wore a hat of such unsightliness as to rival one of Ivy's more favored investments. It was white and peaked, boasting yet another red cross emblazoned on the front and gold brocade about the edge.

Floote stood at Alexia's side. Leaning over, he whispered in her ear, "Whatever you do, madam, please do not tell him about the child." Then he straightened to his stiffest and most butlerlike pose.

The man bared his teeth when he reached them, bowing slightly. It could not possibly be a smile, could it? He had very straight white teeth, and a lot of them. "Welcome to Italy, daughter of the Tarabotti stock."

"You are *speaking* to me?" Alexia said dumbly.

"I am preceptor of the temple here in Florence. You are considered a small risk to *my* eternal soul. Of course, there will be five days' cleansing and a confessional after I have terminated contact with you, but until then, yes, I may speak with you."

His English was simply too good. "You are not an Italian, are you?"

"I am a Templar."

At a loss over what to do next, Alexia resorted to politeness and proper etiquette. Trying to hide the fuzzy slippers under the frilly hem of her nightgown, she curtsied. "How do you do? Allow me to introduce my companions, Madame Lefoux and Mr. Floote."

The preceptor bowed a second time. "Madame Lefoux, I am familiar with your work, of course. I found your recent paper on the aerodynamic adjustments needed to compensate for aether currents quite intriguing."

Madame Lefoux looked neither flattered nor inclined to make small talk. "Are you a man of God or a man of science?"

"Sometimes I am both. And, Mr. Floote, how do you do? I believe I am familiar with your name as well. You are in our records, yes? You have maintained an unwavering connection to the Tarabotti stock. An intriguing display of loyalty not normally engendered by preternaturals."

Floote said nothing.

"If you would all please follow me?"

Alexia looked at her companions. Madame Lefoux shrugged and Floote appeared only slightly more stiff than usual, but he was blinking apprehensively.

Alexia figured there was nothing for it but to play along.

"With pleasure," she said.

The preceptor led them through the temple, all the while talking to Alexia in a mild, silky voice.

"And how do you like Italy, My Soulless One?"

Alexia did not like his use of the possessive, but nevertheless tried to answer this question. Since she had not, as yet, seen very much of the country, it was difficult. Still, from what she had glimpsed out of her window that morning, she had formulated one ready opinion. "It is very orange. Is it not?"

The preceptor gave a little chuckle. "I had forgotten how extremely prosaic the soulless are. Here we sit in Florence, the most romantic city on God's earth, queen of the artistic world, and she finds it *orange*."

"Well, it is." Alexia gave him an inquisitive look. Why should she be the only one on the defensive? "I read somewhere that the Templars have an initiation ritual involving a dead cat and a duck made from a rubber tree. Is that true?"

"We do not discuss the secrets of the brotherhood with outsiders. Certainly not with a soulless."

"Well, certainly, you *would* like to keep that a secret." He looked dismayed but did not rise to the bait. Apparently, he was unable to. He could not refute her statements without discussing the very secrets he hoped to hide. Alexia relished her small victory.

The rest of the temple, as it turned out, was just as richly furnished and religiously decorated as the parts Alexia had already observed. There was a certain sparseness to the design and a complete absence of personal items that gave the place the unmistakable aura of a monastery despite its luxuriousness. This feeling of piety was helped along by the general hush and quiet all about.

"Where have all the other gentlemen gone?" Alexia asked, surprised not to have encountered any of the many men they had seen in the dining courtyard.

"The brothers are practicing, of course."

"Oh?" Alexia had no idea what their host was talking about, but he clearly believed that she ought to. "Um, practicing what, exactly?"

"The fighting arts."

"Oh." Alexia tried a new tactic after that, asking about some of the artifacts on display in an effort to get him to reveal more about his agenda.

The preceptor explained one or two with the same smooth calmness. "Salvaged from the treasury at Outremer," he said of an entirely unremarkable piece of rock raised in glory atop a marble column, and, "The letter written by Preceptor Terric of Jerusalem to Henry II" of a papyrus scroll yellowed with age.

Madame Lefoux paid attention with the interest of a bluestocking. Alexia was intrigued by the history but mostly mystified; she found religious relics rather dull, so the meaning was generally lost on her. The preceptor failed to reveal any useful secrets despite her cross-examination. Floote strode stoically behind, disregarding the artifacts being described and focusing on the Templar leading them.

Eventually, they ended their tour in a massive library, which Alexia supposed must pass for the relaxation area. The Templars didn't seem like the type of men to boast a card room. Not that she minded; Alexia had always preferred libraries herself.

The preceptor rang a little hand bell, like those Alexia had seen worn by cows, and within moments a liveried servant appeared. Alexia narrowed her eyes and drummed her fingers. After a rapid conversation in Italian, in which the preceptor did most of the talking, the servant left.

"Did you catch that?" Alexia asked Madame Lefoux in a whispered tone.

The Frenchwoman shook her head. "I do not speak Italian. You?"

"Apparently not well enough."

"Really? Italian *and* French?"

"And a little Spanish and some Latin." Alexia grinned. She was proud of her academic achievements. "We had this fantastic governess for a while. Unfortunately, Mama found out that she was filling my head with useful information and dismissed her in favor of a dance instructor."

The servant reappeared with a tray covered in a white linen cloth. The preceptor lifted this with a flourish to reveal not tea but a piece of mechanical gadgetry.

Madame Lefoux was immediately intrigued. She apparently preferred such things to tea. There was no accounting for taste.

The preceptor allowed the inventor to examine the device at length.

Alexia thought it looked . . . uncomfortable.

"Some sort of analog transducer? It bears a passing resemblance to a galvanometer but it isn't, is it? Is it a magnetometer of some kind?"

The Templar shook his head, face stiff. Alexia realized what it was that bothered her so excessively about this man—his eyes were flat and expressionless.

"You are clearly an expert in your field, Madame Lefoux, but no. Not a magnetometer. You will not have seen one of these before. Not even in one of England's famed Royal Society reports. Although, you may know of its inventor, a German: Mr. Lange-Wilsdorf?"

"Really?" Alexia perked up at *that* name.

Both Floote and Madame Lefoux shot her dirty looks.

Alexia backed hurriedly away from any show of enthusiasm. "I may have read one or two of his papers."

The preceptor gave her a sharp glance out of his dead eyes but seemed to accept her statement. "Of course you would have. He is an expert in your field; that is"—the man flashed her another nonsmile of perfect teeth—"in the field of *you*, as it were. A remarkable mind, Mr. Lange-Wilsdorf. Unfortunately, we found his faith"—he paused meaningfully—"inconsistent. Still, he did devise this wonderful little tool for us."

"And what is it designed to detect?" Madame Lefoux was still troubled by her own inability to understand the gadget.

The Templar answered her with action. He cranked a handle vigorously, and the machine whirred to life, humming softly. A little wand was attached to it by means of a long cord. There was a rubber stopper at the wand's base, which corked up a glass jar in which the end of the wand resided. The preceptor pulled off the glass, exposing the wand to the air. Immediately, the small contraption began to emit a metallic pinging noise.

Madame Lefoux crossed her arms skeptically. "It is an oxygen detector?"

The Templar shook his head.

"A methane detector?"

Yet another shake met that guess.

"It cannot possibly be aether. Can it?"

"Can't it?"

Madame Lefoux was impressed. "A miraculous invention, indeed. Does it resonate to alpha or beta particles?" Madame Lefoux was a follower of the latest theory out of Germany that divided up the lower atmosphere into various breathable gases and divided the upper atmosphere and its travel currents into oxygen and two types of aetheric particles.

"Unfortunately, it is not that precise. Or, I should say, we do not know."

"Still, any mechanism for measuring aether ought rightly to

be considered a major scientific breakthrough." Madame Lefoux bent once more over the contraption, enraptured.

"Ah, not quite so important as all that." The preceptor reined in Madame Lefoux's enthusiasm. "It is more a device for registering the *absence* of aetheric particles, rather than measuring their presence and quantity."

Madame Lefoux looked disappointed.

The Templar elaborated further. "Mr. Lange-Wilsdorf referred to it as an aether absorption counter. Would you allow me to demonstrate its application?"

"Please do!"

Without further ado, the man placed the wand into his mouth, closing his lips about the rubber stopper. No change occurred. The machine continued to emit the same metallic clicking noise.

"It is still registering."

The preceptor removed the wand. "Exactly!" He carefully wiped the wand down with a small piece of cloth soaked in some kind of yellow alcohol. "Now, My Soulless One, if you would be so kind?"

Eyebrows arched with interest, Alexia took the wand and did as he had done, closing her lips about the end. The wand tasted pleasantly of some sweetened lemony liquor. Whatever the preceptor had used to clean it was mighty tasty. Distracted by the taste, it took Alexia a moment to notice that the clicking noise had entirely stopped.

"Bless my soul!" exclaimed Madame Lefoux, perhaps not so wary as she should have been over her use of religious language in the house of Christ's most devout warriors.

"Merph!" said Alexia with feeling.

"Well, then, it cannot possibly be registering aether. Aether is around and inside of everything, perhaps in more minor quantities groundside than it is up in the aether-atmospheric layer, but it is here. To silence it like that, Alexia would have to be dead."

"Merph," agreed Alexia.

"So we have previously thought."

Alexia was moved by a need to speak and so removed the wand from her mouth. The device began ticking again. "Are you saying the soul is composed of aether? That is practically a sacrilegious concept." She cleaned the end as the preceptor had done, with more of the yellow alcohol, and passed it to Madame Lefoux.

Madame Lefoux turned the wand about, examining it with interest before popping it into her own mouth. It continued ticking. "Merfeaux" was her considered opinion.

The preceptor's flat, blank eyes did not stop staring at Alexia. "Not exactly. More that the lack of a soul is characterized by increased absorption of ambient aetheric particles into the skin, much in the way that a vacuum sucks air in to fill its void. Mr. Lange-Wilsdorf has theorized for years that preternatural abilities are the result of a lack of internally produced aether, and to compensate, the preternatural body seeks to absorb ambient aether from the outside. He invented this machine to test the theory."

Floote shifted slightly from his customary stance near the door, then stilled.

"When it is in my mouth, it detects nothing because I have nothing to detect? Because I am absorbing it all through my skin instead?"

"Precisely."

Madame Lefoux asked brightly, "So could this device detect excess soul?"

"Sadly, no. Only the absence of soul. And since most preternaturals are registered with the local government, or are at least known, such an instrument is mainly useless except to confirm identity. As I have just done with you, My Soulless One. I must say, your presence presents me with a bit of a conundrum." He took the wand back from Madame Lefoux, cleaned it once more, and switched the machine off. It let out one little wheeze and then the metallic clicking noise stopped.

Alexia stared at it while the preceptor capped the wand with the little glass jar and then covered the machine with the white linen cloth. It was odd to encounter an instrument that existed solely for one purpose—to tell the world that she was different.

"What do you Templars call that little device?" Alexia was curious, for he had specified that "aether absorption counter" was Mr. Lange-Wilsdorf's name for it.

The preceptor did not flinch. "A daemon detector, of course."

Alexia was decidedly taken aback. "Is that what I am?" She turned to look accusingly at Madame Lefoux. "You would tell me if I suddenly developed a forked red tail, wouldn't you?"

Madame Lefoux pursed her lips provocatively. "Would you like me to check under your skirts?"

Alexia backpedaled hurriedly. "On second thought, I think I should notice such a protuberance myself."

Floote wrinkled one corner of his nose in a remarkably understated sneer. "You are a daemon to them, madam."

"Now, gentlemen." Madame Lefoux leaned back, crossed her arms, and dimpled at them all. "Be fair. The last I heard was that the church was referring to preternaturals as devil spawn."

Alexia was confused. "But you gave me a bed . . . and this rather excitable nightgown . . . and a robe. That is hardly the way to treat devil spawn."

"Yes, but you can see why none of the brothers would talk to you." Madame Lefoux was clearly finding this part of the conversation amusing.

"And you understand the nature of our difficulty with your presence among us?" The preceptor seemed to think this fact obvious.

Floote interjected, his tone gruff. "You have found good use for her kind before, sir."

"In the past," the preceptor said to Floote, "we rarely had to deal with *females*, and we had the daemons controlled and isolated from the rest of the Order."

Floote acted as though the Templar had inadvertently given

up some vital piece of information. "In the past, sir? Have you given up your breeding program?"

The man looked thoughtfully at Alessandro Tarabotti's former valet and bit his lip as if wishing he could retract the information. "You have been gone from Italy a long time, Mr. Floote. I am under the impression that England's Sir Francis Galton has some interest in expanding our initial research. 'Eugenics,' he is calling it. Presumably, he would need a method of measuring the soul first."

Madame Lefoux sucked in her breath. "Galton is a purist? I thought he was a progressive."

The Templar only blinked disdainfully at that. "Perhaps we should pause at this juncture. Would you like to see the city? Florence is very beautiful even at this time of year, if a trifle"— he glanced at Alexia—"orange. A little walk along the Arno, perhaps? Or would you prefer a nap? Tomorrow I have a small jaunt planned for your entertainment. I think you will enjoy it."

Apparently their audience with the preceptor had ended.

Alexia and Madame Lefoux took the hint.

The Templar looked at Floote. "I trust you can find your way back to your rooms? You will understand, it is impossible for me to ask a sanctified servant or brother to escort you."

"Oh, I understand perfectly, sir." Floote led the way from the room in what might have been, for him, a huff.

They began the long trek back to their quarters. The Florentine Temple was indeed vast. Alexia would have gotten hopelessly lost, but Floote appeared to know where to go.

"Well, he was certainly very chatty."

Floote glanced at his mistress. "Too chatty, madam." Floote's walk was stiff—well, stiffer than normal—which meant he was upset about something.

"And what does *that* mean?" Madame Lefoux, who had been distracted by a crude black onyx statue of a pig, trotted to catch up.

"He does not intend to let us go, madam."

"But he just offered to allow us to explore Florence on our own." Alexia was getting ever more confused by the highly contrary nature of these Templars and by Floote's opinion of them. "We would be followed, you believe?"

"Without question, madam."

"But why would they have anything to do with me? If they see me as some kind of soul-sucking daemon of spiritual annihilation?"

"The Templars couple war with faith. They see you as incapable of salvation but still useful to them. You are a weapon, madam."

It was becoming evident that Floote had had far more exposure to the Templars than Alexia had previously thought. She had read many of her father's journals, but clearly he had not written down *everything*.

"If it is dangerous for me here, why did you agree to the jaunt?"

Floote looked mildly disappointed with her. "Aside from not having a choice? You did insist on Italy. There are different kinds of danger, madam. After all, good warriors take particular care of their weapons. And the Templars are very good warriors."

Alexia nodded. "Oh, I see. To stay alive, I must ensure they continue to think of me as such? I am beginning to wonder if proving to my bloody-minded husband that he is an imbecile is worth all this bother."

They arrived at their rooms and paused in the hallway before dispersing.

"I do not mean to be callous, but I am finding I do not at all like this preceptor fellow," declared Alexia firmly.

"Apart from the obvious, why is that?" Madame Lefoux asked.

"His eyes are peculiar. There is nothing in them, like an éclair without the cream filling. It's wrong, lack of cream."

"It is as good a reason as any not to like a person," replied Madame Lefoux. "Are you quite certain you do not wish me to check for that tail?"

Alexia demurred. "Quite." Sometimes she found the Frenchwoman's flirtations unsettling.

"Spoilsport," said the inventor wryly before retreating into her room. Before Alexia could go into her own, she heard a cry of anger emerge from her friend.

"Well, this is unconscionable!"

Alexia and Floote exchanged startled looks.

A tirade of French outrage flowed out the still partly open door. Alexia knocked timidly. "Are you quite all right, Genevieve?"

"No, I am not! Imbeciles! Look what they have given me to wear!"

Alexia nosed her way in to find Madame Lefoux, a look of abject horror on her face, holding up a dress of pink gingham so covered in ruffles as to put Alexia's nightgown to shame.

"It is an insult!"

Alexia decided her best move at this juncture was a retreat. "You'll let me know," she said with a grin, pausing on the threshold, "if you need, perhaps, assistance with—oh, I don't know—the bustle?"

Madame Lefoux gave her a dirty look, and Alexia departed in possession of the field, only to find, across her own bed, a dress of equally layered outrageousness. *Really*, she thought with a sigh as she pulled it on, *is this what they are wearing in Italy these days?*

Her dress was orange.

Professor Randolph Lyall had been three nights and two days hunting with very little sleep. The only thing he'd gotten was a lead as to the whereabouts of Lord Akeldama's stolen item, from a ghost agent in good standing assigned to tail the potentate— if one could use the word "tail" when referring to a vampire.

Professor Lyall had sent Lord Maccon off to explore the lead further, arranging it so that the Alpha thought it was his own idea, of course.

The Beta rubbed at his eyes and looked up from his desk.

He wouldn't be able to keep the earl in England much longer. He'd managed a series of investigative distractions and manipulations, but Alpha was Alpha, and Lord Maccon was restless knowing Alexia was out in the world being disappointed in him.

Keeping the earl active meant that Professor Lyall was stuck with the stationary work. He checked every day after sunset for a possible aethograph from Lady Maccon and spent much of the rest of his time reading through the oldest of BUR's records. He'd had them extracted with much tribulation from the deep stacks, needing six forms signed in triplicate, a box of Turkish delights to bribe the clerk, and a direct order from Lord Maccon. The accounts stretched back to when Queen Elizabeth first formed BUR, but he'd been scanning through them most of the night, and there were few references to preternaturals, even less about any female examples of such, and nothing at all about their progeny.

He sighed and looked up, resting his eyes. Dawn was imminent, and if Lord Maccon didn't arrive back presently, he'd be arriving back naked.

The door to the office creaked open, as though activated by that thought, but the man who walked in wasn't Lord Maccon. He was almost as big as the Woolsey Alpha and walked with the same air of self-assurance, but he was fully clothed and clearly in disguise. However, when Lyall sniffed the air, there was no doubt as to his identity—werewolves had an excellent sense of smell.

"Good morning, Lord Slaughter. How do you do?"

The Earl of Upper Slaughter—commander in chief of the Royal Lupine Guard, also known as Her Majesty's Growlers; sometime field marshal; holder of a seat on Queen Victoria's Shadow Council and most commonly known as the dewan—pushed his hood back and glared at Professor Lyall.

"Not so loudly, little Beta. No need to broadcast my presence here."

"Ah, not an official visit, is it? You haven't come to challenge for Woolsey, have you? Lord Maccon is currently out." The dewan was one of the few werewolves in England who could give Lord Maccon a fight for his fur and had reputedly done so, over a game of bridge.

"Why would I want to do a thing like that?"

Professor Lyall gave an elegant little shrug.

"The trouble with you pack types is you always assume us loners want what you've got."

"Tell that to the challengers."

"Yes, well, the last thing I need is the additional responsibility of a pack." The dewan fussed with the hood about his neck, arranging it to suit his taste.

The dewan was a man who had taken the curse later in life, resulting in a permanently jowly face, lined about the nose and mouth, with bags under the eyes. He sported a full head of dark hair, with a touch of gray at the temple, and fiercely bushy brows over deep-set eyes. He was handsome enough to have broken hearts in his day, but Lyall had always found the man's mouth a little full and his mustache and muttonchops quite beyond the limits of acceptable bushiness.

"To what, then, do I owe the honor of your visit at such an early hour?"

"I have something for you, little Beta. It is a delicate matter, and it goes without saying that it cannot be known that I am involved."

"Oh, it does, does it?" But Lyall nodded.

The werewolf pulled forth a rolled piece of metal from his cloak. Professor Lyall recognized it at once—a slate for the aethographic transmitter. He reached into his desk for a special little cranking device and used it to carefully unroll the metal. What was revealed was the fact that a message had been burned through—already transmitted. The note was short and to the point, each letter printed neatly in its segment of the grid, and, rather indiscreetly, it had been signed.

"A vampire extermination mandate. Ordering a death bite on

Lady Maccon's neck. Amusing, considering she cannot be bitten, but I suppose it is the thought that counts."

"I understand it is just their turn of phrase."

"As you say. A death order is a death order, and it is signed by the *potentate*, no less." Professor Lyall let out a deep sigh, placed the metal down with a tinny sound on the top of his desk, and pinched the bridge of his nose above his spectacles.

"So you understand the nature of my difficulty?" The dewan looked equally resigned.

"Was he acting under the authority of Queen Victoria?"

"Oh, no, no. But he did use the Crown's aethographor to send the order to Paris."

"How remarkably sloppy of him. And you caught him in the act?"

"Let us say, I have a friend on the transmitter-operating team. He swapped out the slates so that our sender there destroyed the wrong one."

"Why bring it to BUR's attention?"

The dewan looked a little offended by the question. "I am not bringing it to BUR; I am bringing it to the Woolsey Pack. Lady Maccon, regardless of the gossip, is still married to a werewolf. And I am still the dewan. The vampires simply cannot be allowed to indiscriminately kill one of our own. It's not on. Why, that is practically as bad as poaching clavigers and cannot be allowed, or all standards of supernatural decency will be lost."

"And it cannot be known that the information came from you, my lord?"

"Well, I do have to still work with the man."

"Ah, yes, of course." Professor Lyall was a tad surprised; it was rare for the dewan to involve himself in pack business. He and Lord Maccon had never exactly liked each other ever since that fateful game of bridge. Lord Maccon had, in fact, given up cards as a result.

With his usual inappropriate timing, Lord Maccon returned

from his jaunt at that very moment. He marched in, clad only
in a cloak, which he removed in a sweeping motion and flung
carelessly in the vicinity of a nearby hat stand, clearly intent on
striding on to the small changing room to don his clothes.

He stilled, naked, sniffing the air. "Oh, hello, Fluffy. What
are you doing out of your Buckingham penitentiary?"

"Oh, for goodness' sake," said Professor Lyall, frustrated. "Do
hush up, my lord."

"Lord Maccon, indecent as always, I see," snapped the dewan,
ignoring the earl's pet name for him.

Now, bound and determined to remain nude, the earl marched
around Lyall's desk to see what he was reading, as it clearly
had some connection with the unexpected presence of the second
most powerful werewolf in all of Britain.

The dewan, showing considerable self-restraint, ignored Lord
Maccon and continued his conversation with Professor Lyall as
though the earl had not interrupted them. "I am under the impression the gentleman in question may have also managed to
persuade the Westminster Hive to his line of thinking, or he
would not have sent that order."

Professor Lyall frowned. "Ah, well, given—"

"Official extermination mandate! On *my wife*!"

One would think, after twenty-odd years, Professor Lyall
would be used to his Alpha's yelling, but he still winced when
it was conducted with such vigor so close to his ear.

"That lily-livered, bloodsucking sack of rotten meat! I shall
drag his sorry carcass out at high noon—you see if I don't!"

The dewan and Professor Lyall continued their conversation
as if Lord Maccon weren't boiling over next to them like a
particularly maltreated porridge.

"Really, by rights, preternaturals," Lyall spoke coldly, "are
BUR's jurisdiction."

The dewan tilted his head from side to side in mild agreement. "Yes, well, the fact remains that the vampires seem to
think they have a right to take matters onto their own fangs.

Clearly, so far as the potentate is concerned, what that woman is carrying is *not* preternatural and thus no longer BUR's jurisdiction."

"*That woman* is my wife! And they are trying to kill her!" A sudden deep suspicion and sense of betrayal caused the Alpha to turn upon his Beta in accusation. "Randolph Lyall, were you aware of this and yet didna tell me?" He clearly didn't require an answer. "That's it. I'm leaving."

"Yes, yes, well, never mind that." Professor Lyall tried unsuccessfully to calm his Alpha down. "The question is, what do they think she *is* carrying?"

The dewan shrugged and pulled his cloak back up over his head, preparing to leave. "I rather think that is your problem. I've risked enough bringing this to your attention."

Professor Lyall stood, reaching over his desk to grasp the other werewolf's hand. "We appreciate you giving us this information."

"Just keep my name out of it. This is a domestic matter between Woolsey and the vampires. I wash my fur of the entire debacle. I told you not to marry that woman, Conall. I said no good could possibly come of it. Imagine contracting to a soulless." He sniffed. "You youngsters, so brash."

Lord Maccon began to protest at that, but Professor Lyall shook the dewan's hand firmly in the manner of pack brothers, not challengers. "Understood, and thank you again."

With one last mildly offended look at the naked, red-faced, sputtering Alpha, the dewan left the office.

Professor Lyall, drawing on long years of practice, said, "We have got to find Lord Akeldama."

Lord Maccon sobered slightly at that abrupt change in subject. "Why is that vampire never around when you need him, but always around when you don't?"

"It is an art form."

Lord Maccon sighed. "Well, I canna help you find the vampire, Randolph, but I do know where the potentate has his object stashed."

Professor Lyall perked up. "Our ghost overheard something significant?"

"Better, our ghost *saw* something. A map. I thought we might just go steal the object back, before I leave to fetch my wife."

"And you still haven't told me where you sent Channing."

"It's possible I was too drunk to remember."

"It's possible, but I think not."

Lord Maccon took that as an opportunity to get dressed, leaving Professor Lyall in possession of the field but not the information.

"So, about this theft?" Lyall was always one to cut his losses and move on when necessary.

"It should be fun." Lord Maccon's voice emerged from the little changing closet.

When the Alpha reemerged, Professor Lyall wondered, not for the first time, if gentlemen's garb was not made complex through vampire influence as a dig at werewolves who, by their very nature, were often in a tearing hurry to get dressed. He himself had mastered the art, but Lord Maccon never would. He stood to go around his desk and help his Alpha rebutton a lopsided waistcoat.

"It should be fun, you said, this reacquisition operation, my lord?"

"Especially if you like swimming."

CHAPTER ELEVEN

Wherein Alexia Encounters Both Pesto and a Mysterious Jar

"Hadn't we better go to the local dirigible station? Didn't Monsieur Trouvé say he would send our luggage there?" Alexia looked down in disgust at the orange frilly dress she was wearing. "I could very much use the comfort of my own wardrobe."

"I could not agree with you more." Madame Lefoux's feelings of maltreatment were equally evident, as she was clearly uncomfortable in her pink frilly version of the same gown. "I should like to pick up some supplies as well." The inventor looked meaningfully at Alexia's parasol. "You understand, for a reconstitution of the necessary emissions."

"Of course."

There was no one around them in the temple hallway, but Madame Lefoux's use of euphemisms seemed to indicate that she felt they were in danger of being overheard.

They made their way to the front entrance of the temple and out into the cobbled streets of Florence.

Despite its generally orange overtones—Alexia's dress fit right in—Florence was indeed an attractive metropolis. It had a soft, rich quality about it that Alexia felt was the visual equivalent of consuming a warm scone heaped with marmalade and clotted cream. There was a pleasantness to the air and a spirit about the town that did not come from its color, but from some inner, tasty citrus quality. It made Alexia wonder fancifully if cities could have souls. Florence, she felt, under those circumstances, probably had extra. There were even little bitter bits of rind scattered about the place: the dense clouds of tobacco smoke emanating from various cafes and an overabundance of unfortunates begging from the church steps.

There were no hansoms, nor any other ready form of public transportation. Indeed, the entire city was apparently possessed of only one means of locomotion: walking. Alexia was a profuse walker. Even though she was a little sore from her mountaintop peril, she was equal to further exercise. After all, she had been asleep for three days. Floote valiantly headed their expedition. He was suspiciously familiar with the city, leading them unerringly through a wide open plaza called the Piazza Santa Maria Novella, which Alexia thought sounded like an assembly of sainted literary pundits; down the Via dei Fossi, which sounded like a fascinating geological discovery; across a bridge; and down into Piazza Pitti, which sounded like a pasta dish. It was a long walk, and Alexia had reason to be grateful for her parasol, for Italy did not appear to notice that it was November and poured sun down upon them with unremitting cheerfulness.

As it turned out, the Italians beyond the walls of the temple were a friendly, excitable bunch. Several of them waved to Alexia and her party. Alexia was mildly put out; after all, these were people to whom she had not been introduced and had no particular interest in knowing, yet they *waved* as she passed. It was most disconcerting. Also, it became quickly evident that Alexia's capable governess had been remiss in the matter of the Italian tongue. She had never taught Alexia that a great majority of communication was achieved through hand gesticulations. Although sentiments were often expressed a tad too loudly for Alexia's refined sensibilities, it was indeed as lovely to watch as it was to hear.

Even with such distractions as shirtless men kicking rubber balls around the bank of the Arno and a language that danced, Alexia noticed something amiss.

"We are being followed, are we not?"

Madame Lefoux nodded.

Alexia paused in the middle of the bridge and looked casually back over her shoulder, using her parasol to disguise the movement.

"Really, if they wanted to hide, they ought not to wear those ridiculous white nightgowns. Imagine going out in public in such a state."

Floote corrected his mistress. "Holy Tunics of Piety and Faith, madam."

"Nightgowns," insisted Alexia firmly.

They walked on.

"I counted six. Do you concur?" Alexia spoke in a low voice, although their followers were still a considerable distance behind and well out of earshot.

Madame Lefoux pursed her lips. "Yes, about that many."

"Nothing to be done, I suppose."

"No, nothing."

Florence's dirigible landing green was part of Boboli Gardens, a robust and extensive terraced park that lay in resplendent glory behind the most imposing castle Alexia had ever seen. In truth, Pitti Palace looked more like a prison of unusually fine proportions. They had to walk around the side of the massive edifice to get to the garden gate, where they were checked by a uniformed customs official.

The grounds were quite lovely, teeming with lush vegetation. The landing green was located directly behind the palace and on the same level. In its center stood an Egyptian obelisk, used as a tethering station, although no dirigibles were currently at rest. The luggage depot and waiting area took the form of a rebuilt ancient Roman gazebo. The official in charge was delighted to show them to the baggage storage area, where Alexia found her trunks, Madame Lefoux's modest assortment of carpet-bags, and Floote's scruffy portmanteau, courtesy of Monsieur Trouvé.

As they began gathering up their possessions, Alexia thought she saw Madame Lefoux snatch at some small item sitting atop her hatbox but could not be certain what it was. She was about to ask when the station clerk approached to have her sign a chit for their belongings.

Once she had done so, the clerk glanced down and made a sudden face as he read Alexia's name. "La Diva Tarabotti?"

"Yes."

"Ah. I 'ave ze"—he waved his hand in the air, apparently incapable of recalling the appropriate English vocabulary— "thing, para you."

At which he bustled off, returning a moment later to hand Alexia something that amazed the entire party.

It was a *letter* directed to La Diva Alexia Tarabotti in round, sprawling script. And it was not, as any person of sense might have surmised, from Monsieur Trouvé. Oh, no, this missive was from Mrs. Tunstell.

Alexia twisted the heavy folded paper about in her hand for a moment in surprise. "Well, doesn't that just go to show that no matter where you go, Ivy will always find you?"

"Perish the thought, madam," replied Floote with feeling before bustling off to hire a cart.

The clerk kindly handed Alexia a letter opener, and she cut through the seal.

"My dearest, darlingest of Alexias," it began in flamboyant style, and went on from there with no hope of sobriety. "Well, it is all go around London with you gone. All go, I tell you!" The missive employed Ivy's preferred abuse of punctuation and reliance upon malapropisms. "Tunstell, my brilliant pip, has gotten himself the lead role in the Winter Season of Forthwimsey-Near-Ham's operatic production of the *HMS Pennyfarthing*! Can you envisage that?" Alexia tried desperately not to. "I am lathe to admit it"—Alexia imagined Ivy spinning round and round like a top—"but I am adapting quite comfortably to life in trade, rather too comfortably for my mother's peace of mind. Please tell Madame Lefoux that her hat shop is doing *extremely* well, and I have even made one or two improvements." Alexia relayed this information to the Frenchwoman, who blanched.

"It has been less than a week. How much damage can she possibly have done in such a short time?" Madame Lefoux sounded as though she were trying to convince herself.

Alexia read on. "I have even, I blush to admit it here in print, inadvertently precipitated a wildly popular new craze in earmuffs for dirigible travel. I had the notion to affix fake hair falls from Paris to the exterior of the muffs so that the Young Lady Traveler might look as though she had an elaborate hairstyle while still staying warm. Such *hairmuffs*, as I call them, have the added benefit of bearing the brunt of the aether breezes' mussing. Well, I don't mind telling you, Alexia, they are selling by the baker's dozen! They have been heralded, only this morning, as the very *latest* in vital travel wardrobe accoutrements by no less than three leading fashion journals! Have enclosed clipping for your perusal." Alexia read this bit of the letter out for Madame Lefoux's continued edification and then handed her the newspaper clipping.

"In other shocking news, the dashing Captain Featherstonehaugh has announced his engagement to Miss Wibbley, who really is only *just* out of finishing school! This has had the unfortunate side effect of putting about the rumor that your younger sister was thrown over for a schoolroom chit, quite the persona au gratin, if you take my meaning. You will hardly be surprised when I tell you, London is all in uproars over the impending nuptials! I do hope this letter finds you well. As always, your dearest friend, Ivy."

Alexia folded the letter up, smiling. It was nice to be reminded of the mundanities of everyday life where there were no Templars stalking one through the streets of Florence, no drones in armed pursuit, and nothing was more worrisome than Miss Wibbley and her "au gratin" antics. "Well, what do you make of that?"

Madame Lefoux gave Alexia a particularly droll look. "Just out of finishing school, indeed."

"I know. Shocking. Most girls recently out of finishing school are like soufflés: puffed up, not very substantial inside, and prone to collapsing at the slightest provocation."

Madame Lefoux laughed. "And earmuffs with hair attached. How is it you English put it? *I say!*"

Floote returned with a pony and trap for their bags.

Alexia smiled, but she was, she hated to admit it, a little disappointed. She could not help noticing that there had been no mention of Lord Maccon, nor the Woolsey Pack, in Ivy's letter. Either Ivy was being circumspect—which was about as likely as Floote suddenly dancing an Irish jig—or the London werewolves were staying well out of the social limelight.

"You may find yourself the exclusive owner of a highly profitable hairmuff business instead."

Madame Lefoux flipped the newspaper clipping over and then stilled, face drawn.

"What is it? Genevieve, are you unwell?"

Mutely, the inventor passed the bit of paper back to Alexia.

It wasn't the whole of the article, just a section of it, but it was enough.

". . . surprised us all with a printed apology to his wife in the *Morning Post*. He has claimed that all previous rumors and accusations were not only false, but his fault, and that the child is not only his, but a miracle of modern science. Speculation is rampant as to the earl's purpose in issuing this retraction. No one has seen Lady Maccon since . . ."

Alexia's knees, previously quite reliable support structures, failed her, and she sat suddenly straight down onto the stone floor of the customs depot.

"Oh," she said, because it was all she could think to say, followed by, "Blast."

Then, surprising everyone, including herself, she started to cry. And not in the elegant, slow-dripping manner of true ladies of quality, but in loud embarrassing sobs like a little child.

Madame Lefoux and Floote stared down at her in stunned silence.

Alexia simply went on crying. Hard as she tried, she couldn't stop.

Madame Lefoux finally reacted, crouching down to wrap her friend in a bony but comforting embrace. "Alexia, my dear, what is wrong? Isn't this a good thing?"

"B-b-b-bastard," blubbered Alexia.

Madame Lefoux was clearly at a loss.

Alexia, taking pity on her, tried desperately to control herself and explain. "I was doing so well, being angry at him."

"So you are crying because you cannot be angry at him anymore?"

"No. Yes!" Alexia wailed.

Floote handed over a large handkerchief. "It is relief, madam," he explained to the Frenchwoman.

"Ah." Madame Lefoux applied said square of cotton to Alexia's blotchy face with tender care.

Alexia realized she was making a spectacle of herself and tried to stand. Too many things were going on in her head at once, and it was causing her eyes to leak. She took a deep, shaky breath and blew her nose loudly into Floote's handkerchief.

Madame Lefoux patted her back, still looking at her in concern, but Floote's attention had shifted.

Alexia followed his gaze. Four robust-looking young men were heading purposefully in their direction across the garden.

"Those are definitely *not* Templars," said Madame Lefoux with conviction.

"No nightgowns," agreed Alexia, sniffing.

"Drones?"

"Drones." Alexia stuffed the handkerchief up one sleeve and got shakily to her feet.

This time the drones looked to be taking no chances: each man held a wicked-looking knife and walked with decided purpose.

Alexia heard a faint shout and thought she could see, some way across the green, their group of Templar shadows running in their direction. They would in no way be fast enough.

Alexia raised her parasol in one hand and the clerk's letter opener in the other. Madame Lefoux reached for her cravat pins. Finding she wore no cravat, she swore and groped blindly for the nearest heavy object, coming up with her stealth hatbox, the heavy one that contained her tools, from the stack of luggage in the cart behind them. Floote relaxed into a kind of loose-limbed fighting stance that Alexia had seen before: in a battle to defend the location of tents between two werewolves on her front porch. What was Floote doing fighting like a werewolf?

The drones attacked. Alexia's parasol whipped out to deliver a crushing blow, only to be deflected by a knife. Out of the corner of her eye, she saw Madame Lefoux swing the hatbox, cracking the wood casing against the side of a drone's skull. Floote balled up his fist and, fast as any boxer—not that Alexia knew much of pugilism, being a lady of good breeding—dodged the knife slicing down toward him and made two quick hits to his opponent's stomach.

Around them, waiting dirigible passengers gasped in shock, but no one did anything to either help or hinder. Italians were reputed to be a people of violent emotions; perhaps they thought this was a lover's spat of some multifaceted variety. Or perhaps they thought the battle was over a ball sport. Alexia seemed to recall hearing one matron complain that the Italians were very passionate in their support of balls.

They could have used some assistance, for Alexia was no formally trained fighter, and Madame Lefoux, whether she was or not, was considerably hampered by her floofy dress. Quicker than Alexia would have thought possible, the drones had her disarmed, parasol rolling away across the stone floor of the gazebo. Madame Lefoux was thrust to the ground. Alexia thought she heard the Frenchwoman's head hit the side of the cart on the way down. She certainly didn't look to be moving anytime soon. Floote struggled on, but he was not quite so young as he once was, and certainly a good deal older than his opponent.

Two of the drones held Alexia fast between them, while the third, having determined Madame Lefoux was no longer a threat, brandished his knife with the clear intention of slitting Alexia's throat. This time they were brooking no delay. They would simply eliminate the preternatural right there in broad daylight and in front of witnesses.

Alexia writhed in the grip of her two captors, kicking out and wiggling as much as possible, making it difficult for them to steady her for the knife. Floote, seeing her imminent peril, fought all the harder, but death seemed embarrassingly inevitable.

And then a very odd thing happened.

A tall masked man, hooded like some parody of a religious pilgrim, leapt into the fray, and he appeared to be on *their* side.

The unexpected champion was a big man—not so big as Conall, Alexia noticed, but then few were—and clearly quite strong. He carried a long sword in one hand, British military issue, and had a mean left punch, which was also, Alexia guessed, British military issue. The masked man certainly was liberal and enthusiastic with his use of both sword and fist.

Finding her captors distracted, Alexia jerked a knee into one in the vicinity of his nether regions at the same time twisting violently, trying to shake off the others' grip. The one she'd kneed backhanded her across the mouth, and Alexia felt a starburst of pain before tasting blood.

The masked man reacted swiftly at that, slicing out with his sword and catching the offender behind one knee. The drone crumpled.

The drones regrouped, leaving only one still holding Alexia while two went back on the defensive, facing off against the new threat. Alexia liked these odds considerably better and did what any proper young lady ought to do: she pretended to faint, collapsing in a sudden dead weight against her captor. The man shifted to hold her with one hand, no doubt reaching for his own knife to slit her throat with the other. Sensing the opportunity, Alexia braced both feet and thrust sharply backward with all her might, knocking both herself and the drone to the floor. Once there, they proceeded to roll about gracelessly on the stone. Alexia had reason to be grateful for her husband's fondness for rolling among the bedsheets, for it had given her some practice wrestling with a man twice this drone's size.

Then, like the knights they had once been of old, the Templars were upon them. *White nightgowns to the rescue*, thought Alexia happily. The drones were forced, once more, to flee from the papal enforcers. Alexia had to admit Templar attire looked much less silly behind flashing, naked blades.

Alexia struggled to her feet in time to see their masked defender, clutching his bloody sword and dashing across the dirigible green in the opposite direction from the drones. In a whirl of dark cloak, he leapt over a row of topiary deer and disappeared into the gardens beyond. Clearly he liked being mysterious, or disliked the Templars, or both.

Alexia checked on Floote, who had not a hair out of place. He, in turn, wanted reassurances that neither she nor the infant-inconvenience had suffered any ill effects from the ordeal. Alexia did a quick internal assessment and discovered that they were both hungry, of which she informed Floote, and then bent to examine Madame Lefoux. The back of the inventor's head was bloody, but her eyes were already blinking open.

"What happened?"

"We were saved by a masked gentleman."

"Pull the other one." Sometimes Madame Lefoux could be surprisingly British in her verbal mannerisms.

Alexia helped her to sit up. "No, really. We were." While she explained what had occurred, she helped the inventor into the cart, and then they both watched with interest as the Templars dealt with the results of the altercation. It was almost like watching BUR at work cleaning up one of Alexia's messes, only faster and with less paperwork. And, of course, there was no Conall marching around waving his massive hands in exasperation and growling at her.

Alexia found herself grinning foolishly. *Conall had apologized!*

The dirigible passengers were clearly uncomfortable with having to deal directly with the Templars and were willing to do anything they were told so long as the men in white left quickly.

Floote disappeared mysteriously and then returned only to offer Alexia a sandwich of what appeared to be some kind of ham on what appeared to be some kind of roll and that turned out to be quite delicious. Alexia had no earthly idea where he had acquired the foodstuff but would not put it past him to have managed to make it during the fight. Having delivered the expected daily miracle, Floote stood in his usual stance and warily watched the Templars work.

"The locals, they are terrified of them, aren't they?" Alexia spoke softly, but she was reasonably certain that no one was paying them any mind. "And they must wield a considerable amount of clout for things to go so smoothly. No one has summoned the local constabulary, even though our little battle occurred in a public arena, in front of witnesses."

"One country under God, madam."

"It happens." Alexia wrinkled her nose and looked about for a scrap of fabric for Madame Lefoux to press against the back of her head. Finding nothing of use, she shrugged and ripped one of the ruffles off her orange dress. The inventor took it gratefully.

"One cannot be too careful with a head wound. Are you certain you are quite the thing?" Alexia watched her with concern.

"Everything is fine, I assure you. Except, of course, for my pride. I tripped, you know. He didn't overpower me. Really, I do not know how you ladies do it, run around dressed in long skirts all day every day."

"Generally, not a whole lot of running is involved. Is that why you dress as a man, then, pure practicality?"

Madame Lefoux looked as though she would like to twirl her fake mustache in thought, although, of course, she wasn't wearing it at the moment. "Partly."

"You like to shock people—admit it."

Madame Lefoux gave her an arch look. "As if you do not."

"Touché. Although we approach the endeavor differently."

The Templars, having concluded their activities, disappeared back into the foliage of Boboli Gardens with an air of hauteur. Even though violent action had been undertaken on Alexia's behalf, they had neither addressed her, nor looked in her direction. Alexia was disgusted to find, once the Templars had gone, that the ordinary Italian folk, including the once affable clerk, now regarded her with suspicion and disdain.

"Persona non grata once more." Alexia sighed. "Beautiful country, as you say, Floote, but the locals. The locals." She climbed into the cart.

"Exactly so, madam." With that, Floote took the driver's seat and, with a steady hand to the reins, guided the pony and trap through Boboli Gardens and out into the city streets. He took the bumpy course slow and gentle in deference to Madame Lefoux's head.

Floote stopped along the way at a small public eatery where, despite the presence of even more of the vile coffee and far too much tobacco, Alexia's opinion of the Italians was greatly improved through the application of the best victuals she had ever eaten in her entire life.

"These little chubby puddings with the green sauce," she declaimed, "must represent the food of the gods. I declare, the Templars may do what they like; I love this country."

Madame Lefoux grinned. "So easily swayed?"

"Did you taste that green sauce? How did they refer to it? Pets-something-or-other. Sheer culinary genius."

"Pesto, madam."

"Yes, Floote, that! Brilliant. Full of garlic." To illustrate her point, she took another mouthful before continuing. "Seems they put garlic in positively everything here. Absolutely fantastic."

Floote shook his head faintly. "I beg to differ, madam. It is, in fact, the result of practicality. Vampires are allergic to garlic."

"No wonder it is so rare back home."

"Terrible sneezing fits, madam. Much in the manner that young Miss Evylin used to come over when faced with a feline."

"And werewolves?"

"The basil, madam."

"No? How intriguing. Same sort of sneezing?"

"I believe it makes the insides of the mouth and nose itch, madam."

"So this pesto I enjoy so much is really an infamous Italian antisupernatural weapon?" Alexia turned accusing dark eyes on Madame Lefoux. "Yet there is no pesto in my parasol armament. I think we ought to rectify that immediately."

Madame Lefoux did not point out that Alexia could hardly go traipsing around toting a parasol that smelled strongly of garlic and basil. She did not have to, as Alexia was distracted by the arrival of some variety of orange fruit—of course it was *orange*—wrapped in a thinly cut piece of pig meat that was almost, but not quite, bacon. Alexia was transported.

"I don't suppose this is a weapon?"

"Not unless you have suddenly taken against the Jews, madam."

It was fortunate that they ate, for no food awaited them upon their return. After a lengthy stop at the alchemist's, which in Italy also stocked pharmaceuticals and fishing equipment, to purchase what Madame Lefoux referred to as "necessary supplies," they returned to the temple. There they found that, despite the early hour—it was not yet six—the Templars were already retired for the evening, undertaking some form of extended silent prayer.

While Madame Lefoux fussed with refilling the parasol and Floote went to do mysterious butler-type duties, Alexia hunted down the library. When no one stopped her, she began reading various books and records with interest. She had Ivy's little clipping with her and paused to reread it now and again. *A printed admission of guilt, imagine that?* She found herself humming from time to time. *You see, infant-inconvenience, it's not so bad.*

She did not find the information she was chiefly interested in: anything pertaining to the preternatural breeding program or concerning Templar use of soulless agents. However, she did find enough entertaining reading matter to keep her occupied well into the night. It was far later than she thought when she finally looked up to find the temple utterly silent around her, and not in the way of an edifice filled with prayer and soft movements. No, this was the silence of sleeping brains that only ghosts were comfortable experiencing.

Alexia padded toward her room, but then, sensing a presence she was not quite certain she could name, she shifted in her purposeful tread and veered down a small hallway. It was undecorated: there were no crosses nor any other religious effigies, and it ended in a tight stairwell that she might have thought only used by servants, except that it was arched and mossy and had the feel of immense age about it.

Alexia decided to explore.

This was, it must be admitted, probably not the most intelligent decision of her life. But how often is one given the opportunity to investigate an ancient passageway in a sacred temple in Italy?

The stairs down were indeed steep and slightly wet, as the back ends of caves will get no matter the climate. Alexia steadied herself with one hand against the damp wall, trying not to think about whether said wall had been cleaned recently. The stairs seemed to go down a very, very long way, ejecting her at the end into another undecorated hallway that in turn ended in what was possibly the most disappointing little room imaginable.

She could see that it was a room because, and this was peculiar, the door to the room was glass. She walked up and peeked through.

A small chamber lay before her, walls and floors of dingy limestone, with no paint nor other form of decoration. The only piece of furniture was a small pedestal in the center of the room, on top of which stood a jar.

The door was locked, and Alexia, resourceful as she was, had not yet learned to pick locks, though she mentally added it to her list of useful skills she needed to acquire, along with hand-to-hand combat and the recipe for pesto. If her life were to continue on its present track, which, after twenty-six years of obscurity now seemed to mainly involve people trying to kill her, it would appear that acquiring a less savory skill set might be necessary. Although, she supposed, pesto-making ought to be termed *more savory*.

She squinted through the door. It was paned with small squares of old leaded glass that were warping and sagging in their frames. This meant that the room within shifted and wiggled, and she squirmed around trying to see. She just couldn't quite make out what was inside the jar, and then finally she got the correct angle and was abruptly rather queasy to her stomach.

The jar held a severed human hand. It was floating in some liquid, probably formaldehyde.

A tactful little cough sounded behind her, just soft enough not to startle.

Alexia still jumped practically out of her frilly orange dress in surprise. Upon landing, she whirled around.

"Floote!"

"Good evening, madam."

"Come look at this, Floote. They have a human hand in a jar in the middle of an empty room. Aren't the Italians strange?"

"Yes, madam." Floote didn't come over, only nodded as though every house in Italy had such a thing. Alexia supposed this might be possible. Gruesome, but possible.

"But don't you think, madam, it may be time for bed? It would not do for anyone to find us in the Inner Sanctum."

"Oh, is that where we are?"

Floote nodded and extended a gracious arm for Alexia to precede him back up the tiny staircase.

Alexia took his advice, as there was apparently nothing else to see besides the random human body part. "Is it very common, in Italy, to keep a jar full of hand, just lying about?"

"For the Templars, madam."

"Uh, why?"

"It is a relic, madam. Should the temple come under serious threat from the supernatural, the preceptor will break the jar and use the relic to defend the brotherhood."

Alexia thought she might understand. She had heard of holy relics in connection with some Catholic cults. "Is it the body part of some saint?"

"They have those, too, of course, but in this case, it is an *unholy* relic, a weapon. The body part of a preternatural."

Alexia shut her mouth on her next question with a snap. She was surprised she hadn't been physically repulsed by the hand as she had been by the mummy. Then she remembered the daemon detector. She and the disembodied hand hadn't been sharing the same air. She supposed that was why the jar had to be broken in case of emergency.

They proceeded the rest of the way to their rooms in silence, Alexia mulling over the implications of that hand and becoming more and more worried as a result.

Floote stopped Alexia before she retired. "Your father, madam, was fully cremated. I made absolutely certain."

Alexia swallowed silently and then said fervently, "Thank you, Floote."

He nodded once—his face, as always, impassive.

CHAPTER TWELVE

The Great Scotch Egg Under the Thames

Much to Lord Maccon's annoyance, the acquisition operation, as Professor Lyall had termed it, was taking far longer than intended. Impatient to be off after his errant wife, the Alpha was instead stalking back and forth in the drawing room of Buckingham Palace awaiting an audience with Queen Victoria.

He was still unsure as to how Lyall had, in fact, managed to keep him in London all these days. Betas, in the end, were mysterious creatures with strange powers. Powers that, when all was said and done, seemed to involve nothing more than a continued battery of civilized behavior and an excess of manners. Effective, blast him.

Professor Lyall sat on an uncomfortable couch, one stylishly clad leg crossed over the other, and watched his Alpha pace.

"I still don't see why we had to come here, of all places."

The Beta pushed at his spectacles. It was nearing the afternoon of his third day awake in a row, and he was beginning to experience the effects of prolonged daylight exposure. He felt drawn and tired, and all he wanted to do in the world was return to his tiny bed at Woolsey Castle and sleep the afternoon away. Instead, he was stuck dealing with an increasingly edgy Alpha. "I have said it before, and I shall say it again—you will need sundowner authorization for this, my lord."

"Yes, but couldn't you have come and gotten it for me afterward?"

"No, I couldn't, and you know it. This is too complicated. Stop complaining."

Lord Maccon stopped for the simple reason that, as usual, Lyall was correct. It *had* gotten very complicated. Once they'd discovered the location of the stolen object, they'd sent a river rat in to assess the place. The poor lad had come back soaking wet and in an absolute panic, justly earned, as it turned out. Their quick theft and retrieval operation had turned into something far more problematic.

Professor Lyall was a wolf who liked to look on the practical side of any given situation. "At least now we know why Lord Akeldama went into such a tizzy, pulled in all his drones, and ran."

"I didn't realize roves could swarm, but I suppose they have the same protective instincts as hives."

"And Lord Akeldama is a particularly old vampire with a peculiarly large number of drones. He is liable to be overprotective when one is stolen."

"I cannot believe I'm stuck here involving myself in vampiric tomfoolery. I should be hunting my wife, not one of Lord Akeldama's drones."

"The potentate wanted Lord Akeldama panicked for a reason. Your wife is that reason. So, essentially, this *is* your problem, and you have to deal with it before you leave."

"Vampires."

"Exactly so, my lord, exactly so." Professor Lyall's calmness covered his genuine worry. He had met Biffy only once or twice, but he liked the lad. Generally acknowledged as Lord Akeldama's favorite, Biffy was a pretty young thing, calm and capable. He genuinely loved and was loved by his outrageous master. For the potentate to drone-nap him was the height of bad taste. The greatest unwritten law of the supernatural set was that one simply didn't steal someone else's human. Werewolves did not poach clavigers, for the key-keepers were vital to the safety of the greater population. And vampires did not take each other's drones, because, quite frankly, one doesn't interfere with another's food source. The very idea! And yet, they were now in possession of eyewitness testimony to the fact that this was exactly what the potentate had done to Lord Akeldama. Poor Biffy.

"Her Majesty will see you now, Lord Maccon."

The earl straightened his spine. "Righty'o."

Professor Lyall checked his Alpha's appearance. "Now *be polite*."

Lord Maccon gave him a dour look. "I have met the queen before, you know."

"Oh, *I know*. That is why I am reminding you."

Lord Maccon ignored his Beta and followed the footman into Queen Victoria's illustrious presence.

In the end, Queen Victoria granted Lord Maccon sanction in his attempt to rescue Biffy. She refused to believe the potentate was involved, but if, in fact, a drone *had* been kidnapped, she thought it only right that the earl, in his capacity as head of the London BUR offices and chief sundowner, rectify the situation. It was untenable, she claimed, given her experience with vampire loyalty and trust, even among roves, that any vampire would steal another's drone.

"But supposing, Your Majesty, just this once, it has accidentally occurred? And that Lord Akeldama has swarmed as a result."

"Why, then you should carry on, Lord Maccon, carry on."

"I always forget how short she is," the earl commented to Professor Lyall as they readied themselves to "carry on" later that evening. Lord Maccon took the queen's tacit permission to mean he could use his Galand Tue Tue, which he was busy cleaning and loading. It was a graceless little revolver, portly with a square grip and hardwood bullets caged and capped with silver—the Sundowner model designed to kill mortals, vampires, or werewolves. Lord Maccon had designed a watertight, oiled leather case for the gun, which he wore about his neck so that it might be with him whether he was in wolf or human form. Since they would be traveling fast, wolf seemed the most sensible way to get through London.

Biffy, they had learned, was imprisoned inside a rather fantastic contraption. Lord Maccon was still upset that the installation of this device had escaped BUR's notice. It was, according to the trusty river rat, a man-sized sphere made of glass and brass with one large tube coming out its top. The tube was to conduct breathable air, because the sphere had been sunk into the middle of the Thames just under the Charing Cross Rail Bridge near Buckingham Palace. Not unsurprisingly, it had sunk not just into the water, but some way down into the thick mud and garbage at the bottom of the river as well.

When they arrived at the spot, Lord Maccon dove with alacrity off the newly completed Victoria Embankment and into the filthy water. Professor Lyall was more fastidious and thus more reticent. Nothing the Thames could throw at him could damage him permanently, but that didn't prevent his shuddering at the inevitability of the smell he was destined to produce: wet dog mixed with Thames river water.

Lord Maccon's brindled head appeared, fur slicked back like a seal, and he barked at his Beta imperiously. Professor Lyall locked his jaw and leapt stiffly into the water, all four legs extended in disgust. Together, looking like nothing so much as two stray dogs after a stick, the two made their way under the bridge.

Since they knew what they were looking for, they managed to find the breathing tube affixed to one of the piers. It was stretched upward well out of the high-tide mark. It looked as though it could have also been used as a drop for food and water bags. At least the potentate had no intention of actually killing poor Biffy. Still, it was carelessly done. Should the tube fall, some misguided boat crash into it, or one curious animal climb up and stopper it over, Biffy would suffocate to death.

Lord Maccon dove down to investigate the contraption. This was hard to do in wolf form, and it was hard to see much in the blackness of the river. But he had supernatural strength and wolf night vision helping him. He surfaced looking pleased with himself, tongue lolling.

Professor Lyall winced at the very idea of tongue having any proximity to the Thames.

Lord Maccon, being Lord Maccon and good at such things, then changed, right there in the Thames, from dog-paddling wolf to large man treading water. He did so flawlessly, so that his head never went under the water. Professor Lyall suspected him of practicing such maneuvers in the bathtub.

"That is one interesting little contraption he has down there, like some species of mechanical Scotch egg. Biffy's still alive, but I have absolutely no idea how to get him out, short of simply muscling the blasted thing open and dragging him up through the water. Do you think a human could survive such an experience? There seems to be no means of attaching a crank or pulley to the sphere, nor of getting a net underneath, even if we had ready access to such things."

Professor Lyall sacrificed his meticulousness to the winds and changed form. He was not so good as Lord Maccon, sinking down slowly in the process so that he bobbed up, sputtering and disgruntled, to his Alpha's amused gaze.

"We could raid Madame Lefoux's contrivance chamber, but I think time is of the essence. We are werewolves, my lord. Muscling things is our specialty. If we can open it fast enough, we should be able to get him out with relatively little harm."

"Good, because if I do damage him, my wife will never let me hear the end of it. Once she decides to speak to me again, that is. She is awfully fond of Biffy."

"Yes, I recall. He helped with the wedding."

"Did he really? Well, what do you know? So, on the count of three? One, two, three."

Both men inhaled deeply and dove down to crack open the sphere.

It was constructed in two halves, joined by means of large metal ribs, screwed tightly together. From these stretched a cage-like lattice with glass in between, each square far too small for a man to squeeze through. Each werewolf grabbed at one bolt and began to unscrew it as fast as possible. Soon enough, the pressure of the air within caused the upper half of the sphere to separate from the bottom. Air began to escape and water rushed in to fill the vacancy.

Professor Lyall caught sight of Biffy's panicked expression, his blue eyes wide in a face bushy with weeks' worth of beard. He could do nothing to help free himself. Instead he fought the inrushing water, trying to keep his head afloat and tilted toward the air tube as long as possible.

With two bolts gone, the two werewolves wedged their bodies into the opening and began to physically push, muscles screaming, tearing the sphere apart bodily. The metal buckled, glass broke, and water filled the small compartment.

Even in all the chaos, Professor Lyall heard several out-of-context noises and, moments later, saw from the corner of his eye as the earl popped out of the sphere and began wildly thrashing about. But Lyall maintained his focus on Biffy. Pushing forward with both legs off the edge of the sphere, he dove for the drone, grabbed him around the waist, and with another tremendous push, shot upward toward the surface.

He emerged, panting, Biffy clutched against him. The young man was suspiciously limp, and Professor Lyall could think of nothing but the need to get him to shore as quickly as possible. Drawing on every last iota of his werewolf strength to give him the necessary speed, he plowed through the water, reaching the Westminster side of the Thames in record time and dragging the drone out onto the bottom of a filthy set of stone steps.

Professor Lyall was no medical doctor, but he could say with confidence that the best thing for Biffy at that moment would

be to get the water out and the air into his lungs. So the werewolf stood, lifting the young man up by his feet. Lyall had to
dangle him off the side of the steps; Biffy was taller than he.
Then the Beta proceeded to shake the limp drone vigorously.

As he was shaking, Professor Lyall looked over at the midpoint
of the river. The moon was only a few days past full, and it had
risen enough for his werewolf eyes to see everything clearly.
His Alpha was engaged in a splashy battle with three assailants.
Much frothing of the water, yelling, and growling was involved.
Lord Maccon was in his Anubis Form, his head that of a wolf
but his body still human. This allowed him to tread water but
still apply the trademark werewolf savaging. It seemed to be
working. His opponents were human, and, while they were armed
with silver knives, they were not so adept at striking and swimming as Lord Maccon.

Professor Lyall returned to his task. As the shaking was
proving to be ineffective, he positioned the young man carefully
on a higher step and bent over him.

He was at a loss. Werewolves breathed, but not so deeply,
nor so frequently as mortals. He wasn't convinced his next idea
would even work. But, blushing furiously—after all, he and
Biffy had only met casually a few times; they were hardly on
terms of any intimacy—he bent forward and sealed the young
man's mouth with his. Breathing out in a powerful blast, he
attempted to physically force air into the drone's lungs. Nothing
happened. So he did it again. And again.

A loud cry caused him to look up, although not stop in his
attentions to young Biffy's survival. The figure of a man, a
gentleman by his top hat and tails, ran along the rail bridge, faster
than was humanly possible. The figure stopped and, in one impossibly quick and smooth movement, drew a gun and fired down
into the churning mass of combatants.

Professor Lyall's protective instincts reared up. He had no
doubt that the vampire, for that is what the newcomer must be,
was firing silver bullets at *his* Alpha. Desperately, he breathed

harder, hoping against hope that Biffy would revive so that he could go to his Alpha's aid.

Behind him, Lord Maccon behaved in an unexpectedly sensible manner. Abandoning his roughhousing, the Alpha dove under the surface of the Thames and began swimming toward the steps and his Beta. He stuck his muzzle up for air only once and briefly.

Unfortunately, with his first target underwater, the vampire simply moved on to the second best option. He fired at Professor Lyall and his charge as they hunched unprotected against the embankment. The bullet whizzed by perilously close to Lyall's head and struck the stone wall, causing fragments of rock to pellet downward. Lyall curled himself over the drone's body, shielding it with his own.

Then Biffy began to cough and sputter, spewing out Thames river water in a manner that Professor Lyall felt, while inelegant, was most prudent of him. The drone's eyes opened, and he stared up into the werewolf's sympathetic face.

"Do I know you?" Biffy asked between coughs.

Lord Maccon reached the steps at that point and hauled himself up, still in Anubis Form. He reached for his neck, unclasping the leather case safely fastened there, and pulled out his gun. The case had served its purpose, for the Tue Tue was still dry. He took aim at the vampire silhouetted against the moon and fired.

He missed.

"I'm Professor Lyall. We have met before. Remember the aethographor and the tea? How do you do?"

"Where's—?" But Biffy did not get to finish his thought, for the vampire's return shot scooted right past both Lord Maccon and his Beta, striking the poor drone in the stomach. Biffy's sentence stopped midquestion with a cry, as his body, emaciated from weeks in confinement, convulsed and writhed.

Lord Maccon's second shot back at the vampire did not miss. It was a lucky one, for at such a distance, even his trusty Tue Tue was unreliable. Nevertheless, the bullet struck home.

The vampire fell from the bridge with a shout, hitting the Thames with a loud splash. Immediately his agents—or were they drones?—ceased paddling about, recovering from their altercation with the earl, and swam over to him. From the resulting cries of distress, what they discovered was not to their liking.

Lord Maccon's attention remained fixed on the tableau in the water, but Professor Lyall was once more focused on Biffy. The blood leaking from the young man's injury smelled divine, of course, but Lyall was no pup to be diverted by the scent of fresh meat. The drone was dying. No doctor in Britain could patch up a damaged gut like that. There was really only one solution and no one, in the end, was going to be happy with it.

Taking a deep breath, the Beta reached into the wound, fishing about for the bullet with no care for Biffy's finer feelings. The young man conveniently fainted from the pain.

Lord Maccon came to kneel on the step below them.

He gave a confused whine, unable to talk, as his head was still that of a wolf.

"I'm trying to get out the bullet," Professor Lyall explained.

Another whine.

"It's *silver*. It must come out."

The earl began violently shaking his shaggy brindled head and backing slightly away.

"He is dying, my lord. You have no other choice. You're already in Anubis Form. You might as well make the attempt."

Lord Maccon continued to shake his wolf head. Professor Lyall fished out the offensive bullet, hissing in pain as the vile silver thing burned his fingertips.

"Don't you think Lord Akeldama would rather have him still alive, or at least partly alive, than dead? I am aware that it is not done. Unheard of, even, for a werewolf to poach a drone, but what else can we do? You have to at least try."

The Alpha cocked his head to one side, ears drooping. Professor Lyall knew what he was thinking. If this failed, Biffy would be found dead, savaged by a werewolf. How could they possibly explain that to anyone?

"You metamorphosed a female recently. You can do this, my lord."

With a small shrug that said as clearly as any words that if this didn't work, he would never forgive himself, the Alpha bent over the boy's neck and bit.

Normally, metamorphosis was a violent savaging of flesh, an infliction of a curse as much as a conversion to immortality, but Biffy was so very weak and had lost so much blood already that Lord Maccon took it slowly. He was able to. Conall Maccon had more self-control than any other Alpha Lyall had ever met, for all his Scottish heritage and grumpy temper. Lyall could only imagine how sweet the boy's blood must taste. In answer to that thought, Lord Maccon stopped biting and bent to lap at the bullet wound. Then he went back to biting. The idea of metamorphosis, most scientists believed, was to get the were-wolf saliva, carrier of the curse, into the petitioner and to get sufficient human blood out. This would break mortal ties and tether the remnant soul. Supposing there was, of course, excess soul present.

It seemed to take a very long time. But Biffy kept breathing, and so long as Biffy kept breathing, Lord Maccon resolutely continued his repetitive action: bite, lick, bite, lick. He was not to be distracted even by the sloshing arrival of their opponents.

Professor Lyall stood to defend their position, prepared to change form if needed, the moon well overhead and the smell of human blood giving him added strength. But the three young men emerging from the water were obviously uninterested in any further hostility. They hauled themselves out onto the bottom step and held up empty hands at Professor Lyall's threatening stance. Their faces were lined with distress—one was crying openly, and another was keening softly at the limp form cradled in his arms. The third, a grim-faced boy holding one mostly gnawed hand against his chest, spoke.

"We've no reason to fight you further, werewolf. Our master is dead."

Drones, then, and not hired muscle.

Professor Lyall sniffed, trying to catch the scent of the vampire over the smell of human blood and putrid water. The horror of it hit him broadside, and he stumbled back against the stone of the embankment. It was there, the faint odor of old blood and decay that meant vampire, mixed with almost alcoholic overtones that, like the subtle difference between fine wines, indicated lineage. And Lyall smelled an old lineage, with a film of pine resin to the wine, and no ties to the modern hives. It was a scent long since lost and no longer emitted except by this one man. Lyall could have guessed the identity of the vampire from that scent, even were he not already familiar with its owner—the potentate. Or, as the vampire was dead and no longer a denizen of the Shadow Council, Lyall supposed he must be remembered now under his old name, Sir Francis Walsingham.

"Queen Victoria," he said to his Alpha, "is *not* going to be happy about this. Why the hell didn't he send someone else to do his dirty work?"

Lord Maccon did not look up from his self-prescribed penance: bite, lick, bite, lick.

Together, the three drones hefted their dead master and made their way slowly up the stairs around the earl and Biffy's still form. Even in their grief, they winced away from the sight of an Anubis feeding. As they passed, Professor Lyall noticed that Lord Maccon's bullet had hit Walsingham directly in the heart— a lucky shot, indeed.

A vampire was dead. There weren't enough of them around to forgive a transgression like that, even from BUR's chief sundowner. The potentate was a rove, with no major hive connections, and for that Professor Lyall was grateful. But there would be blood payment due to the greater community regardless, and it was the potentate's relationship with Buckingham Palace that was the real stickler. Even if, by his actions, this vampire had shown himself a traitor to his own kind, kidnapping another's drone, his absence left a gap Queen Victoria would find hard to fill. He had served as adviser to the throne since Queen Elizabeth's day. It was his knowledge of Roman strategy and supply management that drove the expansion of the British Empire. For someone like that to die because he had made a mistake, because Alexia Maccon, soulless, had become pregnant by a werewolf and he panicked, was a loss to every British citizen. Even the werewolves would mourn him, in their way.

Professor Lyall, who was cultured and not given to profanity, watched the drones cart the disanimated potentate away and said curtly, "What a bloody awful mess."

After which he stood, silent and waiting, wary and alert, for five long hours while Lord Maccon, stubborn to the last, held Anubis Form and worked over the dying drone.

The earl's stubbornness was rewarded when, just before dawn, before all his labor would be lost to the sun, Biffy's eyes opened, as yellow as buttercups. He howled out his pain and confusion and fear as his form shifted, and he lay there, shuddering but whole, a lovely chocolate-brown wolf with oxblood-red stomach fur.

Lord Maccon changed out of Anubis Form and grinned hugely at his Beta. "And there's another one for the howlers to sing about."

"What is it with you, my lord? Can you only metamorphose the difficult cases?" Professor Lyall was impressed despite himself.

"Yes, well, he is your charge now." Lord Maccon stood and stretched, his spine popping as it realigned. His tawny eyes turned with surprise toward the rapidly lightening sky.

"Best get him indoors right quick."

Professor Lyall nodded and bent to pick up the newly made wolf. Biffy struggled halfheartedly before sagging weakly into the Beta's strong arms. Metamorphosis took even the best of them like that.

Lyall made his way silently up the steps to the top of the embankment, thinking hard. They would have to find shelter nearby. A new pup couldn't take direct sunlight without considerable damage, and poor Biffy had been through more than enough for one night. Just as he figured out a destination and headed purposefully north toward Charing Cross Station, he noticed his Alpha wasn't following him.

"Now where are you going, my lord?" he hollered after Lord Maccon's rapidly retreating back.

The earl yelled over his shoulder without breaking stride. "I have a boat to catch and a wife to find. You can carry on from here."

Lyall would have rubbed his face with his hands, except his arms were full. "Oh, yes, certainly, feel free to depart. And me with a drone changed into a werewolf and a dead potentate. I am certain I have had Alphas leave me with worse messes to tidy up, but I cannot recall them at the moment."

"I am sure you will do very well."

"Wonderful, my lord. Thank you for your confidence."

"Toodles." And with that, Lord Maccon wiggled his fingers in the air in the most insulting way and disappeared around the side of a building. Presumably, he was heading for a busier part of London where he might stand a better chance of hailing a hackney post-haste for Dover.

Professor Lyall decided not to remind him that he was completely naked.

CHAPTER THIRTEEN

Picnicking with Templars

Alexia took a moment before breakfast to drag Floote into a secluded corner.

"We must get a message to the queen on this relic business. Or at least to BUR. I cannot believe you knew about it and never told anyone. Then again, I suppose, you never tell anyone anything, do you, Floote? Even me. Still, I know now and so should the British government. Imagine using preternatural body parts as weapons. Just think what they could do if they knew how to mummify."

"You are no longer muhjah, madam. The supernatural security of the empire is not your concern."

Alexia shrugged. "What can I say? I cannot help myself. I meddle."

"Yes, madam. And on a grand scale."

"Well, my mama always said, one should do what one is best at on as large a scale as possible. Of course, she was referring to shopping at the time, but I have always felt it was the only sensible sentence she ever uttered in her life."

"Madam?"

"We have managed to keep the mummy business mum, even from Madame Lefoux. The point being, we cannot let anyone know that mummies are useful as a weapon. There would be a terrible run on Egypt. If the Templars are using dead preternatural body parts and they figure out the mummification process, I am in real trouble. Right now it is only natural decomposition, and the fact that they have to preserve tissue in formaldehyde, that keeps preternatural-as-weapon limited to special use." Alexia wrinkled her nose. "This is a matter of supernatural security. Italy and the other conservative countries must be kept from excavating in Egypt at all costs. We cannot risk them figuring out the truth behind the God-Breaker Plague."

"I see your reasoning, madam."

"You will need to develop a sudden malaise that prevents you from attending this picnic the preceptor is dragging me on. Get to the Florentine aethographic transmitter by sunset and send a message to Professor Lyall. He will know what to do with the information." Alexia rummaged about in the ruffle of her parasol until she located the secret pocket and extracted the crystalline valve, which she handed to Floote.

"But, madam, the danger of you traveling about Italy without me."

"Oh, fiddlesticks. Madame Lefoux has entirely refitted my parasol with the necessary armaments. I shall have the preceptor and a cadre of Templars with me, and they're bound to protect me even if they cannot look at me. I even purchased this." Alexia exhibited a clove of garlic dangling from a long ribbon about her neck. "I shall be perfectly fine."

Floote did not look convinced.

"If it will help allay your fears, give me one of your guns and some of the spare bullets you purchased yesterday."

Floote did not seem at all mollified. "Madam, you do not know how to shoot."

"How difficult can it be?"

Floote ought to have known after a quarter century of association with Alexia that he could not hope to win any argument, especially as a gentleman of few words and even less inclination to use them. With a faint sigh of disapproval, he accepted the responsibility of sending the transmission and left the room, without giving Alexia one of his guns.

Professor Lyall spent the last hour before dawn coping with the consequences of Biffy's sudden change into a werewolf and the potentate's sudden change into a corpse. He began by seeking out the closest safe house, where no one else would think to look for him and his new charge. And since Charing Cross Station was just south of Soho, he headed north toward the Tunstells' apartments, in all their pastel glory.

While midnight was considered quite an acceptable hour for calling among members of the supernatural set and among the younger, more dashing mortal crowd—drivers of phaetons and the like—dawn was *not*. In fact, dawn might be considered the rudest time for anyone to call upon anyone else, with the possible exception of groups of hardy fishermen in the backwaters of Portsmouth.

But Lyall felt he had no choice. As it was, he had to bang on the door a good five minutes or so before a bleary young maid opened it cautiously.

"Yes?"

Beyond the maid, Lyall saw a head stick out of a bedroom far down the hall—Mrs. Tunstell in an outrageous sleeping cap that resembled nothing so much as a frothy lace-covered mushroom. "What has happened? Are we on fire? Has someone died?"

Professor Lyall, still carrying Biffy in wolf form, muscled his way past the astonished maid and into the house. "You might put it like that, Mrs. Tunstell."

"My goodness, Professor Lyall! What do you have there?" The head disappeared. "Tunny! Tunny! Wake up. Professor Lyall is here with a dead dog. Arise at once. Tunny!" She came bustling down the hallway wrapped in a voluminous robe of eye-searing pink satin. "Oh, the poor lamb, bring him in here."

"Please do forgive me for the presumption, Mrs. Tunstell, but yours was the nearest house." He lay Biffy down on the small lavender couch and quickly reached behind it to draw the curtains over the window, just as the sun's first rays peeked above the horizon. Biffy's previously still form stiffened and then began to shudder and convulse.

Throwing all decorum to the winds, Professor Lyall rushed at Ivy, got one arm firmly about her waist, and hustled her to the door. "Best you not be here for this, Mrs. Tunstell. Send in your husband, would you, once he awakens?"

Ivy opened and closed her mouth a couple of times like an affronted poodle, and then whirled to do as he had bidden. There was a woman, Lyall thought, forced into efficiency through prolonged exposure to Alexia Tarabotti.

"Tunny!" she called, trotting back down the hallway, and then with far greater sharpness, "Ormond Tunstell, wake up. Do!"

Professor Lyall closed the door and turned back to his charge. He reached into his waistcoat for one of his trusty handkerchiefs, only then remembering he was wearing no more than a greatcoat, retrieved from the shore, having dressed for change, not company. Wincing at his own temerity, he grabbed one of Ivy's pastel throw pillows and wedged a corner of it into the new werewolf's mouth, giving Biffy something to bite down upon and also muffling his whimpering. Then Lyall bent low, bracing the shuddering form of the wolf with his own body, curling about him tenderly. It was partly Beta instinct, to protect a new member of the pack, but it was also sympathy. The first time was always the worst, not because it got any better, but because it was so unfamiliar an experience.

Tunstell let himself into the room.

"God's teeth, Professor, what is going on?"

"Too much to explain fully right now, I'm afraid. Can that wait until later? I've got a new pup on my hands and no Alpha to handle him. Do you have any raw meat in the house?"

"The wife ordered steak, delivered only yesterday." Tunstell left without needing to be pressed further.

Lyall smiled. The redhead fell so easily back into his old role of claviger, doing what needed to be done for the werewolves around him.

Biffy's chocolate fur was beginning to retreat up to the top of his head, showing skin now pale with immortality. His eyes were losing their yellow hue in favor of blue. Clutching that writhing form, Lyall could feel as well as hear Biffy's bones breaking and re-forming. It was a long and agonizing shift. It would take the young man decades to master any level of competency. Rapidity and smoothness were markers of both dominance and age.

Lyall held Biffy the entire time. Held him while Tunstell returned with a large raw steak and fussed about with varying degrees of helpfulness. Held him until, eventually, he was left with an armful of nothing but naked Biffy, shivering and looking most forlorn.

"What? Where?" The young dandy pushed weakly against the Beta's arms. His nose was twitching as though he needed to sneeze. "What is going on?"

Professor Lyall relaxed his embrace and sat back on his heels next to the couch. Tunstell came over with a blanket and a concerned expression. Just before he covered the young man over, Lyall was pleased to notice that Biffy appeared to be entirely healed from the bullet wound, a true supernatural, indeed.

"Who are *you*?" Biffy focused fuzzily on Tunstell's bright red hair.

"I'm Tunstell. Used to be a claviger to Lord Maccon. Now I'm mostly just an actor."

"He is our host and a friend. We will be safe here for the day." Professor Lyall kept his voice low and calm, tucking the blanket about the still-shivering young man.

"Is there some reason we need to be? Safe, I mean."

"How much do you remember?" Lyall swept a lock of brown hair back behind Biffy's ear in a motherly fashion. Despite all his transformations, his nudity, and his beard, the young man still looked every inch the dandy. He would make an odd addition to the gruff soldiering masculinity of the Woolsey Pack.

Biffy jerked and fear flooded into his eyes. "Extermination mandate! I found out that there is a . . . Oh, dear God, I was supposed to report in! I missed the appointment with my lord." He made as if to try and rise.

Lyall held him back easily.

Biffy turned on him frantically. "You don't understand—he'll swarm if I don't make it back. He knew I was going after the potentate. How could I have gotten caught? I'm such an imbecile. I know better than that. Why, he'll . . ." He trailed off. "How long was I down there?"

Lyall sighed. "He did swarm."

"Oh, no." Biffy's face fell. "All that work, all those agents pulled out of covert placement. It'll take years to reintegrate them. He's going to be so very disappointed in me."

Lyall tried to distract him. "So, what do you remember?"

"I remember being trapped under the Thames and thinking I would never escape." Biffy brushed one hand over his face. "And that I really needed a shave. Then I remember water flooding in and waking in the darkness to shouting and gunshots. And then I remember a lot of pain."

"You were dying." Lyall paused, searching for the right words. Here he was, hundreds of years old, and he could not explain to one boy why he had been changed against his will.

"Was I? Well, good thing that didn't take. My lord would never forgive me if I up and died without asking permission first." Biffy sniffed, suddenly distracted. "Something smells amazing."

Professor Lyall gestured to the plate of raw steak sitting nearby.

Biffy tilted his head to see, then looked back at Lyall in confusion. "But it's not cooked. Why does it smell so good?"

Lyall cleared his throat. As a Beta, he'd never had to perform this particular task. It was the Alpha's job to acclimatize the newly turned, the Alpha's job to explain and be there and be strong and be, well, Alpha-ish for a new pup. But Lord Maccon was halfway to Dover by now, and Lyall was left to deal with this mess without him.

"You know that dying issue I just mentioned? Well, it did take, in its way."

At which juncture, Professor Lyall had to watch those beautiful blue eyes turn from dazed confusion to horrified realization. It was one of the saddest things he had ever seen in all his long life.

At a loss, Lyall handed Biffy the plate of raw steak.

Unable to control himself, the young dandy tore into the meat, gulping it down in elegant, but very rapid, bites.

For the sake of his dignity, both Professor Lyall and Tunstell pretended not to notice that Biffy was crying the entire time. Tears dribbled down his nose and onto the steak while he chewed, and swallowed, and chewed, and sobbed.

The preceptor's picnic, as it turned out, was a little more elaborate than Alexia and Madame Lefoux had been led to believe. They trundled a sizable distance into the countryside, away from Florence in the direction of Borgo San Lorenzo, arriving eventually at an archaeological excavation. While the antiquated carriage attempted to park on a hillock, their Templar host announced with much pride that they would be engaging in an Etruscan tomb picnic.

The site was lovely, shaded with trees of various bushy Mediterranean inclinations that took being leafy and green quite seriously. Alexia stood up while the carriage maneuvered around, the better to take in her surroundings.

"Do sit down, Alexia! You shall fall, and then how will I explain to Floote that you had—" Madame Lefoux stopped herself before she inadvertently mentioned Alexia's unfortunate condition in front of the preceptor, but it was clear her worry was largely for the child's safety.

Alexia ignored her.

They were surrounded by a series of tombs: low, circular, and grass covered, almost organic in appearance, quite unlike anything Alexia had ever seen or read about. Never having visited anything more stimulating than a Roman bathhouse, Alexia was practically bouncing with excitement—if a lady once more corseted and trussed up to the height of proper British fashion and encumbered by both parasol and pregnancy could be described as "bouncing." She sat down abruptly when their carriage went over a bump.

Alexia refused, on principle, to admit that her new high spirits were on account of Conall's printed apology, but the world certainly seemed a far more fascinating place today than it had yesterday.

"Do you know anything of these *Etruscans*?" she whispered to Madame Lefoux.

"Only that they came before the Romans."

"Were they supernaturally based or a daylight exclusive society?" Alexia asked the next most important question.

The preceptor overheard her.

"Ah, My Soulless One, you ask one of the most troublesome questions of the great Etruscan mystery. Our historians, they continue to investigate this matter. I did think, however, that given your peculiar skill set, you might . . ." He trailed off meaningfully as though intentionally leaving the thought unfinished.

"Well, my dear Mr. Templar, I fail to see how I could possibly be of assistance. I am no trained antiquarian. The only thing I can identify with any consistency is my own kind. I—" It was Alexia's turn to leave a thought unfinished, as she realized the implications of his statement. "You believe there might be a preternatural focus to this culture? How remarkable."

The Templar only shrugged. "We have seen the rise and fall of many great empires in the past, some run by vampires, others by werewolves."

"And some that have been founded upon the persecution of both." Alexia was thinking of the Catholic Inquisition, an expurgation movement the Templars were rumored to have taken a keen and active interest in promoting.

"But never yet have we found evidence of a civilization built to incorporate your kind."

"As difficult as that kind of proximity might be?" Alexia was puzzled.

"Why do you think the Etruscans might be the exception?" Madame Lefoux asked.

The coach stopped and the preceptor stepped down. He did not offer Alexia a hand, allowing Madame Lefoux to jump out and take over that dubious honor. Some distance away, the Templar cavalry dismounted as well and stood about as though waiting for orders. The preceptor gave them one of those hand signals, and the men relaxed into a casual milling group. The silent efficiency was unsettling, to say the least.

"Don't say much, do they?"

The preceptor turned his emotionless eyes on Alexia. "Would you ladies prefer to explore or eat first?"

"Explore," said Alexia promptly. She was wildly curious to see the inside of the strange round tombs.

The preceptor led them down into the dry, dim interior of the already cracked tomb. The underground walls were lined with limestone. Steps led into a single chamber, not much bigger than Alexia's drawing room back at Woolsey Castle. The limestone was elaborately carved to look like the inside of a house, with nooks, stone columns, and even ceiling beams picked out in the sandy, porous rock. It was the interior of a home, frozen in stone. Alexia was reminded of the elaborate jelly sculptures she had eaten at fancy dinner parties, made of aspic and formed with the aid of a mold.

There was no furniture, nor any other artifacts inside the tomb, the sole object being an extremely large sarcophagus in the center of the room. On the top lay two full-sized clay figures: a man lounging on his side and leaning up on one elbow behind a woman doing the same, his free arm draped affectionately over her shoulder.

It was a lovely sculpture, but despite what the preceptor had said, Alexia experienced no sense of repulsion, no feeling about the place that she would have expected when in the presence of a preserved preternatural body. Either there was none present, or the remains had long since decomposed beyond effectiveness. The Templar was staring at her, monitoring her reactions closely.

Face impassive, she walked about, self-conscious under his dead-eyed scrutiny, examining some painted images on the walls.

The place smelled musty, in the same way that old books do, only with an overlay of dirt and cold stone. But there was nothing there that engendered any adverse reaction in Alexia. In fact, she found the ancient abode quite comforting and restful. She was glad of this. She would hate to have to hide her instinct to run if there *had* been some kind of preternatural mummy in residence.

"I am sorry to say, Mr. Templar, I do not think I can be of any help. I do not even see why one might associate this culture with my kind."

The preceptor looked disappointed.

Madame Lefoux, who had been watching him while he watched her friend, turned sharply to stare down at the sarcophagus.

"What were they holding?" she asked.

Alexia wandered over to see what Madame Lefoux was on about. She was struck by the pleasantness in the almond-shaped eyes of the statues, but upon looking closer, she realized what it was that had drawn Madame Lefoux's attention. The man was leaning on the elbow of one arm, the hand of which was up and flat as though offering a carrot to a horse. His other hand, behind the woman's neck, had thumb and forefinger curved in the act of holding some small object. The woman had both hands curved in such a way as one might pour libations or offer up a flask of wine.

"Good question."

Both ladies turned to look at the preceptor inquiringly.

"The woman held an empty ceramic flask, its contents long since dried and evaporated into aether. The man was offering a piece of meat on his open palm. The archaeologists found an animal bone resting there. He was holding something very strange in his other hand."

"What was that?"

The Templar shrugged and fished about his high collar with one finger, finally pulling out a chain that was around his neck. Carefully he lifted it out from underneath nightgown, jacket, waistcoat, and shirt. All three of them moved toward the light streaming down from the entrance. A small gold charm dangled from the end of the chain. Alexia and Madame Lefoux bent to examine it.

"An ankh?" Alexia blinked in amusement.

"From Ancient Egypt?" Madame Lefoux arched one perfect black eyebrow.

"Were the two cultures chronologically comparable?" Alexia scrabbled to remember the dates of Egyptian expansion.

"It is possible they had some form of contact, but it is more likely that this little object came into Etruscan hands through trade with the Greeks."

Alexia studied the small piece of gold closely but, uncharacteristically, pursed her lips and said nothing. She found it odd that an Etruscan statue would offer up the Egyptian symbol for eternal life, and while, to be sure, she had many theories on the subject, she was unwilling to share them with a Templar.

The preceptor tucked his charm away when neither lady had anything further to say and led the way back up the limestone stairs and out onto the sun-dappled hillside. The other tombs were much the same, only in not quite such good repair.

The picnic that followed was an uncomfortably silent affair. Alexia, Madame Lefoux, and the preceptor were seated on a square of quilted gingham spread atop the tomb while the other Templars enjoyed their own meal a short distance away. One of the Templars did not eat, but instead read from the Bible in lugubrious tones. The preceptor seemed to feel this was an excuse not to engage in any conversation with his two companions.

Alexia ate an apple, two rolls of crunchy bread spread with some kind of tomato sauce, and three hard-boiled eggs dipped in more of the green stuff that had so delighted her the day before.

With meal finished and Bible put away, the party prepared to leave. There was one benefit to picnicking, Alexia realized. As she had used no utensils, nothing needed to be destroyed because of contamination.

"It is not a bad life we lead here, is it, My Soulless One?" The preceptor spoke to her at last.

Alexia was forced to admit that it didn't appear so. "Italy *is* a lovely country. And I cannot fault your cuisine or climate."

"You are—how do I say this politely—unwelcome back in England?"

Alexia was going to correct him and boast of Conall's public apology but then thought better of it. Instead she said, "That is a very diplomatic way of putting it, Mr. Templar."

The preceptor smiled his horrible cheerless grimace. "Perhaps, My Soulless One, you might consider staying here with us, then? It has been a long time since we of the temple at Florence had a preternatural in residence, let alone a female of the species. We would make sure of your every comfort while we studied you. Provide for you your own, more isolated quarters."

Alexia's face soured as she thought back to her unfortunate encounter with Dr. Siemons and the Hypocras Club. "I have entertained such an offer before."

The Templar tilted his head, watching her.

Since he seemed, once more, to be in a chatty frame of mind, Alexia asked, "You would put up with devil spawn permanently in your midst?"

"We have done so before. We of the brotherhood are God's best weapon against the supernatural threat. We were made to do what needed to be done no matter what the cost or personal risk. You could be very useful to our cause."

"Goodness gracious, I had no idea I was that appealing." Alexia waggled her eyebrows suggestively.

Madame Lefoux joined the conversation. "If that is the case, why are you not equally welcoming to werewolves and vampires?"

"Because they are not born daemons. To be born with the eternal sin is not much more than to be born with original sin. The soulless suffer, as we all do, under the metaphorical cross, only for them there is no salvation. The vampires and werewolves, on the other hand, have chosen their path voluntarily.

It is a matter of *intention*. They have turned their backs on salvation in a way far more reprehensible, because they once had excess soul. *They* could have ascended into heaven had they only resisted Satan's temptation. Instead, they traded the bulk of their soul to the devil and became monsters. They are offensive to God, for only he and his angels are allowed immortality." He spoke calmly, with no emotion, no inflection, and no doubt.

Alexia felt chilled. "Which is why you wish to see all supernatural folk dead?"

"It is our eternal crusade."

Alexia did some calculations. "Over four hundred years or so. Commendably committed of you all."

"A God-sanctioned purpose, to hunt and kill." Madame Lefoux's tone was full of censure, not unsurprising given her choices in life—she was a creator, an engineer, and a builder.

The preceptor looked from the Frenchwoman to Alexia. "And what do you think *her* God-given purpose is, Scientist Lefoux—a soulless creature whose only skill is in neutralizing the supernatural? Do you think she was not placed on this earth as a tool? We can give her purpose, even if she is only a female."

"Now, wait just a minute there!" Alexia remembered once complaining to Conall, before their marriage, that she wanted something useful to do with her life. Queen Victoria had made her muhjah, but even with that gone, killing vampires and werewolves for a sect of religious fanatics was not precisely what she had been hoping for.

"Have you any idea how rare you are, a female of the species?"

"I am beginning to get the impression that I am more rare than I had thought." Alexia looked about suddenly, feigning physical discomfort. "Do you think I might visit a convenient bush, before we depart for the long drive back?"

The Templar looked equally discomforted. "If you insist."

Alexia tugged at Madame Lefoux's sleeve and dragged her off behind the tomb and down the side of the hill a little ways to a small copse of trees.

"It took Angelique this way," commented Madame Lefoux, referring to her former lover. "During her pregnancy, she always had to . . . well . . . you know."

"Oh, no, that was merely a ruse. I wanted to discuss something with you. That ankh around his neck, did you notice that it had been repaired?"

Madame Lefoux shook her head. "Is that significant, do you think?"

Alexia had never told Madame Lefoux about the mummy nor the broken ankh symbol. But in her experience, it was the hieroglyphic sign of a preternatural.

So she quickly moved on. "I think the terracotta man in the tomb was a preternatural, and the woman was a vampire, and the offering of meat was for the werewolves."

"A harmonious culture? Is that possible?"

"It would be terribly arrogant of us British to think England was the first and only progressive society." Alexia was worried. If the Templars comprehended the significance of the ankh, she was in more danger than she had thought. They would find a way to turn her into a tool, living or dead.

"I do hope Floote managed to send that message to BUR."

"Love note to your werewolf?" Madame Lefoux sounded wistful. Then she looked about the empty hillside, suddenly nervous. "I think, my dear Alexia, we should head back to the carriage."

Alexia, enjoying the countryside and the intellectual advantages afforded by their ancient surroundings, had not registered the lateness of the hour. "Ah, yes, you may be correct."

It was, unfortunately, well into nighttime before they were even halfway back to Florence. Alexia felt awfully exposed in the open-topped carriage. She kept her parasol close and began to wonder if this whole excursion was not an attempt by the Templars to use her as some kind of bait. After all, they fancied themselves great supernatural hunters and might very well risk her safety simply to draw local vampires out. Especially if the Templars had enough foolish pride in their own abilities to believe there was little true peril. The moon was just rising, no longer entirely full but still quite bright. In its silvery light, Alexia could make out a gleam of anticipation in the preceptor's normally emotionless eyes. *You rotten sod, this was all a setup*, she was about to say, but too late.

The vampire appeared out of nowhere, leaping with exceptional speed from the dirt road into the carriage. He was single-minded in his attack, heading straight for Alexia, the only apparent female of the group. Madame Lefoux gave a yell of warning, but Alexia had already thrown herself forward onto the open seat opposite her own, next to the preceptor. The vampire ended up where she had just been sitting. Alexia fumbled with her parasol, twisting the handle so that the two sharp spikes, one wood and one silver, sprang out from its tip.

The preceptor, suddenly brandishing a long, evil-looking wooden knife, gave a yell of pleasure and attacked. Madame Lefoux had her trusty cravat pin already out and in play. Alexia swung her parasol, but all were merely normal humans pitted against superhuman strength, and even fighting off multiple bodies in the awkwardly tiny venue of an open-topped carriage, the vampire was holding his own.

The preceptor dove forward. He was grinning—a real smile for the first time. Maniacal, but real.

Alexia took a firm grip on her parasol with both hands and used a hacking blow to stab with the wooden spike at any part of the vampire that emerged from the wrestling match long enough for her to pin it down. It was a little like trying to hit the heads of ground moles as they appeared out of their holes. But soon enough, Alexia was getting quite into the game of it.

"Touch it!" yelled the preceptor at Alexia. "Touch it so I can kill it."

The preceptor was an excellent fighter, for he was single-minded in his attempt to drive his wooden weapon into the creature's heart or some other vital organ. But he was simply not fast enough, even when Madame Lefoux came to his aid.

Madame Lefoux got in a couple of wicked strikes to the vampire's face with her cravat pin, but the cuts began to heal almost as soon as she had delivered them. With the air of one swatting at an irritating bug, the vampire casually backhanded the inventor with a closed fist. She fell hard against the inside of the carriage and then slumped inelegantly to the floor, eyes closed, mouth slack, and mustache fallen entirely off.

Before Alexia had a chance to react, the vampire managed to heave the Templar up and forward. He hurled the preceptor against the driver so that both fell out of the carriage into the country lane below.

The horses, spooked into screams of panic, took off in a crazed gallop, surging forward, straining against their traces in a most alarming manner. Alexia tried to maintain her footing in the wildly pitching carriage. The four cavalry Templars, who had almost caught up to the ruckus, were left behind in a cloud of swirling dust kicked up by frantic hooves.

The vampire lunged toward Alexia again. Alexia took a firm grip on her parasol and gritted her teeth. Really, she was getting very tired of these constant bouts of fisticuffs. One would think she was a boxer down at Whites! The vampire lunged. Alexia swung. But he batted the parasol away and was upon her, hands wrapped around her neck.

He sneezed. *Aha*, thought Alexia, *the garlic!*

When he touched her, his fangs vanished and his strength became that of an ordinary human. She saw in his beautiful brown eyes a look of surprise. He may have known what she was intellectually but had clearly not experienced the sensation of preternatural touch before. Yet his fingers tightened inexorably around Alexia's throat. He might be mortal but he was still strong enough to strangle her, no matter how she kicked and struggled.

I'm not ready to die, thought Alexia. *I haven't yelled at Conall yet*. And then she thought about the baby really as a baby and not an inconvenience for the very first time. We're *not ready to die*.

She heaved upward, pushing the vampire up and off.

And just then, something white hit the vampire crosswise so hard that Alexia heard bones breaking—after all, the vampire *was* currently quite mortal and lacking any supernatural defenses. The vampire screamed in surprise and pain.

The hit broke his hold around her neck, and Alexia stumbled back, panting hard, eyes fixed on her former attacker.

The white thing resolved itself into the frenzied figure of a massive wolf, growling and thrashing against the vampire in a whirlwind of teeth and claws and blood. The two supernatural creatures scrabbled together, werewolf strength against vampire speed, while Alexia pushed herself and her parasol back into one corner of the seat, protectively shielding Madame Lefoux's fallen form from claws, teeth, and fangs.

The wolf had the advantage, having attacked while the vampire was rendered vulnerable through preternatural contact, and he never lost it. In very short order, he wrapped his powerful jaws about the vampire's neck, sinking his teeth into the man's throat. The vampire gave a gurgling howl, and the smell of rotten blood filled the fresh country air.

Alexia caught a flash of ice-blue eyes as the wolf gave her one meaningful look before he hurled both himself and the vampire out of the moving carriage, hitting the ground with a tremendous thud. The sound of their battle continued but was rapidly lost in the clattering of hooves as the horses raced onward.

Alexia realized it must have been the scent of the wolf that initially panicked the horses. It was now up to her to slow them down before the terrified creatures broke their traces or over-turned the carriage, or worse.

She scrambled up onto the driver's box, only to find that the reins had fallen forward and were hanging down near the shackle, perilously close to the kicking hind legs of the horses. She lay, belly down over the box, holding on with one hand and desperately reaching with the other. No luck. Seized with an inspiration, she retrieved her parasol. It still had the two spikes sticking out from its tip, and she managed to use those to catch the dangling reins and pull them sufficiently close to grasp. Victorious, she only then remembered she had never actually driven a carriage before. Figuring it couldn't be too difficult, she tried a gentle tug backward on the reins.

Absolutely nothing changed. The horses continued their mad dash.

Alexia took a firmer grip with both hands and yanked backward, leaning back and applying all her weight. She was not as strong as a gentleman of the Corinthian set might be, but she probably weighed about the same. The sudden pressure caused the animals to slow, first to a canter and then to trot, sides heaving and flanks lathered with sweat.

Alexia decided there was no point in stopping entirely and kept the horses headed back into the city. It was probably better to attain the relative safety of the temple as quickly as possible in case the rest of that vampire's hive were also after her.

Two of the mounted Templars, white nightgowns floating becomingly in the breeze about them, finally caught up. They took up position, one to either side of the carriage, and without acknowledging or even looking at her, proceeded to act as escort.

"Do you think we might just pause and check on Madame Lefoux?" Alexia asked, but no verbal response was garnered. One of the men actually looked at her, but then he turned aside and spat as if his mouth had been filled with something distasteful. Fear for her friend's well-being notwithstanding, Alexia decided that getting to safety was probably most important. She glanced at her two stony-faced escorts once more. Nothing. So she shrugged and clucked the horses into a more enthusiastic trot. There had been four Templars on horseback originally. She assumed that of the other two, one went back for the fallen preceptor and the other was off hunting the vampire and the werewolf.

With nothing else to occupy her but idle speculation, Alexia

wondered if this white werewolf was the same as the white creature she had seen from the ornithopter, the one that had attacked
the vampires on Monsieur Trouvé's roof. There was something
awfully familiar about those icy-blue eyes. With a start, she realized that the werewolf, the white beast, and the man in the mask
at the customs station in Boboli Gardens were all the same
person and that she knew him. Knew him and was, at the best
of times, not particularly fond of him: her husband's arrogant
third in command, Woolsey Pack's Gamma, Major Channing
Channing of the Chesterfield Channings. She decided she'd been
living too long with a werewolf pack if she could recognize him
as a wolf in the middle of a battle when earlier, as the masked
gentlemen, she had not been able to place him at all.

"He must have been following and protecting me since Paris!"
She said out loud to the uninterested Templars, her voice cutting
into the night.

They ignored her.

"And, of course, he couldn't help us that night on the Alpine
pass because it was *full moon!*" Alexia wondered why her
husband's third, whom neither she nor Conall particularly liked,
was risking his life inside the borders of Italy to protect her. No
werewolf with half a brain would voluntarily enter the strong-
hold of antisupernatural sentiment. Then again, there was some
question, so far as Alexia was concerned, as to the extent of
Channing's brains. There was really only one good explanation:
Channing would be guarding her only if Lord Conall Maccon
had ordered it.

Of course, her husband was an unfeeling prat who should
have come after her himself. And, of course, he was also an
annoying git for meddling in her business when he had taken
such pains to separate it from his own. But the timing meant
he still cared enough to bark out an order to see her safe, even
before he had printed that apology.

He must still love her. *I think he might actually want us back*,
she told the infant-inconvenience with a giddy sense of elation.

CHAPTER FOURTEEN

In Which the Infant-Inconvenience Becomes Considerably More Inconvenient

Eventually Biffy slept and Professor Lyall could afford to do the same. They were safe under the watchful eye of Tunstell, and then Mrs. Tunstell, if such a thing was to be imagined. The two werewolves dozed throughout the day and well into early evening. Eventually, Ivy went off to check on the hat shop, and Tunstell, who had rehearsals to attend, felt it safe enough to wake Lyall.

"I went to the butcher for more meat," he explained as the Beta sawed off a chunk of raw steak and popped it into his mouth.

Professor Lyall chewed. "So I taste. What's the word on the street, then?"

"It's very simple and baldly put, and everyone is talking about it. And I do mean *everyone*."

"Go on."

"The potentate is dead. You and the old wolf had a busy night last night, didn't you, Professor?"

Lyall put down his utensils and rubbed at his eyes. "Oh, my giddy aunt. What a mess he has left me with."

"One of Lord Maccon's defining characteristics, as I recall—messiness."

"Are the vampires very upset?"

"Why, Professor, are you trying to be sarcastic? That's sweet."

"Answer the question, Tunstell."

"None of them are out yet. Nor their drones. But the rumor is they find the situation not ideal, sir. Not ideal at all."

Professor Lyall stretched his neck to each side. "Well, I have been hiding out here long enough, I suppose. Time to face the fangs."

Tunstell struck a Shakespearean pose. "The fangs and canines of outrageous fortune!"

Professor Lyall gave him a dour look. "Something like."

The Beta stood and stretched, looking down at Biffy. The rest was doing him good. He looked if not healthier, at least less emaciated. His hair was matted with muck from the Thames, and his face was streaked with dirt and tears, but he still managed an air of dandified gentility. Lyall respected that in a man. Lord Akeldama had done his work well. Lyall respected that, too.

Without further ado, he swung the blanket-wrapped Biffy up into his arms and headed out into the busy London streets.

Floote was still out when Alexia pulled her panting horses to a stop at the door of the temple. Madame Lefoux was immediately whisked away to the infirmary, which left Alexia to make her way alone through the luxurious building. And, because she was Alexia, she made her way to the calm sanity of the library. Only in a library did she feel completely capable of collecting her finer feelings and recuperating from such a wearying day. It was also the only room she could remember how to get to.

In a desperate bid to cope with the violence of the attack, her discovery of Channing's presence in Italy, and her own unanticipated affection for the infant-inconvenience, Alexia extracted some of Ivy's precious tea. Quite resourcefully, she felt, she managed to boil water over the hearth fire using an empty metal snuffbox. She had to do without milk, but it was a small price to pay under the circumstances. She had no idea if the preceptor had yet returned, or even if he had survived, for

as usual, no one spoke to her. With nothing else to do for the
moment, Alexia sat in the library and sipped.

It was foolish of her not to realize that the all-pervading
silence was not one of prayer but one of impending disaster.
Her first warning came in the form of a volatile four-legged
duster that hurtled into the library, breaking the calm quiet with
a bout of such crazed yipping that a lesser dog would have
become ill at the effort.

"Poche? What are you doing here, you vile animal?" Alexia
fiddled with her snuffbox of tea.

Apparently, Poche's current and sole desire in life was to
launch a vicious attack on Alexia's chair leg, which he got his
little teeth around and was gnawing on passionately.

Alexia contemplated whether she should attempt to shake him
off, kick him with her foot, or simply disregard him entirely.

"Good evening, Female Specimen."

"Why, Mr. German Specimen, what an unexpected surprise.
I thought you had been excommunicated. They let you back into
Italy?"

Mr. Lange-Wilsdorf walked into the room, stroking his chin
with the air of one who has suddenly acquired the upper hand
and was reveling in the state of affairs. "I found myself in the
possession of some, shall we call it, negotiating power, ya?"

"Ya?" Alexia was irritated enough to mimic him.

Mr. Lange-Wilsdorf came to stand near her, looking down.
Which must be a particularly unusual experience for him given
his diminutive stature, Alexia thought nastily.

"The Templars will, with the information I provided, convince
His Holiness Pope Blessed Pius IX to repeal my excommuni-
cation and accept me back into the fold."

"Will they, indeed? I had no notion they possessed such
influence."

"They possess many things, Female Specimen, many things."

"Well"—Alexia was suddenly quite nervous—"felicitations
on your reintegration."

"I have my laboratory back," he continued proudly.

"Good, perhaps you can figure out how—"

The preceptor came into the library. Alexia stopped midsentence and looked him over, noticing bandages about his limbs and scrapes across his face. He was clearly a little worse for his encounter with the vampire and subsequent fall from the carriage.

"Ah, how are you feeling, Mr. Templar?"

Not bothering to answer, the preceptor came over, crossed his arms, and looked down at her as well. Eventually he spoke to her as though she were a recalcitrant child. "I am confused, My Soulless One."

"Oh, yes?"

"Yes. Why is it you chose not to inform us of your delicate condition? We would have taken far greater care of your person had we known of it."

Oh, mercy me. Alexia shifted, wary. She put down the snuffbox and grabbed her parasol. "Would you, indeed? Do you imply that you would not have, for example, used me as bait in a vampire trap?"

The preceptor ignored her barb. "Mr. Lange-Wilsdorf informs us that not only are you with child, but that the child's father is a werewolf. Is this—"

Alexia held up a commanding hand. "Do not even begin that line of questioning with me. My husband *is* a werewolf, and despite any and all accusations to the contrary, he is undoubtedly the father. I will neither argue nor tolerate any insinuations against my integrity. I may be soulless, gentlemen, but I assure you I am faithful. Even Conall, blast him, has finally admitted that."

The Templar snapped his mouth shut and nodded. She wasn't convinced that he believed her, but frankly she didn't care.

Mr. Lange-Wilsdorf rubbed his hands together. "Indeed, in conjunction with your insistence, I have devised a new theory as to the nature of soul that I believe not only supports but indeed *relies* upon your avowal that the child has a supernatural father."

"Are you saying the only way I could still be pregnant is if

I were telling the truth?" Alexia felt her breath quicken in anticipation. *Vindication at last!*

"Well, ya, Female Specimen, precisely."

"Would you care to elaborate?"

The little German seemed a tad taken aback by her calm acceptance. He did not notice how one of Alexia's hands was now delicately fiddling with the handle of her parasol. She was also watching the Templar almost as closely as she watched him.

"You are not angry with me for the telling to the Templars of your little secret?"

Alexia was, but she pretended to be blasé. "Well, it was all over the London papers. I suppose they would have found out eventually. Still, you are a bit of a repulsive weasel, aren't you?"

"Perhaps. But if this theory is correct, I will also be a most famous weasel."

The Templar had taken a fascinated interest in Alexia's snuffbox full of tea and was examining it. Alexia gave him a narrow look, daring him to comment on her idiosyncratic solution to the fact that none of the temple staff would respond to any of her requests. He said nothing.

"Very well, tell me of this theory of yours. And would you mind, terribly, removing your dog from my chair?"

Mr. Lange-Wilsdorf swooped down and scooped up his energetic little animal. The creature immediately relaxed into a floppy, partly comatose state in his master's arms. Draping the dog over one arm as a footman would a dishtowel, Mr. Lange-Wilsdorf proceeded to use the beastie as a teaching tool for his explanation.

"Let us assume that there are certain particles in the human body that bond to ambient aether." He prodded at the dog with one finger unhelpfully. "I shall call these particles 'pneuma.'" He raised his poking finger into the air dramatically. "Supernaturals have broken this bond, losing most of their pneuma. They become immortal by reconfiguring what trace amounts of pneuma they have left into a *flexible* bond with ambient aetheric particles."

"You are saying that the soul is not a measurable substance

after all, but is in fact the type and rigidity of this bond?" Alexia was intrigued despite herself, and she switched the bulk of her attention to the German.

Mr. Lange-Wilsdorf shook Poche at Alexia in his enthusiasm. "Ya! It is a brilliant theory, ya? It explains why we had no luck over the years measuring soul. There is nothing to measure—there is instead only type and strength of bond." He swooped the dog about the room as though flying. "You, Female Specimen, as a preternatural, are born with the pneuma but no bonded aether at all, thus you are always sucking the aetheric particles out of the air. What you do when you touch the supernatural creature is break their flexible bond and suck all the aether out of them, turning them mortal." He made a grasping motion with his hand over the dog's head, as though scooping out the little beast's brains.

"So, when the vampires called me a soul-sucker, they were not so far from the truth of it. But how does this explain the child?" Alexia attempted to refocus the little man on the most important part of his explanation.

"Well, the problem with two preternaturals is that they are both trying to suck aetheric particles at the same time. Thus they cannot share the same air space. But"—and in a triumphant crescendo, Mr. Lange-Wilsdorf held his little white dog over his head in victory—"if the other parent is a *supernatural*, the child can inherit the flexible bond, or as we might think of it, a bit of the leftover excess soul."

Poche gave a funny little howl as though to punctuate his owner's final statement. Realizing he was waving about his pet in a most indiscriminate manner, the German put his dog back down on the floor. Immediately, Poche began barking and bouncing about, eventually deciding to launch a full-blown attack on a small golden throw pillow that was now not long for this world.

Alexia hated to admit it, but Mr. Lange-Wilsdorf's theory was a sound one. It explained many things, not the least of which was why such children as the infant-inconvenience might be so very rare. Firstly, they required a supernatural to preternatural pairing, and the two species had hunted each other for most of recorded history. Secondly, they required either a female soulless, a female vampire, or a female werewolf. Preternaturals were rarely allowed near hive queens, and female werewolves were almost as rare as female preternaturals. There simply wouldn't have been much of an opportunity for interbreeding.

"So, the question is, what kind of child am I going to produce, given Conall's, uh, *flexible bond*?" Said in conjunction with her husband's name, and considering his carnal preferences, Alexia found the terminology salacious. She cleared her throat, embarrassed. "I mean to say, will it be born preternatural or supernatural?"

"Ah, ya, well, difficult to predict. But I am thinking, perhaps, in my theory, that is to say, neither. The child, it could be simply normal. Perhaps possessing less soul than most."

"But I will not lose it as you had previously thought?"

"No, no, you will not. If you are sensible with your own well-being."

Alexia smiled. True, she was still not quite settled into the idea of being a mother, but she and the infant-inconvenience did seem to be arriving at some kind of arrangement.

"Why, that is superb news! I must go tell Genevieve immediately." She stood, with every intention of dashing off to the infirmary, regardless of how this might upset any Templars she barreled into along the way.

The preceptor stood up from his crouch, where he had been trying, unsuccessfully, to wrestle the pillow away from Poche, and spoke. Alexia had almost forgotten his presence. "I am afraid that will not be possible, My Soulless One."

"Why not?"

"The French female was treated for her injuries and released into the care of the Florentine Hospitallers."

"Were her injuries that serious?" Alexia felt a sudden pang of guilt. Had she been enjoying snuffbox-scented tea and good news while her friend lay dying?

"Oh, no, quite superficial. We simply found we could no longer offer her our hospitality. Mr. Floote as well was not invited to return and stay with us."

Alexia felt her heart sink low into her chest, where it commenced a particular variety of rapid thumping. The sudden reversal from what, seconds before, might have been elation caused her to come over almost dizzy. She breathed in sharply through her nose.

Almost without thought, she opened her parasol, prepared to use even the sulfuric acid, undoubtedly the vilest of its armaments, if need be. Madame Lefoux had managed to find some replacement fluids. But before she had a chance to flip it around to the appropriate position, the library door opened.

Summoned by some unseen signal, a ridiculously large number of Templars clattered into the room. And they were *clattering*, for they were fully armored like the knights of the crusades they had been hundreds of years ago—heads covered in helms and bodies in silver-washed chain mail and plate under the obligatory nightgowns. Each had on a pair of heavy leather gloves, no doubt so they could touch Alexia without fear for their heavenly souls. Poche went absolutely crazy, barking at the top of his lungs and gyrating about the room in a succession of crazed leaps. Alexia thought it the most intelligent thing the creature had done in all its useless little life. The Templars, showing great reserves of dignity, entirely ignored him.

Alexia's parasol was good, but it wasn't good enough to take out that many people all at once. She closed it with a snap. "Why, Mr. Templar," she said to the preceptor, "I am honored. All this for me? So very thoughtful. You really shouldn't have."

The preceptor gave Alexia one hard, long look and then, taking Mr. Lange-Wilsdorf firmly by the arm, left the library without responding to her sarcasm. Poche circled the room twice more and then bounced out after them like a fierce feather duster ejected at high pressure from a steam engine. *My last defender, gone*, thought Alexia grimly.

She looked to her opponents. "Very well, then. Take me to your dungeon!" Might as well give a command she was reasonably confident would be obeyed.

Professor Lyall set his precious cargo down upon the sofa in his office at BUR headquarters. Still unconscious, Biffy was as limp as overcooked broccoli. The couch was already covered in various piles of paperwork, aethographor slates, a stack of books, and several newspapers and scientific pamphlets, but Biffy didn't seem to mind overly much. He curled onto one side like a little child, hugging an exceptionally uncomfortable-looking metal scroll affectionately to his chest.

Professor Lyall got to work preparing formal statements for the press, calling in various operatives and agents and then sending them back out again on important information-gathering missions, diplomatic interventions, and secret biscuit-acquisition operations (BUR's kitchen was running low). He also sent a runner to the remaining members of the Woolsey Pack, instructing them to stay alert and stay armed. Who knew how the vampires might choose to retaliate? Usually, they were refined in their reactions, but killing one of them was, as a rule, not considered polite, and they might behave unfavorably. After that, Lyall managed one productive hour of activity before he was interrupted by the first in what he had no doubt would be a long line of offended dignitaries. It was not, however, a member of one of the hives come to complain about the potentate's death. Rather unexpectedly, his first caller was a werewolf.

"Good evening, Lord Slaughter."

The dewan hadn't bothered with a cloak this time. With no disguise and no attempt made to hide his displeasure, either, Lyall had no doubt the dewan was officially representing Queen Victoria's interests.

"Well, you made a dog's bollocks of that, didn't you, little Beta? Couldn't have done worse with it when all's said and done."

"How do you do, my lord? Please, sit down."

The dewan gave a disgusted look at the slumbering Biffy. "Looks like you already have company. What is he—drunk?" He sniffed the air. "Oh, for goodness' sake, have you both been swimming in the Thames?"

"I assure you it was entirely involuntary."

The dewan looked as though he was about to continue his reprimanding tone, but then he sniffed the air again and stopped in his tracks. Twirling about, he lumbered over to the couch and bent over the comatose young dandy.

"Now, that is an unfamiliar face. I know most of the Woolsey Pack has been overseas with the regiment, but I think I remember them all. I am not *that* old."

"Ah, yes." Professor Lyall sat up straight and cleared his throat. "We are to be congratulated. Woolsey has a new pack member."

The dewan grunted, half pleased but trying to hide it with annoyance. "I thought he stank of Lord Maccon. Well, well, well, a metamorphosis and a dead vampire all in one night. My, my, Woolsey has been busy."

Professor Lyall put down his quill and took off his spectacles. "The one is, in fact, tied intimately to the other."

"Since when has killing vampires resulted in new werewolves?"

"Since vampires stole other vampire's drones, imprisoned them under the Thames, and then shot at them."

The dewan looked less like a gruff loner wolf and more like a politician at that statement. He drew up a chair on the other side of the desk from Lyall. "I think you had better start explaining what happened, little Beta."

When Lyall finished his account, the dewan was left looking a mite stunned.

"Of course, such a story will have to be corroborated. With the potentate's illegal kill order out on Lady Maccon's head, you must see that Lord Maccon's motives for killing the man are highly suspicious. Still, if all you say is true, he was within his rights as chief sundowner. Such shenanigans cannot be allowed. Imagine, stealing someone else's drone! So rude."

"You must understand I have other difficulties to deal with?"

"Went off hunting that stray wife of his, did he?"

Professor Lyall curled his lip and nodded.

"Alphas are so very difficult."

"My feeling exactly."

"Well, I shall leave you to it." The dewan stood but walked once more over to look down at Biffy before he left.

"Two successful metamorphoses in as many months. Woolsey may be in political trouble, but you are to be congratulated on the potency of your Alpha's Anubis Form. Pretty young pup, isn't he? He is going to bring down a whole mess of trouble on your head. How much worse will it be to have the vampires think werewolves stole a drone away?"

Professor Lyall sighed. "Lord Akeldama's favorite, no less."

The dewan shook his head. "Mess of trouble, mark my words. Best of luck, little Beta. You are going to need it."

Just as the dewan was leaving, one of Lord Maccon's best BUR agents appeared.

The agent bowed to the dewan in the doorway before coming in to stand in front of Professor Lyall, with his hands laced behind his back.

"Report, Mr. Haverbink."

"'S'not pretty out there, sir. The Teeth are a'stirring up all kinds of toss about you Tails. Them's saying Lord M had a grudge against the potentate. Saying he took him down out'a anger, not duty."

Haverbink was a good solid chap in both looks and spirit. And no one would bet a ha'penny on his having excess soul, but he listened well and got around to places more aristocratic types couldn't. He looked a bit like a farmhand, and people didn't give a man of his brawn much credit in the way of brain. It was a mistake.

"How unsettled?"

"Couple of pub brawls so far, mostly just clavigers giving fist to drones with big mouths. Could get ugly if the conservatives weigh in. You're knowing how they can get: 'none of this would've happened if we hadn't integrated. England deserves it for acting unnatural. Against God's law.' Whine, whine."

"Any word on the vampires themselves?"

"Westminster queen's been dead silent—'scuse the pun—since word on the potentate's death broke. You better believe if she thought she were in the right, she'd be squawking official statements to the press like a hen laying eggs."

"Yes, I would tend to agree with you. Her silence is a good thing for us werewolves. How about BUR's reputation?"

"We're taking the fallout. Lord M was working, not werewolfing, or that's the claim. He should've had more self-restraint." Haverbink turned his wide, friendly face on his commander questioningly.

Lyall nodded.

Haverbink continued. "Those that like BUR are claiming he was within his rights as sundowner. Those that don't like it, don't like him, and don't like wolves—they're going to complain regardless. Not a whole lot would change that."

Lyall rubbed at his neck. "Well, that's about what I thought. Keep talking the truth as much as possible while you are out there. Let people know the potentate stole Lord Akeldama's drone. We cannot allow the vampires or the Crown to cover that up, and we have got to hope both Biffy and Lord Akeldama corroborate the official story or we really will be in the thick of it."

Haverbink looked skeptically over at Biffy's sleeping form. "Does he remember any of it?"

"Probably not."

"Is Lord Akeldama likely to be amenable?"

"Probably not."

"Right'o, sir. I wouldn't want to be in your spats right now."

"Don't get personal, Haverbink."

"Course not, sir."

"Speaking of which, still no word on Lord Akeldama's return or whereabouts?"

"Not a single sausage, sir."

"Well, that's something. Very well, carry on, Mr. Haverbink."

"Jolly good, sir."

Haverbink went out, and the next agent, waiting patiently in the hallway, came in.

"Message for you, sir."

"Ah, Mr. Phinkerlington."

Phinkerlington, a round, bespectacled metal burner, managed a slight bow before continuing hesitatingly into the room. He had the manners of a clerk, the demeanor of a constipated mole, and some minor aristocratic connection that temperament compelled him to regard as an embarrassing character flaw. "Something finally came through on that Italian channel you had me monitoring sunset these past few days." He was also very, very good at his job, which consisted mainly of sitting and listening, and then writing down what he heard without thought or comment.

Professor Lyall sat up. "Took you long enough to get it to me."

"Sorry, sir. You've been so busy this evening; I didn't want to disturb."

"Yes, well." Professor Lyall made an impatient gesture with his left hand.

Phinkerlington handed Professor Lyall a scrap of parchment paper, on which had been inked a message. It was not, as Lyall had hoped, from Alexia but was from, of all people, Floote.

It was also so entirely off topic and unhelpful to the situation in hand as to give Lyall a brief but intense feeling of exasperation with Lady Maccon. This was a feeling that had, heretofore, been reserved solely for his Alpha.

"Get queen to stop Italians excavating in Egypt. Can't find soulless mummies, bad things result. Lady Maccon with Florentine Templars. Not good. Send help. Floote."

Professor Lyall, cursing his Alpha for departing so precipitously, balled up the piece of paper and, after minor consideration for the delicacy of the information it contained, ate it.

He dismissed Phinkerlington, stood, and went to check on Biffy, finding the young man still sleeping. *Good*, he thought,

best and most sensible thing for him to be doing at the moment.
Just as he was tucking the blanket a little more firmly about the
new werewolf, yet another person entered his office.

He straightened up and turned to face the door. "Yes?"

He caught the man's scent: very expensive French perfume
coupled with a hint of Bond Street's best hair pomade and under
that the slow richness of the unpalatable—old blood.

"Ah. Welcome back to London, Lord Akeldama."

Lady Alexia Maccon, sometimes called La Diva Tarabotti, was
quite comfortable with being abducted. Or, as it might better be
phrased, she was growing accustomed to the predicament. She
had led, up until a little over a year ago, quite an exemplary
spinsterish existence. Her world had been plagued only by the
presence of two nonsensical sisters and one even sillier mama.
Her concerns, it must be acknowledged, were a tad mundane,
and her daily routine as banal as that of any other young lady
of sufficient income and insufficient liberty. But she *had* managed
to avoid abductions.

This, as matters would have it, was turning out to be one of
the worst.

Alexia found the experience of being blindfolded and carried
over someone's armor-clad shoulder like a sack of potatoes
unconscionably undignified. She was hauled down a seemingly
endless series of stairs and passageways, musty as only the deep
underground can be. She gave a few experimental kicks and a
wiggle, only to have her legs clamped down by a metal-covered
arm.

Eventually, they arrived at their final destination, which, she
discovered once the blindfold had been removed, was some
kind of Roman catacomb. She blinked, eyes adjusting to the
dimness, and found herself in an underground ancient ruin dug
into the bedrock, lit with oil lamps and candles. The small cell
she now occupied was barred over on one side with modern-
looking reinforcements.

"Well, this is a much inferior living situation," she objected to no one in particular.

The preceptor appeared in the doorway, leaning up against the metal doorjamb, regarding her with lifeless eyes.

"We found we could no longer adequately ensure your safety in your other location."

"I wasn't safe in a temple surrounded by several hundred of the Knights Templars, the most powerful holy warriors ever to walk this earth?"

He made no answer to that. "We shall see to your every comfort here."

Alexia looked around. The room was slightly smaller than her husband's dressing chamber back at Woolsey Castle. There was a tiny bed in one corner covered in a faded quilt, a single side table with an oil lamp, a chamber pot, and a washstand. It looked neglected and sad.

"Who will? No one has so far."

Wordlessly the Templar signaled and, out of nowhere, a bread bowl full of pasta appeared, and a carrot carved to resemble a spoon was handed over by some unseen companion. The preceptor gave them to Alexia.

Alexia tried not to be pleased by the presence of the ubiquitous green sauce. "Pesto will keep you in my good graces for only so long, you understand?"

"Oh, and then what will you do, devil spawn?"

"Ah, I am no longer your 'Soulless One,' am I?" Alexia pursed her lips in deep thought. She was without her parasol, and most of her best threats involved its application. "I shall be *very* discourteous, indeed."

The preceptor did not look at all threatened. He closed the door firmly behind him and left her locked in the silent darkness.

"Could I at least get something to read?" she yelled after, but he ignored her.

Alexia began to think all those horrible stories she had heard about the Templars might actually be true, even the one with the rubber duck and the dead cat that Lord Akeldama had once relayed. She hoped fervently that Madame Lefoux and Floote were unharmed.

There was something eerie about being so utterly separated from them.

Giving in to her frustration, Alexia marched over and kicked at the bars of her prison.

This only served to cause her foot to smart most egregiously.

"Oh, brother," said Lady Maccon into the dark silence.

Alexia's isolation did not last long, for a certain German scientist came to visit her.

"I have been relocated, Mr. Lange-Wilsdorf." Alexia was so distressed by her change in circumstances that she was moved to state the obvious.

"Ya, Female Specimen, I am well aware of the fact. It is most inconvenient, ya? I have had to move my laboratory as well, and Poche will not follow me down here. He does not like Roman architecture."

"No? Well, who does? But, I say, couldn't you persuade them to move me back? If one must be imprisoned, a nice room with a view is far preferable."

The little man shook his head. "No longer possible. Give me your arm."

Alexia narrowed her eyes suspiciously and then, curious, acquiesced to his request.

He wrapped a tube of oiled cloth about her arm and then proceeded to pump it full of air using a set of bellows via a mini spigot. The tube expanded and became quite tight. Pinching these bellows off, the scientist transferred a glass ball filled with little bits of paper to the spigot and let go. The air escaped with a *whoosh*, causing all the bits of paper to flutter about wildly inside the ball.

"What *are* you doing?"

"I am to determine what kind of the child you may produce, ya. There is much speculation."

"I fail to see how those little bits of paper can reveal anything of import." They seemed about as useful as tea leaves in the bottom of a cup. Which made her think yearningly of tea.

"Well, you had better hope they do. There has been some talk of handling this child . . . differently."

"What?"

"Ya. And using you for—how to say?—spare parts."

Bile, sour and unwelcome, rose in Alexia's throat.

"What?"

"Hush now, Female Specimen, let me work."

The German watched with frowning attention as the papers finally settled completely at the base of the ball, which, Alexia now realized, was marked with lines. Then he began making notes and diagrams of their location. She tried to think calming thoughts but was beginning to get angry as well as scared. She was finished with being thought of as a specimen.

"You know, they gave to me complete access to the records of their preternatural breeding program? They tried for nearly a hundred years to determine how to successfully breed your species."

"Humans? Well that couldn't have been too difficult. I am still *human*, remember?"

Mr. Lange-Wilsdorf ignored this and continued his previous line of reasoning. "You always breed true, but low birth rate and rare female specimens were never explained. Also the program was plagued with the difficulty of the space allotment. Templars could not, for example, keep the babies in the same room or even the same house."

"So what happened?" Alexia couldn't help her curiosity.

"The program was stopped, ya. Your father was one of the last, you know?"

Alexia's eyebrows made an inadvertent bid for the sky.

"He was?" *Hear that, infant-inconvenience, your grandfather was bred by religious zealots as a kind of biological experiment. So much for your family tree.*

"Did the Templars raise him?"

Mr. Lange-Wilsdorf gave her a peculiar look. "I am not familiar with the specifics."

Alexia knew absolutely nothing about her father's childhood; his journals didn't commence until his university years in Britain and were, she suspected, originally intended as a vehicle for practicing English grammar.

The little scientist appeared to decide that he ought to say no more. Turning back to his bellows and sphere device, he finished his notations and then began a complex series of calculations. When he had finished, he set down his stylographic pen with a pronounced movement.

"Remarkable, ya."

"What is?"

"There is only one explanation for such results. That you have trace intrinsic aether affixed to the—how to say?—middle zone, but it is behaving wrong, as though it were bonded but also not, as if it were in the state of flux."

"Well, good for me." Then Alexia frowned, remembering their previous discussion. "But, according to your theory, I should have no intrinsic aether at all."

"Exactly."

"So your theory is wrong."

"Or the flux reaction is coming from the embryo." Mr. Lange-Wilsdorf was quite triumphant in this proclamation, as though he was near to explaining everything.

"Are you implying that you understand the nature of my child?" Alexia was prepared to get equally excited. *Finally!*

"No, but I can say with the absolute confidence that I am very, very close."

"Funny, but I do not find that at all reassuring."

*　　*　　*

Lord Akeldama stood in the doorway of Professor Lyall's office, dressed for riding. It was hard to read his face at the best of times and, under such circumstances as these, nigh on impossible.

"How do you do this evening, my lord?"

"La, my dear, tolerably well. Tolerably well. And you?"

They had, of course, met on more than one occasion in the past. Lyall had spent centuries nibbling about the great layer cake that was polite society while Lord Akeldama acted the part of the frosting on its top. Lyall knew a man was smart who kept a weather eye on the state of the frosting, even if most of his time was spent cleaning up crumbs. The supernatural set was small enough to keep track of most members, whether they skulked about BUR offices and the soldier's barracks or the best drawing rooms the ton had to offer.

"I must admit to having had better evenings. Welcome to BUR headquarters, Lord Akeldama. Do come in."

The vampire paused for a moment on the threshold, catching sight of Biffy's sleeping form. He made a slight gesture with one hand. "May I?"

Professor Lyall nodded. The question was a veiled insult, reminding them both of what had been taken from the vampire unjustly. That he must now ask to look upon what had once been his. Lyall let him get away with it. Currently the vampire held all the cards, but Professor Lyall was reasonably convinced that if he just gave Lord Akeldama enough cravat material, he might be able to fashion it into a bow pleasing enough for all parties. Of course, the vampire might also turn it into a noose; it depended entirely on the outcome of this conversation.

Professor Lyall knew that vampires had a limited sense of smell and no clear method of sensing right away that Biffy was now a werewolf. But Lord Akeldama seemed to realize it, anyway. He did not try to touch the young man.

"That is quite the quantity of facial hair. I didn't know he had it in him. I suppose that fuzzy is more appropriate given the current situation." Lord Akeldama raised one long, slim white hand to the base of his own throat, pinching at the skin there. He closed his eyes for a moment before opening them and looking down on his former drone once more. "He looks so young when he is sleeping. I have always thought so." He swallowed audibly. Then he turned and came back to stand in front of Lyall.

"You have been riding, my lord?"

Lord Akeldama looked down at his clothing and winced. "Necessity sometimes demands a sacrifice, young Randolph. Can I call you Randy? Or would you prefer, Dolphy? Dolly, perhaps?" Professor Lyall flinched noticeably. "Anyway, as I was saying, *Dolly*, I cannot *abide* riding—the horses are never happy to seat a vampire, and it plays havoc with one's hair. The only thing more vulgar is an open carriage."

Professor Lyall decided on a more direct approach. "Where have you been this past week, my lord?"

Lord Akeldama looked once more down at himself. "Chasing ghosts while pursued by daemons, as it were, Dolly, *darling*. I am convinced *you* must be aware of how it goes."

Professor Lyall decided on a push, just to see if he might elicit a more genuine reaction. "How could you disappear like that, just when Lady Maccon needed you most?"

Lord Akeldama's lip curled slightly, and then he gave a humorless little laugh. "Interesting query, coming from Lord Maccon's Beta. You will forgive me if I am inclined to see it as my right to ask the questions under such circumstances." He gestured with his head in Biffy's direction, just a little jerk of controlled displeasure.

Lord Akeldama was a man who hid his real feelings, not with an absence of emotions but with an excess of false ones. However, Professor Lyall was pretty certain that there, lurking under the clipped civility, was real, deeply rooted, and undeniably justified anger.

Lord Akeldama took a seat, lounging back into it, for all the world as relaxed and untroubled as a man at his club. "So, I take it, Lord Maccon has gone after *my* dear Alexia?"

Lyall nodded.

"Then he *knows*?"

"That she is in grave danger and the potentate responsible? Yes."

"Ah, was that Wally's game? No wonder he wanted me swarming out of London. No, I mean to ask, Dolly, *dear*, if the *estimable* earl knows what kind of child he has sired."

"No. But he has accepted that it is his. I think he always knew Lady Maccon would not play him false. He was just being ridiculous about it."

"Normally, I am all in favor of the ridiculous, but under such circumstances, you must understand, I believe it quite a *pity* he could not have come to that realization sooner. Lady Maccon would never have lost the protection of the pack, and none of *this* would have happened."

"You think not? Yet your kind tried to kill her on the way to Scotland when she was still very much under Woolsey's protection. Admittedly, that was done more discreetly and, I now believe, without the support of the hives. But they would all still have wanted her dead the moment they knew of her condition. The interesting thing is that you, apparently, do not want her dead."

"Alexia Maccon is my friend."

"Are your friends so infrequent, my lord, that you betray the clearly unanimous wishes of your own kind?"

Lord Akeldama lost some slight element of his composure at that. "Listen to me carefully, Beta. I am a rove so that I might make my own decisions: who to love, who to watch, and, most importantly, what to wear."

"So, Lord Akeldama, what is Lady Maccon's child going to be?"

"No. You will explain *this* first." The vampire gestured at Biffy. "I am forced to swarm because my most precious little drone-y-poo is *ruthlessly* stolen from me—betrayed, as it turns out, by my own kind—only to return and find him stolen by your kind instead. I believe *even* Lord Maccon would acknowledge I am entitled to an explanation."

Professor Lyall fully agreed with him in this, so he told the vampire the whole truth, every detail of it.

"So it was death or the curse of a werewolf?"

Professor Lyall nodded. "It was something to see, my lord. No metamorphosis I have ever witnessed took so long, nor was conducted with so much gentleness. To do what Lord Maccon did and not savage the boy in the heat of the need for blood, it was extraordinary. There are not many werewolves who possess such self-control. Biffy was very lucky."

"Lucky?" Lord Akeldama fairly spat the word, jumping to his feet. "Lucky! To be cursed by the moon into a slathering beast? You would have done better to let him die. My poor boy." Lord Akeldama was not a big man, certainly not by werewolf standards, but he moved so quickly that he was around Professor Lyall's desk, slim hands about the werewolf's throat, faster than Lyall's eyes could follow. There was the anger Professor Lyall had been waiting for and, with it, a degree of pain and hurt he would never have expected from a vampire. Perhaps he had pushed a little harder than was strictly necessary. Lyall sat still and passive under the choking hold. A vampire could probably rip a werewolf's head clean off, but Lord Akeldama was not the kind of man to do such a thing, even in the heat of anger. He was too controlled by age and etiquette to make more than a show of it.

"Master, stop. Please. It was not their fault."

Biffy sat up slightly on the couch, eyes fixed in horror at the sight before him.

Lord Akeldama immediately let go of Professor Lyall and dashed over to kneel by the young man's side.

Biffy spoke in a jumble of words and guilt. "I should not have allowed myself to be captured. I was careless. I did not suspect the potentate of such extremes of action. I was not playing the game as you taught me. I did not think he would use me like that to get to you."

"Ah, my little cherry blossom, we were all playing blind. This is *not* your fault."

"Do you really find me cursed and disgusting now?" Biffy's voice was very small.

Driven beyond his instincts, the vampire pulled the newly made werewolf against him—one predator consoling another, as unnatural as a snake attempting to comfort a house cat.

Biffy rested his dark head on Lord Akeldama's shoulder. The vampire twisted his perfect lips together and looked up at the ceiling, blinked, and then looked away. Through the fall of the vampire's blond hair, Professor Lyall caught a glimpse of his face.

Ah, oh dear, he really did love him. The Beta pressed two fingers against his own eyes as though he might stopper up the tears in theirs. *Curses.*

Love, of all eccentricities among the supernatural set, was the most embarrassing and the least talked about or expected. But Lord Akeldama's face, for all its icy beauty, was drawn with genuine loss into a kind of carved marble agony.

Professor Lyall was an immortal; he knew what it was to lose a loved one. He could not leave the room, not with so many important BUR documents scattered about, but he did turn away and put on a show of busily organizing stacks of paperwork, attempting to provide the two men some modicum of privacy.

He heard a rustle—Lord Akeldama sitting down upon the couch next to his former drone.

"My dearest boy, *of course* I do not find you disgusting—although, we must really have a serious discussion about this beard of yours. That was only a little turn of phrase, perhaps a bit of an exaggeration. You see, I did so look forward to the possibility of having you by my side as one of us. Joined to the old fang-and-swill club and all that."

A sniff from Biffy.

"If anything, this is *my* fault. I should have kept a better watch. I should not have fallen for his tricks or sent you in against him. I should not have allowed your disappearance to cause me to panic and swarm. I ought to have recognized the signs of a game in play against me and mine. But who would have believed my own kind—another vampire, another *rove*—would steal from me? *Me!* My *sweet* citron, I did not see the pattern. I did not see how desperate he was. I forgot that sometimes the information I carry in my own head is more valuable than the daily wonders you *lovely* boys unearth for me."

At which point, when Professor Lyall really felt things couldn't possibly get any worse, a bang came on the office door, which then opened without his bidding.

"What—?"

It was Professor Lyall's turn to look up at the ceiling in an excess of emotion.

"Her most Royal Majesty, Queen Victoria, to see Lord Maccon."

Queen Victoria marched through the door and spoke to Professor Lyall without breaking stride. "He is not here, is he? Wretched man."

"Your Majesty!" Professor Lyall hurried from behind his desk and performed his lowest and best bow.

The Queen of England, a deceptively squat and brown personage, swept the room with an autocratic eye as though Lord Maccon, sizable specimen that he was, might manage to hide in a corner somewhere or under the rug. What her eye rested upon was the tableau of a tear-stained Biffy, clearly naked under his blanket, caught up in the arms of a peer of the realm.

"What is this? *Sentiment!* Who is that there? Lord Akeldama? Really, this will not do at all. Compose yourself this instant."

Lord Akeldama lifted his head from where it rested, cheek pressed against Biffy's, and narrowed his eyes at the queen. He gently let his former drone go, stood, and bowed, exactly as deeply as he ought and not one jot more.

Biffy, for his part, was at a loss. He could not get up without exposing some part of himself, and he could not perform the appropriate obedience from a supine position. He looked with desperate eyes at the queen.

Professor Lyall came to his rescue. "You will have to forgive, uh," he floundered, for he had never learned Biffy's real name, "our young friend here. He has had a bit of a trying night."

"So we have been given to understand. Is this, then, the drone in question?" The queen raised a quizzing glass and examined Biffy through it. "The dewan has said you were kidnapped, young man, and by our very own potentate. These are grave charges, indeed. Are they true?"

Biffy, mouth slightly open in awe, managed only a mute nod.

The queen's face expressed both relief and chagrin in equal measure. "Well, at least Lord Maccon hasn't bungled that." She turned her sharp eye on Lord Akeldama.

The vampire, with a studied, casual air, fixed the cuffs of his shirtsleeves so they lay perfectly underneath his jacket. He did not meet her gaze.

"Would you say, Lord Akeldama, that death was an appropriate punishment for the theft of another vampire's drone?" she inquired casually.

"I would say it is a bit extreme, Your Majesty, but in the heat of the moment, I am given to understand, accidents will happen. It was not intentional."

Professor Lyall couldn't believe his ears. Was Lord Akeldama *defending* Lord Maccon?

"Very well. No charges will be brought against the earl."

Lord Akeldama started. "I did not say . . . that is, he also metamorphosed Biffy."

"Yes, yes. Excellent, another werewolf is always welcome." The queen bestowed a beneficent smile on the still-bemused Biffy.

"But he is *mine*!"

The queen frowned at the vampire's tone. "We hardly see the need for such fuss, Lord Akeldama. You have plenty more just like him, do you not?"

Lord Akeldama stood for a moment, stunned, just long enough

for the queen to continue on with her conversation, entirely ignoring his bemusement.

"We must suppose Lord Maccon has gone in pursuit of his wife?" A nod from Professor Lyall. "Good, good. We are reinstating her as muhjah, of course, in absentia. We were acting under the potentate's advice when we dismissed her, and now we see he must have been furthering his own hidden agenda. For centuries, Walsingham has advised the Crown unerringly. What could have driven such a man to such lengths?"

All around her, silence descended.

"That, gentlemen, was *not* a rhetorical question."

Professor Lyall cleared his throat. "I believe it may have to do with Lady Maccon's forthcoming child."

"Yes?"

Professor Lyall turned and looked pointedly at Lord Akeldama. Following his lead, the Queen of England did the same.

No one would ever accuse Lord Akeldama of fidgeting, but under such direct scrutiny, he did appear slightly flustered.

"Well, Lord Akeldama? You do know, don't you? Otherwise none of this would have happened."

"You must understand, Your Majesty, that vampire records go back to Roman times, and there is mention of only one similar child."

"Go on."

"And, of course, in this case she was the child of a soulsucker and a vampire—not a werewolf."

Professor Lyall chewed his lip. How could the howlers not have known of this? They were the keepers of history; they were supposed to know about everything.

"Go *on*!"

"The kindest word we had for that creature was soul-stealer."

CHAPTER FIFTEEN

Ladybugs to the Rescue

Alexia fought hard. It took some substantial negotiating to convince the German scientist, but in the end all she needed was the right kind of logic.

"I am bored."

"This does not trouble me, Female Specimen."

"This is my heritage we are dealing with, you realize?"

"Ya, so?"

"I believe it may be possible for me to uncover something you and the Templars have missed."

No response.

"I can read Latin."

He pressed down on her stomach.

"Can you? My, my, you *are* well educated."

"For a female?"

"For a soulless. Templar records hold that the devil spawn are not men of philosophy."

"You see, I am different. I might spot something."

The little German pulled out an ear tube from his case and listened to her belly attentively.

"I am telling you, I have excellent research skills."

"Will it keep you quiet?"

Alexia nodded enthusiastically.

"I shall see what I can do, ya?"

Later that day, two nervous young Templars came in carrying some ancient-looking scrolls and a bucket of lead tablets. They must have been under orders to oversee the security of these items, for instead of leaving, they locked the cell door and then sat—on the floor, much to Alexia's shock—crossed their legs, and proceeded to embroider red crosses onto handkerchiefs while she read. Alexia wondered if this were some kind of punishment, or if embroidery was what the Templars did for fun. It would explain the general prevalence of embroidered red crosses everywhere. Lord Akeldama, of course, had warned her. Silly to realize it now that it was far too late.

She bypassed the scrolls in favor of the more intriguing lead squares. They had Latin incised into them and were, she believed, curse tablets. Her Latin was rather rusty, and she could have used a vocabulary reference book of some kind, but she managed to decipher the first tablet after some time and the others came much easier after that. Most of them concerned ghosts and were designed to either curse someone into suffering after death as a ghost or exorcize a poltergeist that was already haunting a house. Alexia surmised that the tablets, in either case, would be entirely ineffective, but there certainly were a large number of them.

She looked up when Mr. Lange-Wilsdorf entered her cell with a new battery of tests. "Ah," she said, "Good afternoon. Thank you for arranging for me to look at this remarkable collection. I did not realize curse tablets were so focused on the supernatural. I had read that they called upon the wrath of imaginary daemons and gods, but not the *real* supernatural. Very interesting, indeed."

"Anything useful, Female Specimen?"

"Ow!" He poked at her arm with a syringe. "So far, they all have to do with hauntings. Very concerned with ghosts, the Romans."

"Mmm. Ya. I had read of this in my own research."

Alexia went back to translating the next tablet.

Having collected a sample of her blood, the German abandoned her once more to the tender mercies of the embroidering Templars.

The moment she started reading the next tablet, Alexia knew she wasn't going to tell Mr. Lange-Wilsdorf about it. It was a small one, and the boxy Latin letters were exceptionally tiny and painfully neat, covering both sides. Where all the previous tablets had been dedicated to daemons or to the spirits of the netherworld, this one was markedly different.

"I call upon you, Stalker of Skins and Stealer of Souls, child of a Breaker of Curses, whoever you are, and ask that from this hour, from this night, from this moment, you steal from and weaken the vampire Primulus of Carisius. I hand over to you, if you have any power, this Sucker of Blood, for only you may take what he values most. Stealer of Souls, I consecrate to you his complexion, his strength, his healing, his speed, his breath, his fangs, his grip, his power, his soul. Stealer of Souls, if I see him mortal, sleeping when he should wake, wasting away in his human skin, I swear I will offer a sacrifice to you every year."

Alexia surmised that the term "Breaker of Curses" must correlate to the werewolf moniker for a preternatural, "curse-breaker," which meant that the curse tablet was calling upon the child of a preternatural for aid. It was the first mention she had yet run across, however minor, of either soulless or a child of a soulless. She placed a hand upon her stomach and looked down at it. "Well, hello there, little Stalker of Skins." She felt a brief fluttering inside her womb. "Ah, would we prefer Stealer of Souls?" The fluttering stilled. "I see, more dignified, is it?"

She went back to the tablet, reading it over again, wishing it might give her more of a clue as to what such a creature could do and how it came into existence. She supposed it was possible that this being was just as nonexistent as the gods of the netherworld that the other tablets called upon. Then again, it could be as real as the ghosts or vampires they were asked to fight against. It must have been such an odd age to have lived in, so full of superstition and mythology, to be ruled by the Caesar's empire hives and a bickering line of incestuous vampires.

Alexia glanced under her eyelashes at the two embroidering men and, in a not-very-subtle movement, tucked the tablet down the front of her dress. Luckily for her, the Templars seemed to find their embroidery most absorbing.

She went on, scanning for the two key Latin phrases "Stalker of Skins" and "Stealer of Souls," but there seemed to be no further mention of either. She weighed her options, wondering if she should mention the phrase to Mr. Lange-Wilsdorf. As it turned out, the preceptor brought her meal that evening, so she figured she might as well go straight to the source.

She took her time working around to the subject. First she asked him politely about his day and listened to the recitation of his routine—really, who would want to attend matins six times?—as she ate her pasta in its obligatory bright green sauce. The preceptor had called the long skinny pasta "spa-giggle-tee" or some such silliness. Alexia didn't rightly care, so long as there was pesto on top of it.

Finally, she said, "I found an interesting tidbit in your records today."

"Oh, yes? I had heard Mr. Lange-Wilsdorf brought them to you. Which one?"

She gestured airily. "Oh, you know, one of the scrolls. It said something about a soul-stealer."

That got a reaction. The preceptor stood so fast that he knocked over the little stool he had been sitting on.

"What did you say?"

"I believe the other term used in the document was 'skin-stalker.' I see you have heard of these creatures before. Perhaps you would care to tell me where?"

Clearly in shock, the preceptor spoke as though his mouth were moving while his mind still coped with the revelation. "Soul-stealers are known to us only as legendary creatures, more dangerous than you soulless. They are greatly feared by the supernatural for their ability to be both mortal and immortal at the same time. The brotherhood has been warned to watch for them, although we have not yet encountered one in our recorded history. You believe that is what your child is?"

"What would you do with one if you caught it?"

"That would depend on whether or not we could control it. They cannot be allowed to roam free, not with that kind of power."

"What kind of power?" Alexia tried to sound innocent as she inched her free hand down the side of her small stool, preparing to grab it out from under her to use as a weapon if need be.

"I only know what is written into our Amended Rule."

"Oh, yes?"

He began to quote, "'Above all this, whosoever would be a brother, you and your profession and faith must deal out death in the name of holy justice against those creatures that stand against God and lead a man unto hellfire, the vampire and the werewolf. For those that walk not under the sun and those that crawl under the moon have sold their souls for the taste of blood and flesh. Moreover, let no brother relax in his holy duty of pure watchfulness and firm perseverance against those unfortunates born to sin and damnation, the devil spawn in soulless state. And finally, the brothers are hereby commanded to fraternize only with the untainted and hunt down the sickness of spirit within those that can both walk and crawl, and who ride the soul as a knight will ride his steed.'"

As he spoke, the preceptor backed away from Alexia and toward the prison door. She was taken by his expression, almost hypnotized by it. As had happened during the battle in the carriage, his eyes were no longer dead.

Alexia Tarabotti, Lady Maccon, had engendered many emotions in people over the years—mostly, she admitted ruefully to herself, exasperation—but never before had she been the cause of such abject revulsion. She looked down, embarrassed. *Guess it is not such a good thing, infant, to be a soul-stealer. Well, never you mind. Templars don't seem to like anyone.*

As she glanced away, her eye was caught by a flash of red coming along the passageway toward her cell—low to the ground.

The two young Templars seemed to have noticed whatever it was as well and were looking in fascination at the object trundling toward them.

Then she heard the ticking noise and the tinny sound of multiple tiny metal legs on stone.

"What is going on?" demanded the preceptor, turning away from Alexia.

Alexia seized the opportunity, stood up, and in one smooth movement, yanked the stool out from under herself and struck the back of the preceptor's head with it.

There was a dreadful crunching noise and Alexia grimaced.

"I do beg your pardon," she said perfunctorily, leaping over his fallen form. "Needs must and all that."

The two embroidering guards leapt to their feet, but before they had a chance to lock the door to Alexia's cell, a large shiny bug, lacquered red with black spots, scuttled directly at them.

Alexia, still brandishing the stool, charged out into the hall.

Queen Victoria had been neither as impressed nor as shocked as she should have been upon hearing the term "soul-stealer" spoken in Lord Akeldama's most salubrious tones. "Oh, is that all?" seemed to be her reaction. Her solution fit the standards of all monarchs everywhere. She made up her mind and then made it someone else's problem. In this case, however, Professor Lyall was pleased to find she had not made it his problem.

No, instead, the queen had pursed her lips and delivered an unsavory verbal package into the elegant alabaster hands of Lord Akeldama. "A soul-stealer you say, Lord Akeldama? That sounds most unpleasant. Not to say inconvenient, considering Lady Maccon will be returned to active service as my muhjah as soon as she can be fetched home. We expect Lord Maccon to have that particular task well under way. It goes without saying, the Crown simply will not tolerate vampires trying to kill its muhjah, however pregnant she may be and whatever she may be pregnant with. You must put a stop to it."

"I, Your Majesty?" Lord Akeldama was clearly flustered by this direct instruction.

"Of course, we require a new potentate. You are hereby granted the position. You possess the necessary qualifications, for you are a vampire and you are a rove."

"I beg to differ, Your Majesty. It must be put to the hive vote, any new candidate to the potentate position."

"You think they will not approve your appointment?"

"I have many enemies, Your Majesty, even among my own kind."

"Then you will be in good company, potentate: so does Lady Maccon and so did Walsingham. We shall expect you at Thursday's meeting of the Shadow Council."

With that, Queen Victoria sailed out of the room, adrift on a sea of self-righteousness.

Lord Akeldama raised himself out of his bow, looking flabbergasted.

"Congratulations, my lord," said Biffy timidly, attempting to stand shakily from the couch and approach his former master.

Professor Lyall hurried over to him. "Not yet, pup. You won't have your legs back for a while longer." He spoke the truth for, despite the fact that Biffy obviously wanted to walk on two legs, his brain seemed set on four, and he pitched forward with a surprised little cry.

Lyall caught him up and deposited him back on the couch. "It will take some time for your mind to catch up to your meta-morphosis."

"Ah." Biffy's voice caught in his throat. "How silly of me not to realize."

Lord Akeldama came over as well, watching with hooded eyes as Lyall smoothed the blanket over the young man. "*She* has placed me in a most insufferable position."

"Now you know how I feel most of the time," said Professor Lyall under his breath.

"You are more than equal to the task, my lord." Biffy's eyes were shining and full of faith as they looked upon his former master.

Wonderful, thought Lyall, *a newly made werewolf in love with a vampire, and more apt to do his bidding than the pack's.* Would even Lord Maccon be able to break such a connection?

"I rather think the queen is getting the better end of the deal," added Professor Lyall, intimating, but not actually mentioning, Lord Akeldama's fashionable yet efficient espionage regime.

Poor Lord Akeldama was not having a good night. He had lost his lover and his comparative anonymity in one fell swoop. "The pathetic reality is, my *darlings*, I am not even convinced the child of a preternatural and a werewolf will *be* a soul-stealer. And if it is, will it be the same kind of soul-stealer as it was when the sire was a vampire?"

"Is that why you remain unafraid of this creature?"

"As I said before, Lady Maccon is my friend. Any child of hers will be no more or less hostile to vampires than she is. Although the way we are currently behaving may sour her against us. Aside from that, it is not in my nature to anticipate trouble with violence; I prefer to be in possession of all the necessary facts first. I should like to meet this child once it has emerged and then render my judgment. So much better that way."

"And your other reason?" The vampire was still hiding something; Lyall's well-honed BUR senses told him so.

"Must you hound him, Professor Lyall?" Biffy looked worriedly from his former master to his new Beta.

"I think it best. It is, after all, in *my* nature."

"Touché." The vampire sat down once more next to Biffy on the settee and placed a passive hand casually on the young man's leg, as if out of habit.

Lyall stood up and looked down at them both from over his spectacles; he'd had enough of mysteries for one evening. "Well?"

"That soul-stealer, the one the Edict Keepers warn us of? The reason for all this twaddle? Her name was Al-Zabba and she was a relative of sorts." Lord Akeldama tipped his head from side to side casually.

Professor Lyall started. Of all the things, he had not expected that. "A relative of *yours*?"

"You might know her better as Zenobia."

Professor Lyall knew about as much as any educated man on the Roman Empire, but he had never read that the Queen of the Palmyrene had anything more or less than the requisite amount of soul. Which led to another question.

"This soul-stealer condition, how exactly does it manifest?"

"I don't know."

"And that makes even you uneasy. Doesn't it, Lord Akeldama?"

Biffy touched his former master's hand where it rested on his blanket-covered thigh and squeezed as though offering reassurance.

Definitely going to be a problem.

"The daylight folk, back then, the ones who feared her, they called her a skin-thief."

That name meant something to Professor Lyall, where soul-stealer had not. It tickled memories at the back of his head. Legends about a creature who could not only steal werewolf powers but become, for the space of one night, a werewolf in his stead. "Are you telling me we will have a *flayer* on our hands?"

"Exactly! So, you *see* how difficult it will be to keep everyone from killing Alexia?"

"As to that problem"—Professor Lyall gave a sudden grin—"I may have a solution. Lord and Lady Maccon will not like it, but I am thinking you, Lord Akeldama and young Biffy, might find it acceptable."

Lord Akeldama smiled back, showing off his deadly fangs. Professor Lyall thought them just long enough to be threatening without being ostentatious, like the perfect dress sword. They were quite subtle fangs for a man of Lord Akeldama's reputation.

"Why, Dolly, *darling*, do speak further; you interest me most ardently."

* * *

The Templars seemed, if possible, less prepared to battle ticking ladybugs than Alexia had been when accosted in a carriage not so very long ago. They were so surprised by their unexpected visitors and were torn between squashing them and handling the now-free Alexia. It wasn't until one of the ladybugs stuck a sharp needle-like antennae into one of the young Templars, who then collapsed, that the brothers took violently against them. Once pricked into action, however, their retribution was swift and effective.

The remaining young Templar drew his sword and dispatched Alexia's noble scuttling rescuers with remarkable efficiency. He then whirled to face Alexia.

She raised her stool.

Behind them, in the cell, the preceptor groaned. "What is going on?"

Since the ladybugs might have been sent either by the vampires to kill her or by Monsieur Trouvé to help her, Alexia could not rightly answer that question. "It would appear you are under attack by ladybugs, Mr. Templar. What else can I say?"

At which moment they all heard the growl. It was the kind of growl Alexia was definitely familiar with—low and loud and full of intention. It was the kind of growl that said, clearly as anything, "You are food."

"Ah, and now, I suspect, werewolves."

And so it proved to be the case.

Of course, Alexia's traitorous little heart hoped for a certain brindled coat, chocolate brown with hints of black and gold. She craned her neck over her brandished stool to see if the growling, slavering beast charging down the stone hallway would have pale yellow eyes and a familiar humor crinkling them just so.

But the creature that bounded into view was pure white, and his lupine face was humorless. He launched himself upon the young Templar, without apparent care for the naked blade, which was, Alexia had no doubt, silver. He was a beautiful specimen of *Homo lupis*, or would have been beautiful had he not been bent on mauling and mayhem. Alexia knew those eyes were icy blue without having to look. She couldn't really follow, anyway, as man and wolf met in the hallway. With a vociferous battle cry, the preceptor charged out of the cell and joined the fray.

Never one to sit back and dither, Alexia grabbed the stool more firmly, and when the younger Templar fell back toward her, she clouted him with the stool on top of the head as hard as she possibly could. Really, she was getting terribly good at bashing skulls in her old age—rather unseemly of her.

The boy collapsed.

Now it was just the werewolf against the preceptor.

Alexia figured that Channing could take care of himself and that she'd better break for freedom while the preceptor was preoccupied. So she dropped the stool, hiked her skirts, and took off pell-mell down what looked to be the most promising passageway. She ran smack-dab into Madame Lefoux, Floote, and Monsieur Trouvé.

Ah, right passageway! "Well, hello, you lot. How are you?"

"No time for pleasantries, Alexia, my dear. Isn't it just like you, to be already escaped before we had the opportunity to rescue you?" Madame Lefoux flashed her dimples.

"Ah, yes. Well, I am resourceful."

Madame Lefoux tossed something at her, and Alexia caught it with the hand not holding up her skirts. "My parasol! How marvelous."

Floote, she noticed, was carrying her dispatch case in one hand, and he had one of those tiny guns in his other.

Monsieur Trouvé offered Alexia his arm.

"My lady?"

"Why, thank you, monsieur, very kind." Alexia managed to grasp it and her parasol and her skirts without too much difficulty. "I am rather grateful for the ladybugs, by the way; very nice of you to send them on."

The clockmaker began hustling her down the hallway. It wasn't until that moment that Alexia realized how large the catacombs were, and how far she had been stashed underground.

"Ah, yes, I borrowed the adaptation from the vampires. I put a doping agent in the antennae instead of poison. It proved an effective alternative."

"Very. Until the swords came out, of course. I am afraid your three minions are no more."

"Ah. Poor little things. They aren't exactly battle-hardy."

They ascended a steep flight of stairs and then dashed down another long hallway, one that seemed to go backward above the one they'd just run up.

"If you don't find it impertinent of me to ask," Alexia panted, "what are you doing here, monsieur?"

The Frenchman answered between puffs. "Ah, I came with your luggage. Left a marker so Genevieve would know I was here. I didn't want to miss all the fun."

"You and I clearly do not share a definition of the word."

The Frenchman looked her up and down, his eyes positively twinkling. "Oh, come now, my lady, I think we may."

Alexia grinned, it must be admitted, a tad more ferociously than genteelly.

"Watch out!" came Floote's shout. He was leading the charge, closely followed by Madame Lefoux, but he had stopped suddenly ahead of them and, after taking aim, fired one of his tiny guns.

A group of about a dozen or so Templars was coming down the passageway toward them, preceded by the tweed-covered, dwarflike form of a certain German scientist. Adding to the generally threatening overtones of the party, Poche led the charge, yapping and prancing about like an overly excited bit of dandelion fluff wearing a yellow bow.

Floote reached for his second gun and fired again, but there was no time to get the first reloaded before the Templars were upon them. Floote seemed to have missed, anyway, for the enemy advanced undaunted. The only member troubled by the shot was the dog, who went into highly vocalized histrionics.

"I would surrender now, ya, if I were you, Female Specimen."

Alexia gave Mr. Lange-Wilsdorf an innocent look from behind

her little group of protectors; after all, it hadn't been her idea to be rescued. She also hefted her parasol. Alexia had faced down vampires. A handful of highly trained mortals would be easy by comparison. Or so she hoped.

The little German looked pointedly at Madame Lefoux and Monsieur Trouvé. "I am surprised at you both. Members in good standing with the Order of the Brass Octopus reduced to this, running and fighting. And for what? Protection of a soulless? You do not even intend to properly study her."

"And that is, of course, all you wish to do?"

"Of course."

Madame Lefoux was not to be outmaneuvered by a *German*. "You forget, Mr. Lange-Wilsdorf, that I have read your research. All of your research— even the vivisections. You were always inclined toward questionable methodology."

"And you have no ulterior motive, Madame Lefoux? I heard you had received instructions from within the highest levels of the Order to follow and learn as much as possible about Lady Maccon and her child."

"I am attracted to Alexia for many reasons," replied the Frenchwoman.

Alexia felt a token protest was called for at this juncture. "I mean to say, really, I am near to developing a neurosis—is there anyone around who doesn't want to study or kill me?"

Floote raised a tentative hand.

"Ah, yes, thank you, Floote."

"There is also Mrs. Tunstell, madam," he offered hopefully, as if Ivy were some kind of consolation prize.

"I notice you don't mention my fair-weather husband."

"I suspect, at this moment, madam, he probably wants to kill you."

Alexia couldn't help smiling. "Good point."

The Templars had been standing in still and, unsurprisingly, silent vigil over this conversation. Quite unexpectedly, one of those at the back gave a little cry. This was followed by the

unmistakable sound of fighting. Poche began barking his head
off even more loudly and vigorously than before. Apparently
less eager to attack when faced with real violence, the dog also
cowered behind his master's tweed-covered legs.

At a signal from the Templar who appeared to be the leader—
the cross on his nightgown being bigger than the others—most
of the rest whirled about to confront this new threat from the
rear. This left only three Templars and the German scientist
facing Alexia and her small party—much better odds.

Floote went about busily reloading his two little pistols with
new bullets.

"What—?" Alexia was mystified into inarticulateness.

"Vampires," explained Madame Lefoux. "We knew they'd
come. They have been on our tail these past few days."

"Which was why you waited until nightfall to rescue me?"

"Precisely." Monsieur Trouvé twinkled at her.

"We wouldn't want to be so boorish," added Madame Lefoux,
"as to arrive unexpectedly for a visit without a gift. So we
brought plenty to go around."

"Very courteous of you."

Alexia craned her neck to try and make out what was going on.
It was appropriately dark and gloomy in the catacombs, and hard
to see around the men standing before her, but she thought she
might just be able to see six vampires. *Goodness, six is practically
an entire local hive!* They really and truly must want her dead.

Despite being armed with wicked-looking wooden knives, the
Templars seemed to be getting the worst of the encounter.
Supernatural strength and speed came in rather handy during
close-quarters fighting. The three Templars still facing them
turned away, eager to join the fight. That helped even the odds
a bit, putting them in a two-to-one ratio. The battle was proving
to be peculiarly silent. The Templars made little noise beyond
the occasional grunt of pain or small cry of surprise. The vampires
were much the same, silent, swift, and lethal.

Unfortunately, the broiling mess of fangs and fists was still

blocking Alexia's only means of escape. "What do you say—
think we can worm our way through?"

Madame Lefoux tilted her head to one side thoughtfully.

Alexia dropped her skirts and lifted her free hand suggestively. "With my particular skill set, such an endeavor could be
quite entertaining. Monsieur Trouvé, let me just show you how
this parasol works. I think I may need both my hands free."

Alexia gave the clockmaker some quick tips on those armaments that might be used under their present circumstances.

"Beautiful work, Cousin Genevieve." Monsieur Trouvé looked
genuinely impressed.

Madame Lefoux blushed and then busied herself with her
cravat pins, pulling out both of them: the wooden one for
the vampires, and the silver, for lack of anything better, for the
Templars. Floote cocked his pistol. Alexia took off her gloves.

They had all forgotten about Mr. Lange-Wilsdorf—an amazing
achievement considering that his absurd excuse for a dog was
still yapping away at the top of its lungs.

"But you cannot possibly leave, Female Specimen! I have not
completed my tests. I did so want to cut the child out for dissec-
tion. I could have determined its nature. I could—" He left off
speaking, for he was interrupted by a loud growling noise.

Channing came dashing up. The werewolf was looking a tad
worse for wear. His beautiful white fur was streaked with blood,
many of his wounds still bleeding, for they were slower to heal
when administered by a silver blade. Luckily, none of the injuries
appeared to be fatal. Alexia didn't want to think about how the
preceptor might look right about now. It was a safe bet that one
or more of his injuries *were* fatal.

Channing lolled a tongue out and then tilted his head in the
direction of the pitched battle going on just ahead of them.

"I know," said Alexia, "you brought the cavalry with you.
Really, you shouldn't have."

The werewolf barked at her, as if to say, *This is no time for
levity.*

"Very well, then, after you."

Channing trotted purposefully toward the broiling mass of vampires and Templars.

The German scientist, cowering away from the werewolf, yelled at them from his position, flattened against the side wall of the passageway, "No, Female Specimen, you cannot go! I will not allow it." Alexia glanced over at him, only to find he had pulled out an extraordinary weapon. It looked like a set of studded leather bagpipes melded to a blunderbuss. It was pointed in her direction, but Mr. Lange-Wilsdorf's hand was by no means steady on the trigger. Before anyone had a chance to react to the weapon, Poche, seized with a sudden bout of unwarranted bravery, charged at Channing.

Without breaking stride, the werewolf swiveled his head down and around, opened his prodigious jaws, and swallowed the little dog whole.

"No!" cried the scientist, instantly switching targets and firing the bagpipe blunderbuss at the werewolf instead of Alexia. It made a loud splattering pop sound and ejected a fist-sized ball of some kind of jellied red organic matter that hit the werewolf with a splat. Whatever it was must not have been designed to damage werewolves, for Channing merely shook it off like a wet dog and gave the little man a disgusted look.

Floote fired in the same instant, hitting the German in one shoulder and then pocketing his gun, once more out of ammunition. Alexia thought she would have to get Floote a better, more modern gun, a revolver, perhaps.

Mr. Lange-Wilsdorf cried out in pain, clutched at his shoulder, and fell back.

Madame Lefoux marched over to him and grabbed the peculiar weapon out of his limp hand. "You know the truth of the matter, sir? Your ideas may be sound, but your research methods and your moral code are both highly questionable. You, sir, are a *bad scientist*!" With that, she clocked him in the temple with the muzzle of his own bagpipe gun. He fell like a stone.

"Really, Channing," remonstrated Alexia, "did you have to eat the man's dog? I am convinced you will experience terrible indigestion."

The werewolf ignored them all and continued on toward the pitched hallway battle, which showed no signs of being firmly decided in either direction. Two to one were clearly good odds when the two were highly trained warrior monks and the one was a vampire.

Alexia ran after Channing to stir things up a bit.

While the werewolf proceeded to clear them a path via the simple expedient of eating his way through the fighters, Alexia, gloves off, tried to touch any and all that she could. The vampires were changed by her touch and the Templars repulsed; either way, she had the advantage.

Vampires dropped their opponents as they suddenly lost supernatural strength or found themselves viciously nibbling someone's neck, having entirely lost their fangs. The Templars were quick to follow up any advantage, but they were distracted by the presence of a new and equally feared enemy—a werewolf. They were also startled to find their quarry, supposedly a complacent Englishwoman of somber means and minimal intelligence, busily plying her art and touching them. Instinct took over, for they had been trained for generations to avoid a preternatural as they would avoid the devil himself, as a grave risk to their sacred souls. They flinched and stumbled away from her.

Following Alexia came Monsieur Trouvé, who, having utilized some of the parasol's armament, had reverted to swinging the heavy bronze accessory about like a club, bludgeoning all who got in his way. Alexia could understand his approach; it was her preferred method as well. Could that technique, she wondered, be legitimately referred to as a "parassault"? Following him was Madame Lefoux, bagpipe blunderbuss in one hand, cravat pin in the other, slashing and bashing away merrily. After her came Floote, bringing up the rear in dignified elegance, using the dispatch case as a kind of shield and poking at people with Madame Lefoux's other cravat pin, borrowed for the occasion.

Thus, undercover of an uncommon amount of pandemonium and bedlam, Alexia and her little band of gallant rescuers made their way through the battle and out the other side. Then there was nothing for it but to run, bruised and bloody as they were. Channing led them first through the Roman catacombs, then through a long modern tunnel that housed, if the steel tracks were any indication, a rail trolley of some kind. Finally, they found themselves clambering up damp wooden stairs and tumbling out onto the wide soft bank of the Arno. The town obviously observed a supernatural curfew after nightfall, for there was absolutely no one to witness their panting exit.

They climbed up to street level and dashed a good long way through the city. Alexia developed a stitch in her side and a feeling that, should her future permit it, she would spend the rest of her days relaxed in an armchair in a library somewhere. Adventuring was highly overrated.

Having reached one of the bridges over the Arno, she called a stop halfway across. It was a good defensible position; they could afford a short rest. "Are they following us?"

Channing raised his muzzle to the sky and sniffed. Then he shook his shaggy head.

"I cannot believe we escaped so easily." Alexia looked about at her companions, taking stock of their condition. Channing had sustained only a few additional injuries, but all were healing even as she watched. Of the others, Madame Lefoux was sporting a nasty gash on one wrist, which Floote was bandaging with a handkerchief, and Monsieur Trouvé was rubbing at a lump on his forehead. She herself ached terribly in one shoulder but would rather not look just yet. Otherwise, they all were in sufficient form and spirits. Channing appeared to have reached the same conclusion and decided to shift form.

His body began that strange, uncomfortable-looking writhing, and the sound of flesh and bone re-forming itself rent the air for a few moments, and then he rose to stand before them. Alexia gave a squeak and turned her back hurriedly on his endowments, which were ample and well proportioned.

Monsieur Trouvé took off his frock coat. It was far too wide for the werewolf, but he handed it over for modesty's sake. With a nod of thanks, Channing put it on. It covered the necessaries, but was far too short and, coupled with his long, loose hair, made him look disturbingly like an oversized French schoolgirl.

Alexia was perfectly well aware of what she was required to do at this juncture. Courtesy demanded gratitude, but she could wish it was someone other than Channing Channing of the Chesterfield Channings who was to receive it. "Well, Major Channing, I suppose I must thank you for the timely intervention. I am confused, however. Shouldn't you be off somewhere killing things?"

"My lady, I rather thought that was what I just did."

"I mean officially, for queen and country, with the regiment and everything."

"Ah, no, deployment was delayed after you left. Technical difficulties."

"Oh?"

"Yes, it was technically difficult to leave a heartbroken Alpha. And it is a good thing for you I wasn't overseas. Someone had to extract you from the Templars." He entirely ignored the rest of Alexia's rescue party.

"I should have managed perfectly well on my own. But thank you, anyway. You are always terribly impressed with yourself, aren't you?"

He leered. "Aren't you?"

"So why *have* you been tracking me this entire time?"

"Ah, you knew it was me?"

"There aren't a great number of white wolves roaming around safeguarding my interests. I figured it had to be you after the vampire and the carriage incident. So, why were you?"

A new voice, deep and gravelly, came from behind them. "Because I sent him."

Floote stopped attending to Madame Lefoux and whirled to face this new threat, the Frenchwoman was already reaching once more for her trusty cravat pins, and Monsieur Trouvé raised the bagpipe blunderbuss, which he'd been examining with scientific interest. Only Major Channing remained unperturbed.

Lord Conall Maccon, Earl of Woolsey, stepped out of the shadows of the bridge tower.

"You! You are *late*," pointed out his errant wife with every sign of extreme annoyance.

CHAPTER SIXTEEN

On a Bridge over the Arno and Other Romantic Misnomers

"Late! Of course I'm late. You do realize, wife, I've been hunting all over Italy for you? You havna been exactly easy to find."

"Well, of course you wouldn't find me if you took that tactic. I haven't *been* all over Italy. I have been stuck in Florence the entire time. I was even trapped in some horrible Roman catacombs, thanks to you."

"Thanks to me? How could that possibly have been my fault, woman?" Lord Maccon came forward and loomed over his wife, both of them having entirely forgotten about their companions, who formed a semicircle of rapt interest about them. Their voices carried far over the water and through the vacant streets of Florence—no doubt providing entertainment for many.

"You rejected me!" Even as she said it, Alexia experienced once more that glorious sense of profound relief. Although this time, thankfully, it was not coupled with the need to break down and cry. Conall had come after her! Of course, she was still mad at him.

Floote bravely interjected at this juncture. "Please, madam, lower your voice. We are not yet out of danger."

"You sent me away!" Alexia hissed, low and fierce.

"No, I didna—that is, not really. I didna intend it that way.

You should have known I didna mean it. You should have realized I needed time to recover from being an idiot."

"Oh, really? How was I to know idiocy was only a temporary condition, especially in your case? It never has been before! Besides which, vampires were trying to kill me."

"And they didna try to kill you here as well as back home? 'Tis a good thing I had enough sobriety left to send Channing after you."

"Oh, I like that . . . Wait, what did you say? Sobriety? You mean while I've been running across Europe pregnant, escaping ladybugs, flying in ornithopters, landing in mud, and drinking *coffee*, you have been *inebriated*?"

"I was depressed."

"You were depressed? *You!*" Alexia actually started to sputter, she was so angry. She looked up at her husband, which was always a strange experience, for she was a tall woman used to looking down on people. Lord Maccon could loom all he liked; so far as she was concerned, she was not impressed.

She poked him in the center of his chest with two fingers to punctuate her words. "*You* are an unfeeling"—poke— "traitorous"—poke—"mistrusting"—poke—"rude"—poke— "*booby*!" Every poke turned him mortal, but Lord Maccon didn't seem to mind it in the least.

Instead he grabbed the hand that poked him and brought it to his lips. "You put it very well, my love."

"Oh, don't get smarmy with me, husband. I am nowhere near finished with you yet." She started poking him with the other hand. Lord Maccon grinned hugely, probably, Alexia realized, because she had slipped up and called him "husband."

"You kicked me out without a fair trial. Do stop kissing me. And you didn't even consider that the child might be yours. Stop that! Oh, no, you had to leap to the worst possible assumption. You know my character. I could never betray you like that. Just because history says it is not possible doesn't mean there aren't exceptions. There are always exceptions. Look at Lord

Akeldama—he is practically an exception to everything. Why, it took only a little research in the Templar records and I figured it out. Stop kissing my neck, Conall, I mean it. Templars should have practiced more of the scholarly arts and stopped whacking about at everything willy-nilly." She reached into her cleavage and produced the small, now-garlic-scented Roman curse tablet, which she waved at her husband. "Look right here! *Evidence.* But not you, oh no. You had to act first. And I was stuck running around without a pack."

Lord Maccon managed to get a word in at this point, but only because Lady Maccon had run out of breath. "It looks like you managed to build your own pack, anyway, my dear. A parasol protectorate, perhaps one might say."

"Oh, ha-ha, very funny."

Lord Maccon leaned forward and, before she could resume her tirade, kissed her full on the mouth. It was one of his deep, possessive kisses. It was the kind of embrace that made Alexia feel that somewhere in there, even though her touch had stolen all the werewolf out of him, he might still want to gobble her right up. She continued poking him absently even as she curled into his embrace.

Just as swiftly as he had started, he stopped. *"Ew!"*

"*Ew?* You kiss me when I haven't even finished yelling at you and then you say *'ew'*!" Alexia jerked out of her husband's grasp.

Conall stopped her with a question. "Alexia, darling, have you been eating *pesto* recently?" He started rubbing at his nose as though it were itching. His eyes began to water.

Alexia laughed. "That's right—werewolves are allergic to basil. You see the full force of my revenge?" She could touch him and the allergic reaction would probably stop immediately, but she stood back and watched him suffer. Funny that even as a mortal, he had reacted badly to the taste of her supper. She resigned herself to a life without pesto, and with that thought realized she was going to forgive her husband.

Eventually.

The werewolf in question approached her cautiously once more, as if he was afraid if he moved too fast she would panic and bolt. "It's been a long time since I tasted that flavor, and I never liked it, even as a human. I'll put up with it, though, if you really like it."

"Will you put up with the child, too?"

He pulled her into his arms again. "If you really like it."

"Don't be difficult. You are going to have to like it, too, you realize."

Nuzzling against her neck, he let out a sigh of satisfaction. "Mine," he said happily.

Alexia was resigned to her fate. "Unfortunately, both of us are."

"Well, that's all right, then."

"So you think." She pulled away, punching him in the arm, just to make her position perfectly clear. "The fact remains that you also belong to me! And you had the temerity to behave as though you didn't."

Lord Maccon nodded. It was true. "I shall make it up to you." Adding unguardedly, "What can I do?"

Alexia thought. "I want my own aethographic transmitter. One of the new ones that doesn't require crystalline valves."

He nodded.

"And a set of ladybugs from Monsieur Trouvé."

"A what?"

She glared at him.

He nodded again. Meekly.

"And a new gun for Floote. A good-quality revolver or some such that shoots more than one bullet."

"For Floote? Why?"

His wife crossed her arms.

"Whatever you say, dear."

Alexia considered asking for a Nordenfelt but thought that might be pushing it a bit, so she downgraded. "And I want you to teach me how to shoot."

"Now, Alexia, do you think that's quite the best thing for a woman in your condition?"

Another glare.

He sighed. "Verra well. Anything else?"

Alexia frowned in thought. "That will do for now, but I might still come up with something."

He tucked her in close against him once more, running his hands over her back in wide circular motions and burying his nose in her hair.

"So, what do you think, my dear, will it be a girl or a boy?"

"It will be a soul-stealer, apparently."

"What!" The earl reared away from his wife and looked down at her suspiciously.

Channing interrupted them. "Best be getting a move on, I'm afraid." He head was cocked to one side, as though he were still in wolf form, ears alert for signs of pursuit.

Lord Maccon turned instantly from indulgent husband to Alpha werewolf. "We'll split up. Channing, you, Madame Lefoux, and Floote act as decoy. Madame, I'm afraid you may have to don female dress."

"Sometimes these things are necessary."

Alexia grinned, both at Madame Lefoux's discomfort and the very idea someone might confuse the two of them. "I recommend padding as well," she suggested, puffing out her chest slightly, "and a hair fall."

The inventor gave her a dour look. "I am aware of our differences of appearance, I assure you."

Alexia hid a grin and turned back to her husband. "You'll send them over land?"

Lord Maccon nodded. Then he looked to the clockmaker. "Monsieur?"

"Trouvé," interjected his wife helpfully.

The clockmaker twinkled at them both. "I shall head home, I think. Perhaps the others would care to accompany me in that general direction?"

Channing and Madame Lefoux nodded. Floote, as ever, had very little reaction to this turn of events. But Alexia thought she detected a gleam of pleasure in his eyes.

Monsieur Trouvé turned back to Alexia, took her hand, and kissed the back of it gallantly. His whiskers tickled. "It has been a pleasure to make your acquaintance, Lady Maccon. Most enjoyable, indeed."

Lord Maccon looked on in shock. "You are referring to my wife, are you not?"

The Frenchman ignored him, which only endeared him further to Alexia.

"And you as well, Monsieur Trouvé. We must continue our acquaintance sometime in the not too distant future."

"I wholeheartedly agree."

Alexia turned back to her faintly sputtering husband. "And we shall go by sea?"

He nodded again.

"Good." His wife grinned. "I will have you all to myself. I still have a lot to yell at you about."

"And here I thought we were due for a honeymoon."

"Does that mean quite the same thing to werewolves?"

"Very droll, wife."

It wasn't until much later that Lord and Lady Maccon returned to the topic of a certain infant-inconvenience. They had had to make their formal good-byes and escape out of Florence first. Morning found them secluded in the safety of an abandoned old barn of the large and drafty variety, at which point things had settled enough for them to undertake what passed, for Lord and Lady Maccon, as serious conversation.

Conall, being supernatural and mostly inured against the cold, spread his cloak gallantly upon a mound of moldy straw and lounged back upon it entirely bare and looking expectantly up at his wife.

"Very romantic, my dear," was Alexia's unhelpful comment.

His face fell slightly at that, but Lady Maccon was not so immune to her husband's charms that she could resist the tempting combination of big-muscled nudity and bashful expression.

She divested herself of her overdress and skirts.

He made the most delicious huffing noise when she cast herself, swanlike, on top of him. Well, perhaps more beached-sea-mammal-like than swanlike, but it had the desirous upshot of plastering most of the length of her body against most of the length of his. It took him a moment to recover from several stone of wife suddenly settled atop him, but only a moment, for then he began a diligent quest to rid her of all her remaining layers of clothing in as little time as possible. He unlaced the back and popped open the front of her corset, and stripped off her chemise with all the consummate skill of a lady's maid.

"Steady on there," protested Alexia mildly, though she was flattered by his haste.

As though influenced by her comment, which she highly doubted, he suddenly switched tactics and jerked her against him tightly. Burying his face in the side of her neck, he took a deep, shuddering breath. The movement lifted her upward as his wide chest expanded. She felt almost as though she were floating.

Then he rolled her slightly off him and, incredibly gently, pulled off her bloomers and began stroking over her slightly rounded belly.

"So, a soul-stealer, is that what we're getting?"

Alexia wriggled slightly, trying to get him back into his customary, rather more forceful handling. She would never admit it out loud, of course, but she enjoyed it when he became enthusiastically rough. "One of the Roman tablets called it a Stalker of Skins."

He paused, glowering thoughtfully. "Na, still never heard of it. But, then, I'm na all that old."

"It certainly has the vampires in a tizzy."

"Following in its mother's footsteps already, the little pup.

How verra charming." His big hands began moving optimistically in a northward direction.

"Now what are you about?" wondered his wife.

"I have some further reacquainting to do. Must evaluate size differentials," he insisted.

"I hardly see how you could tell the difference," pointed out his wife, "considering their oversubstantial nature to start with."

"Oh, I believe I am more than equal to the task."

"We all must have goals in life," agreed his wife, a slight tremor in her voice.

"And to determine all the new particulars, I must apply all the available tools in my repertoire." This comment apparently indicated Conall intended to switch and use his mouth rather than his hands.

Alexia, it must be admitted, was running out of both token protests and the ability to breathe regularly. And since her husband's mouth was occupied, and even a werewolf shouldn't talk with his mouth full, she determined that was the end of their conversation.

So it proved to be the case, for some time at least.

extras

about the author

Ms. Carriger began writing in order to cope with being raised in obscurity by an expatriate Brit and an incurable curmudgeon. She escaped small-town life and inadvertently acquired several degrees in higher learning. Ms. Carriger then traveled the historic cities of Europe, subsisting entirely on biscuits secreted in her handbag. She now resides in the Colonies, surrounded by a harem of Armenian lovers, where she insists on tea imported directly from London and cats that pee into toilets. She is fond of teeny tiny hats and tropical fruit. Find out more about Ms. Carriger at www.gailcarriger.com

Find out more about Gail Carriger and other Orbit authors by registering for the free monthly newsletter at www.orbit books.net

if you enjoyed
BLAMELESS

look out for

DEATH MOST DEFINITE

book one of the Death Works series

by

Trent Jamieson

1

I know something's wrong the moment I see the dead girl standing in the Wintergarden food court.

She shouldn't be here. Or I shouldn't. But no one else is working this. I'd sense them if they were. My phone's hardly helpful. There are no calls from Number Four, and that's a serious worry. I should have had a heads-up about this: a missed call, a text, or a new schedule. But there's nothing. Even a Stirrer would be less peculiar than what I have before me.

Christ, all I want is my coffee and a burger.

Then our eyes meet and I'm not hungry anymore.

A whole food court's worth of shoppers swarm between us, but from that instant of eye contact, it's just me and her, and that indefinable something. A bit of *déjà vu*. A bit of lightning. Her eyes burn into mine, and there's a gentle, mocking curl to her lips that is gorgeous; it hits me in the chest.

This shouldn't be. The dead don't seek you out unless there is no one (or no thing) working their case: and that just doesn't happen. Not these days. And certainly not in the heart of Brisbane's CBD.

She shouldn't be here.

This isn't my gig. This most definitely will not end well. The girl is dead; our relationship has to be strictly professional.

She has serious style.

I'm not sure I can pinpoint what it is, but it's there, and it's unique. The dead project an image of themselves, normally in something comfortable like a tracksuit, or jeans and a shirt. But this girl, her hair shoulder length with a ragged cut, is in a black, long-sleeved blouse, and a skirt, also black. Her legs are sheathed in black stockings. She's into silver jewellery, and what I assume are ironic brooches of Disney characters. Yeah, serious style, and a strong self-image.

And her eyes.

Oh, her eyes. They're remarkable, green, but flecked with grey. And those eyes are wide, because she's dead – newly dead – and I don't think she's come to terms with that yet. Takes a while: sometimes it takes a long while.

I yank pale ear buds from my ears, releasing a tinny splash of 'London Calling' into the air around me.

The dead girl, her skin glowing with a bluish pallor, comes towards me, and the crowd between us parts swiftly and unconsciously. They may not be able to see her but they can *feel* her, even if it lacks the intensity of my own experience. Electricity crackles up my spine – and something else, something bleak and looming like a premonition.

She's so close now I could touch her. My heart's accelerating, even before she opens her mouth, which I've already decided, ridiculously, impossibly, that I want to kiss. I can't make up my mind whether that means I'm exceedingly shallow or prescient. I don't know what I'm thinking because this is such unfamiliar territory: total here-be-dragons kind of stuff.

She blinks that dead person blink, looks at me as though I'm some puzzle to be solved. Doesn't she realise it's the other way around? She blinks again, and whispers in my ear. 'Run.'

And then someone starts shooting at me.

Not what I was expecting.

Bullets crack into the nearest marble-topped tables. One. Two. Three. Shards of stone sting my cheek.

The food court surges with desperate motion. People scream, throwing themselves to the ground, scrambling for cover. But not me. She said run, and I run: zigging and zagging. Bent down, because I'm tall, easily a head taller than most of the people here, and far more than that now that the majority are on the floor. The shooter's after me; well, that's how I'm taking it. Lying down is only going to give them a motionless target.

Now, I'm in OK shape. I'm running, and a gun at your back gives you a good head of steam. Hell, I'm sprinting, hurdling tables, my long legs knocking lunches flying, my hands sticky with someone's spilt Coke. The dead girl's keeping up in that effortless way dead people have: skimming like a drop of water over a glowing hot plate.

We're out of the food court and down Elizabeth Street. In the open, traffic rumbling past, the Brisbane sun a hard light overhead. The dead girl's still here with me, throwing glances over her shoulder. Where the light hits her she's almost translucent. Sunlight and shadow keep revealing and concealing at random; a hand, the edge of a cheekbone, the curve of a calf.

The gunshots coming from inside haven't disturbed anyone's consciousness out here.

Shootings aren't exactly a common event in Brisbane. They happen, but not often enough for people to react as you might expect. All they suspect is that someone needs to service their car more regularly, and that there's a lanky bearded guy, possibly late for something, his jacket bunched into one fist, running like a madman down Elizabeth Street. I turn left into Edward, the nearest intersecting street, and then left again into the pedestrian-crammed space of Queen Street Mall.

I slow down in the crowded walkway panting and moving with the flow of people; trying to appear casual. I realise that my phone's been ringing. I look at it, at arm's length, like the monkey holding the bone in *2001: A Space Odyssey*. All I've got on the screen is Missed Call, and Private Number. Probably someone from the local DVD shop calling to tell me I have an overdue rental, which, come to think of it, I do – I always do.

'You're a target,' the dead girl says.

'No shit!' I'm thinking about overdue DVDs, which is crazy. I'm thinking about kissing her, which is crazier still, and impossible. I haven't kissed anyone in a long time. If I smoked this would be the time to light up, look into the middle distance and say something like: 'I've seen trouble, but in the Wintergarden, on a Tuesday at lunchtime, c'mon!' But if I smoked I'd be even more out of breath and gasping out questions instead, and there's some (well, most) types of cool that I just can't pull off.

So I don't say anything. I wipe my Coke-sticky hands on my tie, admiring all that *je ne sais quoi* stuff she's got going on and feeling as guilty as all hell about it, because she's dead and I'm being so unprofessional. At least no one else was hurt in the food court: I'd feel it otherwise. Things aren't *that* out of whack. The sound of sirens builds in the distant streets. I can hear them, even above my pounding heart.

'This is so hard.' Her face is the picture of frustration. 'I didn't realise it would be so hard. There's a lot you need—' She flickers like her signal's hit static, and that's a bad sign: who knows where she could end up. 'If you could get in—'

I reach towards her. Stupid, yeah, but I want to comfort her. She looks so pained. But she pulls back, as though she knows what would happen if I touch her. She shouldn't be acting this way. She's dead: she shouldn't care. If anything, she should want the opposite. She flickers again, swells and contracts, grows snowy. Whatever there is of her here is fracturing.

I take a step towards her. 'Stop,' I yell. 'I need to—'

Need to? I don't exactly know what I need. But it doesn't matter because she's gone, and I'm yelling at nothing. And I didn't pomp her.

She's just gone.

2

That's not how it's meant to happen. Unprofessional. So unprofessional. I'm supposed to be the one in control.

After all, I'm a Psychopomp: a Pomp. Death is my business, has been in my family for a good couple of hundred years. Without me, and the other staff at Mortmax Industries, the world would be crowded with souls, and worse. Like Dad says, pomp is a verb and a noun. Pomps pomp the dead, we draw them through us to the Underworld and the One Tree. And we stall the Stirrers, those things that so desperately desire to come the other way. Every day I'm doing this – well, five days a week. It's a living, and quite a lucrative one at that.

I'm good at what I do. Though this girl's got me wondering.

I wave my hand through the spot where, moments ago, she stood. Nothing. Nothing at all. No residual electrical force. My skin doesn't tingle. My mouth doesn't go dry. She may as well have never been there.

The back of my neck prickles. I turn a swift circle.

Can't see anyone, but there are eyes on me, from somewhere. Who's watching me?

Then the sensation passes, all at once, a distant scratching pressure released, and I'm certain (well, pretty certain) that I'm alone – but for the usual Brisbane crowds pushing past me through the mall. Before, when the dead girl had stood here, they'd have done anything to keep away from her and me. Now I'm merely an annoying idiot blocking the flow of foot traffic. I find some cover: a little alcove between two shops where I'm out of almost everyone's line of sight.

I get on the phone, and call Dad's direct number at Mortmax. Maybe I should be calling Morrigan, or Mr D (though word is the Regional Manager's gone fishing), but I need to talk to Dad first. I need to get this straight in my head.

I could walk around to Number Four, Mortmax's office space in Brisbane. It's on George Street, four blocks from where I'm standing, but I'm feeling too exposed and, besides, I'd probably run into Derek. While the bit of me jittery with adrenaline itches for a fight, the rest is hungry for answers. I'm more likely to get those if I keep away. Derek's been in a foul mood and I need to get through him before I can see anyone else. Derek runs the office with efficiency and attention to detail, and he doesn't like me at all. The way I'm feeling, that's only going to end in harsh words. Ah, work politics. Besides, I've got the afternoon and tomorrow off. First rule of this gig is: if you don't want extra hours keep a low profile. I've mastered that one to the point that it's almost second nature.

Dad's line must be busy because he doesn't pick up. Someone else does, though. Looks like I might get a fight after all.

'Yes,' Derek says. You could chill beer with that tone.

'This is Steven de Selby.' I can't hide the grin in my voice. Now is not the time to mess with me, even if you're Morrigan's assistant and, technically, my immediate superior.

'I know who it is.'

'I need to talk to Dad.'

There are a couple of moments of uncomfortable silence, then a few more. 'I'm surprised we haven't got you rostered on.'

'I just got back from a funeral. Logan City. I'm done for the day.'

Derek clicks his tongue. 'Do you have any idea how busy we are?'

Absolutely, or I'd be talking to Dad. I wait a while: let the silence stretch out. He's not the only one who can play at that. 'No,' I say at last, when even I'm starting to feel uncomfortable. 'Would you like to discuss it with me? I'm in the city.

How about we have a coffee?' I resist the urge to ask him what he's wearing.

Derek sighs, doesn't bother with a response, and transfers me to Dad's phone.

'Steve,' Dad says, and he sounds a little harried. So maybe Derek wasn't just putting it on for my benefit.

'Dad, well, ah . . .' I hesitate, then settle for the obvious. 'I've just been shot at.'

'What? Oh. Christ. You sure it wasn't a car backfiring?' he asks somewhat hopefully.

'Dad . . . do cars normally backfire rounds into the Wintergarden food court?'

'That was you?' Now he's sounding worried. 'I thought you were in Logan.'

'Yeah, I was. I went in for some lunch and someone started shooting.'

'Are you OK?'

'Not bleeding, if that's what you mean.'

'Good.'

'Dad, I wouldn't be talking to you if someone hadn't warned me. Someone not living.'

'Now that shouldn't be,' he says. He sounds almost offended. 'There are no punters on the schedule.' He taps on the keyboard. I could be in for a wait. 'Even factoring in the variables, there's no chance of a Pomp being required in the Wintergarden until next month: elderly gentleman, heart attack. There shouldn't be any activity there at all.'

I clench my jaw. 'There was, Dad. I'm not making it up. I was there. And, no, I haven't been drinking.'

I tell him about the dead girl, and am surprised at how vivid the details are. I hadn't realised that I'd retained them. The rest of it is blurring, what with all the shooting and the sprinting, but I can see her face so clearly, and those eyes.

'Who was she?'

'I don't know. She looked familiar: didn't stay around long

enough for me to ask her anything. But Dad, I didn't pomp her. She just disappeared.'

'Loose cannon, eh? I'll look into it, talk to Morrigan for you.'

'I'd appreciate that. Maybe I was just in the wrong place at the wrong time, but it doesn't feel like that. She was trying to save me, and when do the dead ever try and look after Pomps?'

Dad chuckles at that. There's nothing more self-involved than a dead person. Talking of self-involved . . . 'Derek says you're busy.'

'We're having trouble with our phone line. Another one of Morrigan's "improvements",' Dad says. I can hear the inverted commas around improvements. 'Though . . . that seems to be in the process of being fixed.' He pauses. 'I *think* that's what's happening, there's a half-dozen people here pulling wiring out of the wall.' I can hear them in the background, drills whining: there's even a little hammering. 'Oh, and there's the Death Moot in December. Two months until everything's crazy and the city's crowded with Regional Managers. Think of it, the entire Orcus here, all thirteen RMs.' He groans. 'Not to mention the bloody Stirrers. They keep getting worse. A couple of staffers have needed stitches.'

I rub the scarred surface of the palm of my free hand. Cicatrix City as we call it, an occupational hazard of stalling stirs, but the least of them when it came to Stirrers. A Pomp's blood is enough to exorcise a Stirrer from a newly dead body, but the blood needs to be fresh. Morrigan is researching ways around this, but has come up with nothing as of yet. Dad calls it time-wastery. I for one would be happy if I didn't have to slash open my palm every time a corpse came crashing up into unlife.

A stir is always a bad thing. Unsettling, dangerous and bloody. Stirrers, in essence, do the same thing as Pomps, but without discretion: they hunger to take the living and the dead. They despise life, they drain it away like plugholes to the Underworld, and they're not at all fond of me and mine. Yeah, they hate us.

'Well, I didn't see or sense one in Logan. Just a body, and a lot of people mourning.'

'Hmm, you got lucky. Your mother had two.' Dad sighs. 'And here I am stuck in the office.'

I make a mental note to call Mum. 'So Derek wasn't lying.'

'You've got to stop giving Derek so much crap, Steve. He'll be Ankou one day, Morrigan isn't going to be around forever.'

'I don't like the guy, and you can't tell me that the feeling isn't mutual.'

'Steven, he's your boss. Try not to piss him off too much,' Dad says and, by the tone of his voice, I know we're about to slip into the same old argument. Let me list the ways: My lack of ambition. How I could have had Derek's job, if I'd really cared. How there's more Black Sheep in me than is really healthy for a Pomp. That Robyn left me three years ago. Well, I don't want to go there today.

'OK,' I say. 'If you could just explain why the girl was there and, maybe, who she was. She understood the process, Dad. She wouldn't let me pomp her.' There's silence down the end of the line. 'You do that, and I'll try and suck up to Derek.'

'I'm serious,' Dad says. 'He's already got enough going on today. Melbourne's giving him the run-around. Not returning calls, you know, that sort of thing.'

Melbourne giving Derek the run-around isn't that surprising. Most people like to give Derek the run-around. I don't know how he became Morrigan's assistant. Yeah, I know *why*: he's a hard worker, and ambitious, almost as ambitious as Morrigan – and Morrigan is Ankou, second only to Mr D. But Derek's hardly a people person. I can't think of anyone who Derek hasn't pissed off over the years: anyone *beneath* him, that is. He'd not dare with Morrigan, and only a madman would consider it with Mr D – you don't mess with Geoff Daly, the Australian Regional Manager. Mr D's too creepy, even for us.

'OK, I'll send some flowers,' I say. 'Gerberas. Everyone likes gerberas, don't they?'

Dad grunts. He's been tapping away at his computer all this time. I'm not sure if it's the computer or me that frustrates him more.

'Can you see anything?'

A put-upon sigh, more tapping. 'Yeah . . . I'm . . . looking into . . . All right, let me just . . .' Dad's a one-finger typist. If glaciers had fingers they'd type faster than him. Morrigan gives him hell about it all the time; Dad's response requires only one finger as well. 'I can't see anything unusual in the records, Steve. I'd put it down to bad luck, or good luck. You didn't get shot after all. Maybe you should buy a scratchie, one of those $250,000 ones.'

'Why would I want to ruin my mood?'

Dad laughs. Another phone rings in the background; wouldn't put it past Derek to be on the other end. But then all the phones seem to be ringing.

'Dad, maybe I should come into the office. If you need a hand . . .'

'No, we're fine here,' Dad says, and I can tell he's trying to keep me away from Derek, which is probably a good thing. My Derek tolerance is definitely at a low today.

We say our goodbyes and I leave him to all those ringing phones, though my guilt stays with me.